TERMINAL BREACH

STEVE BRADSHAW

TERMINAL BREACH©

1st Edition 2018

FORENSIC MYSTERY/THRILLER

ISBN: 978-1-948059-58-9

Library of Congress Cataloging-in-Publication Data

TERMINAL BREACH/Steve Bradshaw

Printed in USA

TERMINAL BREACH© is a work of fiction.

Names, characters, businesses, organizations, places, institutions, events, and incidents either are the product of the author's imagination or use is fictitious. Any resemblance to actual persons, living or dead, events, or locals is entirely coincidental and fictitious.

BOOKS BY STEVE BRADSHAW

The Bell Trilogy
Bluff City Butcher
The Skies Roared
Blood Lions

Evil Like Me

Serial Intent

Terminal Breach

DEDICATION

A special thanks to Kimberly Jace, Mike Primeaux, and Eli Collier for helping me craft a story of chilling possibilities, on the stage of international mystery and suspense. I thank my friends, family, and my readers for their encouragement and support—they are the reasons I write. TERMINAL BREACH made me an even greater fan of the thousands of men and women of the Air Force Global Strike Command, people dedicated to defending the United States with safe and secure intercontinental ballistic missiles; a daunting responsibility of unimaginable force we pray will never be needed. And last but not least, I dedicate this novel to the proud Lakota Indians, one of the seven Sioux tribes of the Great Plains. The extraordinary lives and legends of the American Indian are forever a part of us.

"No man ever steps in the same river twice, for it is not the same river and he is not the same man."
Heraclitus

Bell, Albert — Billionaire patriarch
Busey, Milton — Pingree inmate
Cage, Morgan MD — M.E., North Dakota
Duncan, Mathew — Autopsy assistant
Egerton, Frank — 91st Wing Command missileer
Gibbs, Raymond — Ward County sheriff's deputy
Graham, Frank — Secretary of Defense
Hayes, Daniel MD — M.E., Monroe County, FL
Herbert, James — Director of CIA
Jamison, Brandon (Buck) — Chief General, Joint Chiefs of Staff
Landon, William Alsbury — President of the United States
Malone, Mack — Monroe County Sheriff
Nye, Maureen MD — Director of Homeland Security
Pierce, Michael Glenn — Vice President of the United States
Ramsey, Helen — Secretary, Bowman Weller & Garcia
Rice, Frank — Pingree psychiatrist
Scofield, Cameron (Cam) — Retired Dallas County sheriff
Smith, Chankoowashtay — Belden, ND founder
Sumner, Elliott — Forensic pathologist
Turpin, Harold — Scotland Yard Profiler
Wilcox, Tony — Spyglass PI

THE**LEGEND**

On the seventh day of the seventh winter, the flying eagle drops her head and the gray wolf howls ...

Long ago, on the frozen banks of the Yellowstone River, the one is given the name *Jumping Badger*. He reveals courage and vision and patience. He displays a deep understanding of human existence. He would lead the resistance of the peaceful, nomadic hunters against the erring ways of the flying eagle. And he would be known to all of the Standing Rock Sioux Nation as Tatanka Iyotake—Lakota language for the Buffalo Bull Who Sits.

The elders also spoke of another worthy nomadic hunter of the Great Plains, the one who stood vigil the first day on the frozen banks of the Yellowstone and on the prairie the night *Tatanka* took his last breath and his spirit soared. *Canis lupus*—the Gray Wolf, knows all the world's beginnings and all the world's futures. Gray Wolf is the follower of an ever-changing course, hearer of the clouds passing overhead, and seer of two looks away.

On the seventh day of the seventh winter, the Gray Wolf speaks to the moon, touches the spirit of Sitting Bull, and roams the Great Plains to evict evil and protect the descendants of peaceful men. It is said the sacred mission of the gray wolf can be heard in the whispering winds, but only in the tongue of the Lakota—*Kté iyúha* **hė Iya**.

PROLOGUE

WASHINGTON D.C.

"**M**r. President, we have a situation."

Cameron Scofield would never enter the private quarters of the POTUS for his own purposes, but now he had to. Explicit instructions had been left the day William Landon stepped into the White House—*Cam is the only man allowed to poke me in the middle of the damn night.*

The retired Dallas County Sheriff had lost his wife to ovarian cancer ten years earlier. Then senior Texas Senator (great grandson of Horace Alsbury Landon, the courier sent from the Alamo upon the arrival of the Mexican troops) had removed a gun from Cam's shaking hand and got him back onto his feet. From that day forward, the two were inseparable. Few would ever know Scofield returned the favor a year into Landon's second term. No one would have considered the possibility of a sitting President taking his own life.

"Mr. President," Cam whispered as he turned on the lamp by Landon's head. "They need you now."

He had heard the door open. He rarely slept anymore—not since Barbara. Through one slitted eye, he watched his old friend creep across the room, bumping into furniture. If Barbara were still alive, she would have pinched his backside and played dead. Instead, there was nothing but cold sheets, bulky blankets, and Cam feeling his way along. In the fog of the early morning, President Landon reveled in the fond memory of his wife until he would have to do more.

She had talked him into the second term. Barbara always told him to ignore the negative people. She said there were not that many—they were just a tiny bit louder than the rest of us. Then Barbara had died, a month after the second inauguration. Now he slept alone in the White House. After Cam had stopped him from ending his life, Landon decided he would do the best he could for the country over the next three years. Then he would disappear—no libraries and no pontificating.

Cam leaned inches from the President's chiseled face and poked his shoulder with one finger. "I know you're awake, Bill," he whispered so the Secret Service could not hear his familial tone. Everything had to be "presidential."

Cam cleared his throat and spoke louder. "Mr. President, they need you."

Landon opened his eye all the way. "What's going on?"

"North Dakota, sir." Cam straightened and held out the President's pants.

"Lord Jesus," Landon huffed, swinging his legs from the bed. There was only one reason to get a President of the United States out of bed for *North Dakota*.

The cold, early morning silence swallowed the room as he stepped into his pants and backed into his shirt. Seconds later—surrounded by dark suits, narrow ties, and ear pieces—they walked a stiff pace down the main hall in the private-quarters of the White House.

"Are we in the bunker?" Landon breathed.

Cam passed the note and watched the transformation as Landon digested the words. His brow dipped. His eyes narrowed. And his face hardened like cut granite. The most powerful man in the world seemed to grow six inches as he turned the next corner and dropped the balled paper to the floor.

PART ONE

CANARIES DIE
Five Days Earlier – Somewhere south of Minot, North Dakota

CHAPTER 1

"Death is the solution to all problems."
Joseph Stalin

T*hey're not gonna kill me...*
I gotta be the smallest cog in the whole operation. But someone thought enough of us to give me more money than I make in ten years.

Still, I'm just not important. Maybe they won't come after me.

If I wasn't the son of a stinkin' criminal—especially someone with his resume'—I bet I wouldn't have even gotten the call.

But I am, and I did.

I shoulda' listened to the old man this time. He's not that crazy. But I never trusted him. He's evil. He chose to live in hell with all the other monsters.

They're gonna kill me ...

Roan threw the chrome skull forward, ramming his knuckles into the dash. As blood came to the surface of his ragged fingers, he slammed his boot on the gas pedal and leaned into the curve. Rounding the north end of Lake Vernon, he increased speed and did all he could to hold the old truck onto the snow-dusted road, the only visible line in the endless white landscape.

The frozen plains of North Dakota would never change. They would forever be an unsung graveyard of men. Over the centuries, many men had dropped in its vast emptiness and died a hideous death. Legend says they were killed by the real monsters. Their carcasses were dragged away by the gray wolf and their bones picked clean by the red-tailed hawk. Some men are missed. All men are lost forever, their mangled remains swallowed by an indifferent world.

Roan's familiar lease, the 1952 B42S Mack tow truck, whined and moaned. It did not like going over forty. The rebuilt Cummins diesel engine, cradled two feet above the frozen tarmac on iron mounts, screamed bloody murder as the vintage pile of rusty, red-painted metal neared seventy for the first time in decades. Roan had to get far away, fast.

He kept his boot to the pedal and eyes on the road as the last of the sun dipped below the horizon behind him. The kaleidoscope of oranges and reds reached across the endless snowfields, changing into greens and purples and blues. Although bathed in a spectacular wonderland, Roan knew the realities ahead. Dangers come with a rapid temperature drop after a winter sunset in North Dakota. In minutes, the world drops to twenty-below and all the rules change. The air sucked into the diesel gets choking thick, the shatter-point of the windshield is reached, and the rock-hard tires on the frozen asphalt lose traction—just a few of nature's hurdles to test a man's true desire to live. Roan knew that if he let up, or if his truck gave out, he would be the next warm carcass torn to shreds and dragged away to the middle of nowhere.

He tried to focus on the road. The hundred times he'd traveled the frozen, desolate plains of North Dakota, he'd always thought about being eaten alive by a drove of toothy predators with constant smiles. Each time the flesh-tearing images tormented him until he had reached civilization. This time, Roan did not need to repress Indian legend, or ignore superstition, or block his overactive imagination. This time, real monsters hunted him. He knew because he had seen them.

Several long minutes and empty miles passed. The eastern horizon had darkened and the old tow truck had settled into its once-intolerable speed. Roan's white knuckles on the cold steering wheel stopped bleeding, and his skin started to regain color. At the very moment when he started to believe he had a chance, an explosive impact rolled through the vehicle from behind. It lifted its rear end and propelled the tow truck forward with enormous force.

The violent collision whipped Roan's head back into the cab window. A hundred cracks shot in a hundred directions from its bloody epicenter. Roan was thrown into the passenger seat and slammed against the door. The whirling eruption sent the wounded truck down the frozen highway in a slow tail spin and imminent death roll. Every rusty bolt strained as the freshly crumpled metal rocketed forward, shedding glass and shrapnel onto the frozen tarmac.

As the smoking heap moaned, Roan climbed back to the steering wheel. Like an elk bull asserting dominance, the intensity of the collision had delivered a chilling message—the monsters had arrived. Roan cringed. Unsure of what bones were broken and organs bruised, he squirmed into position and grabbed the wheel. He cut it into the sideway slide, down shifted, popped the clutch, and stomped the gas. The disoriented diesel coughed and came alive. Its tail slid back where it belonged—Roan had retaken control of the crippled truck. His heart pounded in his throat as he rebooted his brain. He knew he had to escape the fog of confusion or accept his imminent death.

Whatever hit me is onboard, he thought as he looked over his shoulder. The back of the truck hung low with the added weight. He could see a spray of sparks that shot ten feet into the sky. He attempted to keep the speed above fifty. The diesel could just not lose the battle.

Roan grabbed the dangling mirror. He studied the large shadow sitting behind the bent, twenty-ton winch. *What are you?* He squeezed the mirror in his bloody hand and moved it around in a desperate attempt to understand. *Are you fused to me? Are you dead?*

He threw down the mirror and looked straight ahead. *Fight or flight? Flight!*

Roan rejected the existence of monsters. He rejected his impending death like a child refusing to eat vegetables. There *had* to be another explanation. *Why do I always go to worst case? Maybe this is just an accident. Maybe the friggin' cold is messin' with my head, making me think unclearly. This could be a random person in the wrong place at the wrong time. Maybe they ran into me by pure accident. They were speeding in the middle of nowhere, like a lot of people do. My taillights are not the best—very easy to miss. Hell, they're always covered with grease and mud and ice. I never clean this old rental truck. Why should I? It's not mine. Granted, I do rent the thing a lot ...*

His head kept saying *maybe*. His heart kept saying *no way*. Roan continued to rationalize away his fears until he ran a cold, trembling hand over his wet face. *How can I be wet? It's freezing outside and almost as cold in here, for God's sake. How can I possibly be sweating?* Under the flickering dash lights, he found the blood on his hand. Then he spotted his reflection in the windshield. The diesel coughed. Roan's rationalizations began to fade as reality took hold. The old tow truck would die soon—and so would he.

Don't be stupid. Nobody runs into the back of a big-ass tow truck goin' seventy on a flat damn prairie at sundown. I got hit on purpose. They want me. He squeezed the wheel and bit his lip. New blood rolled down his chin. *The monsters are here!*

He folded his aching body over the steering wheel, his nose inches from the ice-flecked glass. Hot breath fell from his bloody mouth as he looked through his reflection and got lost in the sliding lights on the empty road.

Stay calm. If I'm lucky, the collision killed the bastards, he thought. *This truck is tougher than she looks. Joe's always sayin' they don't make 'em with real iron anymore. That's what happened; those bastards hit a damn iron wall back there. It coulda' been just enough to break their collective, over-aggressive necks.*

He glanced into his side mirror. Nothing moved except a swinging cable hanging from the bent winch. *I gotta get to Minot! It's not that far—ten to fifteen miles. This old truck can make it. I bet it got through a lotta worse shit over the years.*

When I get to Minot, I'm goin' straight into the Ward County Sheriff's Office. I'm gonna tell 'em everything. I'm gonna tell 'em exactly what's goin' on here. I'll tell 'em what I did, too.

He swallowed hard. *I didn't do anything real bad. I just got 'em to the place that nobody remembers, the place my old man showed me when I was a kid—back when I didn't know he was a monster, too. Yeah ... I got 'em inside that place. That was not easy. Way more complicated than I remembered. I sure as hell earned my money—but they were never going to pay me. When we got inside, they had all they needed. It was pretty much over right then. I could tell. The way they looked at me. I wasn't important anymore. They treated me real good for a year, and then it was time for me to be eliminated. I was just one more fattened pig for their luau.*

I even went through all the ritual shit! Never bought into any of it. Roan pulled up his shirtsleeve and rubbed his tattoo—it burned. He stared at the beams on the snow-dusted asphalt. *All that time, I was with some real teeth-gnashing predators. I heard them talkin.' I know what they do to people. I shoulda known they'd get around to me sooner or later.*

His eyes dropped to the speedometer. The cracked glass had fallen out when the Mack got hit. Now the bent needle wobbled below fifty. Roan leaned to the side mirror. The sparks still sprayed into the night and the rear end still dragged on the asphalt. The diesel could not handle the stress much longer. Smoke had started to pour from the hood and seep into the cab.

Reality crept in. Even if Minot was only one mile away, it no longer mattered. Roan choked on the diesel fumes. His end neared. He would black out first. Then the truck would run off the road and plow into a snowdrift. Roan would die the horrible death he had feared for years. He would be the helpless victim of the monsters clinging onto the back of his truck or the toothy scavengers of the Great Plains. As his fingers numbed and his hopes faded, the horrific images of his worst nightmare grew.

Through the smoke-filled cab, the Lake Vernon Quarry loomed in the distance—the only sign of life on the snow-covered prairie. He saw a dozen enormous mounds of gravel and sand covered in white. It looked like an elephant graveyard on the Serengeti in a snowstorm. Roan had passed the same quarry a hundred times before, but he'd never given the place a second thought. Now everything was different. Still, the small flash of hope died. Roan knew the Lake Vernon Quarry would be closed during these winter months. There would be no employees, no witnesses, and no one to help him. The small business on the desolate highway would not save him from his terrible fate. There were no humans. He could only stare at the winter ghost town.

Maybe his deepest fear of being dragged away and eaten alive made him think more. Maybe the monsters clinging to his tail helped spawn the idea. *The old truck could handle it*, he thought. He created the plan in a split second. *I will maximize speed and drive head-first into the piles of rocks. At sixty, the sheer momentum will take me through at least two piles. The impact and the tunneling will kill and scrape off my passengers.*

He fastened his seatbelt, tightened the strap, and swallowed his fear. He glanced up at the fat roll-bars on the inside roof of the cab. *Always wondered why you guys were up there.* He patted the dash. "You may be old as hell, but you're built strong. Hope Joe forgives me."

Roan downshifted and floored it. To his surprise, the Mack lurched forward like a bear bolting from the brush for prey. Roan picked up speed. Smoke bellowed from the hood. The strained metal whined in the freezing wind.

"I hear ya. Let's shake off these sons-of-bitches!"

At fifty-yards from the piles, the rear window exploded. Shattered glass flew throughout the cab. The choking smoke rushed out. Roan took a deep breath as the spastic speedometer needle climbed to sixty. "I need all hundred-fifty horses to kick some ass now!"

He pounded the clutch to the floor and threw the chrome skull into the last gear, reopening his wounds on the jagged dash. When he hit the gas and popped the clutch, the Mack leaped forward a second time. "I knew you had more to give," he boomed with blood dripping into his eyes and rolling down his neck. This time a hand-wipe of the face would not matter. Roan's newest wound lay open on the side of his head. Raw flesh hung from his grazed skull.

At twenty yards from the snow-covered piles the front windshield exploded—he had no time to understand why. Roan saw his bloody face in the swinging mirror. Before he could blink, the nose of the Mack found the first mound. In a millisecond, the rock-lined snowdrift exploded in a volcanic eruption. The rusted chrome grill and red-painted metal hood collapsed like a crushed beer can. The rebuilt diesel tore off its iron mounts. Sand and rock and ice poured into the cab. Then the duel fifty-gallon tanks torpedoed the piles, followed immediately by the bent winch, and then the monsters.

CHAPTER 2

"The true mysteries of the world are the visible, not the invisible."
Oscar Wilde

Day two – Bismarck, North Dakota

I t arrived hours after midnight. The morgue clerk in Bismarck had specific instructions: Let them store it in the decomposition room, turn the thermostat to seventy, and lock the door. This one would be off-limits to everyone but the medical examiner.

God! The moment I walked in, your frozen-marble eyes found me. He leaned closer to the carnage as if befriending a tortured freak. *I know. I see your terror. You were with a monster.*

With his eyes locked on the dead, Morgan Cage lifted his head and exhaled like a man at the starting line waiting for the gun. The scant light from the hall that spilled into the room revealed little. He rocked on worn heels. In his over-starched, white lab coat with his name sewn in red cursive over his breast pocket, like the first archaeologist to unearth Tutankhamun, Dr. Cage perused his newest mystery one frozen inch at a time. His eyes crawled the glistening terrain of death. *It is too early,* he thought. *You may not be ready for me for several days.*

The macabre presence would paralyze most. It was the stuff nightmares are made of. But Dr. Cage saw only a puzzle to solve, a wrong to right. When he touched one finger to the glassy side of the grotesque block of human flesh, he whispered the words he said to each one who came to see him. "I will listen to you."

Cage spun around and adjusted the thermostat down another ten degrees. The thaw process needed to be slower. He turned out the light and locked the door behind him and then, as he had a thousand times before, he walked the long hall of cracked linoleum and water-stained ceilings. His eyes left the elevator doors ahead as he turned into the hall leading to the swinging metal doors. His autopsy room waited. But this time, Cage struggled with the prep calculations and the horrific image he had just left behind. This time, his inner voice would not be silenced. This time, he knew a real monster had come to North Dakota, and if he could not untangle the twisted mystery soon, many more were going to die hideous deaths.

First, he had to retake control. He was a forensic pathologist, a scientist, and instincts were not science. Cage did not have the luxury of jumping to conclusions. When his hand touched the cold metal door leading into his autopsy room, he closed his eyes and swallowed hard. The frozen block of carnage on the gurney in the Decomp Room would have to wait its turn. When Cage opened his eyes, he needed to be ready to focus on the others waiting to tell their stories. They were the prior day's traumatic deaths from all across North Dakota. They each came to Bismarck, to the state Medical Examiner's office, to tell their story. Cage served a population of 800,000 people. It was his job to determine cause and manner of death without prejudice. Dr. Cage's autopsy room was where the American jurisprudence system was fed its raw meat.

On this cold December morning, seven bodies waited in the walk-in refrigerator. Each lay naked on a cold gurney in the supine position beneath a paper sheet. The identity of each corpse was reduced to a toe tag. Each waited their turn to be alone with the state Medical Examiner. Some would have little to say about their departure. Albeit tragic and inconvenient, their death may have been expected. Almost 90 percent of the deaths in the country were the result of disease and natural causes. Others found their way onto Cage's autopsy table as accident victims. Still others came because they had chosen their fate, ending their own lives through suicide.

Dr. Cage spent most of his time with the people who had no reason to die, the ones who had awakened with no plans to be on an autopsy table the next day. They had not wanted to stretch out, naked and mutilated, in a refrigerator with strangers. They hadn't wanted to leave their friends and families. They certainly hadn't asked to be shot or stabbed or strangled or beaten to death. These people were the homicide victims. Someone else took their life. Although all of them got to speak to the Medical Examiner from the autopsy table, the homicide victims got most of Cage's time. Their stories were often complex. Cage was determined to stop the monsters in North Dakota.

Dr. Morgan Cage, the North Dakota State Chief Medical Examiner, was a tall, lanky man from Key Largo. He had come to the Great Plains after his residency in forensic pathology, arriving in one of the most desolate places in the country to do his specialized research. He'd wanted to study the effects of extreme temperature and climatic exposure on the decomposition process of human tissue. The record lows and highs—from sixty below zero to 120 degrees above—had made North Dakota the perfect laboratory.

Soon after his arrival, the state had recruited Cage to be their medical examiner. He'd agreed to take on the position for one year. Twenty-four years and thousands of cases later, he was still serving the people of the fourth most sparsely populated state in the union, while he continued his groundbreaking research on the codification of climate-induced, postmortem changes, today a standard forensic reference guide—*Extreme Elements and Human Decomposition.*

* * *

"Not counting today, how long have you worked for me?" Cage poked.

"Sorry, Doc. I checked it last night. It worked fine then." The young diener kept his back to the ME and his head in the stainless-steel drawer.

After a long, quiet minute, Cage pulled his head from the blood-filled thoracic cavity and found his diener. With a gloved hand waving in the air, he barked, "I need it now, Mr. Duncan."

Mathew slapped the shiny scalpel into the waiting palm of the ME, then darted into the shadows where he disposed of the sterile packaging and wiped his wet face with a towel.

"I never liked those electric scalpels," Cage growled as he sank deeper into the gaping wound with one hand and reached up with the other to adjust the surgical lamp overhead. Except for the autopsy table, which was bathed in white light, he kept a cold, dark autopsy room. It helped him focus.

"I need to feel the tissue, the lines of demarcation, the texture. It can be important, lest we forget. Electric scalpels just don't give me—"

"Yes, sir," Mathew mumbled on autopilot as his trembling hands fiddled with instruments on the tray next to him and he stared at the swinging metal doors. Something had shaken him to the core. He had seen something he was not supposed to see. He'd broken a rule. The sheriff would be the next one to push through the metal doors, and Mathew had to get his nerves under control.

For two years, he cracked countless chests and passed hundreds of bloody organs to the medical examiner without a hint of angst or despair—a trait Dr. Cage considered a major asset. But on this day, halfway into the first case, sweat dripped from Duncan's paper hat.

Although the *electric scalpel* banter served as a diversion, it did not calm the diener. It only bought him time. Duncan kept his head in the shadows to avoid the eyes of the man who missed nothing. Rules at the North Dakota Medical Examiner's Office were to be followed at all times, without exception. Maintenance of the *chain of evidence* was everything. Duncan knew when he had looked inside the Decomp Room—and he touched *it*—he had put his career on the line. But that was not why he avoided eye contact with the ME. That was not why his knees trembled, his heart raced, and sweat rolled down his face. That frozen *thing* from Ward County sat in the dark behind a door that had never been locked before. That door drew him in.

Now Duncan had seen and touched what nightmares are made of. Now the most horrible thing in his life had climbed into his head, something even the darkest minds could never conjure up. He knew it would be with him forever.

When he'd arrived at work, there had been only two employees present. The night morgue clerk told him the story right away. He said Dr. Cage had called in the middle of the night with some very cryptic instructions—something the ME had never done before. Ten minutes later a white, unmarked van backed up to the loading dock. Like silent zombies, two skinny men in dark suits and thin ties stood under the floodlights in the swirling snow. They pointed and nodded as they unloaded something big onto a gurney. It looked like a large crate under a tarp—three feet in all directions, and with sharp edges. They kept it covered. It came without the routine paperwork.

The night morgue clerk had followed Dr. Cage's instructions. He asked zero questions. He led the two men and their *covered thing* on a gurney to the Decomp Room. They rolled it inside, the lights kept off. They uncovered it, set the thermostat on seventy, and locked the door. One finally spoke. He said he would give the key to Dr. Cage, and effective immediately no one was to go near the Decomp Room.

After hearing the morgue clerk's story, Mathew Duncan had mulled over the cloaked mystery while prepping the autopsy room for the day's cases. The *Decomp Room* mystery tugged at him. He had always been in the know, in the inner circle, had the privilege of a life behind the scenes. His friends revered him—he had professional swag. Duncan enjoyed a degree of local star status. He had an important job working with the state's chief medical examiner. Duncan always had the tantalizing *inside story* on the most horrific homicides in the news. He dominated conversations at all the parties. This time was different. This time the amazing story was sitting in the dark behind a locked door. What could possibly be so important? And why was it delivered by strange people in the middle of the night? And why no paperwork?

He realized he had to know what got Dr. Cage out of bed in the middle of the night. Once Duncan had made the decision to investigate the mystery in the Decomp Room, he moved like a programmed robot in the basement of the Medical Examiner's Office. He turned left at the only elevator into the basement and walked down the long hall with eyes glued on the door to the infamous Decomp Room. When he arrived, he hesitated. Duncan had a key, but ... if he used it he would put his job at risk.

I will look and leave before anyone gets here, he thought. *They forgot I have a key. No one will know.* Duncan finally inserted the key. The door popped open. He turned on his trusty flashlight as warm air moving into the cold hallway lifted his hair. The familiar smell of dead flesh climbed into his nostrils. Duncan approached the gurney and the massive, frozen cube. His beam cut through the dark. His feet stuck to the floor. He touched the flat glass surface and saw the eye looking back at him.

* * *

"As far as I'm concerned, you can wheel that electronic scalpel equipment to the dumpster when we get done here," Cage said, his head still deep in the peritoneal cavity. "I'll never use it again. And I'm pretty confident Rafferty and Kelton won't miss it. We should be using standard scalpels around here. I'm going to make it a rule."

Duncan blinked, when he heard the word *rule*. His head shot back into the autopsy room. "Ah. Yes, sir. I will take care of it." His eyes stayed on the swinging metal doors as he wiped more sweat from his face with a wet sleeve.

Cage pulled his head out of the bloody hole and held up a flabby organ like a newborn child. He flipped it over, patted it, and rinsed off the blood. "There you are," he said to his newest find as he brought the overhead light down for a closer look. The wet organ flopped in the air a few feet from Duncan. He could see bruises and a long laceration.

"Is that what killed him, Doc?"

Cage flipped it over. "In a word, yes."

"Sorry. I shouldn't have said anything."

Cage flipped his magnifying loupe to his forehead and turned to Mathew standing at the edge of the light. "Blunt force trauma." His mask puffed with each word. They watched and waited for the blood stream—from the liver back into the abdominal cavity— to stop. Cage rinsed and weighed.

With his back to his diener, he said, "So, you've been inside the Decomp Room."

"Ah ... Yes, sir."

Cage turned back to him. "Tell me. What are you thinking right now?"

Mathew swallowed hard. "I'm thinking it's the worst thing

I've ever seen in my life. The thing thawing out back there is a nightmare. I won't ever be the same. It—"

Cage nodded and tapped the side of his head mic, Mathew's signal to stop talking.

"Case number 4 2 9 8, postmortem addendum 1.6, on today's date at 9:42 a.m. Central Standard Time. A normal, healthy liver weighing 1.93 kilograms presents a severe, transverse laceration to the left lobe, 7.2 centimeters in length, 1.5 to 3.5 centimeters in depth, a grade five, 80 percent parenchymal disruption."

Cage rolled the organ in his hand like a prize fish he could not drop back into the icy stream. "There is a perforation of the inferior vena cava and severed hepatic artery." He muted his mic. "Mathew. Blood recovered from abdominal cavity—volume?"

"2.7 liters, Doc."

Cage tapped his mic. "The deceased experienced massive internal bleeding. 2.7 liters recovered. Estimate 60 percent of total blood volume. The rapid hemorrhage led to death within three to five minutes after traumatic injury sustained. Cause of death, ruptured liver and rapid exsanguination from external, blunt-force trauma. The liver is torn along the falciform ligament, severely violating the hepatic arterial process."

The ME turned off his mic. His eyes found his diener. They stared in long silence. Mathew expected to be fired on the spot. "The *frozen thing* you were not supposed to see is a person, Mathew." Cage returned to slicing the liver into sections like carving a Christmas turkey. In cold silence, he fanned the quarter-inch thick filets on the bed of the autopsy table and inspected each as if it was the most important piece to the puzzle. He selected portions of two and dropped them into a vial of 10 percent buffered formalin. The histology examination would be completed before the end of the day.

"I didn't mean any disrespect," Mathew whispered. "I've never seen—"

The metal doors popped open. Six-foot-five Sheriff Raymond Gibbs ducked slightly to clear the doorway as he entered with a battered coffee thermos in one fist, a gnarled leather binder in the other, and a scowl that swallowed his otherwise puffy, unshaven face.

CHAPTER 3

"There are no necessary evils in government. Its evils exist only
in its abuses."
Andrew Jackson

Dr. Cage waited for the squeaking doors to stop swinging
before he turned from his pile of sliced liver and the
naked corpse. "Good morning, Ray. We've been expecting you."

Gibbs huffed as he raised his tattered notebook and pointed
at the body lying under the only lights in the room. Stomping
snow from his boots, he tilted his head and squinted at the corpse,
which was opened from neck to groin with bloody racks of ribs
hanging on each side of the opened chest. "That can't be my
guy," he puffed.

Cage turned back to his filets. "No, Ray. Yours will not be on
my table for a while."

Gibbs shrugged off the error and looked around the otherwise
dark room like a child lost in a mall. He dropped his arms to his
guns. "Well. Good. I'll get outside, then." When his shoulder
found the metal door, he paused. "Sorry for bustin' in on ya, Doc.
Do need to talk."

"Almost done here," Cage said. "I'll meet you in the break
room in a few."

When the doors settled, Cage turned back to Duncan. "I
want you to finish up with Mr. Forde. Expedite his tissue samples
to histology. Take the rack of tubes to toxicology. I'll sign off so
the body can be released. Tell Maggie to prepare the death
certificate—I'm not anticipating anything new from the histo or
tox screen. If I get a surprise, I'll amend later. I don't want to hold

onto the body. Family's been through enough. You got everything?"

"Yes sir," Duncan said, pulling on a fresh pair of surgical gloves.

"No mistakes, Mathew. Close him up neat as a pin. Double check all the numbers and paperwork. Mr. Forde is a homicide. I don't want a process problem in the courtroom."

"I understand, Doctor Cage."

"Good."

"Ah, Doctor Cage?" Duncan whispered.

"When you're done, tell Maggie no one comes down here until I say different. The morgue basement is off limits to everyone, regardless of their story. When you're done dropping off Mr. Forde's paperwork and specimens, get back down here with the camera. Come alone. I know you have your master key. It works more than the Decomp Room. It works in the elevator, too. But you already know that."

"I don't know how to work the camera—"

"It's time you learn. You're taking some pictures for me, Mr. Duncan."

Mathew stared at the only man he feared in life—for all the right reasons. "But—"

"The frozen corpse in the Decomp Room will not be ready for an autopsy for several days, Mathew. For reasons that will become obvious later, the thaw process must be slow. You cannot discuss with anyone what you see, hear, or know about this case. Can you do that, Mathew?"

He folded his arms to hide his shaking hands. "Yes, sir. I think. I mean, yes, I can do that."

Cage nodded and leaned into his face. "It's okay to be scared sometimes, Mathew. The secret is to learn how to keep fear from paralyzing you." Cage winked.

"Yes sir, not paralyze—"

"Good." Cage pulled off his gloves and dropped them on Forde's naked legs. Mathew watched him push through the metal doors and disappear down the hall.

Did I just get a promotion? he wondered. *I thought I was gonna get fired, but Doc didn't seem that mad. And he didn't explain anything. He just said do all the new stuff and don't be afraid of things.*

Duncan gathered the remnants of Forde's viscera and returned them to the peritoneal cavity. He flipped the ribcage sections back in place, sewed closed the chest, and rinsed off the blood. *Did you know the person who killed you...?* He wondered. *Did it hurt—I mean death...? Where are you now, Mr. Forde?*

Mathew always asked the same questions, when he got alone time with a corpse. It always felt new. Each time, in some strange way, he felt one day the answers would come. He would often wait a long time in silence in the empty autopsy room for an answer, or until someone came in on him. But this time would be different. This time, more than ever before, he could not mess around. He had to focus. The Doc had been very clear. Duncan had to get everything right.

He double-checked the histology and toxicology specimen numbers with the official paperwork and went through the process: take Mr. Forde to the refrigerator, deliver specimens to the lab and paperwork to administration, tell Miss Maggie that Dr. Cage said the basement (morgue) was off limits, and do not forget the medical camera. Duncan had to get down to the Decomp Room STAT—the Doc and Sergeant Gibbs would be waiting.

He rolled Mr. Forde into the refrigerator and checked the toe tag a third time. Duncan was certain he had done everything, but when he got to the elevator, he froze. For no apparent reason his heart had started to pound out his chest, and his right eye started to twitch. *I'm movin' up the ladder today, of all days? I don't think*

I'm ready for more responsibility, he thought. *I think I'm gonna puke!* The elevator doors opened. The light spilled into the morgue hall. Like a zombie he stepped inside, turned around, and stared at the door to the Decomp room at the other end of the hall —his nightmare.

The elevator doors closed and the aged motor in the wall started to rumble. The car jerked into motion. *Maybe I know too much. Maybe Doc's gotta be nice to me 'cause I saw stuff I should not have seen, things only a few know about. Maybe they gotta keep an eye on me. Shit. Maybe they don't want me leavin' the—*

The light flickered and went out. The elevator jerked to a stop rattling the rack of toxicology tubes. Mathew Duncan bent over and puked.

* * *

Dr. Cage sailed into the break room, pulling on his white lab coat. He locked the door and drew the blinds, then poured himself a cup of a coffee as he watched Sergeant Gibbs fiddle with a dozen large, glossy, black-and-white photographs spread out on one of the long tables.

Sergeant Gibbs looked like a professional wrestler—towering, bulky, broad shoulders, thick arms, no neck, and a crooked nose from too-many untreated breaks. Although he was a gentle-natured man, his visual presence made people nervous. Size came natural to the Gibbs men. Strength came from hard work— growing up on a farm, working dawn to dusk and eating healthy. After a four year stint in the USAF Security Forces, Gibbs returned to North Dakota and joined the Ward County Sheriff's Office. Although he had other opportunities, *sergeant* would be all he wanted. Keep life simple. Gibbs knew his limits. He hated telling people what to do, and he hated people telling him what to do. Sergeant seemed about right.

Gibbs knew Dr. Cage better than most in law enforcement. Each year, Ward County sent the state medical examiner the most bodies. Ward County, one of the seven counties accounting for more than eighty percent of the violent crime in the state, had a worn path to Bismarck. Automobile and farming accidents, suicides, and the occasional homicide kept Gibbs on the road from Minot most every week. But unlike his usual trips to spend time with Cage, this one had him scratching his head.

Stepping up to the table with his nose in a mug, Cage perused the glossies. Gibbs started talking as he touched each one. "Our crime scene is on the south side of the 7000 block of 247th Avenue Southwest, Douglas, North Dakota—22.3 miles south of Minot. Found the 1955 Mack tow truck at Lake Vernon Quarry. It was sittin' behind leveled mounds of sand and gravel."

"That explains some things," Cage said as he leaned closer to study the truck. All the windows were gone and the cab filled with sand, gravel, and snow. *How'd you get in that quarry?* Cage wondered.

"You can see the front and rear end damage," Gibbs said. "The crushed metal is new."

"Where'd you find our victim?"

"About a hundred yards southeast of the truck. Damn miracle. Pitch black and snowing out there, with ten inches of snow on the ground. Like the dark side of the moon. We froze our asses off—twenty-three below zero with a ten-mile wind."

He pushed two pictures toward Cage. "Let's stay with the truck a minute. All of this may make better sense. This truck belongs to a guy named Joe Harbinger out of Stanley."

"Our victim?" Cage asked.

"No. Joe died a year ago. Strange circumstances I need to get back into, but that's another story. I got my people sniffing around. We do know Joe rented out his tow truck a lot. We're

getting the list of customers. We'll find out who was drivin' it."
He shifted in discomfort and readjusted his belt around his waist.

"This truck tells a story, Doc. Looks like a rear-end collision followed by front-end crash in the Lake Vernon Quarry—the mounds of gravel and sand. No other vehicles found in the area."

"Hit and run. Middle of nowhere," Cage sighed.

"What's strange is that the tow truck got hit almost four miles before it crashed into that quarry."

"Our victim was on the run?" Cage said.

"Looks that way. We figure, the truck got hit hard from behind. Bent the hell out of a twenty-ton towing winch. Appears after the rear-end collision, the vehicle that hit him got lodged between the winch and bed of the tow truck. The tow truck dragged it all of the 3.7 miles."

Gibbs pushed more photos at Cage. "You can see the damage to the road all the way. It musta sprayed sparks into the sky like the Fourth of July. Hell of a show for the prairie varmints." He looked up for a reaction.

"I see bullet holes on the back of the cab." Cage pointed with a pen. "Here, here, and here. You catch those?"

"Good eye. Yup. Windows shot out. Safety glass holds together to some degree. We have sections with complete bullet holes. We found plenty of debris on that stretch of road."

"Can we assume the uninvited passenger did the shooting?" Cage asked.

"Yes, for now. We'll get ballistics to confirm. But I think it's safe to say close range, not sniper range. Based on the rear-end debris and gouges in the tarmac, we know a vehicle rammed the tow truck when both were travelin' near seventy. Our victim here, the tow truck driver, was sure as hell on the run."

"And the pursuer was determined to get him," Cage said under his breath.

"Tow driver left the road here," Gibbs said, running a finger down the road to the quarry. "I don't think he lost consciousness. No signs of trying to stop. I think he had it floored."

"He drove into those piles for a reason—maybe to rid himself of the unwanted passenger that rammed him and was shooting at him," Cage said.

Gibbs nodded. "He drove like a man runnin' from a swarm of hornets."

Cage took a sip of coffee. "Okay. Tell me about my body."

The sergeant gathered the first set of photos and slid them into his notebook. He pulled out another set and placed one eight-by-ten glossy in front of the ME. After a big swallow from his thermos, he wiped his wet chin and said, "We were lucky to find this one, doc—for a lot of reasons."

"Why am I not surprised?"

"One of our dogs got the scent wanderin' 'round in the dark snowfield. Like I said, we found our victim a hundred yards from the crash site, a football field." Gibbs set down the next photo like it was the winning card in a poker game. "My deputy thought he was lookin' at a block of concrete. His dog kept yappin' at it as he dusted off the snow. He got close with a light. I think he realized it wasn't cement. It was a big block of ice. I think it was when his light found the eyes in that block of ice—my deputy blacked out right then. Fell like a tree—out cold."

"I can imagine it had to be a frightening moment."

"The dog dragged him all the way back to us."

"God," Cage sighed as he studied the photograph and half listened.

"Good thing Deputy Blithers is a skinny man. If he had weighed another ten pounds, I'm pretty sure Leo would have left him."

"Leo?" Cage looked up.

"The police dog ... Leo," Gibbs said. "We wouldn't have missed Deputy Blithers 'til mornin'. In an hour, he woulda been under another four inches of snow. We'd go back up there and look and all, but still don't know if we'd find him. Poor guy woulda probably been eaten by wild animals before the spring thaw ..."

Cage smiled in his coffee mug at Gibbs' wild imagination and emotional ramblings. It was one more thing he liked about the people in the Dakotas. "Okay. I think I have enough on the discovery story, Ray. Tell me why the U.S. Border Patrol is involved."

Gibbs ran a hand down his face and blinked back into the room. "Those boys got to the quarry minutes after our people called in the accident scene. Damnedest thing, six white vans pull up and park in a line next to our squad cars, their lights flashin' and all. I'm still not sure who they are, for real. Lot of cloak-and-dagger goin' on if you ask me."

"Looks like the federal government's monitoring you," Cage chided.

"I didn't think we were that important. Like I said, not sure about these guys. They say they're a mix, border patrol and a special-ops division of Homeland Security, workin' off the grid. We were told in no uncertain terms to stand down. They were takin' over. If you ask me, I'm thinkin' CIA. They act like CIA— secretive, holier-than-thou, dark suits, and white vans."

"You could be right, Ray. And you did say you were looking into Joe Harbinger and truck renters. That's not standing down." Cage shoved the pile of pictures away and carried his cup to the sink giving his friend time to process.

Gibbs gathered the photos back into his tattered, leather notebook and zipped it with a resounding yelp. "We will do what we always do," he huffed. "No government's gonna change our sworn duty to serve and protect the people of Ward County— CIA or not."

Cage nodded his unofficial approval as they moved into the

hall and headed for the Decomp Room where the nameless, mystery corpse thawed behind a locked door.

"From my experience, I doubt Homeland Security or the CIA is going to share anything with us," Cage said. "Agent Frank Barth got me up in the middle of the night. It was a cryptic exchange, to say the least."

"What was his story?" Gibbs asked as they approached the door to the Decomp Room.

"Well, he assured me the bizarre death that was on its way to my morgue was a routine government matter. Told me not to overthink it. Agent Barth said the unique status of the corpse was part of a messy conflict between savage criminal elements—a scare tactic. Told me the incident at the quarry was tied to an illegal trafficking operation, contraband crossing the Canadian border into the U.S., something he was not at liberty to discuss."

"Hell, that's more than I got," Gibbs groused.

"And that's *all* I got," Cage said. "Barth did apologize for the late hour and any inconvenience."

"Why even send the body to you? Why not take it themselves?" Gibbs asked.

"They need a paper trail through the state medical examiner's office. Even Homeland Security and the CIA have to cover their butts in case of a Senate subcommittee hearing one day. I think oversight is our last bastion of protection for some of these cloaked agencies. Even that is getting weaker every day."

"When they got in my face at the quarry, they didn't explain themselves. Flashed their badges and passed papers officially taking over. I scanned the list of statutes and legal mumbo jumbo —seen it before. Minot Air Force Base people carry it around all the time to shut us down."

"What does it say?" Cage asked.

"In legal terms it says we are to stick our collective heads up our collective asses and leave them there until they tell us we can pull them out," Gibbs said. Cage chuckled as he unlocked the door and Gibbs looked over his shoulder at the elevator doors, the motor churning.

"You sure this place is secured?" Gibbs asked. "Can anyone get down here?"

"The two stairwells from the first floor and dock doors are locked with deadbolts and three-inch steel crossbars. The elevator requires a key. Every time someone inserts a key, the security camera snaps a picture and logs the time. The protection of physical evidence held by the state is vital. Maintaining chain-of-evidence is our job here."

"I guess some cases don't get to the courts for years," Gibbs said.

"You should know something. Agent Frank Barth passed me a piece of paper, too. I have been officially instructed to conduct a confidential and proprietary inquest," Cage said. "I am supposed to notify them in advance of the postmortem examination so a government representative can be present. And my findings are to be sealed."

"So they got to you, too," Cage said.

"No city, county, or state law enforcement personnel are authorized to attend the autopsy, nor are they permitted to view any information pertaining to this case until it's released by the federal government."

Cage pushed open the door. "If they didn't need my signature on their paperwork, I would not get a look at this."

"They just want to check your box, Doc." Gibbs peered into the dark room. "Too late, I'm here and I'm not going away. You can tell the federal bastards I held my gun on you."

Cage smiled as he hit the switch. When the light filled the room, their mood changed. Cage and Gibbs stood in silence a few feet away from the work of demons.

In the warm room, the frozen block of human flesh had begun

to transform into a mass of hideous carnage. A thousand tiny gray stones were embedded over the entire surface, each stone surrounded by a blood-red, oozing jell and dusted with a thin layer of white sand like a sick jelly donut. The arms and legs were gone. Stubs had started to break free and protrude from the melting mass. The head, crushed like a rubber mask, floated under the glossy surface.

The eyes found both Cage and Gibbs. The nose was grotesquely flattened and the nostrils packed with sand, five inches apart. The lips were stretched into a thin rubber band surrounding a toothless hole packed with sand. As it thawed, the odious human mound on the stainless-steel gurney had begun to release streams of an amber viscous fluid that flowed into a slimy pool, filling a dedicated drip pan on the floor. The flattened base of the human blob released gases—they bubbled and moaned as if alive.

"I was not expecting this," Gibbs said with his mouth in his armpit. "I saw the frozen block, but—"

"He's still frozen at the core," Cage said. "Humans were not intended to be cubes." Cage reached up and adjusted the thermostat back to fifty degrees. "I need to slow down the thaw or we will lose what little evidence we've got."

"I guess the gravel and sand happened when he plowed into the mounds. What a terrible way to die—being crushed and buried like that."

"He was dead when the truck came to rest, Ray."

"Someone pulled him out of the truck."

"Yes."

"What made him a block of—?"

"They put him in some kind of compressing device, like a garbage compactor."

"The kind they use in restaurants?" Gibbs asked.

With the inquisitive eyes of a forensic pathologist, Cage

studied the dead mass and whispered, "Every bone has been crushed, pulverized under intense pressure. His body mass filled the rectangular chamber moments after the pressure was applied."

"Why would someone *do* that?" Gibbs asked.

"I can only speculate. Someone went to great lengths to stop him. Ramming into a tow truck at a high rate of speed is risky. They were motivated, and they came prepared. I would assume a compactor device capable of handling a human being would be substantial both in size and weight. The requirements to power the compressive pneumatics would be substantial."

"So from the start, they planned to crush him and leave him in that field?"

"It is obvious they did not intend to take the body with them."

"Wonder why," Gibbs said as he covered his nose.

"If your dog had not found him, we probably never would have."

"I'll be damned," Gibbs muttered. "Made him into a human saltlick."

"Detectable by wild animals from miles around," Cage said. "I suspect his remains would have been gone in days—a supersized frozen TV dinner."

"You're right. Wild animals can find a dead mouse in five feet of snow."

"Everything's hungry out there, especially in the winter. Whatever is not eaten is swallowed by the Great Plains, my friend."

Gibbs leaned closer to the corpse. "You think a gray wolf pulled off the arms and legs?"

"Hard to say until we get a look under a microscope. Although every bone is granulized and floats in a ruptured-tissue puree, there may be enough tissue fragments for us to reconstruct some of the story."

Cage shined a penlight on a stub. "There is evidence of straight line cuts mixed with torn tissue edges. That tells me the arms and legs were removed by a cutting instrument, not the teeth of an animal."

"Removed. Why?" Gibbs asked as he struggled to find some fresh air in the room.

"Don't know yet. But it might be important."

"Why do you say that?"

"Because appendages would not have been a problem for the compactor."

The door to the Decomp Room opened behind them. They watched Mathew Duncan take a step into the room with the medical camera at his side and eyes locked on the floor.

Cage patted Duncan's shoulder. "We're only taking a few pictures. No autopsy today." He turned back to the mound of human flesh. "Our victim needs more time to thaw."

"We got some sick people out there," Gibbs growled. "Hate to wait on anything."

"This is bigger than you're thinking, Ray." Cage shined his penlight into the eyes of the deceased. "We've got a shrouded government agency breathing down our necks minutes after an accident scene is discovered in the middle of nowhere. They force their way into this with no explanation."

"I know, and I don't like it."

Cage moved his light across the half-frozen and half-gelatinous mound. "Whoever did this—why were they so determined to kill this man and prepared to dispose of his body *this way?*"

"And why is this important to the United States Government? You're right, Doc. This is not a typical homicide."

"We all may be in danger," Cage murmured. *I need to slow this thaw process way down. The cells and tissue closest to the core will have a story to tell. The external trauma is too great. Cells and*

tissue at and near the surface are most damaged—won't give us
enough. Elliott Sumner has seen some of the most heinous kills in
the world. Maybe I can get him to fly up here and take a look. I'm
going to need some help on this one.

"Doctor Cage," Duncan whispered with eyes on the floor still refusing to look at the carnage. "There are people in suits upstairs. A lot of 'em."

Cage blinked back into the room. "Okay, and—?"

"They know you're down here. They are demanding access. I stepped out of the office and went to the storage room. When no one was looking, I came down the old laundry chute."

"We have a laundry chute?" Cage asked.

"Yes, sir. I saw six white vans outside—I counted 'em. There were a lot of men in suits standin' around outside. Some were redirectin' traffic. Others just watchin' everything. I don't think Miss Maggie can hold 'em very much longer."

On Mathew's last word came the pounding on the dock doors. "Shit," Gibbs blurted.

"Why didn't you speak up?" Cage huffed as he checked his watch. *I need time to think.*

"What the hell's goin' on?" Gibbs demanded, unsnapping the strap over his gun.

"I don't think we need to shoot anyone, Ray." Cage turned back to the melting human cube. "We're at the front end of something big. This body can tell a story if we handle it correctly. I need time for a proper thaw and postmortem. They can't move him until I am done."

Mathew hesitated. "Dr. Cage, you said for me to speak up. This thing, this man, I mean. He has a name now. I heard it before—"

"Who said it's got a name?" Gibbs shot back.

"One of the guys in a suit said the name. He was on his

cellphone facing the wall. He didn't want anyone to hear, but I did. He repeated it real slow like he had to get it perfect."

"Mathew, who is this man?" Cage demanded.

"He is—"

The pounding on the dock doors stopped. They jerked their heads from the body to the door. The deafening silence had returned. It crept down the empty halls of the state morgue like an evil presence. Eyes widened the moment the elevator motor came alive again. This time it would not be Mathew Duncan.

Cage turned off the light and lowered the thermostat to forty. They stood in the dark Decomp Room staring down the empty hall at the elevator doors. The hum of the elevator got louder. Then the light appeared at the top of the crack. They watched it descend. The line of light touched the cracked linoleum and grew until it reached the Decomp Room. The elevator stopped.

CHAPTER 4

"The right thing and the easy thing are never the same."
Kama Garcia

W hen the thin line of light touched the Decomp Room door, Mathew backed up against the wall and Deputy Gibbs reached for his gun. With his eyes on the elevator doors, Cage reached over and patted Gibbs hand and whispered, "Wait."

The elevator doors opened. From the dark room, they watched through the small glass window. Three suits stepped off and ran into the left hall. Three more suits stepped off and ran into the right hall. One suit stepped off and stared at the Decomp Room, a hundred feet away.

What are you doing here? Cage thought. *The federal government has no right to enter this secured floor without my authorization—we have sovereign rights. This body belongs to me by law. He died in my state. He is my legal jurisdiction. I cannot let you take him. We're not going to have another Kennedy fiasco. There are new laws on the books.*

Cage watched the suit approach. When the man passed under the first ceiling light, Cage recognized Agent Frank Barth. Then Cage saw the bulge under the coat. Barth walked straight and steady, keeping his eyes locked on the little window on the door at the end of the hall. At the halfway point, someone appeared behind him. "Sir, the autopsy room is empty."

Barth continued to walk. Three more suits merged at the elevator and watched.

Gibbs started again to pull his gun from his holster. Cage

again applied a hand over his. Barth stopped at the door. "Dr. Cage?" he called. "I've been looking for you."

"You found me," Cage replied as he opened the door.

Barth squinted. His narrowed gaze found Gibbs and Duncan in the shadows, Gibbs' hand on his gun.

"You're not authorized to be on this floor, Agent Barth," Cage said.

Barth's thin lips stretched into an awkward grin as he looked left and right. "Yes. Of course, you are technically correct. But I'd like to think of us as on the same team. What is standard protocol for team members?" He leaned in to see the frozen body. "Is that our victim?"

"Your idea of *team* is very different from mine," Cage said. "You need to go."

"No, we need to talk. No one can leave this floor."

On his last word, another suit appeared at the end of the hall. "Agent Barth, they are in place, sir," he shouted and then joined the others at the elevator doors.

"What's in place?" Cage asked.

"What we need to talk about, Doctor. Please, all of you, follow me."

Barth pivoted and walked away. Cage and Gibbs looked at each other. Cage pulled Duncan behind him and followed Barth. Gibbs followed Duncan. They passed the suits at the elevator— no heads turned. They walked down the hall and through the double metal doors into the main autopsy room. All lights were on. The three stopped in their tracks. There were three gurneys. On each gurney was another frozen human block, each measuring the same dimensions as the one in the Decomp Room, but these were not covered in gravel and sand. They were glistening, bloody, frozen human cubes.

Mathew Duncan threw up. Sergeant Gibbs leaned back against the wall with his hand on his gun and eyes closed. Cage took in the frozen carnage, his grim expression revealed nothing.

"We found that one at Willow Lake National Wildlife Refuge. Don't ask me how." Agent Barth pointed to the next. "We found that one at J. Clark Salyer National Wildlife Reserve. Again, don't ask."

Dr. Cage pointed to the third human cube. "And ...?"

"Compliments of the Royal Canadian Mounted Police," Barth said. "It's a little different. Some X-treme hunters looking for a wild adventure in Manitoba came across it a hundred feet off a trail in the Turtle Mountain Provincial Park in Canada. They were certain aliens were turning people into blocks of ice. Let's just say they are being held somewhere nice until we are ready for any of this to get out—national interests."

"What is going on?" Cage asked.

"I apologize for our pushy and somewhat shrouded behavior, Dr. Cage, Sergeant Gibbs, and ... whoever the one vomiting is."

"That's Mathew Duncan, my diener. A medical assistant," Cage said.

"I see. He will be staying with us a while," Barth said. "All of you will. As I was saying, I apologize for the stealth nature of things. I can tell you, we believe we are at the front end of a developing national crisis. I am charged with the task of directing the forensic investigation on the ground up here as it unfolds. Our objective is to get ahead of it if possible."

"So the government is concerned about a 'national crisis'?" Cage asked.

"Yes," Barth replied.

"I have no idea what that all means. Now I have four unidentified human ice cubes in my morgue. You're talking about a crisis, yet you break laws and get in the way of the people who could help most." Cage drew a deep breath and seemed to grow an inch taller. "Who the hell do you think you are, Barth? What makes you think you can come in here and push around a state medical examiner's office?"

"I should shoot you," Gibbs growled.

The agent's eyes sized-up Gibbs, and then he turned back to Cage. "If we do not uncover meaningful information soon, our nation might be in grave danger. That is all I am authorized to say. Trust me when I tell you this: No one will ever know what happened here if we do not want them to know."

"What does that mean?" Cage asked, although he knew exactly what it meant.

"We need your help, not your judgment," Barth said with a sigh. "We need a detailed forensic autopsy performed on these four people as soon as possible. My job is to keep a blanket over this until I am told otherwise. Others have the task of identifying the ... *threat* connected to these bodies."

Cage nodded. "I see." He was sure of one thing: Arguing would be fruitless. The government had legitimate reasons to keep national security matters under wraps. Regardless of the politics of it all, Cage wanted to do the autopsies to get answers, too.

Barth stepped closer to Cage and studied his face. "You are known for your work on the effects of extreme temperatures on dead human tissue. I've done my research on you, Dr. Cage. Why are you concerned about this work, these autopsies? Or am I misreading you?"

"I am an expert in some areas, not all. When human tissue is treated with lysing agents, irradiated, crushed into a gelatinous slush, frozen, and thawed, there are enormous variables at play. There may be no useful information here. These people have been crushed. Their bones have been pulverized and tissues destroyed at the cellular level. The thaw process must be very slow, or we lose what little we have a chance to find."

"You are the expert. We are limited by biology. I understand that a proper thaw process gives us the best chance for meaningful information."

"And it also gives you the time to get me the help I need."

"What help?"

"These homicides may have international implications. I need someone with global forensic experience to do the autopsies with me. They will see things I do not even look for in North Dakota."

"We will get them here. Do you have someone in mind, Dr. Cage?" Agent Barth asked.

Cage nodded. "Dr. Elliott Sumner."

CHAPTER 5

"Lack of money is the root of all evil."
George Bernard Shaw

Day three – Pingree State Hospital

D r. Frank Rice pulled the bent Chesterfield from the gold case his father left him. Each time he straightened another cigarette, he had the same thought—*Death by a hideous disease would be better than a slow death in hell or a shank in the gut.*

The Pingree State Hospital for the insane opened its doors in 1910. The altruistic ethos of the times funded the construction of a sprawling campus and the hiring of top professionals in the emerging fields of psychiatric medicine. But in the first decade, the *insane* population proved to be a much greater challenge than anyone had anticipated. Their complex and often frightening mental conditions often worsened, and their numbers only grew. By the end of the first decade, the best of intentions had been overwhelmed by the harsh realities—overcrowding and chaos. Public interest waned and funding dried up. Pingree soon slid into the dark abyss of terrifying epidemics, rumors of patient abuse, and horrible deaths. When pictures of shackled, naked, malnourished patients found their way into the newspapers, the *hell on the hill* went dark.

The state relocated the patients and their attorneys prosecuted those who had committed crimes against these vulnerable individuals. A few patients without options stayed behind, but most of the Pingree buildings stayed empty. Not until the late 1900s did the state legislature see an opportunity to save money and relieve overcrowding at their state penitentiary. The criminally insane and moderate-risk inmates were sent to Pingree, which became an unsecured prison site. Some say the state's action was the second Pingree mistake. The portal to hell reopened.

Dr. Rice tamped his cigarette on his gold case and gazed across the battered metal table at the old man he had treated for three of the last five years. He had almost given up on Milton Busey, an old man beyond repair. Rice did not update his diagnosis in the patient file, nor did he share his conclusions with the warden. Rice had to maintain his patient roster. The dwindling numbers threatened his sole source of income.

The once-successful psychiatrist had spent most of his life taking care of a wife diagnosed with multiple sclerosis a few months after their wedding. Their only child, a son, was born with cerebral palsy and other medical problems that eventually took his life. After their deaths, alcohol took his medical license. Just one week before he was to lose his house, Pingree called. The state required a *maintenance-of-affiliation* (MOA) contract with a doctorate of psychiatric medicine. Their longtime MD had died, creating the vacancy. Paltry fees and a terrible history had hampered efforts to replace him.

If Pingree failed to comply with the MOA, the state might void their charter and jeopardize their existence. In a desperate attempt to save the facility, the warden agreed to overlook Dr. Rice's medical license *inconvenience*. In turn, Rice agreed to overlook Pingree in general.

"You're not allowed to smoke in here," Busey whined. Like a wounded rodent caught in a trap, he wobbled on his metal chair and tugged at the chains bolted to the floor.

Rice smiled with the Chesterfield in his lips and flame dancing at its tip. He puffed and blew smoke across the table into Busey's snake eyes. In an hour, Rice could return to his bottle.

"It's late, Milton. What did you want to tell me that could not wait for Tuesday?"

"When're they gonna get these things off me?" Busey seethed. "Rules are, no chains on inmates over seventy while in the goddamn medical conference room."

Rice took a long drag. Smoke fell from his mouth and nose. "Relax. They need to put checkmarks in their boxes. You know that."

The first day Rice visited Pingree, he took the tour and was struck by the lack of security. Instead of prison cells, there were bedrooms and opened doors. Instead of walls and fences and barbed wire, there were manicured hedges and open fields. Instead of armed guards, there were attendants carrying clipboards and wearing casual clothes—no badges, no weapons. Rice was told the Pingree Correctional Center was an experiment. The state was testing a new way to reduce recidivism rate. Building more prisons was not an option because prisons were expensive. Instead of confinement, control, and punishment, the criminal population at Pingree would be treated with trust, respect, and freedoms.

Rice decided early not to get involved. He would not educate the naïve state legislature or underfunded board of corrections, both of which were desperate to find an economical solution to an impossible problem. Someone else could explain the mountains of psychoanalytical data on the behavior of the deviant criminal that preys on the weak. Someone else could explain that for these patients, every thought was aimed at creating another opportunity to hurt or kill. Rice, hardened by decades of dealing with psychopaths, rejected any possibility for rehabilitation of a class of human predators. But he would not share his view. The only effective measures he knew to work on psychopaths were cages, electric chairs, and a hangman's noose.

Instead, he decided he would stick to his job description. Rice visited Pingree every Tuesday, sat with the criminally insane for eight hours, and updated patient records. Every fourth Tuesday, he picked up his paycheck, purchased a case of vodka and three cartons of Chesterfields, and returned to his dark house at the end of a dark road. There he drank, smoked, and waited to die, until an unexpected opportunity came along.

On this empty Friday, he'd gotten a phone call from Pingree. The message was short—*Milton Busey needed to discuss a personal matter with his psychiatrist and it could not wait.* Rice put down the phone and turned to the suitcase of money. He had been waiting for this moment. Nothing in life was free.

"Why am I here, Milton?" Rice had asked again as he gazed out the window at his new Lexus. He didn't care as much about the car as he did the bottle under the towel on the front seat. "It's past my dinner time."

"Your dinner is vodka," Milton joked, his head down and dark eyes dancing beneath his nappy brows.

A short, muscular attendant came in unannounced and removed Milton's chains, and then unlocked the door that opened to the snow-dusted patio. "If you two want to smoke, you need to do it outside." He reached for the smoldering Chesterfield hanging in Dr. Rice's mouth. "I'm sorry, sir. I will need to take that. It's the rules."

After one more drag, Rice passed his smoke to the fat-fingered attendant. He and Busey watched the attendant leave the room, his pinched fingers in the air like he was transporting a dead fly by its wings.

The door closed. Busey rubbed his wrists as his eerie chuckle turned into a hacking cough. Rice knew the monster better than anyone. Busey had told him everything in the third year of therapy. Busey had admitted to killing five people in five states, but there had never been enough evidence to bring formal charges. The serial killer was proud of his skills—hiding bodies and covering his tracks. Busey often boasted he was the perfect killing machine, an unemotional perfectionist like the sick, bastard father that beat him.

Patient/doctor privacy laws tied Rice's hands, making it impossible to share what he knew about Busey with the police. But Rice could live with it, because Busey had accumulated enough other criminal offenses to keep him in prison well beyond his normal lifespan. He had been convicted of two counts of attempted murder of a law enforcement officer, three counts aggravated assault, armed robbery, and two counts of rape. Even better than the consecutive fifty-year sentences, Busey's kidneys were shot from a life of drinking and drugs. The old man would drop dead on his own within six months.

"Start talking, Milton," the weary Rice said now. "I'm not spending my whole evening with you."

"I got a phone call from a friend."

"And what did your *friend* have to say?" Rice rolled his fingers on the table.

"They killed Roan."

He stopped. "They killed Roan?"

"They killed Roan."

Rice focused on the evil man with the disgusting tufts of hair protruding from his nostrils and the deep crevices on his face. He stared at a man who—if what he was saying was true—had just lost his only son, yet showed no emotion.

"How can you be certain your friend is telling the truth?"

"Let's just say we've worked together on projects. We got a history. He made a lot of money with me. My friend is connected, has access to information."

"How exactly does he know Roan is dead?"

"A guy at the state morgue told him."

"Bismarck?"

"Yeah, Bismarck."

"The state medical examiner's office is a tight operation, Milton. Nothing gets out of that place. I doubt—"

"What're you talkin' about?" Busey growled.

"I seriously doubt anyone could obtain information from the state ME office before it was officially released. If he got it at all, it is probably public information. Milton, your contact would know you don't get a newspaper in here. He may have an agenda. If the information is public, I can look into it for you and get the details. When did it happen?"

"He does not have an agenda. Happened a couple days ago. You know who killed him. The bastards got what they needed and killed my boy." Busey kicked the table leg.

Rice jumped. He took a deep breath. "Okay. Let's just say your friend knows your son's body is at the state morgue. Even if that's true, he would not know the cause of death. Milton, your contact would not know if it was a homicide, accident, suicide, or something natural like a heart attack. He would not know *how* your son died. That information is held confidential by the ME until it's released to family. You're the only next of kin. They would come here and tell you, Milton."

Busey leaned back in the metal chair and looked at the ceiling. He rubbed his face with a gnarly hand and a grunt. "Anyone who saw the body would know he got killed, Rice."

"Well, I don't know about that either. Maybe they would know he was bleeding. They wouldn't know how or why. I'm just saying all this could be supposition or a trick."

"The bastards put my son in some kind of crushin' machine. My friend said they used one of them industrial compactors. They crushed Roan to death. Turned him into a meat cube!"

Oh my God! Rice thought. *He was executed and disposed of ...*

"Them foreigners tortured and killed my boy."

What have I gotten myself into? "Why would they do that?"

Rice asked. "Milton, you need to tell me everything. Tell me the nature of the secret information you gave these people."

"They didn't need Roan after they got it done," he said.

Rice waited for Busey's answer. He turned to the windows and looked across the empty field of snow toward his new Lexus. This time, the bottle waiting for him did not cross his mind. *Why did I get involved in this—the money, a way out of this place? I should have known only dangerous people pay that kind of money for—*

"I'm gonna kill 'em all," Busey seethed.

Dr. Rice had arranged the meeting that started it all. He would learn different later. At first, he had rejected Busey's request to set up a meeting with his son in the medical conference room, the only place at Pingree without surveillance. Something clandestine was in the works. Milton said he had information people wanted and would pay a lot of money for. Busey had reached a point where he now needed to pass this information through Roan. When he said Rice would get $100,000 for setting up the meetings at Pingree, Rice was shocked. Then he started to think about it with a bottle in his hand. That kind of money could finance his way out of Pingree hell. And so, he got involved.

Rice had some second thoughts until he picked up a duffle bag at an airport locker, as instructed. It contained $400,000 in banded, small bills. $300,000 was for Milton. $100,000 was for him. He then learned Milton had been involved with his *unnamed* clients for almost a year before needing Roan meetings set up at Pingree. One night Rice poured all the cash onto his dining room table and got drunk. After staring at it a long while, he realized he could keep Milton's money too. Milton's kidneys were shot. Milton would be dead in less than six months. That night Rice decided to say nothing and just wait.

"I'm startin' with the lawyer. I'll find her and I'll get Roan's money and kill—"

"You're not going anywhere, Milton. You'll die in Pingree and you know it. You'll be dead by the spring, if not sooner. You need me. I can help. I now have a vested interest."

"Maybe you're wrong. Maybe I'll beat this kidney thing. Stranger things have happened, Rice. I appreciate the offer, but I don't think—"

"It would take a miracle in your case, Milton. Look. I can be your eyes and ears while you focus on your health miracle. I do not want these people coming for either of us. It's been almost a year for you. Maybe they think they can kill all of us. I certainly do not want to be executed like Roan, nor do you. For me to help you, I need to know more about your deal."

"I always thought you were a smart man," Busey sneered.

"What does that mean?"

Busey got to his feet like an injured grasshopper, his skinny legs carrying his bent body to the door leading to the snow-dusted patio. He stood inches from the cold glass with a boney hand on the knob. "You're supposed to know everything about me," he said. "Maybe you've been in a drunken stupor most the time."

"That's not helpful. You benefit little by taking out your frustrations on me."

"If you had paid closer attention, you would be able to answer your own questions."

"I did listen to you. I still have questions."

"What could a guy like me possibly know that would be worth a million bucks? I told you Roan was gonna get six hundred thousand, you a hundred, and me three hundred." Busey dropped his head and snarled, "But the bastards didn't pay Roan."

"You're a criminal, Milton. You've killed a lot of people. I assumed you provided other criminals with information that would make them money. I guess I did not want to know more."

"Wrong, doctor. I grew up in Cooperstown, North Dakota. Before my life of crime, I was in the U.S. Air Force. That's where I acquired my expertise in demolition. I got real good at destroying things. It's an art. I found it challenging. I like danger. You gotta know about all kinds of explosives, what they do under all sorts of conditions. Obliterating things is easy. Obliterating specific things without killing people and obliterating everything around your target is difficult. They called me the *Brain Surgeon*, Dr. Rice. I surgically removed things so well that the government asked me to come back in the '90s to do some work for them— secret of course, the Belden area."

"We've never talked about any of this," Rice said.

"It's in my file if you'd ever opened it up."

"Your military record in the '60s and government work in the '90s is in there, but it's heavily redacted. No one at Pingree or the State Penitentiary can know the details. It is classified. I recall one notation—you were once stationed at the Minot Air Force Base, the 94th Wing Command."

"Guess my work was important," Busey said with a twisted grin.

Rice joined him at the door to the patio. They stood inches from the cold glass watching snow drift onto the open field and cars in the distant lot. "Forecast says another four inches by morning." Rice rubbed a thumb on the gold case deep in his pocket as he weighed his desire for nicotine to standing in the freezing cold. He hated smoke-free environments.

"I guess the government felt safe knowing you were in prison the rest of your life."

"I signed up during the Bay of Pigs," he said. "The Berlin Wall was bein' built then. The next year, the Cuban Missile Crisis. The world was a very different place. Every nation had a bomb and an itchy trigger finger. Nobody trusted anybody."

"I remember," Rice said, nodding. "I was in medical school. A

U-2 spy plane got shot down over Russia. China detonated an atomic bomb. I remember the Bay of Pigs and Cuban Missile Crisis. The Soviets invaded Czechoslovakia and Kennedy was assassinated. Turbulent times."

"The country's missile program changed. We were on alert a lot: in '62 the Minuteman One, in '66 Minuteman Two, and in the seventies Minuteman Three." Busey rubbed his whiskers and stretched his turkey neck. He looked like a dead man in prison cottons.

"The Three carried a nuclear warhead with 170 kilotons," Busey continued. "That's ten times the destructive force we dropped in World War Two."

Rice swallowed hard. "Are you telling me your demolition expertise and military background provided you with the *insider information* you sold, Milton?"

"Yup. That's what I'm tellin' you." Busey smiled. His fingers found the razor-sharp shank with the taped handle. "I'm tellin' you, I was an important part of building some of the 150 missile silos we got spread-out across an area around Minot the size of New Jersey. I was not always a loser, Dr. Rice."

You sold secret government information to—? Rice shuddered.

"And like everything else our stupid government does, everything changes. The SALT Agreements, the Berlin Wall comin' down, Reagan's Star Wars dream, and the START Treaty, they screwed up everything. The feds brought me back with a bunch of other guys to demolish a bunch of the silos we had built. It was another waste of goddamn time."

Rice decided on a cigarette. Now he had second thoughts about giving Milton the shot. "The world's a complicated place, Milton. We can't let that change us. We've talked about that many times—the source of your anger."

I think we pretty much figured out my old man is the source of my anger. "They shoulda' stopped with all the talkin' in the '60s,"

Busey spewed. "We just let our enemies get stronger, like the bastards who killed Roan." *I can cross that field, take that Lexus, and get a hundred miles out of Pingree before they check on us.*

"You told someone about the Minot missile silos," Rice said. He turned to Busey. Their eyes met. "Who did you tell, Milton? What are they planning?" *I can't leave this alone. I gotta tell someone.*

"You know, when I was in Australia years ago, I learned 'bout the tiger snake. Not a particularly attractive thing to look at. It doesn't like encounters. Stays to itself unless it's bothered. Did you know its venom can kill a person in thirty minutes? Affects the nervous system—shortness of breath, paralysis, a painful death." *All I need is them keys to that Lexus.* "Seventy percent of the people bitten by the tiger snake die even after antivenin treatment."

"What're you talking about?" Rice pulled a bent Chesterfield from his gold case and stepped closer to the door to the patio that Busey now blocked.

He kept staring out the window. "When pushed enough, the tiger snake attacks." Busey gripped the shank in his pocket.

"I'm sure there is a lot of symbolism in all that, but we don't have the time. We have a real problem, Milton. If your son was executed, these people are coming for you and me. We need a plan. I cannot help if I don't know what information you sold and who you sold it to."

Busey's darting eyes found the bump in Rice's pocket—the keys to the Lexus for sure. "If I tell you, I gotta kill you."

"Very funny. Focus, Milton. Please, just answer my questions."

"You don't want to irritate a tiger snake," Busey snarled as he looked up at Dr. Rice. Milton Busey showed his stained yellow teeth as his cheeks ballooned and sparse whiskers poked from the edges of his perverted smile.

CHAPTER 6

"The hardest thing of all is to find a black cat in a dark room,
especially if there is no black cat."
Confucius

Day Four – London, England

"I'm afraid this one has been *purged*, gentlemen."
Harold Turpin winced as he shifted weight onto his 19th
century English walking cane with the ebonized shaft. The
gnawing pain in his left hip eased as the brass tip sank into the
carpet. "He is not like the others. Belongs to someone else."

After three decades of simplifying the horrifically complex,
Scotland Yard had learned to listen to Turpin. Randolph Pepper,
standing at the window next to the retired profiler, sucked his
pipe. The smoldering bowl remained perfectly still, locked in the
iron bite beneath his sweeping mustache. "Are you still
suggesting we seek outside help on this one, Harold?"

"*Suggesting* is such a timid word, Randolph. *Instructing* is
much better." Turpin stared out the window of the brownstone
on Bayley across from Bedford Square in downtown London.

Mesmerized by the cascading sheets of rain beneath
flickering streetlamps, the three stood in a line. The inclement
weather on the other side of the glass served as a welcomed
distraction for the two returning from another gruesome
homicide.

"You have another opportunity to properly guide the Yard,"
Turpin chided.

Pepper rolled his eyes at the acerbic wit. Over two decades of working together, they both had learned to ignore the other's peculiarities most of the time. "I suppose your *guidance* would include the engagement of that American lad, the one you cannot stop fawning over, the one they call the world-renowned forensic fellow—Dr. Elliott Sumner."

"You must be psychic, old man," Turpin shot back.

"Old man? Codswallop! I'm younger than you, sir," Pepper puffed.

"Elliott Sumner is forty. I would say that qualifies as a man. He knows the *Camden Cutter* better than anyone. But this new victim is work of another—not the Cutter."

"I must agree with Harold," Bennett interrupted. Of the three, Bennett Stotsbury would appear to be contributing the least. However, the Detective Chief Inspector saw his job as managing Turpin's pugnacious pontifications and Pepper's despotic sarcasm.

Stotsbury knew the two men standing beside him possessed brilliant investigative minds. He also knew they approached each mystery from opposite ends of the deductive-reasoning spectrum. Although they predictably met in the middle, the tumultuous ride always ran the risk of derailing. Stotsbury's role was to keep the two sleuths on the tracks.

While looking over his notes, Stotsbury repositioned himself between the two standing at the bay windows—the time for separation had come. "Superintendent Pepper," he said. "We have established that the Camden Cutter does not remove an *even number* of appendages from his victims. Of the eleven cases, the Cutter took one appendage from seven and three from four. That, along with day-of-death, street addresses, and ages of victims, birth orders, and the number of slashes counted on each victim, led to our conclusion: the Camden Cutter always works in odd numbers for still unknown reasons. And our new victim has four amputations."

"Thank you for reminding Mr. Pepper of the obvious," Turpin said, looking over his glasses at his intellectual opponent.

"I am not in disagreement with the facts, Bennett," Pepper barked. "I'm inclined to believe our *John Smith* is not a Camden Cutter victim. However, I fail to see a good reason to take this homicide outside the Yard."

"John Smith, Joe Bloggs, John Q. Public—for God's sake, Randolph, what is your aversion to *John Doe*, the universal place-holder originated in the Middle Ages?" Turpin asked. "It has served the United Kingdom and bloody rest of the civilized world quite well for more than a century, sir. Why do you insist upon inserting your claptrap terminology?"

Pepper stared at the empty park, revealing nothing. Stotsbury also ignored the lecture and flipped another page in his small notebook. "When the Camden Cutter removes a body part, the dissection is flawless, tantamount to a delicate surgical procedure."

Turpin slid his wire spectacles into his tight breast pocket and fished for a small cigar. "Yes. This kill is anything but. It appears to have been sloppy and rushed. It was an execution and hurried process to meet some sort of standard and deadline, not a ritual."

"I think we can all agree this was a *substandard kill* as compared to the Camden Cutter's work," Stotsbury said. "Would you agree our perpetrator seemed to be on assignment?"

"I agree, Bennet," Turpin said. "This butchery was intended to eliminate a person and alter physical evidence."

"I too agree, Bennet," Pepper said. "These amputations are substandard, comparatively."

"Gentlemen, I am quite confident—even after our very capable forensic team completes their work—we will not see the big picture until it is too late for someone else," Turpin said quietly.

"What does that mean?" Pepper asked.

"It means, sir, we do not possess a crumb of relevant background data. We have no viable avenues to pursue." He lit his small cigar. "Something is going on here that is much bigger than we can appreciate. This kill is likely far more meaningful to someone else, and it is that someone who we need to find in haste. We do not want Scotland Yard acting as an impediment, one that launches another's peril."

"Are you saying this homicide is *irrelevant* to the Yard?" Stotsbury asked.

Turpin blew a smoke ring. It exploded on the cold glass. "Other than this body being found in the streets of London, everything tells me it is not a case we should worry about, and not likely the work of the Camden Cutter. I am convinced it is simply a horrific deposit."

"And therein lies your basis of international linkage?" Pepper inquired.

"Yes. Need I itemize the other factors, sir?"

"Nationality, is that one, Harold?" Stotsbury asked.

"Yes. Our *John Doe* is of North African descent."

"And why is Dr. Sumner the best one to bring in on this?" Stotsbury asked.

Turpin observed his glowing ash like the one who created fire. "Dr. Sumner has the best view. His work is in the global arena. He will see international connections faster than anyone. This dreadful mutilation is but a piece of a larger puzzle. We just happen to be in the path."

"We have witnessed Dr. Sumner's work—the Serpentine Strangler," Stotsbury said. "What we failed to unravel in fifteen years, Sumner accomplished in eleven days. I have never witnessed a stronger set of investigative skills."

"I don't know about all that," Pepper murmured with his chin held high.

"Please. Clearly, there are enormous benefits to be derived from a perfect photographic memory," Turpin said. "That, coupled with an unmeasurable IQ and advanced forensic training, helps. Elliott Sumner's global view matters. This strange homicide ties to others elsewhere and served a purpose. There is an *incidental* reason why it surfaced in London."

Randolph Turpin still had a sharp mind and interest in ridding the world of evil. He considered himself lucky his Parkinson's had waited until age sixty to rear its ugly head. The loss of balance came first. It took him out of the field—the center of his universe. He resisted leaving the Yard. After a year of sitting behind a desk, he decided to retire.

His exquisite criminal mind, profiling skills, and miscreant logic were an irreplaceable combination. Instead of finding Harold Turpin behind a desk in a stuffy office on 10 Broadway, the top brass routinely met him on a park bench in Bedford Square. Only during the most inclement weather could he be found in his study. Even on those occasions, Turpin was at his bay windows watching the world.

"If you look above the treetops to the right, you can see the dome of the British Museum. Did you know that, Harold?" Pepper asked, knowing the answer. Changing the subject was his signature method of moving beyond tension.

Everything about Randolph Pepper defined him as a proud, upper-class Brit—always the perfect-pressed pinstriped suit, trimmed handlebar mustache, polished round glasses, and flat belly with the draping gold chain attached to a gold pocket watch. His annoying attention to detail and stubborn pursuit of criminals had moved him up the ladder to Superintendent. With retirement now five years away, he held little interest in other positions.

"Thank you for pointing that out," Turpin said, tongue-in-cheek. All three knew the view of the dome from Adeline Place could be appreciated by a blind man at night. And all three accepted Pepper as the one who had to move conversations beyond the verbal jousts.

"Harold, I believe Dr. Sumner may be unavailable," Stotsbury said. "I recall a confidential memorandum circulated some time ago—a mental breakdown."

"I spoke with Albert Bell yesterday," Turpin said.

"The billionaire patriarch in Memphis, Tennessee?" Pepper asked.

"Yes, and Elliott Sumner's biological father," Turpin shot back.

"After the Serpentine Strangler case, Sumner was hospitalized in Texas," Pepper said. "His recovery was defined as miraculous, but the prognosis remained guarded. After release from the hospital, Sumner terminated his global forensic enterprise and disappeared."

"Yes, I know all that. It was a year ago," Turpin said. "Since the stint in the hospital, the Memphis Police Department engaged Dr. Sumner to hunt a legendary serial killer—the Bluff City Butcher. The assignment was successful, but there was an emotional cost. The last I'd heard, Dr. Sumner went off the grid. He had worked on a veiled international project."

"Did Albert Bell know how to reach him?" Stotsbury asked.

Turpin looked down for the first time. "He said he would try—"

"Jolly good," Pepper spouted. "You say Albert Bell will *try* to locate his son. That certainly fits our expeditious needs. Nothing can stand in our way now. We can take John Smith off the books —solved. Oh. I'm sorry, old man. I meant to say John Doe."

Stotsbury held up a hand, stopping Pepper's rant. "Harold, maybe a backup plan is to engage INTERPOL now. When Albert Bell locates Dr. Sumner, he can join us."

"I don't think that would be wise."

"I don't understand why not."

"Maintaining confidentiality with INTERPOL is questionable. Involving them could create more problems. We do not know what we are dealing with. Our information may help them with their agenda but not benefit the case or those most exposed."

"I know you, Harold. Something else has you worried," Pepper said.

Turpin closed his eyes. "John Doe's cell phone. There were only two calls made—both to North Dakota."

"How did I miss that?" Stotsbury asked as he flipped pages. "You say a cellphone was recovered and only two calls were made, and those were to the U.S.?"

"Yes, it was a disposable phone. I thought you knew."

"Are you proposing CIA as a backup?" Stotsbury asked.

Turpin sighed. "There is no suitable backup option. We must find Elliott Sumner."

Pepper turned red. "What am I missing? Calls to North Dakota—so what?"

"The first call was six hours before John Doe was carved up. The second call was six minutes before. I had the Yard check into those calls for me. We learned they were made to the Pingree Correctional Center in North Dakota, to an inmate named Milton Busey."

"Okay. I'm listening. I need more. What is this Mr. Busey's story?"

"I don't know his story yet. However, I do know he is a heathen."

"You don't know the man's story, but you do know he is a heathen? Wonderful. Harold, I do believe you are on one of your tangents once again. I am starting to get concerned your Parkinson's has moved to your brain, old man."

"Mr. Pepper, that is not helpful," Stotsbury said with his most stern voice.

"I am sorry, but we do not have the time to go down another rabbit hole with Mr. Turpin. The North Dakota connection is interesting, but it's not enough. We have just one option available to keep this case moving forward responsibly. I will engage INTERPOL tonight."

Turpin turned from Pepper to the window and sucked his cigar.

Stotsbury looked at his notes. "He has a point, Harold. CIA has shared recent chatter arising from Istanbul. There could be a connection. We may be dealing with Islamic Terrorists."

"It is a possibility, but far from confirmed," Turpin agreed.

"What is it, Harold?" Stotsbury asked. "Something more is bothering you. It is unlike you to push hard without good reason. You must tell us what it is."

Turpin snubbed out his cigar in the full ashtray on the windowsill as if it would be his last smoke in life. He turned back and leaned on his cane. "Milton Busey is gone, gentlemen."

"Gone?" Pepper huffed.

Stotsbury held up his hand. "Continue."

"The prison psychiatrist was found dead, stabbed in the gullet."

"Good God! The man killed a bloody doctor," Stotsbury breathed.

"The private session was in a medical conference room. Significant because there is no surveillance equipment—privacy and all that rot." Turpin turned back to the window and cold rain. "There was a patio for smoking. It appears inmates at Pingree possess certain freedoms—another ridiculous rehabilitation experiment, I suppose."

"Rubbish," Pepper groaned.

"No prison cells, no armed guards, no compound walls or barbed wire," Turpin said. "The Pingree staff reports they fully complied with protocol and visual observation schedules. They thought the two were smoking on the patio—not an unusual thing. That was where Mr. Busey killed the poor doctor. Propped up the old boy against the patio door."

"It is winter. I heard the northern portion of the states can go well below freezing. I don't know about me taking a smoke outside," Stotsbury said.

"Freezing is quite correct, sir. The doctor froze solid in an upright position. I believe it added to the illusion. He blocked the door to the patio, his back to the conference room."

"This Busey chap must be one sick bastard," Pepper seethed.

"He took the doctor's car and left the state before Pingree knew what happened."

"Bloody awful," Stotsbury said.

"There is a reason Busey killed the doctor and left Pingree that night," Turpin said. "It was the same day he received two calls from our John Doe. We need to know what transpired. The content of those conversations motivated a heinous act and prison escape."

"God knows to where and for what."

"We need to act when *the canaries die*," Turpin said. "This is a sign of things to come."

"You have any more surprises, Harold?" Pepper asked.

"One more for now. Dr. Sumner knows Milton Busey."

Turpin's phone rang. As Pepper and Stotsbury processed the shocking revelations, Harold fumbled with his phone and pressed it to his ear. "Yes," he said. "Yes, this is Harold Turpin ... I am sorry. We have a poor connection. Please repeat, sir."

"Who is it?" Pepper whispered, eager as a boy on the stairs on Christmas morning.

Turpin straightened and turned to Pepper and Stotsbury, his small phone buried in his fat hand pressed against his head. "You say you have a message from Albert Bell—"

CHAPTER 7

"Monsters are real, and ghosts are real, too."
Stephen King

Day Five – Key West, Florida

L ong legs and red lipstick emerged from the shadows of the narrow office. As she approached, the morning sun found the stapler in her right hand. The old man relaxed the hand in his coat pocket.

"May I help you?" she asked with a hint of irritation. Her furtive eyes looked beyond him and out the front window, as if she'd been expecting someone more important. She set the stapler on the desk as she passed. She clutched a legal notepad to her bosom like her only child as she approached and extended her hand. "I am—"

"Which one?" he blurted. His tone was toxic. He panned the room. His eyes climbed the dank walls, stacks of unopened boxes, and two desks with computer monitors. He had expected more.

"I'm sorry, but I don't—"

"Name's on the window," he shot back. "Bowman, Weller & Garcia?"

She blinked away the uncomfortable tone and studied the old man's boney, white legs. He wore a trench coat buttoned to his neck and stared at her through his oversized sunglasses beneath a wide-brimmed hat with an odd red feather, the last hat on the rack at the last gas station.

It dawned on her the sign had gone up the day before. *Bowman, Weller & Garcia, Attorneys at Law* now hung above the picture window on Caroline Street for all the world to see. Although the vacated retail space was not ideal for a law firm, BW&G was not the typical law firm. The partners explained to their new office administrator they wanted to keep a *low profile.* They had snapped up the site on Caroline two weeks earlier. Their abrupt move from Kansas City had limited their options. They would live with loose ends a while—like how to handle walk-ins. BW&G did not need new clients.

She watched the old man's hand sink into his coat pocket. "I'm sorry. I am not an attorney. I am a legal secretary. My name is Helen Ramsey." Forcing a smile she extended her hand a second time. "And you are—?"

He winced as if she had aimed a gun at his belly. He took a step back. "I need Bowman, now."

She kept smiling. He did not know if she was just being professional or if she was an airhead. Either way, she was not Bowman, and that made her another obstacle to eliminate. Kansas City was in his plan. Key West was not. He was tired and angry.

"Do you want to meet with Miss Bowman? I can help you with that. First, I need certain administrative information to conduct business. It is in accordance with our standard operating procedures." She lowered her hand and backed out of the morning sun that poured in the storefront window.

Accordance. Conduct business. Standard operating procedures, he thought. *Those are some big words and they're out of place, comin' from a fake legal secretary in a sham law office sandwiched between Key West Marine Supply Emporium and Jocko's Fish Deli. Give me a break.*

"Please. Come and sit. This will only take a minute."

You people must have been in a big damn hurry to get out of Kansas City—wonder why? I can tell you this; you should have cleaned up better. I found your Key West address in the garbage. Thought you rich people were smarter than that.

She moved behind one of the desks and pointed to a chair. He followed with nostrils flared. The place smelled like a farmer's market—fruity. *Probably couldn't survive the tourist attractions 'round here—docks and eateries.*

"What is your name, sir?" Ramsey asked as she moved her mouse and pecked at the keyboard, opening a protected search field on the internet. As she entered the law firm's code and her password, she noticed the old man jerked every time someone walked by the front window. "Would you like me to close the blinds? The shadows can be disturbing at this time in the morning, with the sun still at its lowest level."

He did not answer. He'd learned long ago to keep his thoughts to himself. He sat so he could both see her legs and keep an eye on the entrance. If the door opened, he would be ready. He was out of view from the window.

Her legs were tan, firm calves and hard thighs. *She's one of those runners,* he thought as another shadow crossed the room. Her arms were muscular, too, but feminine. *Man-muscles on a lady are an abomination.*

"Sir—"

Her high cheekbones and large eyes were signs of natural beauty in his book, and her long, brown hair—now fashioned into a neat bun—reminded him of his sister, back when she was young and alive. *Damn sick way to die,* he thought. *I shoulda' killed the bastard before he raped her.* He swallowed hard and pushed the rest of his nightmare back into the darkness, the place he tried not to go, the place where his perverted father hunkered down in his brain, the man who made Milton a monster.

"Your name?" Ramsey asked again as she searched for the correct field to begin the process. The unsettled office and odd old man had only added to her pressure. She had to hit the right keys on the restricted site. One error would shut it down.

Her breasts were average size, but filled her tight blouse. *She wants someone to appreciate 'em,* he thought. *They always leave enough unbuttoned to mess with a man, but if ya look, it's some kinda' crime—damn crazy world today.* He opposed breast implants and all forms of plastic surgery—unless one had to disappear.

She found her screen. "Sir, I need your name so we can get started," she said as the timed box opened and blinked. She caught his eyes perusing her body. As she casually adjusted her hem and blouse, he blinked back into the room. He had no intention of letting anyone control him.

"I got a problem sayin' anything to you. I want attorney-client privilege before I say a word. Get me Bowman."

"I understand that concern. Many of our clients share your feelings at the beginning of their time with us. I am a representative of this law firm. Anything you say to me *is* protected under attorney-client privilege. You can answer my questions with absolutely no exposure or risk. Everything you share with me is protected. This is a necessary step. I must open a file for you and obtain basic information so Miss Bowman can help you in an efficient manner. Now, I need your name." The box blinked.

"Milton T. Busey," he said with an irritated tone. But at his age, everything he said came across as irritated, or repulsive, or senile. Even when he was younger, he had sounded angry. His short temper and cutting tongue had always driven people away.

Most of his life, Milton's pure existence made him sick. Even after he killed his father, he still felt dirty. After the man, who raped him and his sister throughout their childhood, was gone Milton knew he would never fit in the world. After Roan and Rice and Pingree, Milton was ready to die. He was ready to leave his misery and pain behind. For a long time he'd convinced himself he was normal, from another universe. He was an alien visiting a horrible planet. People did not matter to him. They were just alien animals. But now even that didn't work for him.

As Milton sat in the long, narrow legal office on Caroline Street, he realized it was one of the few times in his life he had told someone his real name. But now it didn't really matter. He was on a death mission. Milton would not allow cancer or anyone to get in his way before he got justice for his son—and all the money coming to him.

"Thank you, Mr. Busey. Now, I need a permanent address," she said with her eyes locked on her monitor and painted fingers poised. "It's another box I must fill. We don't have many."

He kept one hand in his coat and fidgeted with the worn edge of the desk. He didn't hear her. He was thinking about his miserable life again. Milton never had a place he called home—nothing about him was permanent. When he was a kid, he'd spent time in Belden working on his aunt's farm and hunting rabbits. He grew up. Lived in hotels or his car for as long as he could remember. After they closed the missile silos, and after he finished his work for the Air Force, he'd signed a lot of documents with tiny print and went back to moving around. Nobody wanted Milton talking about what he knew. The government thought his knowledge of things demolished posed some kind of risk to the country, one Milton did not understand. But all that was before Pingree and the people who came with money.

"Mr. Busey, a permanent address please?"

"Cooperstown, North Dakota, is the closest thing I got to permanent," he said. He had stayed there on and off over the years, most the time sleeping on a porch in the summer or a basement in the winter. Nobody liked him much, but he was family. Now everyone was dead except a grandfather in Belden, the only one who had ever cared about him—Tay Smith, a ninety-year-old Lakota Indian living alone in an abandoned gas station in a ghost town. Now, with Roan dead, Milton couldn't even trust Tay anymore. Milton couldn't trust anybody.

"I don't have no street number." *And I don't remember no street,* he thought.

Miss Ramsey loaded Cooperstown, North Dakota. When she hit enter, 2167 Rollin Avenue populated the next box. She would not need to ask any more questions. She had enough information to trigger a background check. For a hefty fee, the advanced search services were available to an elite clientele. In seconds, Milton T. Busey's life would be itemized and categorized: employment history, two family generations, financial history (banking and cash flow analysis), international travel, major transactions, and criminal history.

"Thank you, Mr. Busey," she said as she waited for the screen to populate. Her eyes drifted to the man still wearing the hat with the scarlet-red feather. If he had been even a little bit normal, maybe she would have started a conversation, perhaps asked about the feather and his plans in Key West—sightseeing, fishing, visiting friends. Instead, she looked forward to being done with him. The search took longer than usual. "And what do you need Miss Bowman for, Mr. Busey?" *Please. Just answer one question without making it an impossible, uncomfortable matter.*

"I need to change my will," he said with his lips not moving.

That wasn't so hard. "I see. Did you bring your will today, Mr. Busey?" she asked as she looked at the bulge in his coat pocket, the one his hand had stayed in since he arrived.

"No."

"Okay. Did Miss Bowman prepare your will?"

"No."

"Was Miss Bowman recommended to you?"

His eyes found hers. Busey said nothing.

"Well, I guess it wouldn't matter either way. Miss Bowman is an estate planner. She specializes in property rights, taxes, and last wills and testaments."

"I answered enough questions. I need to see her now. Call her."

"I'm sorry, Mr. Busey. That is not possible at the moment. All of our legal partners are in a meeting. But Miss Bowman will be out in two hours, and I can adjust her schedule so you will be her first appointment. Would 1:30 today be convenient?" Ramsey started to stand.

Busey did not move. "That does not work for me. I must see her." He looked over his shoulder out the picture window, and then back to her. "Now."

The search screen popped up and caught Ramsey's eye. Busey's background populated. Under his name were dozens of lines of criminal offenses filed over a twenty year period in multiple states. Convictions were highlighted.

"Did you hear me?" Busey growled.

She read that he'd been sentenced in 2005—three consecutive fifty-year terms. They had sent him to the North Dakota State Penitentiary. In 2012, the state had transferred him to the Pingree Correctional Center. She sat and scowled. "Let me see if there is something I can do." Her fingers froze on the keyboard. She read the flashing message on the screen:

WANTED – MILTON T. BUSEY – PRIME SUSPECT IN KILLING OF PINGREE CORRECTION CENTER PSYCHIATRIST, DR. FRANK RICE – BUSEY ESCAPED AND IS BELIEVED TO HAVE LEFT THE STATE, DESTINATION UNKNOWN. BUSEY IS ARMED AND DANGEROUS. DIAGNOSED MENTAL ILLNESS. DO NOT ATTEMPT TO DETAIN OR

APPREHEND. CONTACT LOCAL FBI OFFICE
IMMEDIATELY.

"This is the last time I ask polite-like," Busey seethed as he got to his feet.

Ramsey tapped the screen asleep and got to her feet with a smile. "I understand, sir. I think I have enough to interrupt the meeting. You are right. We must be sensitive to client needs. Please wait here. I will get Miss Bowman now."

Milton had no intention of waiting. Ramsey had already cost him too much time. Now she was pretending to help. He rounded her desk. Like a cobra strike, he grabbed her arm. Their faces met. He tapped the keyboard. The dormant screen came alive. He saw the pulsating message.

Everything changed in an instant.

Ramsey struggled to get free, but she could not break the iron grip or escape the sour breath of the wiry old man. His snake eyes climbed her cleavage and slender neck and red-painted lips. They stopped on her big blue eyes. There his perverted smile grew and revealed his crooked, yellow teeth. Milton pulled the blood-encrusted shank from his coat pocket. It was time to eliminate another obstacle.

A flash of light outside the window caught Busey's eye. He turned and watched the crack climb the storefront glass. Blood sprayed Ramsey's desk and monitor.

CHAPTER **8**

"The only secrets are the secrets that keep themselves."
George Bernard Shaw

Day Five – Key West, Florida

E lliott leaned on the front counter at the Key West Marine
Supply Emporium. "I need my transducer," he whispered
to the top of the head of the bushy-haired clerk, who was deep
into his tattered comic book.

"You're the guy that bought the new Commander 44."

"Well it's not new, really—"

"You're Mr. Sumner. I never forget a face."

Elliott knew he should have changed his name when he got to
Key West a year ago, but to him, changing a name is what
criminals do to disappear. His objective was different. He wanted
to extend his natural life on the planet.

"That would be right, my friend."

Disappearing might have been a good idea, too. Elliott's idea
of disappearing was to move to a remote location. His idea of
blending in was to do anything out of character, but it had to be
convenient. He grew a beard, let his hair go long, and got a pair of
Aviator Ray Bans and a Miami Dolphins ball cap—even though
he was a Cowboys fan and never liked to wear shades. He already
had half a dozen white, cotton, button shirts, as well as plenty of
khaki shorts and flip-flops. If he was not wearing the standard
disguise, he would be in jogging shorts, a pair of Adidas, or his
faded beach attire: black La Perla Echo swim shorts and a white
T-shirt.

"To be perfectly accurate, the boat I purchased is not new. It is a year old," Elliott whispered beneath the din of shoppers. "That being said, the *used* navigation system on the fritz is still under warranty. You owe me a transducer."

"You don't have it yet?" the clerk asked.

"We're now entering Week Three. I was told a few days. I'm sure you can appreciate my loss of confidence in your operation. Until I have a reliable and functioning navigation system, my seafaring adventures are somewhat limited."

"I'm sorry, man." He pulled over a water-stained ledger chained to the counter and started flipping pages. Halfway through, he stopped and ran his finger down the smudged-ink entries with his nose deep in the log. "That boat is totally rad, man—a Commander 44." He looked up. "I mean, Mr. Sumner."

Elliott smiled. Not at the clerk's comments, but at the *mister* tag. He had heard *Doctor Sumner* for the last twenty years. Now, that no longer mattered. Now the *doctor* tag fell into the "emotional pressure cooker" category—stressful expectations. Elliott's objective in Key West was to avoid all forms of stress.

The clerk's finger stopped. "Here we are—Elliott Sumner, Commander 44 cabin cruiser, Twin Volvo IPS 435 horses. Has the Garmin 8000 series electronic package. That's top-of-the-line."

Elliott rolled his eyes and looked out the storefront window beneath the painted letters—KEY WEST MARINE SUPPLY EMPORIUM. A steady stream of tourists wearing sunburns and clutching souvenirs strolled by. Shops across Caroline blocked the burning ball on the horizon, but the blinding blanket of morning sunlight streamed down Williams Avenue and spilled over the rooftops of the Waterfront Market.

"Garmin 8000 electronic package," Elliott said, struggling to control his impatience. "Yes. And we have been here before, Mr. —"

"Call me Randy." The clerk's elbow accidentally knocked his comic to the floor.

Elliott nodded, but his eyes stayed with the pedestrians as Randy dropped behind the counter. An old man reading a note edged into view, inches from the glass. He wore a wrinkled trench coat buttoned to the neck, women's sunglasses, and a fedora with a bright red feather. *Aren't you an odd fellow?*

Randy popped up between Elliott and the old man. "Mr. Sumner, look what I just found."

"A comic book and dusty sheet of pink paper?" Elliott asked as he leaned around Randy to see more of the odd old man. But the man was gone.

"Not just *any* pink paper," Randy said with pride. "I found the root cause of our problem." He wiggled it like a long worm on a small hook. "This is your waybill. It shows delivery of the transducer eleven days ago. And this notation here tells me where it is in back—aisle, shelf, and bin. Somehow, this paper got lost under the counter." His sneakers chirped as he rounded the counter and shot to the back of the store.

Maybe this fiasco can be over, Elliott thought. *Maybe I can take my boat out and break my boredom.* When he looked back out the window, he spotted the old man now standing on the curb next door. *What is it with you, old fellow? You look like a giant bird, with those long, skinny legs poking out your coat,* he mused. *Do I know you?* Elliott scratched his beard. *And what's with the bright red feather? Is it an identifier? Are you meeting someone?*

The new mystery was just a game for the international forensic investigator on sabbatical. It was a mental exercise, one he could not have stopped if he tried. It was in his nature to solve mysteries, untangle webs of intrigue, and to find the missing pieces to the puzzles of life—large and small.

... And the coat is out of place here. The temp's already above ninety degrees. You gotta be burning up. I suspect that's what you

were wearing when you arrived here from wherever you came from —the north, probably, one of the cold states. You came directly here. You drove all the way. Along the way, you purchased shorts and sunglasses, but you didn't think about the rest of your Floridian wardrobe. That suggests your trip was unplanned—spontaneous. What brought you here? There is a specific reason you are standing outside a law firm. The hat, the sunglasses—those are a last-minute disguise. You don't want to be recognized, except by the one looking for you maybe—the red feather and the rendezvous. No. You're looking for someone.

Elliott blinked away when a cluster of tourists blocked his view, but his brain continued to churn. *Either I'm close, or you lack taste in attire. If I'm right, you lack appreciation for the art of blending. That suggests you are not used to this, not used to the outside world. You're too old to be a novice. You are a criminal, one who spent a lot of time in confinement—a prison. That's it. You tossed your prison stripes. You borrowed someone's trench coat. You bought that ridiculous hat and those oversized sunglasses. Hmm. What are you doing here, old man?*

"Excuse me, Mr. Sumner," Randy said as he approached from behind with a box in his hand. He could not know his customer was a serial killer hunter. In Randy's eyes, Mr. Sumner was just another wealthy boat owner in the Keys—and there were many.

"I have your transducer," he announced as he rounded the front counter. This time, he paused so as not to cross the line of his customer's intent stare out the window.

When the old man pushed up his hat and took off his sunglasses, Elliott knew him immediately. A familiar, macabre cloud grew in Elliott's brain. A blanket of impending danger fell over the blissful island in the Straits of Florida. *I know of only one man who adjusts his hat with the pad of his left thumb arched from a gnarled fist. And those snake eyes could never be mistaken. It's been fourteen years. You should be in prison or dead.*

"Mr. Sumner?" Randy prodded with a gentle tap on Elliott's shoulder. He then slid the small cardboard box across the counter with the tip of a screwdriver.

Elliott nodded his awareness of Randy's presence, but his eyes stayed on the man standing on the curb. He was holding a small piece of paper inches from his nose. Elliott watched him put on his sunglasses and leave the curb. *You've reached your destination.*

"Mr. Sumner, your transducer? I need a few minutes in the back to finalize your paperwork and to retrieve the installation instructions. We have a file. While you wait, please help yourself to coffee." He pointed to the pot. "I'll be right back."

Five minutes flew by after the old man had left the curb and Randy had slipped into the back. *I can't get involved,* Elliott thought. *It is not my business anymore.*

He poured another coffee, stared out the window, and stewed. *You would not have been released from the North Dakota Penitentiary. Although you did get away with killing five people— the five bodies never found—you blessed us with a long criminal record, one in which you had dodged justice a very long time. Thank God we had enough crimes on the books to lock you up for the rest of your life. You were tucked away so nobody else would get hurt. We put away another monster.*

Now I'm outside the loop on purpose. I know nothing and don't want to know. You are someone else's problem. I can't get involved. Not anymore. I can't risk it. Elliott blinked away from the sun and the mystery, and he found his coffee cup. Looking into the steaming brew, he ended his game. *Just get the transducer and walk away.*

Randy returned and tucked the installation instructions into the box. "Sorry we messed up, Mr. Sumner. You're good to go."

The first rolling explosion rattled the store window. Elliott jerked up from his box and watched people in the streets duck heads and flee in all directions. He dove over the counter and pulled Randy to the floor beneath him.

The second rolling explosion came like a distant sonic boom. The giant storefront window rattled even more and dust filled the sun pouring in. "What *is* that?" Randy asked with his back pinned to the floor and Elliott's face inches away.

"Do you have a cell phone on you?" Elliott asked.

"Yes, sir."

"Call 911. Tell the police there's been a shooting. Tell everyone in your store to stay down. Do not look out the window. Someone could get hurt. Got it?"

"Yes, sir. What're you gonna do?"

"I am going to help."

"Mr. Sumner, you should stay here, too. You could get shot."

"I need to go," Elliott said as he started to move.

"Are you a cop or doctor or somethin'?" Randy asked.

"Yes," Elliott said as he started to get up, his eyes stopping at the edge of the glass. "I need you to do exactly as I said."

Randy started punching numbers on his cell. Elliott climbed over the counter and moved to the store entrance. He shoved open the door and stepped outside—the street was eerie and empty, except for a few stragglers scrambling for cover.

Next door, he saw a giant triangular shard of glass on the sidewalk, and more fractured sheets leaning against the now empty storefront window. Shattered, painted letters had reached into the street and a wooden chair lay on its side at the curb. Elliott immediately saw the splintered bullet hole in its seat.

Now what have you done, Milton?

CHAPTER 9

"There's nowhere you can be that isn't where you're meant
to be."
John Lennon

The 911 call was brief. *"This is the Marine Supply
Emporium. We heard two explosions."*

Spinning blue lights washed over storefronts at the
intersection of Caroline and Telegraph. They poured in the
demolished window frame of the block's newest tenant—
BOWMAN, WELLER & GARCIA, ATTORNEYS AT LAW.
Shaken tourists were jammed together peering out shop windows
and packed alleys as paramedics picked their way through the
broken glass and headed to the center of attention. Monroe
County Sheriff cars blocked all roads as deputies secured a two-
block perimeter.

Sergeant Mack Malone knelt inside with his gun on the
target. When two paramedics entered behind him, he held up a
hand. They knew to back out and wait—the crisis was still
unfolding.

His target was behind a desk, covered in blood. Malone could
only see the top of a man's head, a Miami Dolphins cap.

"I said, hold up your hands," Malone ordered. His two
deputies moved in an attempt to triangulate the target.

"We don't need to do this," Malone said. "Just put your hands
up and we can—"

"I cannot put my hands in the air," the man said with a steady
voice.

"Are you injured?" Malone asked.

"No."

"Then you'd best do as I said. I don't have to tell you this is a very sensitive situation. There is a lot of blood in here. Someone is hurt or worse. Your failure to cooperate is not a good idea. I can't let you leave here. Don't make me shoot you—"

Malone swallowed, calming himself. "Okay. Listen to me. There's no negotiating your way out of this mess. You need to show your hands so we can get this resolved and all go home."

"If I raise my hands, she will die."

Malone was closest. He had the best shot. He moved to his right with his gun on the target. He could see a lady's legs covered with blood. *Oh God! You do have a hostage and she's hurt or worse. I got no room for talkin' this thing out.*

"Someone's lost a lot of blood already," Malone said, his voice steady. "I'm thinkin' it's your hostage." The standoff could now be a matter of life or death. *I gotta get to her.* Malone aimed. He had a clean shot—the top three inches of the man's head. Malone would put a bullet right under the Dolphin logo.

"You need to let the lady go, right now," Malone ordered.

He cocked his 357 Magnum—the one he'd only taken out of his holster once a week at the practice range over the last twenty years.

"You got no options here, mister. Do not make this go a bad way." Malone closed one eye and aligned the bead on the tip of his barrel. At the shooting range, twenty feet was easy. He always put the bullet exactly where he wanted.

Malone steadied his hand, held his breath, and started to squeeze.

"I'm a doctor. The lady I'm holding has been shot."

Malone relaxed his finger and opened his eye. "You're a doctor?"

"Yes. I came in here to help. This young woman is badly injured."

"How do I know you're tellin' me the truth? How can I be sure this isn't some trick?"

"We don't have much time. Her left subclavian artery is severed. I am pinching one end with my fingers. I can't find the other end. I have reduced but not eliminated her internal hemorrhaging. The loss of blood is now critical. She could go into shock. If I let go of this artery she will bleed out in two minutes and we will lose her. I need paramedics over here, STAT!"

Stat was enough for Malone—he didn't understand the rest, but he knew no scumbag would use that word in any sentence. Still holding his gun on the target, he rose to his feet and took a chance on trusting his gut. He made his way to the desk. Their eyes met.

"Please hurry," Elliott said.

Malone rounded the desk and holstered his gun. "Get those paramedics in here pronto," he yelled to his deputies. "How is she?" Malone asked Sumner.

He cradled the girl on his lap. Her head rested on his stomach and his right hand was pressed against her left chest, the fingers deep inside a bloody wound. His left hand held her shoulder steady so he could maintain his grip on the lacerated artery.

"She's unconscious, on the edge. We need to push fluids and get her blood pressure up." The paramedics arrived and took positions on each side of the victim. Malone backed off and the deputies pulled the desk away.

"I'm a doctor," Elliott repeated. "Give me two surgical-clamp forceps and get your sterile dressings prepped. I need an IV setup now."

As the paramedics scurried to grab the supplies requested, Elliott continued. "You're going to push 500 ccs Ringers lactate. She's lost a lot of blood, at least two pints—30 percent of her blood supply. We're on the edge. I want three units of O-neg waiting at the ER door. She won't make it inside. You got that?"

"Yes, doctor," said the lead paramedic as he passed the first clamp and took over bracing the victim so Elliott could focus on the severed artery.

"Okay. I got one. Next clamp," Elliott ordered. The paramedic slapped it into his waiting hand like a surgical nurse assisting an open-heart procedure. "Good." Elliott blindly probed for the other end of the severed artery. "Ah, there you are." He clamped. "Give me a bottle of sterile saline." The paramedic passed it and Elliott poured it onto the open wound, washing away blood and debris.

"Surgical tape," he ordered. Three, six-inch strips hung from the EMTs arm thrust near the doctor's face. Elliott took each strip and sealed the wound, leaving the two pairs of clamped forceps sticking out.

"Go. That'll hold to surgery. No other injuries. No signs of trauma from her fall after the bullet. We have an exit wound, too. Transport Code Red, gentlemen. Thank you. Good job."

Malone and his deputies watched them roll the young woman out the door to the waiting ambulance. "What the hell happened here?" he asked as the ambulance sirens came alive and the flashing lights passed by the shattered picture window.

"I don't know much," Elliott said, as he wiped his hands on some paper towels.

"Why are you here?" Malone asked. "And who *are* you?"

"I was next door getting something for my boat when we heard the shots. I came over to see if I could help. I found her and went to work."

"She's lucky. If you hadn't been nearby, she might have bled to death."

Thanks for the amateur medical opinion. "Possibly," Elliott said.

"Never seen this much blood. Not in this town. Not Key

West. Did you see anybody come in or leave this place?" Malone asked, looking around the room.

Elliott glanced down at the blood all over him and, for a moment, forgot he was not at one of his own death scenes. "As I sat here waiting for paramedics, I looked around. Someone shot through the storefront window. They hit the girl by mistake."

Malone smiled at the amateur detective. Everyone thinks they can do his job. "Thanks for your theory, doctor, but I will need a lot more information before I can go there. We need to know everything we can about the crime scene—and about you, sir. And your name is—?"

"I'm not important. I'm sure we'll have plenty of time to talk later. Right now, you have an active crime scene. I suggest you and your people investigate behind that backdoor, the one with the bloody hand print. And I'd look upstairs, too."

Malone spun around and zoomed-in on the bloody print on a door thirty feet away. "Holy shit," he huffed. "Men, come with me. Doctor, you stay put." As Malone and the deputies ran to the back, Elliott could hear the sergeant say, "Get another ambulance out here. I got a bad feeling about this."

With guns held high, the three disappeared into the dark hall and the door closed with a muffled click. Elliott turned back to the shattered storefront window. Giant, pointed shards of glass hung from the upper molding. He felt like he was looking out from the belly of a shark.

Elliott stood where he'd found the girl. He looked out the window, a straight line. He saw a two-story building three blocks away. There were four dark windows and a flat roof. Any one of them could have been the sniper's nest.

Were they hunting you, Milton? Elliott thought as he heard the ceiling creak under the weight of the sergeant and his deputies.

What're you doing down here from North Dakota? Elliott wiped more of the girl's blood from his face as he looked back at the desk. The pool of blood told him someone had been standing next to her. *You were the target, Milton. This poor girl took your bullet.*

Elliott picked up the nameplate. "Helen Ramsey, Legal Secretary." *Looks like you were in the wrong place at the wrong time.* He walked to the window to further scrutinize the line of fire. *Milton Busey ... there was a day when you were too smart to walk into a trap like this. You must have had a very important reason to be here. Or was your guard down? No. You just didn't think anyone would look for you down here in Key West. But you were wrong.*

Malone came back into the room. With a dipped brow and cell pressed to his head, he studied his mystery doctor and continued to whisper into his phone.

"You need me up there, sergeant?" Elliott asked

Malone pocketed his cell. "How'd you know there even was an *upstairs,* doctor? You been up there?"

"Every building on Caroline has an upstairs. It's logical to assume a law firm would need additional office space to accommodate three lawyers in addition to this reception area."

Malone nodded. "Okay," he said with a sigh. "Unless you can bring *people* back from the dead, we won't need your medical services up there—"

"More than one lawyer died upstairs?" Elliott asked.

Malone spun back around. "And you know that how?"

"Know what?"

"That there's more than one lawyer dead upstairs!"

"I didn't know until you told me. I assumed your use of the noun *people* was plural. Are you certain they are dead? Sometimes they look dead but are not. Do you need me to check?"

Turning red, Malone looked at the ceiling. "No, sir. You don't have to be a doctor to know the two guys upstairs are dead. They were hacked up pretty good—throats cut. One's head is hanging by a thread. Whoever did this is one sick SOB. Place looked like a slaughterhouse."

"I'm sorry to hear that."

Malone could only shake his head. "We don't see things like this 'round here," he repeated. "You got anymore little tidbits of information you want to share, like the bloody handprint on the door? Anything you think is *time sensitive*. After all, you've been here the longest."

"I have a suggestion or two."

"Excellent. Please share," Malone said, narrowing his discerning eyes.

"Standing where the girl was shot and looking on a line out the window, it appears the shooter was either in one of those windows or on the roof, three blocks away." Elliott pointed and Malone followed his finger. "I doubt you will find much helpful now, but I would still get your forensic people up there before too much time gets away."

"So you doubt we'll find anything," Malone said under his breath as he scrutinized the doctor, who seemed to know way too much. "Why?" *Maybe you will make a mistake.*

"Based on the crime scene, I suspect the shooter is a professional. They don't leave evidence behind. They are a *precise breed*."

"Based on the *crime scene* and a *precise breed* you say." Malone rubbed his chin. "Tell me why you think we're dealing with a shooter outside this room. Why eliminate the possibility of a shooter inside the room? Maybe a bullet broke the window from inside."

"Are you serious?" Elliott asked.

"I'm always serious!"

"The caliber and the window, for starters."

"You did notice the chair on the sidewalk outside the window, right?" Malone asked.

"Yes. I did," Elliott said.

"Maybe one of our victims threw a chair at the shooter *in this room*, missed, and the chair broke the window. That scenario would place a shooter right here. It explains the broken window and puts the chair at the curb."

"I saw a hole in a large piece of shattered glass lying on the sidewalk. You will find it to be well-defined—a 50 caliber. That caliber holds a true line for 2,500 yards, three blocks easily." Elliott pointed to the back wall. "You will find a slug there. It passed through *Miss Ramsey* like a hot knife in butter. That actually minimized her injury."

"You know Miss Ramsey, do you?" Malone asked.

Elliott pointed to the nameplate on the bloody desk.

Malone smiled. *You're about to hang yourself. Let's see how much you really know about my crime scene. You already know too much for a doctor who happened by. You nuts are all alike. Sick arsonists who come back to their fires so they can watch 'em burn.*

"Thank you, sir. We will look for that slug," Malone said as a polite diversion. "But help me with the chair on the curb. Why would it be out there?"

"I saw a bullet hole in the seat. Someone used that chair to deflect the second projectile."

"*Deflect*, you say? I missed the hole. Tell me more?" Malone urged.

"The shooter intended the first shot fired to take out the window glass and the second shot fired to take out the target—a head shot. Storm glass windows in the Keys are thick and strong because of hurricane building codes. That fact is problematic to a sniper. Thick glass can deflect a projectile three to five inches depending on the quality of glass, distance the bullet travels, and angle of impact. An experienced hitman would eliminate the glass first."

"Please continue," Malone said. *Please continue to paint yourself into a cell.*

"The first shot missed the primary target and hit Miss Ramsey, who was in the error zone. She was *collateral damage.* Because she was hit in the chest, I can hypothesize the primary target was standing next to her and was five-five in height. Miss Ramsey is about five-nine.

"The primary target knew immediately what was happening —a sniper. He or she knew another bullet would be on its way, this time on an uninterrupted line of fire. The shooter only allowed enough time for the shattered glass to drop from the window frame. That gave the primary target enough time to throw a chair into the line of fire to disrupt the second round. The chair deflected the second shot on its way out the window to the curb.

"It looks like the target escaped out the backdoor. At this point, I can only assume the target killed two lawyers upstairs and took one lawyer as a hostage."

"Very interesting reconstruction for an amateur, doctor," Malone said, chuckling. "You must watch a lot of crime TV."

I've said too much. What am I doing here? "Well then, I think you have enough from me. I must go. I have things to do."

Malone put a hand on Elliott's shoulder. "I think it best you stay with us a little longer, if you don't mind. The medical examiner should be here any moment. You two can speak Latin and save me mountains of time. I'm sorry; I still don't know your name—"

The front door opened and the Monroe County Medical Examiner rushed into the room. "I'm in a hurry. What do we have, Mack?" he said with eyes on his watch.

Malone spun around. Elliott backed into the shadows.

"Daniel! I was just thinking about you," he said with an awkward laugh. "Yes. We have two bodies upstairs, their necks cut." He opened his arms to the room like preparing for a bow. "And this mess, a young lady shot. The receptionist. We suspect collateral damage. She's on her way to the hospital as we speak.

"I know you're on a tight schedule today," Malone said as he turned to his deputies. The ME discovers the doctor standing in the shadows. "Stay here with our good Samaritan. I'll be back shortly." Malone turned back to the ME and a puzzled look. Malone waved him to follow. "I'll fill you in upstairs."

The Sergeant led the way. Dr. Hayes passed by the deputies and paused as he neared the doctor. Hayes smiled, nodded, and continued with Malone through the backdoor. The two walked to the end of the dark hall and stopped at the narrow staircase.

"I suggest you invite the doctor to join us, Mack," Hayes said.

Malone turned back to the ME with a confused look. "I think that man might be involved, Daniel," he whispered. "I don't question he's a doctor. He may have saved the life of the lady shot out there. But he is someone we do not know much about. He knows way too much about this whole damn mess and has avoided identifying himself. I find him very suspicious."

The ME chuckled. "You find him very suspicious, you say? How's that, Mack? How is that doctor behaving in a suspicious manner?"

"He recreated the crime scene based on little evidence and a dozen possible scenarios. It is obvious he knows more than he should. Right now, he's a prime suspect."

"Before we go up, I want you to tell me exactly what he told you, Mack."

Malone stepped back down into the hallway and met Hayes's stare. "He said the girl that took a bullet was not the target—used the words *collateral damage*. He said there was a sniper three blocks away that was going after a *primary target* who got away.

Someone left that room with blood on their hands. They went up these stairs, killed two attorneys, and possibly took a third hostage. That doctor got all that from sitting on the floor in blood with his hands in the chest of a lady supposedly bleeding to death."

"He was pinching-off a severed artery," said the medical examiner.

"Yes. That's what he said. How'd you know?" Malone asked with eyes wide.

"He's done it before," Hayes said, scratching his head. "I guess it's been almost two years now. He saved a homicide detective in Memphis doing precisely the same emergency procedure. An unstoppable serial killer—the Bluff City Butcher—carved up the poor fellow. Left the detective for dead. Your suspicious doctor saved the man's life. Someone wrote it up for the *Journal of American Medicine* after the doctor described the *in-the-field* emergency procedure in great detail. Medics use it today in Afghanistan and Syria—save countless lives."

"Okay. Fine. But that does not explain his knowledge of this crime scene, Daniel."

"You don't know who he is, do you?"

"No. I told you that. He is not telling us who he is."

"In the room out there is possibly the most gifted forensic pathologist in the world."

Malone leaned to look through the small window on the back door. "You gotta be making a mistake here, Daniel. He looks like he's still in college."

"Early forties actually, Mack. That man is a world-renowned serial killer hunter. He holds the record. Personally taken over fifty of the most horrific serial killers off the streets all around the world. He only hunts the most prolific monsters."

"He's a doctor not a cop. How does he catch these killers?" Malone asked.

Hayes pulled Malone from the window. "He is a gifted man —genetics and study. He possesses an unmeasurable IQ, a perfect photographic memory, and an advanced education. This produces a man with unparalleled investigative skills. This man can see in minutes what takes a forensic team days. Mack, your *prime suspect* is your gift in this case. He is Dr. Elliott Sumner."

Malone looked back out the window and watched Sumner stare out the shattered storefront window. "If he's that good, what's he doing in Key West in shorts and flip-flops?"

"I did not know he was down here, Mack. He disappeared some time ago. Rumors were he went on a self-imposed sabbatical. Dr. Sumner has issues. He carries a lot of baggage. If you deal with enough twisted killers, they start moving into your head and haunt you. They can drive a man insane. He has seen more than most. His photographic memory won't let him forget the gruesome details or the pain. He needed to get away from his life of carnage before it all came crashing down. I understand it, and I'm only dealing with a small fraction of the pain and horror that man carries around. I can tell you the medical examiner offices and law enforcement agencies around the world that have worked with Elliott Sumner are giving him space so he can get healthy."

As Malone listened with his back to the little window, he knew there was no way he could have known some genius forensic sleuth would walk into his double homicide and piece things together so fast. Nor would he know the man already had information that would put Malone on the trail of the sniper's target and a killer. But Elliott had already moved beyond Caroline Street. He knew the events at the law offices in Key West were just the tip of an iceberg of death and destruction, one he could not survive. It was time Elliott disappeared again.

"Mack, we've got a multiple homicide, and we don't get too

many of those around here," Dr. Hayes said. "I think we should see if we can talk Dr. Sumner into giving us a hand."

"I have no reason to question you, Daniel. Let's do it together."

They turned and pushed through the door and entered the room. The two deputies were on their cell phones as a crowd gathered outside.

"Men," Malone shouted. "Deputy Bunt. Where is the doctor?"

"He left, sir."

"You let him go? What were you thinking?"

"He said they needed him at the hospital. The girl is asking for him."

CHAPTER **10**

"All that is necessary for the triumph of evil is for good men to do
nothing."
Edmund Burke

T his time, walking away felt right.

They would not know how to find him, even if they
saw the waybill at the Marine Supply Emporium—because
Elliott had never left an address. After weeks of waiting for a
transducer, he could handle a few more days without a boat. And
his phone was untraceable—another perk of having been an
international serial killer hunter. And he shaved his beard.
Maybe Malone would lose interest in the innocent bystander
who helped and did not leave a name.

Over the previous year, his night runs had ended on South
Roosevelt Boulevard at Bertha Street. After five miles, he would
hop the railing, drop onto the beach, and walk the last mile to his
obscure dwelling in the dense, tropical foliage. On this night, his
last mile would be more important than ever before. After the
perilous morning on Caroline Street—the kind of experience he
came to Key West to *avoid*—Elliott needed to get back to his self-
imposed isolation like a junky needed a fix. Walking an empty
beach next to a vast ocean—beneath an infinite night sky—
seemed to give him the ability to control his inner demons.

His unique genetic assets had come with lethal liabilities.
Elliott's advanced sensory gifts made it possible for him to see the
smallest detail and solve the most complex homicide—but they
also opened him up to the agonizing pain of his victims. His

genius intellect and perfect photographic memory allowed him to successfully hunt the most horrific serial killers in the world, but it also made room in his head for the monsters. They were always there to torment him. Sometimes, they seemed determined to break down his doors of sanity.

For more than a year, Elliott had walked the same empty beach after running the same five-miles. The enormity of the universe overwhelmed him—that profound reality and his insignificance in the world revealed a path to a normal life, one without terror and pain, where his inner demons went silent. On this night, as the full moon hung over the Atlantic Ocean and a soft blanket of fog crawled onto the sand, eyes followed him. With hands on his hips and sweat dripping from his chin, he walked the hard sand and tasted the ocean air. But this time, he felt eyes. This time, he scoured the shadows. This time, he put his holistic journey on hold.

The five-square-mile resort town provided few places to hide. Elliott's departure from Caroline Street, without clearance from Malone, could be in play. *I did leave without permission, I suppose. Malone, are you looking for me? If I were you, I'd put resources on the beaches to find me. But you weren't very interested in my input this morning. Why waste time with some opinionated bystander, unless Daniel told you about me?*

Elliott had met Dr. Hayes in Boston at a forensic pathology conference—The National Association of Medical Examiners. *They just had to recognize my achievements. So I caught number fifty in London—the Serpentine Strangler. Guess it was a milestone. But an award just never felt right. We're all trying to catch the bad guys and save the innocent. I remember my presentation:* The Unpredictability of the Predictable Serial Killer. *It was one of my better lectures,* Elliott mused. *I remember Dan Hayes had some good questions. I was a bit surprised. He was the ME with the string of resort islands on the tip of Florida and the lowest homicide rate in the country. I also remember Hayes felt his luck was running out. He wanted to be ready, he said.*

Oh, Dr. Hayes. Caroline Street must be your worst nightmare. After you got a look upstairs and figured it was a sniper-and-hostage situation, maybe you changed your mind about keeping me your little secret. You knew I had left the business for a reason. Maybe your nightmare is more important than my privacy now.

Who opens a law firm in a Key West tourist center? Elliott wondered, as he kept an eye on his surroundings—the uninterested runner cooling down. *The location is suspicious. Why not put your law firm in the business district? There's dozens of better places. If I was Malone, I'd get homicide looking into that first thing. I'd wanna know everything about the Bowman, Weller & Garcia law firm: history, background checks, areas of expertise, client list, where they came from and why. Since two are dead and one's kidnapped, I'd get back in there and dive into those boxes along the back wall. Most of them were still sealed. And why the high-priced background-check web agency? That kind of resource is used by the top levels of law enforcement and international security agencies. Why a little law firm in Key West?*

I hope you don't need me to point to the Milton Busey profile on Ramsey's computer screen. Poor girl, she had to be blind-sided. The old man walked in off the street and asked for an attorney— probably Bowman. Maybe he wanted an in and out. Ramsey launched the standard client registration process, entered Milton's name and address—and boom. There's the chilling FBI alert. Ramsey's shaking in her heels. She's alone with a man who killed someone and escaped prison. There's no way to hide that kind of terror from a serial killer. Milton saw it in her eyes. He made his move. Stepped in front of the window. The sniper found his target.

A shadow moved. The wind tickled the foliage. Elliott watched in his periphery. The shadow stiffened and then melded into the curve of a palm tree. *Are you trying to hide from me for a reason, or are you trying to maintain your privacy? God knows, I tend to overthink things.*

There's a chance you're just a tourist. That's a reasonable and logical assumption, Elliott said to himself. *But the business suit and tie are atypical—not normal beach attire. Although there is a Sheraton across the street. You could be attending a function—a wedding or party or some business event. Maybe you left your function to take a walk on the beach—you are in Key West. Maybe you needed a break, some alone time. There you are and here comes a jogger. I'm crowding you. You want me to just mosey on by—*

Elliott side-stepped another far reaching wave. He looked up at the night sky with a forced sense of relief. He sucked in the warm ocean air and tried to let go of his suspicions. *I don't have to figure this out.* But as soon as he exhaled, he knew he could not leave it alone. His analytical, investigative, problem-solving brain would not allow it. Instead of a holistic journey down the beach, Elliott fell into yet another investigative process that would take him to the edge, just like a hundred times before. He could not turn it off until he reached a plausible endpoint. Thus far, the percolating scenarios were nonviable. Something did not fit.

His thoughts turned to his companion/stalker. *What if you're not a tourist? What if you're here for me? I can rule out a sheriff deputy because they don't wear suits and ties, although homicide detectives do. So I rule the county back in. You could be someone from my past. That could be good or bad, likely bad after last year. I would need to meet you face-to-face to know. Standing by the palm tree on the narrow path to my secret bungalow is telling. You didn't choose that spot with blind luck. You've been watching me. Therefore, I now eliminate the county sheriff's office. All other possibilities remain.*

Turning around would not be prudent. Elliott was too close

to the shadow and too exposed to potential unknowns. Walking alone on an isolated beach late at night had its disadvantages. An abrupt change in direction could trigger something bad—like a bullet in the head. Or trigger nothing. *The Caroline Street sniper is still out there,* Elliott thought. *Probably saw me enter and leave. They could want to eliminate me. I'm an unwanted variable.*

Elliott's only option was to stay the course and hope for the best. A cigarette moved. A face glowed by the palm tree in Elliott's path. Elliott approached, his eyes straight ahead.

"Dr. Sumner, we need to talk." The words cut through the night air and answered Elliott's first question—the mystery man was not a random tourist.

"Who are you?" Elliott asked.

"I'm CIA." The man in the suit shined a penlight on his credentials and badge—Special Agent Richard Keswick.

"I'm retired." Elliott kept walking.

The light clicked off. "Mr. Turpin sent me."

Elliott stopped in the shadow of the palm tree.

"They have a messy homicide in London. It connects to Milton Busey, Dr. Sumner." Elliott turned. Keswick dropped his cigarette, kicked sand over it, and lit another.

He knows Milton was there. "They should talk to Sheriff Malone," Elliott said.

"You were at the law firm where two people died," Keswick shot back.

Elliott stood his ground a few feet away. "The CIA should already know I was at the Marine Supply Store picking up a transducer for my boat," he said. "There was an explosion. As a concerned citizen, I went outside and saw the broken window next door. I went in to help the injured. That is the extent of my involvement." He started to leave.

"You saved Helen Ramsey's life by holding her subclavian artery between two fingers, Dr. Sumner. You're not what anyone would call the 'typical concerned citizen.' That woman would have died if any other person had found her. We know your capabilities."

"Any doctor could have—"

"And we know you had enough time at the Caroline Street crime scene to sort through the chaos and put things together—things the Monroe County Sheriff's Office would not put together for days if not weeks or ever. Time is of the essence, Dr. Sumner. We need to know what Miss Ramsey said to you. It might be important to our international case."

"Ask Miss Ramsey."

"She's unconscious. Blood loss, you know. Intensive Care."

"What makes you think she talked to me at all?"

"When you got to her, she was conscious. We know she passed out after the blood loss and shock—but that takes a while. We know you can't help yourself—the enduring investigator. You asked questions. That's what you were born to do—solve puzzles. We know she told you something. Tell me what she said and we will be done. You can return to your quiet life."

"I suggest you wait for Miss Ramsey to regain consciousness and ask her. I'm sure she can be of far more help than I."

Keswick took a long drag off his cigarette. Smoke rolled out his nose as the moonlight found the whites of his eyes. "Please don't do this, Dr. Sumner. I'm just trying to do my job. I need a fraction of your time. Help us. If you do, I can promise when I finish this cigarette, we will be done and you will be on your way."

Elliott looked around. *Why would the CIA be on the ground in Key West prior to the shooting on Caroline? Why this kind of interest? And why would Milton talk to London?*

"How'd you find me?" Elliott asked as he considered the new pieces to the puzzle.

"We never lost you. We've always known your whereabouts.

You may be the best in the world at hunting serial killers, but you're not good at hiding."

"We're done here," Elliott said as he turned into the elephant ears and parted the bamboo shoots. He could not be drawn into another horrific homicide case. His doctors in Dallas were adamant. The next traumatic event could be his last. The emotional overload could launch his ultimate mental breakdown without warning. It could trigger a spontaneous cardiac arrest. Elliott had no control over it. His autonomic nervous system would take over. Like everything else about him, the doctors had never seen anything like it before. They could not explain it.

"You know they will kill Helen Ramsey next, Dr. Sumner."

Elliott stopped in his tracks. The agent continued. "Harold Turpin in London—his homicide victim phoned Milton Busey and was butchered minutes later. Busey put a shank in Dr. Frank Rice's gut a few hours later—sliced him from his bellybutton to his throat. Dr. Rice was the prison psychiatrist. The man froze solid standing on a patio outside a medical conference room at the Pingree Correctional Center. Had a cigarette in his hand and a frozen stream of blood from his gut to the floor. Gets real cold up there in North Dakota. Rice's blood had filled his trousers. Stopped steaming long before they found him."

"I can do without the details," Elliott replied. With eyes on the moon, he swallowed hard.

"Right. Sorry. I know you're tryin' to manage—well—I know why you're down here."

Keswick took another long drag off his cigarette with an odd smile. His face hardened. "Mr. Busey left Pingree that night, Dr. Sumner. He took Rice's new Lexus—not even two weeks old. Rice is an interesting character. The psychiatrist lost his medical license years ago. He was an alcoholic. Lived alone. The man was broke and drunk most the time. Wonder how he could afford a $70,000 Lexus on his paltry wages from Pingree?"

"You're wasting my time," Elliott whispered. "I don't need this information."

"Milton Busey took the Lexus and drove to Key West. He helped himself to a few more cars along the way. Aren't you a little bit curious why, Dr. Sumner?"

"I am not."

"Just maybe you know something that could save Miss Ramsey's life. It would be a shame for her to die through no fault of her own, especially after you worked so hard to give her a chance at life. Now she's one of those victims you carry around in your head. You don't want to deal with her death if you can help it—right, Dr. Sumner?"

Elliott turned to Keswick with burning eyes.

"The homicide in London connects with one in Istanbul and another in Canada. You're getting this before the POTUS. This is international shit, Dr. Sumner."

"I'm sure the Royal Canadian Mounted Police, Scotland Yard, and INTERPOL can sort this out without my help," Elliott said, his calm voice revealing nothing.

"They connect to three more murders in North Dakota, Dr. Sumner. That's not counting Dr. Rice. That's six homicides in four countries in three days. Now you can add two more—from Caroline Street. Something is going on, Dr. Sumner. We need to know what you learned today."

"Did Harold Turpin invite INTERPOL in on the London homicide?" Elliott asked.

"In a roundabout way."

"That would be a *no*."

"Well, technically."

"Tell me how the CIA got involved. Don't lie, or I am gone this time."

"Excellent. We're making progress. To be brutally honest, we listened in on a private conversation between Mr. Turpin and your father—Albert Bell."

"I know my father's name."

"Of course you do."

"Good to hear the CIA is violating our civil rights," Elliott scoffed.

"The agency has an ongoing interest in certain high-profile Americans who interact with high-profile people across the pond. Mr. Bell is a multibillionaire with considerable influence in the world. Harold Turpin—although retired and ill—continues to live up to his exceptional profiling reputation. The man pretty much stays ahead of everyone. He sees an international connection, when the rest of Scotland Yard does not."

"Your justification to wiretap is weak and illegal."

"Our interests justify—"

"The hell with civil liberties," Elliott puffed as he studied the man. Keswick did not behave like a CIA operative. Keswick's explanation of clandestine surveillance practices was creative but amateur—a pro would never share that information. Elliott knew the agency had obtained court clearances before surveilling any and all American citizens, and he knew the process was rigid with oversight. His description of off-the-grid, illegal surveillance sounded like it came from a Clancy novel.

"We walk a fine line honoring civil liberties while protecting the country from terrorists, rouge nations, and superpowers with unacceptable geopolitical agendas. It is a dangerous world."

"Gee. I've been more isolated than I thought," Elliott chuckled. "Who do you work for?"

"Graham Pucket."

"Have you been with Mr. Pucket long?"

"Three years."

"Are you friends? Been to his house for dinner, met the family?"

"Yes," Keswick said, his eyes looking down for the first time.

"Good. Then you know Jenny's daughter's names."

Keswick smiled. "Melissa, Manda, and Yvonne."

Elliott nodded. "You've got three minutes. Then I leave."

"Did Helen Ramsey speak to you?"

"Yes."

"What did she say?"

"Don't let me die," Elliott said.

"I don't need that kind of information. What did she say about Busey, doctor?"

Elliott could tell Keswick had had plastic surgery—his eyes, chin, and hairline. "I was a little busy at the time, so I'm not sure I heard her."

"You know Milton Busey. You know the man's background. And you were at the crime scene on Caroline for thirty-one minutes—eleven alone with Miss Ramsey and twenty with the sheriff. Comparably, that's a whole day at a crime scene for a CSI team. What did you learn?"

"You timed me?" Elliott asked, watching Keswick's eyes.

He looked away. "We're organized."

"I see."

"Answer my questions, doctor. You said you would."

"Milton Busey is a serial killer who hid his victims and physical evidence well. In all five cases, he avoided prosecution—not enough to convict. Fortunately his checkered past proved to be enough to get him off the streets for the rest of his life. Last I heard, drinking and drugs had damaged his kidneys, further diminishing his time in this world."

A breeze slid off the water and up the beach, lifting a spray of sand. The foliage stirred. Elliott rubbed the back of his neck and looked up the beach. A chill ran down his spine. Something was wrong—out of place. "You know why Busey was here," Keswick said. "Tell me where he is now. I know you know."

"I suspect Milton Busey conducted some sorted business from prison. Something happened that upset him."

"Go on," Keswick pushed.

"Possibly he had a deal with someone on the outside. Possibly the law firm—Bowman, Weller & Garcia—acted as intermediary. Possibly Milton Busey learned something on the phone call from London that set him off, triggered his escape and trip down here."

If I can keep you talking, you will help me find Busey, Keswick thought. *I need to know what Ramsey told you about the deal.* "Makes sense. This is helpful."

Elliott nodded. "You need to find out what was said on the London call. That is the key."

"Why?"

"It motivated Milton to kill again and to come here. He left with a goal to locate the law firm. He thought he was going to Kansas City. They had moved. He tracked them to Key West. The law firm was running from something. Maybe you people know what."

"How can you be so sure of all these conclusions?" Keswick asked.

"Milton's never been the type to do a deal with people far away—like Key West. Labels on boxes at the law office had a Kansas City address crossed out. The site selection in the middle of a tourist center suggests they were not looking for new clients. And Miss Ramsey is a local girl. She's not involved."

"How could you possibly know she is local?"

"Her Key West tan. It's not from a Kansas City tanning bed," Elliott said.

"Logical."

"Milton Busey's motivators are respect, money, and family. I suspect someone stepped on one or more of them. Probably did not adhere to terms of their agreement. Good way to irritate a psychopath."

"How can you be so sure?" Keswick asked.

"I'm not sure. I'm logical. Milton would die in prison in less than a year. He had a pretty good deal for a tired, sick old man—walk-around time, free meals, free medical, free smokes, and unlimited TV in his pajamas. The man was waiting to die. Something motivated him to kill again and to leave Pingree. He did not have the energy or health to run around the country. He also knew he would be caught, and then spend the rest of his life in solitary confinement or be killed on the outside. Something significant motivated Milton Busey."

Keswick dropped his second cigarette and stepped it into the sand. "Did Helen Ramsey say anything to you about the law firm?"

"No." *Why are you fishing that hole?*

"Where is Milton Busey now, Dr. Sumner?"

"I don't know. Why ask me?"

"Because you know how Busey thinks. You're a profiler and world-renowned forensic pathologist and psychologist, among other things. The kind of analysis I'm talking about is not much of a reach for you. You just explained why Busey killed, left prison, and came down here. You know he gutted two lawyers and took Bowman with him. Where is he hiding, Sumner? I know you know."

I never said which lawyer Milton took, Elliott thought. *I never knew. Unless he spoke to Malone and Hayes, he wouldn't know. That kind of information would be closely held for at least forty-eight hours.*

"Are you going to answer me, Dr. Sumner?"

"Fair point," Elliott said. "Perhaps if you share some of the information you obtained from Malone and Hayes, it would help me zero in on where Milton might be. This is a relatively small area with few exit routes. If you've been watching the exits and haven't seen him, there's a good chance he's still here."

"We have not connected with law enforcement or the medical examiner. They don't know the CIA is down here, and we would like to keep it that way for now. The Caroline Street homicides are part of a bigger picture. We do not intend on bringing the local yokels along for the ride, Dr. Sumner."

"I see." Elliott shifted his weight for an anticipated sprint into the foliage.

"This part of our investigation is a long shot. Pucket sent me down on a hunch. He didn't like the London-Pingree connection. We tracked Busey here. Then this mess happened. Guess Pucket was right. Looks like the proverbial tip of another iceberg from hell," he said.

"So, you two are working *outside* the agency?" Elliott asked.

"I guess you could say that," Keswick replied. He turned to the ocean. "When Pucket confirmed Busey was headed here, I got on a plane."

The only way Keswick could have known Milton Busey was in Key West would be through a connection with Bowman, Weller & Garcia, Elliott mused. Keswick must have been on Caroline before, during, and after the shooting if he timed me at the crime scene. Keswick must have known Milton would show up at the law firm.

Elliott leaned onto his push-off foot. "I never said Milton took Bowman."

"You didn't?" Keswick said. "I must have heard it on the street. Doesn't matter which lawyer he took. They're all educated vermin, right?"

Elliott looked left, right, and back at Keswick. "And Jenny's three daughters—"

"Yeah. What about 'em?"

"There's no Jenny. It's Karen Pucket. Seems you should know that."

Keswick's eyes froze as his smile melted.

"Who are you?" Elliott pushed. "And why are you in Key West looking for Milton Busey? Do you work for Bowman, Weller & Garcia?"

Keswick's smile returned with evil eyes. "You're as good as they say. I knew it would be risky talking to you, but I didn't have a lot of options. I gotta find Busey. The old man avoided sniper fire and got out of the law office too damn fast. I knew the Keystone Cops couldn't help me. Hell, they couldn't find their way off a six-foot dingy with a floorplan in hand." He shook his head and snickered. "That moron Busey is screwing things up for some important people. He's got their attention now, Dr. Sumner. That old man needs to die."

Keswick reached into his coat and pulled out a Glock. "You were right. This thing with Busey is about family and money. I'm impressed. But I don't know which got in his craw the most. Probably when they killed his son. Timing fits."

Keswick gloated—he had just solved another complex puzzle. "Although, there was a lot of money involved, it was money Busey and his son would never see. They should have known."

"What are you talking about?" Elliott prodded.

"Busey couldn't do much sitting in prison. The money was used to rope in the son and Rice so the information Busey possessed could be utilized over a period of time."

"You're not making sense."

"Busey was key. Who would have thought that old guy—a serial killer dying in prison—would be walkin' around with some of the most guarded military secrets on the planet?"

"I still have no idea what you're talking about."

"You mean to tell me the world-renowned forensic sleuth could not put this one together? You know the man's life story. You hunted him. I know when you were sittin' on that bloody floor on Caroline, you were puttin' things together. You had to know Busey was the reason for all this shit. He's the major crack in the armor."

Elliott shook his head. "Sorry. You're still not making sense."

"Think, Sumner. Years ago, Busey signed government papers pledging his damn allegiance to the goddamn flag. Probably the same papers our military boys signed at Area 51 in Nevada while working with those UFOs the feds deny exist. Those government papers are meant to scare a man into a life of silence. If they spoke a word, the United States Government would come down on them—hellfire and brimstone. Those threats work most the time, but there were always whistleblowers and entrepreneurs. Busey falls into the entrepreneur category. His expertise threatened national security. He has information that's valuable stuff in the right markets."

"National security ... the right markets?"

"You're good," Keswick chuckled. "Got me ramblin' on in the ocean air without a care in the damn world. I think I've said enough, even though you won't be tellin' anyone this shit."

"What have you done to Graham Pucket?" Elliott asked.

"He's crab bait in the Chesapeake. Poor Jenny—I mean Karen—she thinks her old man's on another secret mission. CIA spouses don't miss their husbands for months."

"You're a very sick man, Keswick."

"And we were being so civil," he sneered. "Guess our little friendly chat is over. You don't seem willing to help me anymore. It's time we both go." He looked up and down the beach. "Well, your way is a bit more permanent."

He lifted his Glock and touched Elliott's nose. "Sad. I bet you never thought your illustrious forensic career would end on a beach in Key West by little ole me—"

The first hollowpoint whistled through the salt air and

pierced the left temple. The right side of the head exploded—brain tissue, blood, and splinters of bone rained down on the giant elephant ears and sprayed the lush bamboo shoots. The vacant body went limp and collapsed onto the sand as another hollowpoint zipped over the water and sand toward the target.

PART TWO

UPSIDE-DOWN PYRAMID
Early Morning Day Five

CHAPTER 11

"Maybe this world is another world's hell."
Aldous Huxley

Day Five – WASHINGTON D.C.

"Are we in the bunker?" The President asked.

"No, sir." Cameron Scofield passed another paper and watched the president's eyes scan each line. When he looked up, Cameron said, "The Oval Office."

"Good, for now." They turned the corner and walked a brisk pace down the next hall. The deep royal blue carpet runners were centered on polished, stained-wood floors, and the windowless walls were lined with dark oil paintings—a century of gifts from around the world. It all added to the darkness of the early morning crisis. "Who's here?"

Cameron glanced at smeared scribbles on his right palm. "The Vice President, Secretary of Defense, and the directors of the CIA and Homeland Security."

"I want the Air Force here, Cam."

"Chief General Jamison is at Wright Patterson. He said it would be more productive for him to head northwest, not southeast for an hour 'to pontificate'. His words, not mine. The Chief General did add that, if you saw it differently, he would dutifully turn around his *goddamn* plane. Again, his words—"

"—not yours. I got it." Secret Service led down the first flight of stairs.

"He is leaving Dayton for Minot Air Force Base."

"Can't argue with good sense," Landon agreed. "I want Buck on the box."

Cameron nodded. "That has been arranged, sir."

Cam opened his left hand and squinted at the smaller print—more words to fit. He knew the president well. He knew the questions and the order and depth of answers required within the first five minutes of any crisis. After that, no one could predict President Landon. He stood alone as a leader. This would be his greatest test.

"Other than my cabinet members, who else knows?" asked the POTUS.

"Seven high-clearance military staff members at Minot Air Force Base. Chief General Jamison has three in the know on his team. The Vice President put a lid on early."

"Fifteen, by my count."

"Not including me and Secret Service, Mr. President."

"I don't think we need to include you and secret service, Cam." He patted his friend's back on the next turn. "Let's see if we can keep the lid on this better than the others. A leak this time could create a serious problem. I don't give a damn about the politics."

"Yes, sir."

"Who would have thought the day would come when the most powerful office on earth couldn't keep a damn secret?" the POTUS murmured. "It's a new world. Uncompromising ideologies have turned everything upside-down. What happened to just getting it right?"

"A terrible problem, Mr. President," Cam confirmed out of habit.

"This thing got a code name yet? Everything around here gets a code name."

"GRAY WOLF," he said.

President Landon nodded as they marched into the next hall

with Secret Service around them. His protection increased with identified threats. "GRAY WOLF. Interesting choice, the animal kingdom terrorist of the Great Plains. It's gotta be Buck. He named the thing, didn't he?"

"Yes he did, sir."

"Buck's from those parts. Knows his Indian legends and zoology."

"Zoology, Mr. President?"

"Study of animal life: evolution, behavior, distribution, classification. Like the American Indians, at one time the gray wolf occupied most habitats on the continent. They particularly liked the Great Plains. In modern times, people moved in and the gray wolf moved out. The animal was hunted to near extinction in the seventies. Ranchers believed the gray wolf fed on their livestock. Fact was, they did not. Actually preferred deer and moose." The POTUS smiled. "But I bet that's not why Buck named it GRAY WOLF."

"No? Then why?"

"Like the American Indian, the gray wolf had more to do with this country and our future than most people know. I'll let Buck choose the time and place to elaborate."

Moving onto the West Colonnade, Landon looked across the Rose Garden at the heads in his Oval Office.

"Michael was one of my best decisions." His words shot into the crisp air.

"Mrs. Landon saw the good in him from the start," Cam said, forgetting the intensity of the moment. Flustered, he turned to the president. "I'm sorry. I should not have said that."

The POTUS smiled, setting aside the imminent danger for a moment of renewal. Barbara had been the love of his life—his entire world—and the reason he even sat in the Oval Office. The successful oil baron and international entrepreneur had everything he ever wanted in life—health, wealth, and his

Barbara. William Alsbury Landon had no desire to become a political animal. But Barbara had seen it differently. In her way, she'd urged the man she loved and respected to help the nation he loved. It was time to give back. A landslide election made him a Texas Senator. Seven years later, he would become the surprise President of the United States. Then Barbara pushed him into a second term. He initially refused, but he always did what Barbara said.

He lost her to uterine cancer a month after his second-term inauguration. Now, when he faces a crisis, President Landon remembers Barbara's last whisper in his ear: *"You will always do right when you trust your instincts over other's intellect, my love."*

"Michael can be a challenge on occasion. The man's not afraid to wear me out."

"He's also a loyal patriot who believes in you, Mr. President. I know it is a little old-fashioned to say, but he would fall on his sword for you."

Landon put his hand on Scofield's shoulder. "Like you, my dear friend."

They reached the glass-paned double doors leading into the Oval Office. Cam stepped aside and bowed to his best friend, who happened to be the nation's leader. Landon's soft eyes left Cam as he turned to the doors. Everything transformed as the light from the sacred chamber washed over the President of the United States.

The door opened. Landon paused. All heads turned. The Oval Office rose to its feet. Secret Service spilled in and fanned out, touching their earpieces. After the lead agent nodded, the President entered. His six-five stature and chiseled, Lincolnesque presence brought an immediate calm to the room of distinguished, dedicated, capable, and worried national servants. The POTUS nodded with a soft smile. His eyes found each cabinet member. In the brief moment, each knew why the country had elected the man two times. Before he uttered a single word, his intense eyes embraced each member of his dedicated team. They felt his respect and confidence, like the sun breaking through a cloud, as they faced another impossible moment.

After a cacophony of *"Good morning, Mr. President,"* Vice President Michael Pierce stepped forward. With a firm handshake, he passed around copies of the half-inch thick classified report. The President glanced at the cover—GRAY WOLF. The room fell silent as he opened and read the first-page brief.

Protocol: The Vice President would open the meeting. The POTUS would ask questions along the way and then take the lead when ready. The orchestration of the first few minutes had to put everyone on the same page of a clearly defined situation facing the nation.

"We have a *terminal breach*, sir. An unidentified and unquantified entity entered the United States through Canada five days ago. They commandeered one or more Minuteman III ICBM silos in and around Ward County—Minot, North Dakota. One message has been received at Minot Air Force Base, 0200 Eastern Time. The message: *Minot AFB is our hostage. No planes take off. No planes land. No one enters or leaves the base. We are monitoring.*"

"How was the message received?" the President asked.

"Text to the base commanding officer," Pierce said. "He was at the 91st Missile Wing, 740th Strategic Missile Squadron headquarters investigating a potential breach."

"And why do we believe this message is not a hoax?" asked Landon.

"GRAY WOLF sent a command to the silo doors of asset High Tech A-7, forty miles southeast of Minot, a little more than four miles southwest of Balfour, North Dakota. The silo door hydraulic pressure went up, an action preceding opening. We have a MRBM in there."

Medium-range ballistic missile ... "My introduction to GRAY WOLF," the POTUS said.

"This action lit up the boards at the Air Force Global Strike Command Center," Frank Graham (Secretary of Defense) said. "Raising the door is an impossible feat unless you're sitting inside a silo and have hacked second-tier codes controlling operational functions such as locking and unlocking doors, opening and closing gates, regulating environments, and gaining access to selected military operational servers."

"Thank you for that clarification, Frank." The President motioned for all to sit. "Let's get comfortable. We're going to be here a while. Thank you for getting this started, Michael." He turned to the speakerphone. "Buck. You on the box?"

"I'm here, Mr. President," said the Chief General of the Air Force.

"Good. I'd like to start with silos in North Dakota. What do we have up there?"

The room stared at the speakerphone. "Mr. President, we have 135 operational missile silos in North Dakota. We nest two medium-range ballistic missiles. We nest 133 Minuteman III ICBMs capable of delivering a nuclear warhead three-thousand-five-hundred miles away. The Minuteman III is our most advanced ICBM. It is a three-stage booster capable of delivering a W62 nuclear warhead anywhere in the world."

"Remind all of us of the potency of the Minuteman III, Buck," said the President as he fanned through the GRAY WOLF document. His request was for the benefit of the attending cabinet members. Landon had been briefed in detail the day he took office. He would never forget the chilling realities.

"The Minuteman III has the most accurate trajectory

technology in the world. It will deliver the W62 warhead anywhere with less than a half-kilometer variance from target. The blast yield is 170 kilotons. Order and magnitude, Hiroshima was thirteen kilotons."

The room sat in cold silence as the President flipped pages. After the uncomfortable pause General Jamison said, "Patton was right—*War is hell*. Possessing such outrageous strength has served our country well—deterrence. However, it has never been our intention or expectation to ever use these weapons of mass destruction. As all of you know, we have been downsizing our ground missile program over the last decade. A quarter of the arsenal would be adequate enough to destroy the planet several times over. Downsizing offers substantial financial benefits as well as reduces dangerous maintenance risks and reduces exposure to events such as the one we face today. At times like this, we all will second-guess our strategic nuclear doctrine."

"An arguable premise either way in today's world—necessary deterrence verses potential annihilation," Landon said as he flipped the last pages of the GRAY WOLF document.

"General, can the Minuteman III be stopped?" the Vice President asked.

"This ICBM places the W62 nuclear warhead in a suborbital trajectory. It reenters the atmosphere on a stealth pathway to a preprogramed target. As I said, it is the most advanced technology in the world. It can avoid all known antiballistic missile technology."

"The Minuteman III is unstoppable. Thank you," the Vice President affirmed.

"Undeterred, GRAY WOLF could deliver one or more of our nuclear warheads anywhere in the world," Landon said with icy clarity.

"I recommend we assume the worst until we know different," Jamison said.

"At this time, we do not know if GRAY WOLF possesses the ability to launch, guide, arm, and detonate one of our missiles. Is that correct, Buck?" asked the President.

"That is correct, sir. We know only two things for certain: GRAY WOLF might be able to open one set of silo doors, and they can text the Minot Air Force Base commander's cell phone."

"That could be enough," said the Vice President as he loosened his tie.

"Do we positively know GRAY WOLF is sitting inside one or more of our silos or launch control capsules?"

"No, Mr. President," said Jamison. "At this time, we don't know where they are."

"When will we know?"

"We are employing a wide range of high-tech tools," said the General. "We cannot trust our fixed video assets. They could be manipulated and monitored by GRAY WOLF. We cannot put boots on the ground for obvious reasons. And we will not deploy the standard surveillance technology. However, we do possess classified, undetectable, surveillance technology. We intend to use it now. Until I get up there and know more, we must minimize activity that could trigger a negative response."

"Is it possible the silo doors were opened from a distant location?"

"If you mean outside of North Dakota, the answer is yes."

"So GRAY WOLF could be in another country, for all we know," Landon said.

"Correct," said the General.

"Let me summarize. We do not know who we are dealing with, how many there are, their capabilities, or their intentions. Is that an accurate accounting of the matter, Buck?"

"Yes, sir. I thought you should be brought in now. Our ground nuclear missile program has been breached. The risks are too great. You need to know everything prior to and during discovery, and be in the middle of the early analysis phase. At any moment, lethal action may be necessary—action you must authorize, sir."

"I understand, Buck. Criticism has no place here. Moving heaven and earth to define this terminal breach does."

"Yes, sir. And to do that, I must be on the ground up there."

"GRAY WOLF's stated demand prohibits all traffic into or out of Minot Air Force Base. I assume you have your ways, Buck."

"I do, sir. And be assured, we have a very capable team in place. We prepare for events like this," Jamison said.

"Although we have numerous informational needs, let me be clear on our priority," said the President. "I must know who I am dealing with as soon as possible. The identity of GRAY WOLF will shape our resolution strategy beyond the total annihilation of the threat, which would carry its own terrible consequences."

"Understood, Mr. President," said the General. The cabinet nodded.

"GRAY WOLF can destroy a major city anywhere in the United States with little or no warning," said the Vice President. "There would be no time to evacuate."

The President tapped a finger on the cover of his GRAY WOLF report. All cabinet members turned to him. His stone-cold face stared into the room as if he stood alone with the devil in hell. "We are dealing with an *upside-down pyramid*—our questions vastly outnumber our answers. We must get to work. If one Minuteman III leaves our borders, we will be the ones responsible for starting the last World War."

CHAPTER 12

"If it bleeds, we can kill it."
Arnold Schwarzenegger

Key West, Florida

Covered in blood, Elliott dropped to the sand. The gaping head wound stared up at the night sky like an enormous, oozing eye. Elliott had walked into the perfect kill zone—a skinny, desolate beach late at night. He was fortunate to still be alive.

When Richard Keswick had pulled out his gun and put it in Elliott's face, something unexpected happened. Instead of fearing death, an overwhelming sense of relief engulfed him. At last, a life of terror and torment would be over. His battles with the monsters living in his head would end. Someone else would make the decision for him, the difficult choice he could not make on his own—to end his life once and for all. For a split-second, Elliott had looked into the barrel of Keswick's gun and saw his pathway to peace. Then Keswick's head exploded.

The gun was locked in Keswick's iron grip as the vacated body collapsed. Elliott blinked human debris from his eyes and dropped onto his belly next to him. Another bullet buried itself in the trunk of the palm tree next to Elliott's head—but he was alive. Keswick did not move. Elliott peered through the reeds and saw the shadow of a boat that bobbed beyond the breakers, a hundred yards out. He watched the muzzle flashes of a sniper's rifle. The muffled explosions were swallowed by the folding waves. Each hollowpoint fluttered by and slapped the elephant ears like an injured sparrow falling from the sky.

I guess I'm alive. Ocean swells were enough to alter trajectory, he thought. *Even the best would have trouble hitting a target from a moving platform.*

He crawled to the body, keeping his head low. He felt for the pulse he knew would not be there. The first shot to the head had killed Keswick instantly. *This hit had to be setup on the fly—a last-minute thing,* Elliott thought as he parted the reeds and watched the boat approach shore. *They're coming. Why the desperation? What did Keswick know that warranted this? Was he with you at one time? Did you have to stop him in his tracks? What did he know?*

Elliott pulled back and grabbed Keswick's foot. He had to move deeper to avoid the random flurry of bullets from the bobbing boat. Elliott was not feeling lucky—one might find him. The incoming hollowpoints covered an ever-widening swath of scrub as Elliott crawled on his belly with Keswick in tow.

About twenty yards from the palm tree, he stopped. *I should have known better. I should have taken precautions after Caroline. Why did I leave the Marine Supply store in the first place? And after the disaster at the law offices, why did I resume my routine as if nothing happened? People never leave me alone.*

God, I ran the same route and walked the same beach at the same time I do every night. I'm out of practice—I must have forgotten what it's like to be in danger. What was I thinking? Anyone could have been standing in the crowd downtown—my old enemies and the new ones I don't even know yet. Anyone could have seen me leave that law office. The news cameras were all over. I was covered in blood, leaving the biggest crime scenes in Key West's history.

"What is my problem?" Elliott whispered to himself, as again he peeked through the tall grass. *You people could be anyone. What is your interest in the Caroline Street mystery? Were you here for Keswick, or did you come looking for me? Maybe you know me, my reputation? If that's the case, I can see you not wanting me in your sandbox.*

Elliott rolled the body over. "I'm going to assume all you people are connected to the Bowman, Weller & Garcia law firm. Therefore, like Mr. Keswick you people want to locate Milton Busey," he muttered. "And like Keswick you think I know his whereabouts."

I need to stop talking to myself. He rifled through the dead man's pockets and found a wallet. He flipped it open. Under the moonlight he read, "Florida State Driver's License. Well, hello James Penland. Keswick is your CIA cover name." Elliott pulled out a crisp business card. "You are James Edward Penland of the Penland Private Investigation Agency in Orlando, Florida." *Are you a bad guy? Did you kill my CIA friend? Who are you working for?*

The shooting stopped. Elliott opened the tall grass hoping for the best and expecting the worst. Bad news. The boat had landed. Elliott turned back to the body and found a second wallet, the one with the false CIA ID—"Keswick"—and the badge. He slid everything into his pocket for safe keeping—*I will get this to Malone somehow.* Then he saw the Glock still gripped in the dead man's white-knuckled hand. Elliott pried it loose as he watched from the reeds. *Don't come up here. Just go away.* They approached the palm tree and elephant ears. *You're going to follow the blood trail to Penland's body. Time to go. Let's hope when you find Penland dead you turn around and sail away.*

The next flurry of bullets came from the muzzles of handguns with silencers. The shots were random. Elliott left the corpse behind and crawled another forty yards into a stand of trees on the edge of Atlantic Boulevard. From there, he watched the two trackers marked by a flashlight bobbing on the blood trail. Every few yards, they shot into the scrub ahead.

Elliott crossed Atlantic Boulevard like an untrusting crab in the moonlight. He scurried up the first cinder-block wall he came to. Taking a chance on meeting a guard dog or yapper, he flipped over the top and hung inches off the ground. With his chin on top he saw three silhouettes in the bobbing boat on the shoreline. A fourth silhouette stood in the water holding a line. When the trackers reached Penland's body, they waved their light to the boat.

"Congratulations. You found him," Elliott whispered as he watched a silhouette on the boat raise a rifle and tuck it to his shoulder. It had a scope and panned the beach. *Pretty certain you have night vision,* Elliott thought as he looked back to his trackers. *Okay, gentlemen, may I suggest you turn around and go now? You've got what you came for. Mr. Penland is dead. I'm sure it was not an accident. Your secret's safe with me.* His heart raced. *I'm not in this. I'm more motivated than you to disappear.*

The flashlight darted around Penland's body. Then the beam moved in all directions over the wild brush. When it lined with Elliott's escape route, it began to move forward. They were heading toward Atlantic Boulevard on Elliott's crushed-grass trail.

When he let go, his feet touched the ground and the cinder block above him exploded. Brushing the concrete chips from his hair, he bolted to the opposite end of the small yard and climbed the wall. He dropped into a narrow alley and ran. Not knowing who or why he was being pursued, all he could do was keep moving.

The forensic sleuth had only a collection of observations and thoughts to guide him. He had theories based on random facts, but little to help construct a feasible survival plan. He knew he had to keep moving. Until he learned more, everyone could be dangerous. Of one thing he was certain; something much bigger loomed on the horizon, something that could kill him. At this juncture Elliott could not even put his trust in the county sheriff or medical examiner.

Why did Penland track me? Elliott wondered as he ran down the alley, his eyes darting left and right. *Why execute this man and come for me? Did Milton kill a prison doctor in North Dakota? And what did this law firm mean to him? Hiring a sniper is big-league. The location was setup for a sniper hit. I know Milton killed those two attorneys and kidnapped one, but I don't know why.* Elliott stopped at the end of the next alley, took a deep breath, and checked his pulse. *This gathering storm could kill me, and I don't even know what it's about.*

He crossed George Street and hid in bushes. He skirted concrete-block walls to Blanch and stood in the shadows of an empty garage. Peering back, he found his trackers getting closer. Now they were less than a hundred yards away and closing. He left through a back yard and slipped across Bertha and onto the Key West High School grounds. There he stayed low along the baseball field fence and worked his way to the northern ridge. From there, Elliott dropped into an inland pond and waded along the shoreline staying in the shadows of the moon. When he reached a boat ramp at the end of Juanita, he looked back again. They were still there, just climbing into the pond.

You guys are experienced at this. I'm sure you have shared my line with your associates. They will be closing in from the opposite direction anytime now.

He entered the small house on Juanita, one of many with identical designs. This one was Elliott's safe house. He had two, both of which he had rented a month after arriving at Key West. He'd visited each one several times over the last year with a purpose. He took care of the yard and managed his emergency supplies—items he might need, should he have to quickly disappear. The rental house on Juanita was strategic—it was between his primary residence and the dock where he kept his boat. His other safe house was at the north end of the county, the best location should he have to leave the Keys by land. Elliott knew his primary residence—the bungalow on Patricia—would no longer be an option. Between the county and his pursuers, he was certain it was being watched.

Elliott felt his way through the dark, musty house he had memorized. In the kitchen, he opened the cupboard under the sink, lifted the plywood floor, and reached into the crawlspace for a backpack. Squatting on the floor, he felt the contents—a change of clothes, money, his visa, two throw-away cells, bottled water, and a set of keys. One key was for the boat and the other was for the '82 Ford pickup in the garage.

He didn't have much time. They were close. Somehow, they seemed to anticipate every move he made. Elliott had to slow his heart. He had to get his mind on something else. The fear of being hunted was not the problem; it was the carnage on Caroline Street and Penland's head exploding. His blood, brain tissue, and pieces of shattered skull were still pasted on Elliot's clothes, his face, and in his hair. The sickening kill he had witnessed only added to his excessive load of debilitating memories.

Elliott had no control over when his involuntary nervous system took control. At any moment, it might send the deadly order: shut down the heart now. The doctors in Dallas had told him pain and trepidation were life-ending stimuli he was to avoid at all costs.

He took another deep breath and focused on positive things, his boat. *I will put in the new transducer and take her out for a relaxing day twenty miles from the tip of Florida. I will stop on the way and pick up some food.* He pulled on his jeans and hooded-sweatshirt and stuffed his blood-soaked shorts and t-shirt into the crawlspace. After replacing the section of flooring, he washed up and slid Penland's Glock into his waistband. He dropped Penland's IDs into his backpack.

Elliott turned to leave. The shadow blocked the kitchen doorway. There was no other way out. He froze.

"Where do you think you're going?"

CHAPTER 13

"Everything you can imagine is real."
Pablo Picasso

Washington DC

President Landon stared out the window into the rose garden. The commander-in-chief had aged more in the last year than in any ten before. Each day, the increasing complexities of the world seemed a little heavier. His newest crisis had started to take its toll when Scofield said *North Dakota*. Landon's most dreaded fear had come to roost on his doorstep: a nuclear catastrophe.

In the crisp morning hours before sunrise, the POTUS stared out the window digesting the first wave of intelligence presented by the Chairmen of the Joint Chiefs of Staff. General Jamison was most adept at setting the table for the unfolding nuclear nightmare. As pages of the GRAY WOLF document turned behind him, the President made a fist with the hand he kept in his pocket all morning. Still, it trembled, even after an increased dosage of carbidopa-levodopa. His medical condition had been diagnosed a month after the death of his wife, the first devastating blow. Doctors said at his age, early-stage Parkinson's could be managed. Landon could make it to the end of his presidency, and no one would ever know. He didn't like it, but he did agree to hide his problem. Strength in the White House helped to maintain a level of order in the world. Weakness encouraged desperate nations to do desperate things. Faced now with a nuclear crisis, Landon believed more than ever that the strength of the POTUS had to be unwavering. But to keep a clear head, he had to stop taking his medications and hope for the best.

"Shall I continue, Mr. President?" asked General Brandon Jamison. His voice cracked on the speakerphone as his plane skirted storm clouds en route to the Minot Air Force Base.

"Are there any new demands, Buck?" Landon asked.

"No, sir. Silence."

"It's been a while since the first contact."

Eyes lifted from briefing documents and found the speaker phone as if searching for the general's eyes and some hidden meaning. "GRAY WOLF is looking for needles in our nuclear haystack," Jamison said. "Regardless of what they thought they knew, they are now in the thick of things. Our failsafe security mechanisms are prolific and complex, designed to confound any and all unauthorized attempts to manipulate or hijack our nuclear assets."

"Refresh all of us on some of the security mechanisms, Buck?" asked the President.

"Multilayered coded systems, redundant procedures, and an intricate web of safeguards programed to change on a random basis several times in every twenty-four-hour cycle. Doors of vulnerability once open are closed. New doors do open, unfortunately. Unpredictable change is a key component. GRAY WOLF is attempting to navigate a thousand *Rubik Cubes,* all in continual motion. The effort requires full attention, Mr. President. They cannot afford one error."

"Why does that not comfort me?" Landon asked.

"An error will box them in," Jamison said, "and give us immediate visibility. Our systems or our people will find them. And then the games begin."

"Still not comforting, Buck."

"Nothing I can say will be comforting, Mr. President. We are nervous because there is a rat in our kitchen. Regardless of safeguards, technology, and an abundance of traps ... there is a chance the rat gets the cheese."

Landon turned to Frank Graham, his Secretary of Defense. "Until we know more, our *strategy of containment* continues. Military deployment beyond the ready position remains on hold until forced into action. I need to make some calls. Are you and State ready?"

Landon had surrounded himself with colorful people of high intellect. Frank Graham had become his new Secretary of Defense after Bill Myers died in a tragic private plane crash. Graham, then the Deputy Secretary, had demonstrated an ability to navigate policy and politics with great vision and efficiency, and to the liking of the President. Landon moved him into the vacated cabinet seat without hesitation. The short, stodgy, cigar-smoking, vodka-drinking military strategist had a reputation for creative problem-solving. As far as the president could tell, he also had no axes to grind and no skeletons in his closet. Unlike most politicians, the President demanded his cabinet have their politics under control. In alignment, Graham had already demonstrated he never allowed politics to get in the way of a good idea for the country or onto a field of battle. His stellar military career had taken him to the position of Deputy Secretary. His exceptional grasp of ever-changing world affairs and strategic warfare—and his love of country—took him to Secretary of Defense.

"State and I are working together on the international communications preliminaries," Frank said. "The *usual* leaders are already in the loop, sir."

"Good."

"I will present military options after the forensics, or whenever you say, sir." Graham said. "I agree, strategy is better honed when we know who we're up against."

"Your initial calls—what do they know, Frank? The Russians, China, Israel, our European friends?"

"They know the President of the United States may call with regard to a matter of great mutual importance, sir."

"Great mutual importance," Landon said under his breath.

"Each expressed willingness to cooperate," Frank said.

"Cooperate. Good."

"—Short of turning a blind eye to a Minuteman III coming their way."

"Their words?" Pierce asked.

"In some cases, yes," Frank replied, reaching for his coffee. "Their exact words."

"How could they know?" Pierce asked.

Graham stopped his cup at his lips. "They may know, and they may not know. Either way, we must do what we do and remember we live in a small world."

"Small world," the VP sighed. "I'll bet one of those bastards is involved."

"Respectfully, I suggest we not go there now, Mr. Vice President." Graham set down his coffee cup and pinched the knot of his tie.

"Why not go there? We know the bastards can't be trusted. They're never there for us. All we do is help them with their problems—send military support and billions in aid."

"The comment is fair and to be expected, Michael," Landon said. "It is real. If a missile came toward us, we would react the same way. They have every right to defend their homelands. If they know something, I can assure you, they are more nervous than we."

"You're right, of course," Pierce said. "I'm just tired of the lies. It leads to—"

"Now is not the time. We must focus on North Dakota. Identification of GRAY WOLF is our priority. When we know who is up there, we have a chance to avoid a cataclysmic outcome."

"I concur, Mr. President," Jamison crackled over the box.

Landon took a sip of coffee as the room caught their breath. "We need to hear from Homeland, the CIA, and then Defense. Buck, what do you need to do now?"

"I am thirteen minutes from Minot, Mr. President."

"Do you need to leave this call?"

"Yes. I will reconnect at 0600 unless all hell breaks out."

"Understood," Landon said. "Thank you and—"

"Excuse me," Pierce interrupted again. "I think everyone in this room needs to be reminded what is at stake—if all hell breaks out, Mr. President."

"Buck, please elaborate."

"Very well, sir. GRAY WOLF presents a *terminal breach* threat to the United States of America. This is the highest level danger for our nation. Within this threat classification, there are thresholds of penetration, points of no return. When reached, we are alerted. When the last one is crossed, the threat becomes a termination notice—the imminent end of our existence. This notice triggers a set of *rules of engagement*. They are predetermined, deliberate, and absolute. In this case, the action will be *programmed cataclysmic containment* of the threat in North Dakota."

"GRAY WOLF can trigger this action by accessing certain sensitive files within our system," the President said. "Once triggered, our system takes over and cannot be stopped."

"We cannot stop—?"

"A *terminal breach* by definition is a confirmed nuclear threat against the United States homeland," the General reiterated. "Elimination of U.S. leadership is one of many precepts in this defense calculation. Our programs are designed to implement the same actions we would if we were alive. Unlike human assessments, thousands of data points are processed at multiple locations—the Pentagon, Colorado, and many other sites. The master computer evaluates the penetration and assigns risk. Our systems unleash nuclear assets aimed at GRAY WOLF. Because the Minot nuclear arsenal is compromised—because it has fallen into the hands of the enemy—it is the primary target."

"When and if GRAY WOLF crosses the threshold Buck described, our nuclear response will devastate the Midwest," the President said. His eyes were cold and determined.

"Devastate?" the Vice President breathed.

General Jamison cleared his throat. "The state of North Dakota will be obliterated before one Minuteman III missile can leave a silo. The hits will impact all surrounding states in the Midwest and a large portion of central Canada."

Pierce approached the President and whispered, "Is this what we want? Can we allow a computer to execute thirty million Americans? Up until today, this has been theoretical."

Heads of the cabinet dropped. Like the Vice President, they had been briefed on the dreadful realities of a *terminal breach*. The chilling classified protocol had been debated in secret Congressional committee hearings with the nation's top military minds and strategists. Each president over three prior terms had signed off on the plan. Each year, the protocol was reviewed, and each year, reinstated—a viable alternative not yet found. Unlike all other military actions, nuclear engagements are managed by a computer program.

Landon put his steady hand on the Vice President's shoulder. Their eyes met. Words did not need to be exchanged. Michael Pierce knew the answer to his question. He understood the dire consequences of nuclear warfare. Still, he had to try, for everyone in the room.

"We will get through this. I promise," Landon said.

"Mr. President, I need to sign off," General Jamison said.

"Our thoughts and prayers are with you, General." Landon pressed the speaker phone bar and stared at the picture of Barbary on his desk—a happier time. He took a deep breath and turned to his wide-eyed cabinet. "I want to know who is in my silos. The identity will define our actions. As Buck said, if they do something stupid, all of this is out of our hands and a lot of people die. Let's move to Homeland Security. Maureen, tell us about GRAY WOLF?"

"Mr. President, our trail—at this juncture—begins at Bone Lake in Manitoba, Canada."

As one of the three women in the president's cabinet, Maureen Nye—an accomplished forensic pathologist and Harvard legal scholar—had climbed the ranks to the District Attorney for Washington D.C. and now serves as the first female Director of Homeland Security. Landon met Dr. Nye on the campaign trail during his run for Texas Senator. Their consultations over the years produced a mutual respect, one of great depth and substance with regard to the security needs of the nation. Dr. Nye supported Senator Landon's presidential runs. Her contributions had been described as pivotal in key borderline states. Some said Dr. Nye made Landon's presidency possible. Dr. Nye said the voters made his presidency possible— Dr. Nye only made the introductions.

"How do we know Bone Lake, Maureen?"

"What I have is gruesome, sir."

"I understand. Leave nothing out."

"We have a body in the woods near Bone Lake, a remote location in Manitoba, Canada. The victim is mutilated in a particularly macabre manner, sir: decapitated, dismembered, and crushed—or *compressed* is a better word—sir. The head and appendages of the victim appear to be missing from the primary death scene."

"Did you say *compressed*?"

"Yes, sir. The victim was compressed into a cubic shape measuring three feet by three feet by three feet. The human cube was found frozen solid in the wilderness in subzero conditions."

"I've never—"

Maureen handed photographs to the President. He grimaced and passed them back. Director Nye circulated them to cabinet members.

"*Gruesome* is not a strong enough word, doctor," the President said.

"No it's not, sir," Nye said. "I've never seen anything like this. In my forensic pathology days, there were troubling cases—but nothing like this."

"Why do this?" the President asked. "It seems excessive. Do you believe GRAY WOLF did this? Were they sending some kind of message?"

"This appears to be about the elimination of physical evidence, sir. The deceased was executed, processed, and left in the woods in a remote location."

"Food for wildlife?" the President asked.

"Yes, sir. This disposal methodology is unique, calculated, and telling. It required planning and preparation, and it took into account the environment—weather conditions and wildlife feeding habits and trails. Every aspect of this invasion was well-planned and resourced. The Bone Lake killing allows us to see how GRAY WOLF thinks. In this case, we see their perception of best-practices to terminate and dispose of members of their team, both short- and long-term. Based on this observed thought process, we can reach some conclusions."

"Please continue."

"The mutilated body found near Bone Lake was a member of GRAY WOLF. We believe a border scout. His or her role was to identify and secure a viable route into the United States for the primary GRAY WOLF team. Unknown to the scout, once the assignment had been completed, they were no longer needed."

"Explain your rationale, please."

"The most important part of the GRAY WOLF operation is to access and control the U.S. nuclear missiles in Minot. All tactical elements subordinate to the primary mission are viewed by GRAY WOLF as without value and disposable. We believe they not only want to unload people and things of no value, but they also want to limit their exposure for both the short and long term. I am quite confident we will find more.

"We believe the primary GRAY WOLF team, those engaged in the primary mission, is composed of the experts—systems people, security, nuclear, negotiations and the like. Those people had to know in advance the border scout would be eliminated after the route into the United States had been secured. The compacting equipment and executioner arrived at Bone Lake with the primary team, the people who were needed to confirm suitability of the route into our country before the border scout could be eliminated. This is revealed by four things: one, the execution; two, the presence of compacting equipment at the kill site; three, the dispersal of the remains in a remote location to maximize the rate of wildlife consumption; and four, the stealth entry of GRAY WOLF into the United States, of which we have no sense of timing. It could have been a day, a week, a month, or a year. We only know this scout was terminated recently."

"Apparently, their best-laid plans failed," said the President. "The body was found."

"Hunters stumbled across the victim while tracking wildlife to a food source. However, we can still legitimize GRAY WOLF's disposal calculation. Historically, winter blizzard conditions and subzero temperatures have kept hunters and hikers out of that remote area of the Manitoba Mountains. By fluke or fortune, a few X-treme hunters braved the elements for an adventure, but one they had never counted on. If they had not done so, GRAY WOLF's disposal of physical evidence would have been successful. The cubed body would have never been found—devoured by wildlife, birds, and insects, or melted into the rugged terrain."

"Still seems there are easier ways," Graham scoffed.

"It is clear GRAY WOLF did not want to leave a trail of physical evidence *long term*. That fact alone suggests we could be dealing with a *superpower* on a provocative mission. They are setting up a safety net. If their mission fails, they have maintained plausible deniability."

"We would not expect a rogue nation or radical Islamic terrorist group to have the same concerns," the President said.

"A point to consider, but not yet definitive," Graham added.

"I agree."

"It is another piece to the puzzle," Nye said. "The take-away is, GRAY WOLF wanted devalued members of their team to disappear forever. The short-term risk of discovery was a reasonable assumption that—in this case—turned into a miscalculation."

"And GRAY WOLF does not know we have this information," Pierce said.

The President nodded. "We don't know what will make all the difference." A staff member wheeled a coffee cart into the Oval Office. "Please continue, Maureen."

"We are working with the Royal Canadian Mounted Police, the Canadian Border Services Agency, and the Manitoba Medical Examiner's Office. The Bone Lake crime scene has been secured. The area is being scoured for physical evidence. Interviews are underway in neighboring communities. Maybe someone remembers something or saw something. The body is in refrigerated storage in Winnipeg, pending autopsy. It is best to keep it in a frozen state until we are ready. The provincial medical examiner has extended a formal invitation for us to send our own forensic pathologist or to transport to a location in our country for the inquest."

"I have some thoughts on that," Landon said.

"Dr. Emma Osgard recommends we engage Dr. Elliott Sumner," Nye said.

"Why am I not surprised?" Landon smiled.

"In my view, Dr. Sumner is the only forensic pathologist with the broad international experience we need to put this puzzle together in time to address a terminal breach, Mr. President. If anyone can identify GRAY WOLF from an international forensic trail, it will be him."

"I agree," Landon said.

"However, the last I heard, Dr. Sumner left the profession."

Landon looked at the ceiling of the Oval Office, rubbing his throat. "The man helped me on two occasions during my first term, and both matters still keep me up some nights."

"Matters, sir?" Nye asked.

"Things that confounded my sense of reality," he said as he blinked back into the room. "Elliott Sumner. We need him, no doubt. Mr. Herbolt, please try. He knows you."

"He never liked CIA, sir," James Herbolt replied. "I think Maureen might have better luck, since she's a forensic pathologist and he's a big fan of homeland security."

"You've already tried to rope Elliott in, haven't you, James?"

"Yes, sir. The moment I heard *terminal breach*, I anticipated a blood trail."

"You anticipated correctly. What's the problem, James?"

"We have located Dr. Sumner in Florida—Key West. We have not been in direct contact as of yet, but are working on it."

"And is there a problem?"

"Possibly, sir."

"Are you concerned he may be non-receptive?"

"It is all about who approaches him and how, sir."

"Give me more?" Landon asked.

"Some time ago, we engaged an old friend of Dr. Sumner's. As luck would have it, this old friend is already in Florida. I reached out in anticipation. This friend said he would talk to Elliott. I am hopeful, sir."

"I will call Albert Bell," Nye offered. "He might help."

"Good. See that we get Dr. Sumner on this," Landon ordered. "I will talk to him if it will help. I'm quite sure he will have more questions than any one of us can handle alone."

"Yes, sir." Herbolt punched numbers in his cell and stepped away from the group.

"Good. Dr. Nye, please continue."

"The Manitoba death scene tells us one GRAY WOLF priority is to maintain anonymity as long as possible. I agree with General Jamison's assessment. GRAY WOLF needs time to navigate our nuclear haystack. That is precisely what they are doing now, and we are leaving them alone as they intended. Those two facts tell us GRAY WOLF understands the complexity of their mission. They are too familiar with U.S. behavior and systems. That is disturbing."

"Possible insider?" asked the President.

"Possible, sir."

"GRAY WOLF knows we possess enormous power," Landon said. "And they know we will not use any of it until *we know* who and what we are dealing with. The longer they keep their anonymity, the more time they have to burrow into our strategic command center."

"Those predictable behavior components can be factored into our counteraction plan."

"Agreed, Dr. Nye. Unpredictable action on our part will be of value."

"Excuse me," Susan Dabney interrupted. She had been the

last cabinet member to enter the Oval Office and the last to close the GRAY WOLF briefing document.

With intense eyes and churning thoughts, Landon turned from Nye to his Secretary of State. "Miss Dabney. Please go ahead."

"I apologize for missing the beginning of the meeting. If I repeat something already said, please stop me."

"Fine," the President said, opening and closing his twitching fist under his desk.

"I can see the identification of GRAY WOLF has been prioritized. I can see we all agree a malformed action plan on our end can produce a horrible level of American casualties, one that could go well beyond historical proportions. I'm sure we all agree how we must handle this crisis based on the identity of GRAY WOLF. Anything less will be to the detriment of our country."

"Yes," Landon said. "If we hope to have any chance to avert a major nuclear event, we must know the other side of the equation. GRAY WOLF may or may not share this view. That fact alone could alter our actions and timing."

"In that light, it is important to define the three primary categories of likely enemies. Radical Islamic terrorists have established a horrific track record with the United States. A rogue nation—like North Korea or Iran—are the second category. They have the will and capabilities to disrupt world powers. The third category is the superpowers. I am particularly concerned with one with a new geopolitical strategy. Our world is changing. Some areas face growing internal pressures. Governments are challenged. Sovereignty and continuation are at risk. The Russians are on a road to bankruptcy. A change in their geopolitical strategy would not be a surprise. China sees a strong American economy. They see the development of competitive manufacturing. This is a major threat to their economy, and one that depends on exports. These changes threaten China's long-term stability. They may be compelled to act.

"Each category has a mission based on a different perspective on survival and success. Each has a level of defeat they cannot tolerate. As you know, Mr. President, we are engaged in discussions around the world. Each country faces problems that can redefine their futures. We know the European nations face very serious times. They have civil unrest, out-of-control immigration, changed political identities, failing economies, and increased threats from third-world terrorist organizations that they cannot afford to fight. The days of turning to the United States for help and financial aid have ended. This harsh reality has increased the possibilities of who GRAY WOLF could be. We must not make a move until we know exactly whom we face."

"GRAY WOLF could be a friend," the Vice President said.

"A desperate one," said the POTUS. "Thank you, Susan. I think we are all in agreement. We must identify GRAY WOLF. Maureen, take the forensics into our country. What do we have?"

"After Bone Lake, GRAY WOLF'S next stop is Turtle Mountain Provincial Park on the Canadian border—an isolated cabin. We found two more bodies processed like those in Bone Lake."

"GRAY WOLF crossed into the U.S. in Turtle Mountain Park?"

"Yes. We have evidence they entered North Dakota two-point-seven miles west of the International Peace Garden. The bodies were a mile over the U.S. border. The terrain is remote and rugged. A night crossing would be undetected."

"No surveillance in the area?"

"Not official. Random and private," Maureen said. "A form of transportation waited for the GRAY WOLF team. This time of year, night temps drop to twenty below zero. They would not attempt to cross fifty miles of ice and snow on foot. We are working with area law enforcement to identify and review any and all residential and commercial surveillance in the sector. We should find something helpful soon."

"You said they executed two in Turtle Mountain Park, a mile inside the U.S.," the President said. "Are you certain of the linkage to Bone Lake?"

"Yes, sir," Dr. Nye said. "Dismembered, decapitated, and crushed into blocks of flesh. The kill method is too unique to be more than one entity. And there was one more, sir. We have another found south of Minot—"

Richard Parker leaned his head in the door of the Oval Office and caught the President's eye. "Sir, I'm sorry to interrupt. We need a moment."

The POTUS knew Parker would not interrupt a meeting in the Oval Office unless the matter was critical and timing a factor. "We will pick up on Minot when I return. Please excuse me." Closing the door behind him, Landon saw the angst in Parker's eyes. "How much do you know?" the President asked.

"Enough, sir."

Richard Parker had been with Landon since his early Texas days. Parker joined the team as a junior manager. Now he served as Chief of Staff for the President of the United States. Parker's Harvard education and OCD tendencies helped him control a myriad of responsibilities and the loose ends that moved at lightning speed during an election cycle. He had been through several heart-stopping crises in the past five years. None stopped him from running the tightest ship in Washington D.C. His athletic build, short-cropped hair with a pinch of gray, and perfect attire projected the precision of a well-oiled operation committed to serving the POTUS.

"I have a message from General Jamison, sir. He had only seconds to pass information or he would have interrupted your meeting himself. He wanted you to have this first. There are changes in Minot. Sir, at Viking A-9, a silo off the grid, the hydraulics register is showing an increase in pressure on the silo doors. The general said GRAY WOLF is attempting to open the doors. They abandoned efforts at the High Tech A-7 site."

"What do you mean—a silo off the grid?" The President asked.

"The General will explain. Now he is headed to the 91st Wing Control Center."

"What else, Richard?"

"I wrote this down so I would get it absolutely correct, sir." He looked down at his scribbled notes. "The 91st Missile Wing of the Air Force Global Strike Command—the people responsible for maintaining the Minuteman III missiles—reported to the General a launch control capsule has been breached."

"Breached?" the President huffed.

"The LCC blast doors opened and closed, sir. The General told me about the blast—"

"—doors," the President finished. "Twenty-tons of concrete-and-steel secured by a dozen hydraulic steel pins intended to keep intruders out and to protect our missileers."

"Yes sir, missileers," Richard said. "Designed to take a direct hit—"

"Impenetrable," the POTUS whispered as his thoughts moved to the worst-case scenario.

"General Jamison wanted you to know GRAY WOLF may now be in a secured position. The *terminal breach* threshold could be violated at any time."

Without a word, the President turned to the door to the Oval Office and gripped the antique-gold knob, just as he had a hundred times before. But this time, he felt nauseous. *The containment option decision is out of my hands,* he thought. *The Midwestern United States could be wiped off the map by a damn computer—*

CHAPTER 14

"For a second, I was almost jealous of the clouds."
Kamila Shamsie

Key West, Florida

E lliott froze. The silhouette blocked his only way out. The weight of the Glock grew heavy in his waistband as he considered options. Could he use it? Would this be the time he broke his rule?

Maybe he could talk his way out. Maybe he could explain he had nothing to do with Caroline Street. He was next door getting something for his boat. He's a doctor. He tried to help someone injured, someone he'd never seen before. But none of that really mattered now. They had killed Penland and they were hunting him for a reason. These were not random criminals. Something much bigger was in play, and Elliott had become entangled in the web. The killers would not expose themselves for just any reason. They would not chase a *Good Samaritan* unrelated to their agenda. They wanted to stop Elliott Sumner. If Elliott accepted the situation, he would end up like Penland. If Elliott did not do something fast, he would be Key West's Homicide Number Four.

Elliott inched his fingers to the Glock in his waistband. *Maybe Fenland is rogue CIA. I think he was sent to kill Milton and me. Why? Those guys on the boat, they think I'm CIA too?*

"You're not thinking about shooting me, are you?" The words filled the dark room like bats with full bellies flying into a cave. The silhouette had control. He exuded confidence. It was as if he knew the forensic sleuth would find his gun and do nothing. The suffocating reality washed over Elliott as he tried to figure out what was happening and why.

"You know me," the silhouette said in a raspy voice.

Elliott's finger touched the warm, wet handle of the gun. *That voice*, he thought. *Did they split up? This one found the right empty house first?*

Maybe Elliott's window of opportunity was small. Maybe he had to shoot and take the truck now. It might be his last chance. He gripped the handle and pulled the weapon out, all the while watching the shape in the dark kitchen.

In less than one second, I must chamber a round and get off a shot. It must be perfect. And I need to move to avoid getting hit. He will shoot me when I make my move.

"It's only been a year. Granted, I have a damn cold, but you should recognize me ..."

"Tee?"

"Thank you." The stiff silhouette slouched and leaned against the door jam. "I gotta tell ya, it really hurts a guy's feelings when his best friend—his '*numero uno compadre*'—disappears for a year with no goodbyes, no cards or letters. And then when I come to visit, he pulls a gun at me. I can't believe you did not recognize my voice, Elliott."

"First, you're the last person I expected."

Elliott shoved the Glock back into his waistband and embraced Tony Wilcox—the retired Memphis homicide detective and his best friend for two decades. He patted Tee's cheek, as always. "Second, your cold made you very nasal. I've never heard you nasal. Third, it's dark. Fourth, you did not use profanity. And, for the record, I've been away for a reason."

"I can't remember the last time I got sick as hell," his friend said through the congestion. "I pride myself."

"Not to mention you just stood there—your ominous shadow —giving me one-liners. I'm good, but not that good."

"You're a friggin genius, Elliott. Don't give me that shit. You're nervous for some damn reason. What the hell are you doin' poking around this house in the dark?"

"I'm in the middle of something that has me rattled. We gotta go. I'm being followed. They have guns. You can tell me later how you found me and why."

"Slow down, Tonto, we need to take care of some routine business first."

"We don't have time," Elliott snarled. "They're on my heels."

"I'm talking about your problem, not mine. We'll get to mine later." Tony pulled out a pocket device. "I got to Key West twenty minutes ago. Had no idea how I was gonna find you. Albert told me you were down in this area."

"Albert was supposed to keep that information to himself."

"Don't get upset at Albert. He did the right thing, as usual. Trust me. I will fill you in later." Tony held up the small device. "When I got to Key West, this little guy started to vibrate. Latest thing in scanning technology. Searches for transmissions in a twenty-mile radius. Checks a hundred frequencies in seconds. Finds one and locks. Weeds out cell phones, broadcast radio, Bluetooth, Zigbee and satellite communications, and ignores the legal stuff and routine trash floating across the airwaves. It looks for the high-end stuff: microwaves and things I don't really understand. It's where you can pick up on expensive tracking transmissions—the things used by the Feds, foreign governments, PI's, and high-end criminals. This one's a little pricey, but it has already paid for itself. I got an odd signal when I landed. Had no idea where you were, so I figured it would be a good place to start. Had a hunch you'd be involved."

"I'm *transmitting*?" Elliott asked feeling his chest.

Tony held up the tracking device and swept the room. As it neared Elliott, the beeps increased and red light changed to amber. "Turn around," Tony ordered. He held it to Elliott's backpack. The beeping peaked and the amber light turned green. "Take it off."

Tony rifled through the contents and removed Penland's ID. He felt the leather case. In the lining, he found a flat tracking pod the size of a dime. He held it up with a half-smile. "This puppy is why people have been on your ass."

"I took that from James Penland, the guy who stopped me on the beach. The people hunting me killed Penland. I need to get this information to Sheriff Malone."

"We need to get out of here first. And we need to drop off this expensive little dime somewhere creative—shake these guys once and for all. I've got some very important shit to discuss with you, and time is short."

"I guess I'm out of practice," Elliott said with resignation. "I should have looked closer. I missed that little tracking device."

"Well, you're a serial killer hunter, and those dirt bags don't use expensive tracking devices. You're in my world now. Granted, I've only been in it a year myself, since my homicide days in Memphis. And that's another story for a later time. Let's go."

"I have a pickup in the garage," Elliott whispered as they headed for the carport. "The trackers are close." Elliott jumped in the driver's side and slid the key in the ignition. As Wilcox threw the backpack onto the seat, a man leaped on his back. Elliott watched as he kept turning-over the cold engine. Maybe the second man had split off, checking the house next door. He would be showing up soon.

The engine chugged and coughed and came alive. Elliott eased the pickup out of the carport, the passenger door swinging wide open. He threw it into park—he had to help Tony. When his hand let go of the shift knob, he saw Wilcox flip his attacker to the ground. Tony followed with a rabbit-punch to the throat, and then jumped into the car.

They pulled onto Juanita Street and Elliott threw it into second.

"I think that'll keep that son-of-a-bitch busy a while—trying to breath," Tony crowed as he inspected his torn shirt and rubbed his neck. "Don't go in a straight line out of here."

As they turned off Juanita onto Fifth, Tony watched two men stop at the end of Elliott's driveway with guns drawn as the pickup passed his abandoned rental. "That was close. They're really pissed at you."

"They didn't shoot," Elliott observed as he shifted into third and accelerated. "I wonder why? Maybe it means they gave up on me." Elliott pulled the Glock from his back and laid it on the seat between them. "Take this. I don't use guns."

"You'd better keep it."

"No."

"Elliott, this thing is not over. Trust me. Those guys are determined, not giving up. We need to find a place to talk, somewhere safe. There's something we gotta get to that is bigger than some organized crime problem in Key West." Wilcox pulled out a bent cigarette and slid it into his mouth.

"Your little move back there was new," Elliott poked.

"Yeah. I've been expanding my horizons. Learning a Japanese system, unarmed combat. As a *retired* homicide detective, I am not free to shoot people who try to kill me. I'm a private citizen now, the respected owner of a private investigation firm. I gotta resort to less lethal methods to obtain cooperation, ways that cannot be misconstrued in a courtroom."

"*Obtain.* Nice. Good to hear you are evolving," Elliott said tongue-in-cheek. "A person can do a lot with basic leverage and quickness," he said looking in the rearview mirror.

"Jiu-jitsu is a method of close combat for defeating an armed and armored opponent without the use of weapons. Always heard about it, but never bought in. Then I tried it."

Elliott turned onto Roosevelt Road. "I have a boat nearby. We should get rid of the tracking pod while we have this slight advantage."

"Pull into that worksite, the port-a-potty," Tony said.

"You can't hold it?"

"Please. Just do it."

When Elliott stopped, he turned off the lights and watched Tony run to the port-a-potty and go in. Seconds later he returned to the pickup. "Let's go."

"Really," Elliott chided as he pulled back onto the road. "You tossed it in the commode?"

"They'll surround that port-a-potty for an hour waiting for all their people to get in place," Tony said. "These people are motivated and well-resourced, Elliott. I would not be surprised if they knew you have a boat. We need to check it out from afar very carefully. And we need to get rid of this pickup."

"The boat is not in my name. It's in Carol's name."

"Carol Mason?" Tony asked.

"Yes."

"Is she down here?"

"No."

"Never thought you two would—"

"—split?" Elliott pulled off the road into an empty parking lot.

"Well, yeah. You seemed awfully close."

"We decided it would be best we take a break."

"Why, if you don't mind me askin'?" Tony lit a cigarette.

Elliott looked in the rearview mirror at headlights in the distance. "The last year together, we spent more time worrying about each other than trying to stay alive. It's hard to be surrounded by danger with someone you love. We were vulnerable. It almost got us killed."

"I guess you know what you're doing."

"Right now we need to park this out of view and get to my boat." Elliott pulled into the gravel lot and stopped to consider options.

"Key *damn* West is not a very big place, Elliott. These people will be lookin' for a water escape. And they will have eyes on every road out of here."

"We are close enough. Best we go on foot to the boat," Elliott said.

"Shit. I was hoping not to get all sweaty—"

The back window and the windshield cracked. They saw two bullet holes. Elliott popped the clutch and spun out of the Banana Bay Resort Marina lot. He rounded a cluster of dark buildings and shot down a narrow lane between rows of boathouses. Without looking back, he entered another gravel lot. Elliott turned off the lights and skidded to a stop in a shallow grassy ravine behind a thick stand of trees, leaving behind a cloud and two paved roads into the woods. Within seconds lights popped into view and reached into the empty parking lot. Two cars skidded to a stop. They split up, each taking a paved road. When they disappeared, Elliott and Tony jumped out of the truck and moved into the woods on foot.

"Hope you know this place," Tony said, beginning to sound out of breath already.

"I do."

They ran on the edge of the tree line for a half mile. When they reached a private pier, Tony could see thirty docked boats. It was late. There was no activity. He followed Elliott to the end. The jet-black Commander 44 hardly moved in the unlit slip.

When the engine growled alive, Tony tossed in the ropes and jumped aboard. Elliott backed the sleek vessel into the small bay, running lights off. As they turned the Commander toward the tip of the peninsula and the Gulf, two cars slid to a stop at the end of their pier. Elliott eased the forty-foot yacht by bay rocks and buoys and approached the tip of the peninsula, their bay exit. The towering palms and thick bamboo would soon swallow their dark mass.

Two men left the cars and ran to the end of the pier. Tony watched them raise their guns, but they were too late. They did not have a shot worth drawing attention. They could only watch the tail of the Commander 44 leave the bay and enter the moonlit waters of the Gulf.

"Nice," Tony murmured as he rubbed the polished teak in the aft-cockpit, an unlit cigarette wagging between his lips and hair lifting in the gentle sea breeze. "And I like the name on the back of this bucket."

"I thought it appropriate. This is my new home."

"I'm pretty certain no one else is using BLOOD LION."

"I haven't had it long. It's been sitting in the slip for weeks—a navigation problem. A man can get lost out here fast."

"Oh, pray tell you have resolved your navigation problem," Tony said as he looked for the shoreline, now a quarter-mile away.

Elliott passed Tony the transducer. He had kept it in his pocket since Caroline. "I knew if I set this little guy down, I would lose it." He smiled. "The navigation system will come alive after you slip this transducer into that panel—slot 24F."

"I'm no electrician," Tony complained as he followed Elliott's finger to the navigation panel. He unlatched the cover and searched for 24F.

"If you don't want to be marooned at sea, follow my directions explicitly."

Tony snapped it into place. The navigation panel lit up instantly. Monitors populated and maps took shape. Elliott pointed to one screen. "This blinking dot is us. You can see where we are on the electronic map. You can see coordinates and key landmarks on the grid. I have it preset. Each square on the grid is five kilometers. I can modify the settings up to a hundred." He pointed to another screen. "This is my weather. It shows fronts in a fifty mile radius. I believe I have a depth finder and can monitor boats and airplanes that enter my navigation zone, too."

"All good to know," Tony mumbled as he lit a cigarette. "So the shoreline is now fifty kilometers away?" When he blew smoke, a sharp crack like an errant lightning bolt broke the night with a splintering thud in the aft section of the boat. "Shit! We've been hit."

Elliott slammed the throttle forward and cut sharp turning the smallest target to the shore. Two more cracks and two more projectiles fanned by the boat as the front of the Commander lifted five feet and churning water shot out the back. In five seconds, the sleek vessel had put another mile between them and the shooter.

"Check stern, starboard side. I need to know where we were hit."

"Speak English," Tony shouted. "I'm not a damn sailor."

"Back right side," Elliott shouted as he went for another mile separation.

"Looks like we got hit a foot above deck level, a few inches from the right edge."

"Nothing there to worry about. A foot below the deck would be bad."

"Really," Tony said as he felt the hole with a finger.

"Gas tanks."

With eyes on the shrinking shoreline, Tony moved toward the wheel and Elliott. "It's not gonna take long for these guys to find this boat in coastal waters. They know we're out here, and they know there are only two ways to run. We may no longer have a tracker pod on us, but all they have to do is cover both routes. It's a matter of time, and that shortens if they have a chopper. These people are not messin' around, Elliott."

No, they are not messing around.

Elliott kept the boat at twenty knots and turned toward the southeast tip of Key West. "I do not know why they're after me," he said as he flipped toggles and checked systems. "I simply picked up my transducer, the Marine Supply Emporium on Caroline. There were shots. I went next door to help. The secretary was hit. I stayed with her until the ambulance got there."

"Is it possible, when you were there, you saw something you should not have seen—something incriminating?"

"I always see a lot. You know that."

"And they may know that too, Elliott."

"But I didn't see anything unusual. It was the typical crime scene—bloody and chaotic. I got out of there as soon as I could. After they took the girl, and after the Monroe County ME had arrived, I left."

"Do you know the medical examiner?"

"Yes. Dan Hayes. But I don't think he told the Sheriff he knew me."

"That's peculiar," Tony said as he tried to light another cigarette in cupped hands.

"Hayes covered for me. Several forensic pathologists know I stepped away for personal medical reasons. They know I needed a break, but I don't believe they know the extent of my psycho-physiological condition."

"My two cents—something stinks," Tony said. "Could be your buddy Hayes is involved. Could be the County cop is involved, too. You said yourself you don't know anything about the Caroline Street shooting."

"A double homicide and a critical injury."

"My point. We don't have time for Caroline Street, Elliott. And we don't have time for organized crime and bounty hunters. I'm here for a reason. Something much bigger than anything we have ever dealt with. Bigger than you can imagine, and it is something only you can fix. It deserves a sit-down discussion with no distractions. Soon—

Tony looked around. "Right now we're sitting ducks. These people can disable your nice boat with one weaponized drone. We're in the middle of nowhere. No one's gonna know. They can kill us and throw our bodies overboard—food for the sharks. Then they'll sink your Commander 44 in a New York minute."

"I know," Elliott said as he adjusted settings on the master panel. "We have plenty of fuel—396 gallons. This boat can go a long way fast, Tee."

"These people are now watching the coastal waters, Elliott. It is not a hard thing to do at the very tip of this goddamn state. There's not much else going on."

"You need to relax," Elliott said.

"You do know they're setting their nets for us now. They're waiting for us to swim into one. I hate that there are only two ways on water out of here—up the coast or down the coast."

Elliott turned to Tony with a half-smile. "Maybe there are more—"

CHAPTER 15

"I have heard the language of apocalypse, and now I shall
embrace the silence."
Neil Gaiman

London, England

"Albert Bell said a friend is on his way to retrieve Dr.
Sumner," Turpin said as he put down the phone. "Seems
there is something going on in the states, something he could not
discuss."

"Is that what he said—that he could not discuss the matter?"
Randolph Pepper asked moving to the leather chairs by the fire.

"Albert's words precisely."

"What do you think that's about?" Pepper jabbed.

"I'm not sure at the moment. Possibly a governmental
matter."

"Governmental matter? Political or strategic?"

"International, maybe," Turpin said as he lit another cigar
and watched Deputy Chief Inspector Stotsbury pour a drink.
"One cube for me, Bennett," he said between puffs. "Scotch.
Thank you, sir."

"Carry on, Harold," Pepper prodded. "You're a profiler, sir.
You are supposed to dissect everything, find the hidden buried
within."

The three sat by the smoldering fire staring over the rims of
their glasses at the burning embers. The momentary silence gave
Turpin time to further sort things out.

"Why would someone in the federal government seek Dr.

Elliott Sumner, a forensic sleuth for God's sake?" Stotsbury asked.

"They could have a serial killer problem, right then," Pepper said. "Maybe someone is knocking off beloved senators or threatening the POTUS."

"No to both," Turpin breathed into his glass, and then took a swallow. "Mr. Herbolt is the one who contacted Bell."

"The Director of the CIA—James Herbolt. I'll be damned. It *is* international."

"Yes, international, but not the typical CIA matter," Turpin cautioned. "I sensed it to be something more."

"Well then, out with it," Pepper barked.

Turpin smiled and sucked his cigar. "You're like a petulant child, Randolph. Want all your candy at once. Really an abhorrent weakness, old man."

"I don't know about that. I wish you would refrain from beating around the bloody bush. I have lost ten years of my life waiting for you to get to the bloody point."

"Stop it. Both of you," Stotsbury ordered.

Turpin looked back into the fire. "Albert Bell said Mr. Herbolt was calling before knowing the depth of the gathering storm. He said there would probably be a blood trail and there would be a need to study it to determine what is at its end."

"A bloody blood trail," Pepper huffed. "That could mean anything.

"I don't think Albert knew the extent of *his reveal*."

"The extent of his reveal," Stotsbury mumbled.

"He revealed more than intended," Turpin reworded. "He said Mr. Herbolt felt certain the POTUS would need Dr. Sumner. There was no other man who could assess and interpret the blood trail in time."

"What does that mean?" Pepper asked setting down his glass.

Turpin turned to both men in the dim study, half his face lit by the fire. "Elliott Sumner is possibly the only international forensic investigator able to study carnage from different parts of the world and find linkage. He may be the only man in the world who can understand and ascertain the origin of carnage, and the hidden story it tells. Albert said three things that impart a chilling possibility. He said—"

The phone on Turpin's desk rang. Bennett jumped to his feet. The two turned from the fire and listened.

"Yes, this is Mr. Turpin's home. I am Bennet Stotsbury. Yes. I know you too, sir. It is late. Can this wait ...? I see. May I take a message ...?" Stotsbury gently replaced the phone onto its cradle and lifted his head with glassy eyes.

"What is it, Bennet?" Pepper asked. Turpin puffed his cigar and leaned.

"You know our mutilation; the John Doe we believe is the work of the Camden Cutter?"

"Yes, the one Harold believes is something else," Pepper said.

"Yes. Well. That was Thomas Bernard, INTERPOL, on the phone."

"Well good. We know it isn't a political, military, religious, or racial matter," Pepper chuckled and leaned back in his chair."

"INTERPOL may be politically neutral, Randolph, but there is always a gray area," Turpin corrected. "What did Mr. Bernard want with me?"

"He knows about our victim. He knows details— dismembered and decapitation. It is not something one sees often," Stotsbury said as he took his chair and downed his Scotch. "He knows our victim's cell phone number too."

Stotsbury came to the fire and stared. "The Pertek Kalesi Castle in the Tunceli province, Turkey. I remember studying it in the university. A castle built in the 11th century on a rocky mountain. The Keban Dam built in 1974 flooded the area. Left a rock island with the Kalesi Castle sitting five kilometers out in the artificial lake." He sat and stared into the fire with his empty glass on his knee. "It was built under the Ottoman Empire to control the copper mines."

"Snap out of it, Stotsbury," Pepper ordered. "For God's sake, what did Bernard say?"

"Yes. Well then. There's a body on the crag a hundred meters from the Pertek Kalesi."

"Why has that got you shaken?" Pepper pushed. "We see bodies every day."

"It's like ours, isn't it Bennet?" Turpin said.

"Yes. They found it stuffed into a rock crevice, dismembered and decapitated. There was only the torso."

"So you believe that is enough to tie back to our Camden Cutter kill?" Pepper asked.

"You know the number on our victim's cell that we could not identity—"

"There were only three calls on that disposable cell," Pepper said. "Two calls were made to Pingree Correctional Center. One call was received from an unidentified phone."

"They found that phone in the rock crevice—shattered. They recovered the few numbers placed on that phone. The victim on the Pertek Kalesi Castle grounds talked to our victim moments before our victim placed a call to Pingree, and minutes before the Kalesi death."

Pepper poured another Scotch and passed it to Turpin. "That's not good. Now we have two abhorrent kills on two continents that may connect to the United States. We need to find—"

"—where the blood trial leads and why," Turpin murmured.

"Are you suggesting it ties to your chat with Albert Bell?" Pepper asked.

"Yes. That is precisely what I am saying."

Pepper's smile melted as Stotsbury blinked away from the

fire. "The phone interrupted you, Harold. Bernard's call, it interrupted what you were saying," Stotsbury said. "You were talking about Dr. Sumner. You said he was the only man in the world who could ascertain the origins of international carnage. There was more. What is it? What were you about to say?"

Turpin's eyes narrowed. He downed his drink and leaned back in the warm leather chair like Winston Churchill finalizing a battle plan. The two watched the retired profiler. They knew he was still at the very top of his game. Parkinson's had not yet taken him.

"Albert Bell said three things that take the London and Kalesi Castle homicides to their shores. They point to the worst possible of outcomes."

"What are you saying?" Stotsbury demanded, shuddering.

This time, Randolph Pepper had no words. He was over his head. Knowing Turpin could leave him behind had bothered him throughout his career. Now, blood drained from his face. His stomach wrenched into a twisted knot. Physically crippled, only his eyes could find the profiler. Next to Pepper, Stotsbury perched on the edge of his leather chair like a schoolboy who was just told his parents had died in a terrible accident. Stotsbury swallowed, but had no saliva.

Harold Turpin leaned toward the fire and spoke as if he were one of the disciples. His words hung in the damp, dark room like a biblical truth—impending doom. "Albert Bell said three things to me. Each, on its own merits, means nothing. Together, they are abominable. Laced in his dialogue, albeit intentionally vague, he used words like blood trail, POTUS, and North Dakota."

"What does it mean?" Stotsbury whispered as if hiding under a blanket.

"President Landon—the POTUS—must need a *blood trail* into *North Dakota* investigated by Dr. Elliott Sumner. North

Dakota is one of three sites where the United States maintains their ground nuclear ICBM arsenal."

"Someone has taken control of an intercontinental ballistic missile," Pepper said.

"One or more. The POTUS is tracking kills into North Dakota. They need to know who is in their silos—"

On Turpin's last word, someone pounded on the door, further devastating the moment. Pepper and Stotsbury froze. They stared at the popping fire. Turpin grabbed his cane and grunted his way to the door.

"It is me, Thomas, Thomas Bernard," flowed from the other side.

"Why are you here?" Turpin queried with his hand twisting the brass knob.

"We must—"

Turpin opened the door. The tall, skinny man in the black suit and narrow black tie looked more like a funeral director than an INTERPOL Agent. His magnified eyes behind the round glasses with thick lenses only added to the man's eerie presence.

"I'm sorry. I know it is late," Bernard said with lips not moving and water dripping from his chin. "I should have said I was in London, when I called. I felt it important I see you in person, now, sir."

"Well, you're here. I don't appear to have much to say about the matter, do I?"

"May I come in?"

Turpin opened the door wider and pointed to the fire with his cane. Stotsbury and Pepper managed to snap out of their daze. They got to their feet, but terror hung in their eyes.

"Please. Sit. Dry off." He handed him a towel draped over the umbrella rack. "What is it that cannot wait, Mr. Bernard?"

He sat and stared at Stotsbury and Pepper, and seemed to forget why he came.

"I'm sure you know *The Yard* prefers to operate alone," Turpin barked to get Bernard's attention back onto his agenda and away from the *fear* projected by his colleagues. "INTERPOL has not been the best of partners over the years, sir. And before you get started, let me remind you it is unlikely we will personally engage in cases outside of our jurisdiction—like Turkey. Certainly, we would like notes on the matter at the appropriate time."

"The bodies are being moved, Mr. Turpin," Bernard said with a blank stare.

"Excuse me. Let me be clear. You say your body—the Pertek Kalesi Castle body—is being moved? Why would that matter to me, sir?"

"The Pertek Kalesi Castle body and your body—both—are being moved," Bernard corrected. "They are on planes to Bismarck, North Dakota, as we speak. Mr. Turpin, the Turkish and British Governments have stepped in. Both unidentified remains are gone."

"That request had to come from the White House," Turpin noted.

"I don't know, sir ..."

The four turned to the fire and sat in silence. Waves of rain peppered the windows and the smoldering logs popped. Randolph Pepper sank into his chair. Bennett Stotsbury sat stiff, his eye twitching, and Thomas Bernard removed his thick glasses to wipe fogged lenses.

No one noticed Harold Turpin get to his feet, walk to his desk, and pick up his phone. "Miss Lambert," Turpin said as he pulled the latest Camden Cutter file from the stack. "I know it is late. I need your immediate assistance." He opened the file and pulled out the photograph of the butchered John Doe, a bloody-stubbed torso in an alley next to an overflowing dumpster. As he perused the hideous butchery, the only thing he could be certain of was gender.

"Miss Lambert, schedule the private jet. Sunrise, in a few hours. I am going to Bismarck, North Dakota."

Turpin set down the phone and stared in silence at the grisly photograph. His eyes watered and the hand holding the photo trembled.

CHAPTER **16**

"The more I see, the less I know for sure."
John Lennon

Washington D.C.

P resident Landon returned to the Oval Office not yet ready to share the horrifying update sent by General Jamison. If GRAY WOLF had accessed a launch control capsule, ten missile silos were under their control. The terminal breach had moved to a darker stage. At any moment *controlled-containment* could trigger. Failsafe systems would unleash an irreversible and devastating force. Minot would be the unfortunate epicenter of the most massive nuclear attack in the history of the world. A cluster of Minuteman III missiles would be sent from Montana and Wyoming to end a terminal breach. An estimated 27.9 million lives in the Midwestern United States and Central Canada would be lost.

"Before we continue with the forensic trail into the country, I want more on the Minot missile silos," the POTUS ordered, his tone careful and icy. He struggled to hide the new wave of uncertainty from his cabinet. He would choose the time.

"Major General Gentry, tell us more about the Minot Missile silos, how many are active today, and their structure. Also, give us more on the launch control capsules, please."

Gentry sat along the wall with the other military leaders, and next to Colonel Pent. They wore crisp uniforms adorned with an abundance of gold stars, bars, and medals of Honor. Their combined experience, illustrious careers, and records of success would place enormous weight onto each word they spoke.

"I will provide an overview," Major General Winston Gentry said. "Colonel Charles Pent—the 20th Air Force—will handle the drill downs, sir."

"That will be fine," the President said with his eyes locked on Gentry, the military hero he'd met three years earlier. As the major general got to his feet, cabinet members lowered their cell phones and closed their briefing documents. They turned to the man they had to hear from, but each would stay in touch with their operations. Each would advance in their respective lanes of responsibility. At any moment, they might be called upon to take some action that could affect millions of lives and change the course of history. Only the most current and most accurate information could be used. Like all other Presidents, William Landon had surrounded himself with people who could step in if he fell.

"The Air Force Global Strike Command 91st Missile Wing is responsible for managing the Minuteman III Nuclear Missiles program in Minot," Gentry said. "The 740th, 741st, and 742nd Strategic Missile Squadrons each oversee five flights of ten missiles. Minot Air Force Base is one of three of our ground nuclear operational units. The other two are Malmstrom Air Force Base in Great Falls, Montana, and FE Warren Air Force Base in Cheyenne, Wyoming. For the people in this room only, Malmstrom and Warren went on alert the moment Chief General Jamison learned of the Minot breach. Be assured there will be no extension of this threat beyond Minot. Malmstrom and Warren operations are prepared to respond. Let us hope it is not necessary."

"God forbid," Vice President Pierce said into his coffee cup.

"Contrary to reports in the media over the years, we do not have 400 missiles in North Dakota. We have 133 Minuteman III

ICBMs and two medium-range missiles spread across 8,500 square miles—an area the size of New Jersey. Since the mid-1990s, we have relocated several missiles to our Montana operation and resized our total ground based nuclear asset inventory.

"Each missile is a hundred feet deep, encased in a concrete silo. Each is on an acre with a 1,200-foot easement perimeter. We need a minimum 2,500 square foot area for a rocket fuel-fired launch."

Dr. Nye shook her head. "I'm sorry. I am surprised to hear we do not have 400 ICBMs in North Dakota, Mr. Gentry. I don't know if the reduction is important or not. I'm certain you had a good reason to drop the inventory and to misdirect the outside world."

"The nuclear deterrent game is a blend of smoke-and-mirrors and reality, Dr. Nye," President Landon said. "A fraction of the global nuclear arsenal can obliterate this planet ten times over. Escalating costs, tightened budgets, exposure to malfunctions, accidents, and a world faced with the non-traditional attacks of radical Islam have made unilateral reductions feasible."

"No superpower wants to show weakness," Gentry said. "Make no mistake; ground basing continues to be the most cost-effective option. Notwithstanding our current dilemma, only Russia could effectively attack U.S. ground assets. Even that possibility is not nearly the concern it was during the Cold War."

Graham—Secretary of Defense—interrupted. "The Air Force has successfully demonstrated the viability of extending ground-based nuclear operations. It is the most effective, low-cost, low-risk program. However, because we are in the midst of upgrading these assets, we may have exposed ourselves to this unprecedented invasion."

"How did we expose ourselves?" Pierce asked.

"That will be addressed in detail by the Major General," Graham said.

Gentry nodded. "Moving along, a launch control capsule (LCC) is electronically linked to ten silos. Each silo holds one missile. A strategic missile squadron (SMS) is responsible for five LCCs and fifty missiles. We have three squadrons. Above each LCC is a military-guarded entry building. This is the only access point to an LCC sixty feet underground. There is a secured elevator. It descends to the LCC and a five-ton concrete/steel door designed to protect our crew. The door will withstand the blast effect of a direct hit. I will ask Colonel Pent to continue."

"Thank you, sir," Pent said as he got to his feet. "The Major General took you to the LCC. It is managed by two *missileers*—specially trained service officers on twenty-four-hour shifts—entrusted with launch keys to be inserted and turned in unison upon an order from the President of the United States.

"When and if a verified order is received, the procedure to target and release a missile or missiles is initiated. Launch keys, gateway codes, passwords, and error-free movement through a complex checklist of duties are required before a missile can leave its nest."

"How secure are the LCCs?" Pierce asked.

"The entry buildings are guarded. There are electronic sensors on the perimeter of each missile site: audio, tactile, video, and heat-sensitive surveillance on the ground. Dedicated drone surveillance twenty-four/seven is also part of the program. Our drones are equipped with heat-sensitive and motion sensors, night vision, infrared, and technology we do not talk about. The three ground-based programs (North Dakota, Montana, and Wyoming) are monitored by multiple dedicated satellite resources. All active silos and LCCs are inspected daily."

"With that kind of coverage, how did GRAY WOLF gain access to anything out there?" Secretary of State Dabney asked.

"We have gone over surveillance for the last twenty-four hour period and found nothing. We are now looking at forty-eight and seventy-two hour intervals. It is conceivable the GRAY WOLF incursion took place days or weeks before we were contacted," Colonel Pent said. "Regardless, they found a way to avoid multiple sophisticated surveillance systems."

"Maybe they possess a cloaking technology we don't know about," said Dr. Nye.

"That is a possibility, but unlikely," Gentry said.

"What about the men and women of the U.S. Air Force missileer community?" Pierce asked. "Based on your numbers, there are fifteen LCCs in and around Minot. That means there are thirty missileers and another thirty or more armed guards at the associated entry-point buildings. How did GRAY WOLF avoid them?"

Colonel Pent cleared his throat. "Therein lies a procedural miscalculation on our part. You recall prior comments on upgrading our ground nuclear assets. Over the last fourteen days, six LCCs have been in operation. Nine LCCs are out of service. Three of the nine are being upgraded. Six of the nine are idle, scheduled for upgrade resources next. We believe GRAY WOLF took this opportunity to move into one or more of the idle LCCs."

"How could they know? And how can we let six LCCs—sixty ICBMs—sit idle?" Pierce barked at the colonel.

"It is standard operating procedure, Mr. Vice President. It happens often."

"I don't understand. It's like leaving a loaded gun out for kids to find."

"We often close a significant portion of our nuclear assets for a wide array of reasons: routine repairs and maintenance, equipment upgrades, training, and changes in personnel and procedures. In every case, the fire-power of the idle sites is covered with increased assets at other locations. It is routine to have sixty to ninety silos *collectively idle* at any given time in the three land base operations."

"The multi-layered security surveillance resources are always operational," Graham said. "At any point in time, 70 percent of our ground program is functional, and that is more than adequate for defense purposes."

"If what you say about our advanced surveillance systems is true, we should have picked up something. We did not! Maybe GRAY WOLF is not in a silo or an LCC. Maybe this whole thing is an electronic ruse," Pierce puffed.

"This is not a ruse, Michael," said the President. Motioning to his trusted military men, he said, "Thank you for your information gentlemen." He turned to his cabinet. "I have some disturbing information to share, information that eliminates any possibility of a ruse. General Jamison left a message with Richard, which was the reason I stepped out. It was an update, one he did not have time to give me directly, and one we all need to know. Buck has evidence GRAY WOLF has commandeered an LCC and is trying to open a new set of silo doors."

"Oh my God," Pierce shouted. "How do we—?"

"Alerts at the 99th Wing control center in Minot indicate blast doors opened and closed at one of six vacated LCCs. We do not know which one of the six. To some degree, this new information does allow us to narrow our focus to these six LCCs."

"That's sixty ICBMs," Pierce breathed.

"Fifty-eight Minuteman IIIs. Two medium-range missiles. As the Colonel shared, six LCCs are in operation—staffed. Three are out of commission and staffed with maintenance crews. That leaves six LCCs idle. Any one or more of those six could be occupied by GRAY WOLF."

"This changes everything," the Secretary of Defense boomed.

"If GRAY WOLF is in an LCC, they have access to our network."

"And they are in a protected vault."

Graham whispered, "If they got that far, it is not too much of a reach to—"

"—take control of a missile," Pierce finished the crippling thought as the Secretary of Defense took a phone call on his cell.

"Do you really think an alien force could hack into our complex ICBM launch programs?" Dabney asked. "There are new codes daily, changed procedures, and traps."

Major Gentry cleared his throat. "Although the probability is low, it is a possibility we must consider, given the extent and degree of GRAY WOLF's apparent accomplishments."

"Sir." Frank Graham lowered his cell seeking the President's attention. "I have an update from Minot—just in."

"Go ahead, Frank," the President said. All heads turned to the Secretary of Defense.

"GRAY WOLF has made contact a second time, this time through protected military channels at the base—another daunting feat. We have new demands, Mr. President. GRAY WOLF has given us one hour to evacuate the six operational LCCs, support buildings, and all missile silos. They demand maintenance crews be pulled out of the three renovation LCCs."

"How do they have that information?" the President asked.

"They must have someone on the inside," Pierce said.

Graham continued. "If we fail to comply within the allotted time, GRAY WOLF will demonstrate their capabilities."

"Did they say how they planned to do that?" the President asked.

"Yes, sir. They will send one of our missiles into Canada," Graham said.

"If GRAY WOLF makes a single computer-stroke error, our system will take over."

"Correct, Mr. President. A *terminal breach* can trigger one of several containment options automatically. After that action is triggered, we can no longer intervene. The system makes all the decisions as if we were already gone."

"A goddamn computer can unleash a deadly nuclear barrage of the Midwestern United States and there is nothing we can do about it," Pierce ranted.

"GRAY WOLF is either bluffing or smarter than us," said the President. "At this time, we cannot determine which. We still don't know who we are dealing with. Until we know, we are fumbling for a light switch in the dark."

"Mr. President, we have more GRAY WOLF victims," Dr. Nye said. "More bodies need to be discussed. They are in North Dakota. They connect to the Canadian blood trail. The count is now four on this continent. And we have just learned two more—"

"What chance do we really have, Maureen?" Landon asked as he turned back to the windows and stared into the Rose Garden. GRAY WOLF's new demands weighed heavier than anything he faced before. "What can we really learn from mutilated bodies?"

"I was about to add a body in London and another in Turkey are connected to our four, sir. We have six bodies that lead to Minot. This terminal breach is spawned from an international scheme. GRAY WOLF went to great lengths to cover their tracks.

"I know from experience, no one can think of everything," Dr. Nye said. "These six bodies may be all we ever have to identify GRAY WOLF. I recommend we move heaven and earth to learn as much as we can about these victims."

"You are certain they are connected?" the President asked.

"Yes. And I believe they have something to say."

"The timing is impossible," the President breathed.

"Four are at the North Dakota State Medical Examiner's office. The two from London and Turkey are en route. Dr. Morgan Cage, an accomplished forensic pathologist and expert in the effects of extreme temperature on human tissue, will begin the autopsies as soon as it is technically possible—a proper thawing process is vital. Dr. Cage can subtract temperature-induced anomalies. Dr. Sumner can process the international implications of the forensic evidence better than anyone in the field. If there's a way to identify GRAY WOLF by examining these bodies, these two will find it."

"You speak of Elliott Sumner being on board with all this. Has he been located? Is he engaged?" the President asked.

"We are very close, sir. We found him," James Herbolt said.

"Is he on his way to Bismarck? I want to talk to him."

"Not yet, sir," Herbolt said knowing he did not have the big fish in his net. "I will—"

"You don't have him on board with this, do you?" the President pushed.

Herbolt swallowed. "We are extracting him from a situation. I anticipate success soon."

"Do you anticipate he will be agreeable?"

"Yes I do, sir. He is a patriot."

The POTUS leaned into Herbolt and studied his face. Then he walked to the edge of his desk and paused. "Mr. Herbolt, I wish you success with your efforts. However, we cannot wait. I must deal with the latest demands of GRAY WOLF."

"Understood, sir," Herbolt mumbled, looking at Dr. Nye.

"Get General Jamison on the box," Landon ordered. "I am going to say *no* to GRAY WOLF. We are not standing down. Our people are not leaving the LCCs."

The room reeled.

CHAPTER 17

"Life is what happens to us while we are making other plans."
Allen Saunders

Off the coast of Key West, Florida

"We are about 100 kilometers from Havana," Elliott said as he spun the steering wheel slowly, turning the Commander south.

"Speak English," Tony grumbled. "What's that in miles?"

"Sixty miles, Tee. In these smooth waters, without a headwind, we should be there in an hour.

"Elliott increased speed and flipped a half-dozen toggles. It was the first time he had taken his boat out more than a mile off the coast. The chart plotter's screen glowed, functioning perfectly, showing thier precise location as an orange dot in a turquoise sea.

"They will be looking for us to go to Naples or Cape Coral on the Gulf side, Miami on the Atlantic side." Elliott said. "They won't look at Cuba. Not many pleasure crafts can make the run. I doubt they know the particulars of my boat, although it is possible."

"I'm betting they visited the little Marine Supply store on Caroline," Tony said.

"By the time they put it all together, hopefully we'll be flying."

"Flying?"

"Albert keeps a plane in Havana for business and tax

purposes. I can fly her. We just need to decide where we go to hide until I figure out what this is all about."

"What kind of plane are we talkin' about—one that could maybe get us to Bismarck?"

Elliott turned from the wheel. "Why are you here, Tony?"

"I'll get to that soon enough. Just answer my question. Can Albert's plane get us from Havana to Bismarck, North Dakota? And how fast?"

"It's about 1,900 miles. Albert has a Learjet 75 LXi. Its range is 2,000 miles. The cruising speed is 515 mph. We could fly at 50,000 feet and squeeze a little more out of her. All things considered, we could get to Bismarck in less than four hours."

"That photographic memory comes in handy once in a while," Tony poked.

"Right. Tell me. Does this have anything to do with Spyglass?"

"No." Tony looked out at the waves, offering nothing more.

"Max left you the business." Elliott opened a cupboard and pulled out a bottle of Chivas Regal. He cracked the seal. "It's been a year since we lost him."

"I know ... Max Gregory was one of the best men I ever knew," Tony said as he watched Elliott take a swallow of Scotch and hold out the bottle. He took a swallow and winced at the full moon. "This has nothing to do with the PI business Max left me, which—for the record—I never saw coming. I'd probably still be a miserable homicide detective in Memphis."

"You were an excellent homicide investigator," Elliott said. "And you know, Max didn't have a family. You and Albert were the closest he ever came to one."

Tony managed to light a cigarette on the second try by cupping the flame. He sucked in and exhaled with satisfaction and turned back to Elliott, who was now gripping the wheel of the Commander 44 with eyes straight ahead. "Add your name to the list, my friend."

Elliott smiled as he again reached for the bottle. "Why Bismarck, Tee? What are you trying to get me into?"

Tony looked back at the horizon behind the boat. "I guess we've lost them. Maybe now this is a good time, out in the middle of the damn ocean."

Elliott took another swig and tightened the cap on the bottle. "Talk to me."

"I was in Orlando working a case when I got a call from James Herbolt."

"The director of the CIA," Elliott said under his breath, his eyes still straight ahead. "You know I don't like the CIA."

Tony ignored the comment. "When Herbolt called, he did not have all his information. He was still pulling it together with Susan Dabney and Dr. Nye."

"Secretaries of State and Homeland—"

Tony nodded as he sucked his cigarette. "Herbolt admitted he was jumping the gun, but said he felt—in his gut—the effort to find you had to begin. He said Dr. Nye would also be looking for you, but not until she had her facts in order."

"Sounds like Herbolt, and sounds like Maureen," Elliott muttered.

"Herbolt knows you're not fond of the CIA, by the way. He said he believes time is of the essence. More facts to follow, but it was best to move now with the info we had. This makes sense to me now, because we know Dr. Nye is a forensic pathologist by trade. She only moves with solid facts. Herbolt is a New York detective-turned-CIA director. I'm pretty sure he's not the type to wait on anything."

"Still don't trust Herbolt—never did. Something's not right with that man. Putting that aside, what's this all about and why is Herbolt using you to get me on board?"

Tony lit another bent cigarette with maddening slowness. "It's confidential and it's big," he said with a stream of smoke sliding into the wind. "I don't know about all that other stuff, but I can tell you Herbolt called me on a secured line and said everything he had had to be confidential. Something big is happening in North Dakota, Elliott. His people found three bodies in that state. Dr. Nye found one in Canada. Herbolt believes their blood trail goes through Canada into Minot. At the time of the call they were still looking for the origin prior to Canada."

"And what makes Herbold think these three bodies are connected?" Elliott asked.

"They were all mutilated and frozen in a peculiar way. He could not give details."

"Sounds like they could just as easily *not* be connected," Elliott said. "That would explain why Maureen Nye has not reached out. I know her. Maybe she's got nothing."

"Elliott, Herbolt said he was 100 percent certain the frozen bodies are connected. All are on their way to the Bismarck Medical Examiner's office. They could be there by now."

"That's good to hear. But it sounds like they don't need me, Tony."

"What're you talkin' about?"

"They have a very capable forensic pathologist running the North Dakota State Medical Examiner's Office. I happen to know Morgan Cage. The man is more than competent. He happens to be the subject matter expert on the effects of extreme temperatures and harsh environments on cadavers—human tissue. He is the best person to help the CIA and Homeland with those frozen bodies." He shook his head. "I bet it's already twenty below up there."

"Don't know exactly where they were found, but it is cold as hell up there now."

"And now you have more information and can relax, Tee. Dr. Cage is the perfect forensic pathologist to help the CIA with their 'possibly' connected homicides."

"I don't think—"

"You can rest easy knowing Herbolt, Nye, and Dabney are in good hands," Elliott said.

Tony blew a thin stream of smoke over his shoulder. "How much further to Havana?"

"Fifteen to twenty minutes."

"Is there any way those people hunting you could find us out here? Does your newfangled charting thingamajig or your other gadgets have sonar or any kind of tracking capabilities? I mean, could someone find you if this boat was lost at sea?"

"Everything trackable I know about is turned off, Tony."

"Well then, let's hope the light in the sky approaching us is just a low-flying pleasure craft or a mail run to Cuba."

Elliott turned. Together they watched the light in the sky grow in size and intensity. The narrowing path seemed to be on a course over their boat. Elliott throttled up the engine. The light continued to grow—but faster. Its speed easily exceeded the Commander 44.

"Shit!" Tony huffed, panic edging his voice. "Now what, genius? They found us. We're dead—shit, shit, shit."

Elliott studied the approaching aircraft hovering a hundred feet above the water closing from a quarter-mile out. "I know that shape and those lights. It's a Jayhawk MH-60," he said. "I've seen them flying around Key West."

"What the hell is a Jayhawk MH-60?"

"Helicopter. United States Coast Guard," Elliott said.

Tony squinted. "Could those goons chasing you get their hands on one?"

"No. It's military. But I have no idea why the U.S. Coast

Guard would be so close to Cuban airspace. They're walking the line here." *Why would you risk a Cuban incident?*

"Let's just pray it is the Coast Guard. The hell with Cuba," Tony scoffed.

The chopper moved to a position fifty-yards off the starboard side of the Commander and matched the boat's speed. Elliott and Tony watched it hover thirty feet above the water. They could see heads moving in the helicopter windows. Elliott's ship-to-shore radio light started to flash. With an eye on the chopper and hand on the wheel, he slipped on his headset, adjusted the mic, and flipped the toggle of the communication system. "Who are you?" Elliott asked.

"Am I speaking to Dr. Elliott Sumner?" The words scratched and popped in his headset.

"Who's asking?" Elliott barked.

"This is Captain Edward Cobb, US Coast Guard, Naval Air Station, Sigsbee Annex, Key West. Am I speaking to Dr. Elliott Sumner?"

"Why are you here?"

"We must locate Dr. Elliott Sumner. It is a matter of national security. We know this is his vessel. Is Dr. Sumner on board?"

"What do they want?" Tony asked Elliott.

"How did you find this boat?" Elliott asked Cobb.

"I am not at liberty to answer that question. I repeat, is Dr. Elliott Sumner on board the Commander 44? Time is an important factor."

Elliott paused, just staring up at the helicopter. His silence prompted Captain Cobb to continue. "We have the capability of disabling the boat. I urge you cooperate with the United States Coast Guard. Answer my question, or we will be forced to take another course of action."

On Cobb's last word, the Jayhawk pivoted and aimed its nose

to the boat. It approached the starboard side as both crafts moved on the same line in parallel at forty knots.

"Shit, Elliott," Tony said without moving his lips. "Those are friggin *missiles* pointing at us. What the hell did you say to piss these guys off?"

Elliott's voice was soft, despite the roar of the helicopter rotor. "I am Elliott Sumner."

The chopper held its threatening position. "Dr. Elliott Sumner, I have a call for you."

"A *call?*"

"I request authorization to temporarily seize control of your communications system."

"I guess I don't have much choice," Elliott said.

"There will be a whistle and hum as we patch you into a cloaked frequency."

Tony stared at the spectacle next to the boat. "What the—?"

As described by Captain Cobb, a whistle and hum followed, and then silence.

"This communication is classified, Dr. Sumner," Cobb said.

"Someone wants to talk to me in the middle of the night, in the middle of the ocean, and they are concerned about being overheard? Who is calling me, Captain Cobb?"

As Elliott clamped hands over his ears, a garbled sound emitted from the headset. Elliott could not distinguish words in the transmission.

"You're breaking up. Hello? Can you hear me?" Elliott tapped his headset, looking at the chopper and then his console. The light glowed amber. It should be functioning.

With a cigarette hanging on his lip, Tony could only watch and try to figure things out. The half-conversation, the Jayhawk's determined position, and the two shooting across the moonlit Atlantic in parallel—oddly, it was beginning to make sense to him.

The crackling in the headset stopped. "The President of the United States, William Landon, is now being connected, Dr. Sumner."

Elliott put his hand over his mic. "It's the President of the United States."

"Shit! I knew this thing was big," Tony said.

"—Elliott Sumner ... Bill Landon here."

"Mr. President. It has been a while."

"Yes it has. You are a hard man to find," Landon said.

"I'm sorry about—"

"We have a situation, Elliott, one I think you can help us with. I am concerned for our nation this morning. Something has happened, something we have often worried about as a stabilizing force in a turbulent world. I will bring you up-to-date on the details later."

"I'm listening," Elliott said as he slowed the Commander and watched the chopper pivot its missiles away while continuing to hold a perfect, parallel position.

"You are on the speakerphone in the Oval Office," the President said. "I believe you know most of my cabinet. Many of them are here now: Vice President Michael Pierce, Secretary of State Susan Dabney, Defense—Frank Graham, CIA—Jim Herbolt, and Homeland—Dr. Nye. We also have some top military minds with us, Elliott—Major General Winston Gentry and Colonel Charles Pent of the 20th Air Force. Chief General Buck Jamison is in the field at the moment. I will explain.

"Twenty-four hours ago, an unidentified force commandeered one or more of our nuclear ICBM assets. Someone has taken Minot Air Force Base hostage. As you may know, the United States maintains a substantial ground-based nuclear program in three locations—Wyoming, Montana, and North Dakota. Each holds an inventory of Minuteman III missiles, and each missile is capable of delivering a catastrophic nuclear payload anywhere in the world. We now have good reason to believe this unidentified invading force—code name GRAY WOLF—has advanced in their penetration of our systems. We believe GRAY WOLF has taken control of two launch control capsules. One LCC operates ten missile silos."

"My God," Elliott said.

"We would like to believe our counter-defense systems are capable of preventing this invader from launching EVEN one of our missiles. However, as Chief General Jamison so appropriately put it, even with all the traps set, there is a chance the rat gets the cheese.

"Elliott, this attack on our soil is unprecedented. GRAY WOLF has successfully penetrated United States nuclear defenses and now poses a *terminal threat*—"

"—to our country and the world," Elliott finished the sentence.

"Yes. At any moment, GRAY WOLF could trigger U.S. counter-actions—programmed responses that are not the decisions of men. When and if GRAY WOLF crosses that threshold, our automated defense systems take over. Computers at the Pentagon and three other locations across the country evaluate, select, and implement a *containment option*. Even the least aggressive one is the total and complete annihilation of the threat. Minutemen III missiles will be sent from Wyoming and Montana to North Dakota to destroy GRAY WOLF. That action will devastate a large portion of the Midwestern states. The immediate death toll will be in the millions, Elliott. The prolonged death sentence from nuclear fallout will be even greater."

"Is there a surgical-strike *containment option*?" Elliott asked.

"No—not for a *terminal threat*, the most egregious offensive action posing the most deadly outcome. The containment option I just described is the least intrusive. It is intended to eliminate the threat and leave the Minot nuclear arsenal incapable of starting a third World War."

"I would assume GRAY WOLF could trigger such a horrific event without even knowing it—cross some line in the nation's nuclear defense system," Elliott said.

"Exactly," the President said.

"How do you know they—"

"GRAY WOLF activated silo door hydraulics to get our attention. An hour later, they opened and closed blast doors of one or possibly more launch control capsules. This gives them a protected workspace with direct access to LCC systems and twenty missile silos."

"But I don't know how I can be of help," Elliott said. "I'm not a military strategist."

"I'm not surprised to hear you say that, Elliott. Military matters do not typically call for the expertise of a forensic pathologist."

"But now they might? Why?" Elliott asked.

"We need to know who we are dealing with, Elliott. Who is GRAY WOLF? Who is sitting in my missile silos in North Dakota?"

"I understand, but—"

"Most of our adversaries know us well. They know our ways and the limits of our patience. They know seeking non-military resolution of conflict is our first priority. They also know not to poke a stick into the eye of the tiger. The world understands our strength. That knowledge helps us to manage conflict in the world. Other countries know not to test us. They know if we are cornered, we can and will eliminate any and all threats. Peace through strength."

"That's why this does not add up," Elliott said. "This is a suicide mission."

"Or perhaps it is intended to look that way," the President

said. "This might be something very different from anything we have seen before."

"It appears to be."

"The battleground is here. The risk to our nation is great. GRAY WOLF sits in our heartland. Millions of American lives and more than a hundred nuclear time bombs are in the equation. GRAY WOLF is not only threatening to destroy America, they are threatening global war, one nobody survives, and one that will change the course of mankind."

"The Armageddon," Elliott breathed.

"Without knowing it, GRAY WOLF could make a mistake," the President said. "They could cross a procedural line that launches World War III. We cannot risk that. We must try to identify GRAY WOLF, Elliott. Or we must contain them ... completely."

Elliott fumbled for words, overwhelmed with the magnitude of what he was being asked to do, and his *problem*. How could he walk away? How could he withhold his unique skills at a time of national crisis? Maybe this was his destiny? Maybe this was his end.

"How ... what can I do to help?"

"You possess the international forensic knowledge and skills we need. We have the frozen remains of six people we believe were connected to GRAY WOLF. We believe a forensic assessment may provide information that could help identify GRAY WOLF."

I have spent the last year trying to retake control of my inner demons—but there are so many now. I can feel them stirring. I don't know if I can survive ... but I must try. He let go of the wheel and wiped sweat from his forehead. He caught Tony turning away, but Tony was not fast enough. Elliott saw in his eyes, the concern and the fear.

"Mr. President," Elliott said with a noticeable crack in his voice. "You are pursuing many avenues to identify GRAY WOLF. I would put the forensic track at the bottom of your *hopeful* list. Although a lot can be learned from a corpse, based on the complexity of GRAY WOLF's mission and their demonstrated level of success, I doubt they left much of value for us to find. Like a calculated and prolific serial killer, GRAY WOLF's attention to detail and clarity of mission are core values. Elimination and disposal of operatives along the way is one of their standard operating procedures—carefully constructed to protect the accomplishment of their mission."

"Elliott, this is Maureen Nye."

"Hello, Maureen."

"Our blood trail begins in Turkey, goes through London into Canada, and ends in Minot. We have six bodies I am confident connect to GRAY WOLF—terminated operatives. At this time, four bodies are at the North Dakota State Morgue. The London and Turkey bodies are in route. Dr. Morgan Cage will begin postmortems when properly thawed. We can put you on a plane to Bismarck. While in the air, you will be linked to Dr. Cage."

You are hanging your hat on one telling error, Elliott mused.

"These bodies have been handled in a grisly manner," Nye said. "All were decapitated and dismembered. Four were put into a compacting device, their bodies crushed. They were turned into frozen blocks of human tissue and deposited in the wilderness to be removed by wild animals. Like a serial killer GRAY WOLF has a termination and disposal plan. And like a serial killer, their plan is detailed and with purpose. But Elliott, as you know better than anyone, serial killers make mistakes. Everybody does. One mistake might be all we need."

Elliott's heart beat faster with each logical argument anticipated and then set forth by Nye and the President. The dull pain at the base of his brain felt like a burning coal growing in size. *I am not ready for this—*

He pulled the throttle back. The Commander stopped in the water. He turned on the speaker, slid his headset to his neck, and fell back into his seat staring at Tony Wilcox.

Dr. Nye continued. "You are the most experienced international forensic pathologist in the world. We need you with Dr. Cage. You may find that one thing that helps."

"That's why Bismarck?" Tony whispered. "Herbolt never said—"

"You don't know the half of it," Elliott whispered back. *If I do this, I must accept it could be the last thing I ever do—*

"You are the only one who can examine this bizarre collection of altered human remains and give us a chance to identify GRAY WOLF," Nye said. In the room around her, the President, cabinet members, and military advisers stared at the speakerphone in silence. Each had a job to do. Each knew the significance of identifying GRAY WOLF as soon as possible.

"Who is GRAY WOLF?" Tony whispered as their boat bobbed in the water and the Jayhawk lifted straight up and disappeared into the dark cloud bank. "Are we done here? Where did they go with lights off?"

Elliott's eyes followed the Jayhawk up into the clouds. *I need to say no. I want to help, but I can't do this. Maybe if there was a slight chance I could find something, then I accept this suicide mission. I serve my country. But they don't understand. They are desperate. Maureen knows she is grabbing at straws. What they are asking me to do is impossible. GRAY WOLF is implementing a sophisticated mission. And I'm not the same man I was one year ago—*

"We will continue to develop all tracks to identify the people in our missile silos, Elliott," the President said. "I feel it in my bones. These six bodies are GRAY WOLF's mistake."

"Jesus Christ, the President!" Tony gasped as he recognized the voice. "Missile silos. North Dakota—shit."

The spray of bullets peppered the aft section of the Commander 44. In an instant, the smell of diesel fuel filled the air and painted the water. Elliott pushed forward the throttle and cut the wheel to the right. The boat lifted and arced starboard as another spray of bullets whistled by. The Commander accelerated and the speaker crackled. Elliott and Tony could see a box-shaped shadow on the northwest horizon now. The large boat closed in as Elliott snaked left and right, trying to minimize the damage of the hollowpoints.

"These people are way too motivated," he yelled as a wave hit his face. Spitting out the saltwater, he could only smile. The burning coal at the base of his brain went cold. His demons were quiet. Although his words were lost in the din of the churning diesels and breaking waves and wind, they were not lost to his logical mind. As more bullets sailed through the air, Elliott's course became clear.

"If you're still there, Mr. President," he shouted into his dripping mic, "I will join your team. I will do whatever I can to identify GRAY WOLF—"

Another spray of bullets hit the boat. "Where the hell's the Coast Guard when you need them?" Tony yelled as he was heaved from one side of the boat to the other by Elliott struggling to navigate the choppy water and gunfire.

Their boat pierced a giant wave. In an instant, the deck flooded. Elliott clung to the wheel and reached back for Tony. It happened too fast. The wave swallowed the deck and poured over the sides, taking Tony with it. Elliott could only watch his friend disappear into the dark, turbulent froth and rolling ocean. More bullets riddled the starboard side and thick smoke started to pour from the cabin. The twin diesels had been hit, and they began to fail. The Commander 44 was taking on water.

The box-shadow on the horizon got larger as it closed in on its wounded prey.

CHAPTER 18

"When diplomacy ends, War begins."
Adolf Hitler

When the shooting stopped, the Commander 44 bobbed in the dark water, listing starboard. Billows of black smoke streamed from the cabin and hung over the deck. Gasping for air, Elliott tried to restart the engines as he watched the boat, now just a half mile away, approach.

In an instant, the ocean had taken Tony and the Commander had started to sink. Elliott could only wait to be taken—and probably killed—by the people he had watched kill PI James Penland on the quiet beach in Key West. In the chaos, which was followed by an eerie silence, Elliott missed the knuckles on the port-side railing.

"Hey. A little help, please. Don't want to become shark bait," Tony burbled in a spray of salt water. "Hello over there!"

Elliott pulled him aboard. "I thought you were gone. I know you can't swim."

Exhausted, they both flopped down on the flooded deck. Sitting in five inches of water, they stared at the approaching boat on the horizon.

"I don't know how I got out of that," Tony gasped. "A goddamn wave knocked me on my ass and threw me overboard. Another goddamn wave picked me up and slammed me into the boat. Next thing I know, the rail is in my hand. I'd rather die from a bullet than be dinner for some God awful fish."

"Actually, I prefer neither," Elliott muttered.

"Still don't know why those people are so hell-bent on getting you. What did you do?"

"I'm starting to figure that one out," Elliott said as they stared at the approaching phantom.

"It looks like that boat just stopped dead in the water. What do you think that's all about?" Tony asked, his shivering hands squeezing open a wet pack of Marlboros.

"I think I know the answer to that one, too," Elliott said.

The thumping sound behind them got louder. Like the flapping wings of a Pterosaur, the helicopter was hovering fifty feet above the ocean, a hundred yards behind the Commander.

"I think our new friends don't like us being shot at," Elliott said.

"Yeah, especially after the POTUS said he needed your help and you accepted."

"I erred."

"Speak up. Did you say you erred? You? Never," Tony chuckled, stopping to gasp and spit out more swallowed sea water.

They looked back at the chopper as it held its position. "That's not a Jayhawk."

"What, that helicopter?"

"It's an AH-1Z chopper. I knew when I saw the air-to-ground hellfire missiles."

"What is it doin'?" Tony asked.

"If I'm right, the boat out there is involved in the President's little problem in North Dakota."

"Once again, you've left me in the dust. But that's okay. If we get out of this mess, I have successfully delivered the world-renowned forensic sleuth to the POTUS, my mission has been accomplished. I shall just go back to my case in Orlando and let you boys fix the world."

A fiery missile left the AH-1Z, passed over the sinking Commander, and found the boat on the horizon in three seconds of sizzle. The explosion sent a small mushroom cloud into the early morning sky and rained tiny pieces of nondescript debris in a one-mile radius. In less than a minute, there was nothing floating except the injured Commander 44.

"I could be wrong again," Elliott said as he watched Tony try to light a wet cigarette. "It could be an Apache AH-64. I need to keep up. I guess my sabbatical dulled my senses."

"Really, Elliott?" Tony kept flicking his lighter.

"Really what?"

"Holy hell, Elliott, they just blew the shit out of a private boat. Our government just killed people in front of us. No trial. No discussion. No nothing. That's just not right."

"I suggest you wait for the facts, Tee. I'm sure there is a very good reason."

"Oh. I'm sure they can justify it."

"What if Hitler was on that boat? What if you had thirty seconds to end the war?"

"What the hell are you talkin' about? Hitler is dead."

"It's a hypothetical, Tee."

"I'm not good with hypotheticals. I'm a homicide detective. Killing is not okay."

The radio scratched alive. "Dr. Sumner, can you hear me. Come in. Elliott Sumner."

He grabbed the mic. "Yes. This is Elliott. Captain Cobb?"

"Yes."

The helicopter moved closer to the sinking Commander. "Now that they confirmed we are still alive, I wouldn't be surprised if they just let us sink out here," Tony said, shrugging. "The government does not like witnesses. Doesn't matter who you are."

Elliott rolled his eyes. The speaker crackled again. "We need to get you two off that boat before she goes down," Cobb said.

"I don't like any of this shit," Tony griped as he balled his pack of soaked cigarettes and threw it into the ocean.

CHAPTER **19**

"When we truly realize we are all alone is when we need others
the most."
Ronald Anthony

Flight to Bismarck, 0400 EDT

"Can you handle this?" Albert Bell asked as his Dassault
Falcon leveled at 20,000 feet. He loosened his seatbelt
and leaned closer to Elliott. "I'm concerned about you, son."

Up until two years ago, the billionaire patriarch had been
masterfully manipulated, and the world-renowned forensic
sleuth had spent a lifetime alone with his bizarre gifts. A secret
society on a sinister mission had kept them apart almost four
decades—Albert could never know he had a son, and Elliott
could never know his father. The twisted plan to bring an end to
the Bell family bloodline by eliminating the rightful heir—the
first male born—would have seized control of the vast Bell
fortune.

"I am standing at the edge of a dark abyss," Elliott said into
the small window, his eyes tracking the tops of clouds sliding by
ten thousand feet below.

"So *they* are still bothering you?" Albert asked. He avoided
calling them *inner demons*.

Elliott had hunted the worst of the worst, the double-digit
serial killers of the world. His genetic gifts of intellect and
advanced sensory perception had made him the most successful
forensic sleuth in the world. But now the evil he had hunted lived
in his head. Now the pain of each victim ate at his soul. Elliott

was at emotional capacity. He stood on the edge of an insanity that he was told could lead to his sudden death. He simply could not handle more.

"*They* stir on occasion now," Elliott said. "But they're not beating on the door. Let's hope my year in seclusion, and efforts to manage them, helped."

Some say Albert and Elliott bonded the moment they learned they were father and son—an occasion when their imminent death hung over them. Thoughts of elation had mixed with terror when the words flowed over Albert's speakerphone in Memphis —"Elliott is your first male born, Albert"—because an unstoppable serial killer had his knife pressed against Elliott's throat. When Albert first looked into the eyes of the infamous Bluff City Butcher, and Elliott first saw the eyes of his father, they had reveled in a moment of immeasurable truth and death.

"I knew you would be part of this," Elliott said as he accepted the coffee mug.

"Bill is an old friend," Albert said.

"—and just happens to be the President of the United States."

"Well, that too," Albert agreed. He sipped his coffee and smiled. "He and Barbara often stayed at the Memphis mansion back during his Texas Senator days." Albert turned to his small window as the memories transformed his face. "I saw Bill last at Barbara's funeral. It was a terribly sad time. He took her death very hard. We all worried about him, whether he could finish—"

"—his second term," Elliott said. "I remember."

"We were lucky Cam was there. He will never get credit for saving the life of one of our presidents. Life can be poignant and wondrous at the same time," he whispered.

What great force puts those two extremes together? Elliott wondered. *Is it true? Is there a greater plan for us and this world?* "I would like to believe everything happens for a reason."

"When Bill called, I knew we had a real problem. He did not have to tell me about the missile silos or the terminal breach. I heard catastrophic pain in his voice. Bill has never asked me for anything, so when he asked me to get you to Bismarck, I knew I had to find you. And if you were going into hell, I was going with you. This could be the last thing we do."

Elliott's eyes stayed on the man he most admired and trusted with his life. He never wanted to fall short in Albert's eyes, but he believed this time he would—because he was on an impossible mission. Although Elliott could not turn away, the least he could do was lower Albert's expectations.

"I don't know if I can help," Elliott said.

"What do you mean?"

"Forensic pathologists determine cause and manner of death, Albert. We don't resolve nuclear geopolitical threats. I cannot consult on military strategy or weaponry."

Albert smiled. "You have always sold yourself short, son."

Elliott found his reflection in his coffee mug. "I'm a realist with a pinch of hope."

"You've had enormous success finding the most elusive, diabolical serial killers in the world. You've stopped more than fifty and received the highest recognition from international law enforcement. You've used your gifts wisely, Elliott."

"But that's not who I am *now*," he said. "You need to accept that I have changed."

"I'm sure you've heard of Heraclitus of Ephesus," Albert said.

"Yes. The Greek philosopher who believed fire was the origin of all things?"

"And permanence an illusion," Albert said.

"That, too," Elliott said as their eyes met again.

"Heraclitus said many things. I believe this is my favorite: 'No man ever steps in the same river twice, for it is not the same river and he is not the same man'."

"And how does that homily fit this moment, Albert?"

"I think Heraclitus got it right. Everything in life is in a state of change. That includes you. Change is neither good nor bad, in of itself. What we do with it matters. I have faith. You possess possibly the most advanced perceptive and deductive reasoning skills of any man alive. It is your gift in life. You have many other gifts, and you've taken them further. You've used them in a positive way. They can be applied to all things in your life—not only forensic science.

"In a very short time, you could know more about the United States nuclear triad than anyone. You retain everything. You devour information and categorize it with rational thought. I am confident the new Elliott will step into this new river of life and do what is good and right."

Elliott's reluctance to leave his *lifelong* comfort zone of self-doubt did not seem worth a battle with his father. Both Albert and the President had already ripped him from his safe place. Elliott had been thrown into a hopeless situation, and a deep and dark river he doubted he could survive. No one knew his limits like he.

"Elliott, do you hear me, son?" Alfred whispered to the man in deep thought.

"Yes. I do," he said, ready to move on to other things. "So, you just happened to have a jet sitting on a tarmac in Miami pointing to Bismarck."

Albert chuckled. "Compliments of my beloved brother—may John rest in peace. I suppose we have too many planes in the family now. I need to do something about that."

"Does President Landon know about my *little problem*?"

"I have said nothing. However, it is somewhat public knowledge that you've stepped away from your profession for medical reasons. I'm quite sure Dr. Nye has briefed the President accordingly—in a broader sense, of course."

"Nothing about my battle with my inner demons—"

"That is not public."

"Good. I do not want the President to know. He has enough to worry about."

Albert nodded, watching Elliott with the eyes of a concerned father.

"If my demons are going to kill me, I suppose it should be while I'm trying to save the world," Elliott joked.

"Please don't do that, son."

His smile faded. "I'm sorry."

Albert had not been able to handle the truth about Elliott's potentially lethal psychophysiological condition any more than Carol Mason had. Carol was the only girl Elliott had ever loved, and he'd had to push her away for the same reasons. Until he could manage the monsters in his head, he had to avoid the emotional overload that came with real danger. A sense of terror now had medical consequences for him.

A knock on the cabin door broke the quiet reflection. Albert snapped out of his worry. "That is Harold Turpin and Anthony, I'm sure. I invited them to join us the moment the plane reached a cruising altitude.

"Come in, gentlemen." The door swung open.

"Dr. Elliott Sumner, very good to see you, sir," Turpin said as he slid his cane between the seats and flopped down like a man who had just climbed a mountain.

"Always a pleasure, Harold," Elliott said. "It has been a while."

"Eighteen months since the Serpentine Strangler."

"I recall your man Orca pulling him off me. Happy it worked out for all of us."

"Elliott," Tony said as he found a seat and cup of coffee.

"And you, sir," Turpin said. "I thank you again for the twelve minutes you so graciously allotted me. I was gobsmacked by the headwinds from London. I do believe we were out of petrol after rerouting and finding your peninsula—"

"—Florida. I am quite certain the President would have allowed a man of your stature fifteen minutes, sir." The two chuckled.

Turpin gathered himself. "This is indeed a time of great challenge."

"Yes. A time for great minds to unite," Albert said with a peculiar, somber tone. "Tell me Harold, have you spoken to the President?"

"No, sir. A busy man at the moment, I am sure. I have spoken with Secretary of State Miss Dabney and Defense, Mr. Graham. Both maintain a gracious relationship with our prime minister. I've been privileged on occasion to be 'in the loop,' as it were."

"I see. And what do you know about our situation, Harold?" Albert asked.

"I know it is of international scope and could turn quite grim at any moment," he said. "Although specifics were not shared—unsecured communication over the Atlantic—it did not take this *old profiler* long to construct a theory. Granted North Dakota is most assuredly a wonderful place to visit in the spring, but it is now the dead of winter. The splendors of the Great Plaines are not what commands the undivided attention of your President, his cabinet, and your military. No, it's the crop of Minuteman ICBMs. They are compromised, I believe, and I am quite certain my *John Doe* fits into this disturbing puzzle."

"Impressed," Wilcox said, nodding. As an ugly American, he held little respect for the Brits. However, he did respect investigative prowess.

"We have much to discuss before Bismarck, gentlemen," Albert said.

"First," Elliott interrupted, "Dr. Nye asked I connect with

Dr. Cage for the first autopsy while in flight. There was to be a patch-in arrangement."

"I'm afraid those plans have changed, Elliott. I'm sorry I did not tell you when you boarded. With so much to coordinate, that got lost in the shuffle. Dr. Nye did attempt to reach you on the matter. You were between helicopter and plane at the time."

"Did she say why, Albert?"

"Dr. Cage is displeased with the thaw process. He recommended the first autopsy be delayed a few more hours. I'm sure you know more about the associated issues than I."

"Yes."

Elliott rubbed his chin as he drew upon his photographic memory. In an instant, he reviewed the countless, relevant studies as if he held each document in his hand. Wagster's noted work, *Decomposition and the Freeze-Thaw Process*, confirmed his initial thoughts on the matter and agreed with Dr. Cage's work on the detrimental effects of thawing of frozen cadavers. The risk of losing valuable information in a biological stew of ruptured cells would be too great. Sumner and Cage know they had a tiny forensic opportunity to recover anything that would help identify GRAY WOLF. A too-rapid thaw might destroy their chances before they got started.

"Actually, it is not a surprise," Elliott said. "If Dr. Cage has a problem with the thaw process, that means I also have a problem. Biology has limits."

"We are dealing with *corpsicles*," Wilcox fumed as heads turned. Unable to hide his exasperation any longer, he said, "When the chopper set down in Miami, I let it be known in no uncertain terms I did not want to go to Bismarck. Did anyone listen? No. Did the military escort deliver me to the plane with hands in my armpits and my feet kicking all the way? Yes."

"Tony. You are needed," Elliott said, holding back a smile.

"Being shot at and thrown overboard into the Atlantic was

enough for one day. I do not swim. I do not like fish with big teeth," Tony grumbled. "I am a patriot, but like biology, I have *my* limits too. My job was to get you here. I admit I did get help, but you're here." He turned to his small window. "I'm perfectly satisfied to leave *saving the world* to you smart people."

"There might be a time when your contribution will make a difference," Elliott said. "You are an experienced homicide detective. You know how *bad people* think. Trust me. For some reason, I feel like you need to be with us."

"Thanks," Tony huffed with an unlit cigarette wagging in his lips. "Let me know when that time arrives."

"I certainly shall, my friend."

"Well then," Albert said as he winked at the son who also sold himself short. "We will be in Bismarck in less than three hours. Dr. Cage said more time for the thaw preserves physical evidence and gives Elliott an opportunity to participate in the autopsies from the start. Some of the victims have been slow-thawing for days."

"What about the goddamn nuclear timeline?" Tony barked.

Elliott turned to Albert. "Yes, the risk of triggering a terminal breach—"

"—containment option?" Albert finished. "I don't know. But Dr. Nye concurred with Dr. Cage's recommendations, and the President approved it."

"Then the small possibility of finding something is more important than the automated launch of nuclear missiles," Elliott said. "Delaying the autopsies says a lot."

"What do you mean?"

"The bodies may be all they have to identify GRAY WOLF."

"I assume GRAY WOLF is the *terminal threat*—the code name?" Turpin said.

"Yes," Albert said.

"Identification must be pivotal to the construct of a counter strategy," Turpin said. "One short of nuclear destruction of a third of your country."

"The autopsies are one track of government focus. We do not know about the other initiatives. The President said it is best that way," Albert said.

"Four are thawing in Bismarck," Elliott said. "Mr. Turpin's *John Doe* is en route with the victim from Turkey."

"Yes," Albert said. "They arrive before we land. No thawing issues."

"Do we know if they have identified anyone?" Elliott asked.

"One identified," Albert said, "and the first to arrive at the state morgue—Roan Busey."

Elliott's and Turpin's eyes met. "What are the particulars, Albert?" Elliott asked.

"He was found twenty miles south of Minot, in a quarry closed for the winter. Roan Busey ran his rental tow truck off the road into piles of gravel and sand. His body was found in a field a hundred meters from the crash site." Albert flipped a page. "There is evidence of another vehicle, a rear-end collision. The other vehicle left the scene.

"Do either of you know Roan Busey?" Albert asked.

"Tell me why your government believes this man is connected to GRAY WOLF."

"His body was processed like the three others," Albert said.

"Decapitated, dismembered, and compressed into a frozen cube," Elliott said.

"My God," Turpin gasped.

"Tell me why Roan Busey is important to you," Albert insisted.

Turpin fiddled with his coat cuffs. "My *John Doe* was found in the streets of London. He possessed a disposable cell phone. There was one incoming and two outgoing calls of interest. The incoming was from the dead gentleman in Turkey—that call was placed minutes before his death. Two outgoing calls were made by my John Doe to the Pingree Correctional Center, North Dakota. The first was made hours before my John Doe died. The second call was placed six minutes before he died. I am quite certain his killer (or killers) triangulated the first calls and closed in on the last one. They did not want my John Doe talking to North Dakota."

"Do you know who he spoke to at Pingree?" Elliott asked, with sad certainty he already knew the answer.

"Milton Busey," Turpin said, "Roan's father. Do you know him?"

"Yes, I do. Milton Busey is a serial killer. I hunted him many years ago."

"You put him in jail?"

"I connected him to five murders. I caught him, but he avoided prosecution. The forensic evidence was too weak to take to a grand jury."

"What was he doing at Pingree?" Tony asked.

"His life of felonious crimes caught up to him, and he became quite ill. His criminal history and a successful plea deal put him at the minimal security retention center for the rest of his natural life. The man was off the streets. I thought he was too old and tired to do anything more. I moved on."

"Why are you here, Harry Turpin?" Wilcox asked.

"Harold," Turpin corrected. "I am here because my John Doe spoke to Milton Busey. I believe that conversation triggered the killing of Dr. Frank Rice—the Pingree Psychiatrist—and Mr. Busey's prompt departure."

"Elliott. Why were you startled when I mentioned Roan Busey?" Albert asked.

"Because I saw Milton in Key West yesterday," Elliott said.

"My God, sir," Turpin puffed. "What could he possibly be doing that far from Pingree?"

"I don't know. I saw him outside a marine supply store the morning of the shooting. I was picking up something for my boat ... the one now at the bottom of the Atlantic Ocean."

"No it's not, Elliott. The Coast Guard secured your boat with emergency floats," Albert said. "She's being towed to Key West as we speak."

"Wonderful," Elliott replied. "I saw Milton walking down Caroline. He seemed confused, lost. He kept referring to a note. I assumed an address. Then he walked out of view."

"You followed him into the law offices next door," Tony said.

"It was after a shooting, and not because I was looking for Milton Busey." Elliott closed his eyes. "There was an explosion. At first, I thought it was a sonic boom. I heard glass shatter, and then a second explosion. I knew then it was gunfire. I went outside and saw the glass on the sidewalk next door. That's when I entered the law firm. Inside I found an injured secretary— bleeding. I did what doctors do. I attended to her. I confirmed my suspicions. She had been shot. While I waited for the paramedics, I looked around and put some things together."

"What happened to Milton Busey?" Albert asked.

"I know he went into the law office. He was the target of the sniper fire. Milton Busey was a hunter being hunted, and I think he knew it. After the police came, I learned two of the three attorneys were dead. One was missing—a young woman named Bowman. I'm pretty sure Milton killed the two and took Bowman. That's it. I don't know the whys."

"How do you know Milton Busey killed the two lawyers?" Albert asked.

"Milton did not like guns. He always used a knife. The two on Caroline had their throats cut. They were not important to Milton. There is a reason he took Bowman. Milton is a fox. He knew the law office was a setup, perfect for a sniper hit. He risked it to get Bowman."

Tony sighed. "The man was definitely motivated—"

"—to kill a prison doctor and break out, in his condition," Turpin said, shaking his head. "My John Doe must have told Mr. Busey something that set him off."

"Very few things matter to Milton," Elliott said. "He only cared about money, respect, and his only son. Do we know when Roan was killed?"

"According to this, four or five days ago," Albert said.

"Harold, when did Milton get the phone calls from London?" Elliott asked.

"Three days ago."

"It fits. Someone told Turkey. Turkey told London. London told Milton."

"Why would people in Turkey and London care that a kid named Roan Busey got whacked in Minot, North Dakota?" Tony asked.

"Therein lies the mystery," Turpin said with a sigh. "The answer may give us the identity of GRAY WOLF." They stared into their coffee mugs. The connections and timing made sense.

"Someone ran into Roan Busey's tow truck," Albert said.

"So he was run off the road," Elliott murmured.

"According to this summary report," Albert said, passing the document to Elliott, "the Ward County Sheriff's Deputy Raymond Gibbs described a protracted accident scene. There were three miles of debris before the quarry where the truck was found."

"Roan was on the run," Turpin repeated. "He was being chased."

"And they caught him," Tony said.

"It was twenty below and snowing," Albert said.

"The executioners pulled Roan from the wreckage," Elliott read from the report. "They cut off his head and arms and legs. They loaded all parts of him into a portable garbage compactor.

They took the time to put his frozen remains in a field 100 meters from the truck and waited for snow to cover their tracks."

"The wild damn animals would have seen him as a tasty snack—fresh frozen human tissue," Tony said.

"He would be lost forever—he'd just disappear," Turpin said.

"Shows a lot of sick-ass planning," Tony growled.

"Diabolical," Albert whispered.

"We need to send Tony back to Key West," Elliott said.

"Thank you," Tony said. "Ah, but why?"

"Milton went to Key West to find the people who killed his son. He knows GRAY WOLF. He may be the only man alive who can tell us who they are and what they are doing."

"You think Busey is alive?"

"Yes. He killed five times and got away with it. While Dr. Cage and I conduct six autopsies in Bismarck, you need to find Milton Busey before GRAY WOLF's henchmen do. The people interested in us are definitely interested in Milton. They do not want that loose end talking to anybody."

"The Key West GRAY WOLF henchmen are now at the bottom of the Atlantic off the coast of Cuba," Tony said. "Have your forgotten about their boating accident?"

"I am sure GRAY WOLF has more resources. They will not leave Milton Busey out there. The man knows too much."

"The Milton Busey Factor explains why they've been so determined to stop Elliott too."

"Because they know Elliott's capabilities and history with Mr. Busey," Albert said. "We can all appreciate why GRAY WOLF would not want Elliott to connect with Milton."

"Okay, I will go to Key West," Tony said with a new wave of interest.

A quiet Turpin stared over his glasses at the sun breaking on the horizon. He cleared his throat. "And I will return to Key West with Anthony."

"No you won't, *bloke*," Tony said, sarcastically emphasizing the last word. "I work alone old man. You'll just slow me down."

"London has a vested interest in capturing Milton Busey. We will not sit this out."

"We must find Milton alive, Tony," Elliott said. "He may be our only chance to identify GRAY WOLF. Time is not on our side. We have no room for errors or setbacks. You and Harold might have a chance. If Milton is alive, I know he is still in Key West."

Wilcox turned to the window. "I guess GRAY WOLF won't leave it alone—"

"—until they've completed their mission," Turpin said.

"Let us hope they do not complete their mission," Albert said.

"Excuse me. Do we have a military escort?" Wilcox asked with his nose pressed against his small window.

"No, Anthony. We are traveling solo," Albert said. "The POTUS does not want to attract attention to our plane. We are ten-thousand feet above all scheduled flights."

"Well, we have company, and they're comin' up fast," Wilcox said.

PART THREE

NEEDLEINNUCLEARHAYSTACK
DAY 6, MINOT AIR FORCE BASE

CHAPTER 20

"Information is not knowledge."
Albert Einstein

Minot, North Dakota, 0500 CST

Senior Airman First Class Frank B. Edgerton stared at his monitor in disbelief. The silent red light flashed for the first time. Edgerton flipped a toggle, adjusted his headset mic, and said, "Whistle Pig alert."

The three words cut through the rustle and din of the other airmen at monitors in the dark, cavernous chamber underground. Heads lifted. Edgerton followed protocol. "Viking A-9, coordinates 48-00-34 100-40-22, thirty-two miles southeast Minot, twelve miles east-southeast Velva." The enormous screen on the north wall flickered and connected to Edgerton's monitor. A blurred aerial image took shape. As it sharpened, whispers rolled. Edgerton's next words hung in an eerie silence. "Missile silo doors engaged at 0500."

The world knows the 91st Missile Wing of the Air Force Global Strike Command oversees the nation's ICBM program in North Dakota. And it is no secret the primary tenant at the Minot Air Force Base is the 740th, 741st, and 742nd Strategic Missile Squadrons under the 91st Wing. Each squadron manages five flights of ten Minuteman III ICBMs nested in underground silos across an 8,500 square mile area. It is also public knowledge 1,500 specialists stationed in Minot have one mission: to defend the United States at all costs with a safe and secured ground missile program—the third leg of the U.S. nuclear triad. Only a few knew the 91st Security Forces operated a secret control center in a bunker sixty feet below an abandoned hanger in the southeast quadrant of the base—the real brain of the operation linked to the Pentagon.

Shadows fell over Airman Edgerton's shoulders as he flipped plastic pages in his ops manual. He stopped at the *Whistle Pig protocol*. As his finger moved down the lines on the acrylic page, a hand reached from the dark and gripped his shoulder. The next words were firm but calm. "Take us closer, airman."

Whistle Pig is slang for groundhog or woodchuck, a large, burrowing rodent that whistles when faced with danger. The slang term is disappearing, except in the bowels of the 91st Wing's security apparatus. There it means a burrowing predator (enemy) has entered a den (silo).

Without turning to see who gave the order, Airman Edgerton pounded his keyboard—only the commanders walk. The aerial view enlarged on the enormous screen a hundred feet away. Edgerton's coded instructions traveled from Minot Air Base to a satellite 22,230 miles away. In seconds, the Viking A-9 real estate grew. Soon, the cracked silo doors dominated the screen. When the hand on Edgerton's shoulder squeezed a second time, he stopped typing. "That's good there, son."

The crisp silence in the vast room tempted Edgerton to look up. Instead, he kept eyes on the blue-light images from his monitors. For now, he *was* Viking A-9. A momentary glance away from his *reason for existing* would break more than a dozen rules. Even staff moved with no eye contact in the hole. The rigid rules are in place for reasons—each is purposeful and time-tested. Edgerton's purpose in life was to monitor five missile silos on the farm. When he was on duty, they were his responsibility. He was one of six dedicated airmen in rotation, twenty-four/seven.

"They know what they're doing, sir," whispered the squadron commander to the man with the hand on Edgerton's shoulder.

Edgerton stayed with protocol. He left conversations to circulators, commanding officers, and high-ranking visitors. Edgerton never knew who stood behind him. He was monitored often, but he never looked. Now, he focused on the fact that he had three more pages of procedures to complete after reporting a *Whistle Pig Alert*. Every tap on his secured keyboard codified another message to the Pentagon, and three other unnamed locations around the world.

"The Viking A-9 is an MRBM," said the second shadow draped over Edgerton.

The third shadow kept a relaxed hand on Edgerton's shoulder. *Did you forget?* He wondered as his fingers danced over his keyboard, leaving only to flip a certain toggle switch at a certain time. *Nobody touches people down here. Granted, there is no specific rule forbidding—*

When the third shadow spoke, the hand moved with each word. He was the man who had directed Edgerton to zoom-in. "They threatened to send one into Canada. The medium range ballistic missile would be all they needed."

What the hell? Edgerton thought. *Send one of my missiles into Canada? Are we getting into something with friggin Canada?*

"The fact they know where we keep an MRBM is telling, sir."

Who is they, Edgerton wondered? *And who is touchin' me? Commander Troy is one of the shadows, but he wouldn't touch me. I'm not surprised you're down here. This is one of three things: for real, a malfunction, or a test.*

"They said an hour at 0430."

"They're showing us they can do what they say."

This is not a test, Edgerton concluded.

"Update me on the MRBM in Viking A-9, commander," said the third shadow.

"It's a modified Pershing, sir."

"They went out of service in the '90s."

"We held onto a few, *known alternatives* for our medium-range program. The Pershing has a W85 nuclear warhead with a forty-kiloton blast yield. It has an operational range of eleven hundred miles. Moves Mach 8, vector control with a steerable nozzle and Singer Kearfott Inertial Guidance System."

"Singer Kearfott? That's a little bit dated now, commander."

"But functional. Most important, it's predictable—a safe fallback asset for us."

"Is GRAY WOLF sitting in a McLean County LCC?"

Who is GRAY WOLF? Edgerton wondered as he continued to type.

"That would be a reasonable assumption, but not a definitive one, sir. At this juncture, we cannot rule out anything. We're still reviewing surveillance over the last seventy-two hours."

Surveillance, seventy-two hours, GRAY WOLF—what's going on? Is this—?

"Where are we on the connectivity probe?"

"Thirty percent. No sign of electronic breach. No helpful mapping to GRAY WOLF."

"That means 70 percent is still unknown. This could be real, or smoke-and-mirrors?"

"Assuming the latter is a slippery slope, sir." The commander's reply dropped to a whisper. Airman Edgerton heard the entire conversation. The commander pointed to the airman and touched his lips.

"I understand. When you get anything new, find me commander."

"Yes, sir."

Edgerton turned the last page of guidelines as if he had heard nothing. He would complete the Whistle Pig protocol in another minute, well within processing parameters. The shadow holding his shoulder continued to speak, not bothered an airman could hear his words.

"With the Viking A-9 breach, we are moving into dangerous territory. When I leave, you are to brief this room and activate all 91st Wing personnel. Nobody sits this one out."

"Yes, sir. I will brief central command at 0600."

"We are moving on multiple fronts." He squeezed Edgerton's shoulder with his eye on the big screen. "All options are on the table. Resources are moving into place around the world, and around Minot. You should also know a forensic track to identify GRAY WOLF has been authorized. I don't know if it will help, but we need to try."

Who authorized ... and what is a forensic track? Edgerton wondered.

"—the terminal breach, sir?"

"Yes. GRAY WOLF is on the verge of triggering a containment option. I don't need to tell you what that means for this command."

"We will not allow a single missile to leave Minot."

Edgerton stopped typing. The hand on his shoulder squeezed again. The commander's next words answered all of Edgerton's questions.

"Yes sir, Chief General Jamison," said the commander of the 91st Wing.

The Chief General has his hand on my shoulder, Edgerton thought as he swallowed hard. He blinked sweat from his eyelids, typed the final set of instructions, and closed the procedure manual.

More views of the Viking A-9 silo populated the big screen. They watched the doors open another two inches and a trail of white smoke stream from the silo into the sub-zero air.

"I am surprised this provocative action has not already

triggered a terminal breach containment option," General Jamison said. "What am I missing, commander?"

"We have two medium range ballistic missiles, sir. Both silos are off the grid. They will not register at the Pentagon."

"Since when? How can we—?"

"They were put on mothballs last month, sir. Formally taken out of service. Dismantling is scheduled. However, our first priority is the complete renovation of a 133 Minutemen III ICBM resources in Minot. At the moment, that is taking our resources, sir."

"I'll be damned," Jamison huffed as he pulled his hand off Edgerton's shoulder. "Now I remember signing off. But how could GRAY WOLF know it's off-line?" he asked as he stared at the exit, fifty yards away. "We need to pull out all missileers and ground personnel."

"Is that an order, sir?"

"Not yet. I will talk to the President. This new development matters." Jamison patted Edgerton shoulder. "Keep up the good work, young man. You soldiers are the heart and soul of our operations. We depend on men and women like you in times of great challenge, son."

Edgerton nodded with his eyes locked onto his monitors and hands hovering above his keyboard like a rattlesnake ready to strike. His Viking A-9 silo doors were open five inches on the giant screen—and he could not leave it that way. But why were his commanding officers and the general leaving before giving him his orders?

Minutes later, when the three officers exited the control room floor of the 91st Wing, the whispers of the forty-nine other airmen rolled. They were all of like minds. *"This is not a drill. This is bad. What the hell is going on and what are we gonna do about it?"*

Over the last forty-seven months, Airman Edgerton had lived with his five missiles, five silos, and one launch control capsule.

On this frigid morning, beneath a snow-covered prairie in North Dakota, he knew more about his missiles, his silos, and his LCC than any other person on the planet. He knew his five missiles could kill millions of people in minutes anywhere in the world—but Edgerton saw much more. His missiles were not just horrific weapons of mass destruction ready to scream from their concrete holes, able to wreak havoc and despair on the world. His missiles were his children.

Airman Edgerton knew their personalities. He knew their strengths and weaknesses, their complex anatomy, their nervous systems, and he knew their secrets, too. Like all children, they needed constant care and attention. He understood their imperfections, and he helped them adjust to change—like when they all had to adapt to new missileers, new parts, and new procedures. The top brass at the Air Force Global Strike Command (AFGSC) understood the unique bond between airmen and their missiles—and they even encouraged it. Familial relationships accentuated oversight and reduced errors. The intense training and regimented focus nurtured the bond Edgerton now possessed with each of his five. He could never leave a problem with his missiles unaddressed, unresolved. He could never give up the hunt for a solution. Unknown to the top brass, his devotion included going outside the sacred procedural manual.

After the officers left him alone, Edgerton could not lose any more precious time. He pecked his keyboard like a master pianist in a concert hall—he could not leave his silo doors open. As a drop of sweat left his sideburn and rolled down his jaw and off his chin, he watched his hydraulic pressures continue to climb. Without intervention, his Viking A-9 silo doors would open all the way. If they ratcheted to 100 percent clearance, his nuclear missile would be naked in its nest and ready for flight. His missile would awaken. It would be receptive to launch protocol.

Edgerton hit the last key and leaned closer to his monitor, his eyes locked onto the dreadful image of doors opening. First the throbbing red light on his Viking A-9 console went out. Then the door-expansion pressure stopped its climb and began to drop. Edgerton watched a fat column of green numbers crawl up his screen like army ants on a mission. His smile started to grow as the numbers left his screen and the door-expansion pressure registered zero. He watched his Viking A-9 silo doors close. The enormous aerial image left the big screen. His commands had reversed the provocative orders. The satellite cancelled the Whistle Pig. Chief General Jamison could not have been more correct: the airmen and missileers were the heart and soul of the nation's AFGSC.

Edgerton's smile faded as he poked his head out of his cyber-burrow and peered across the cavernous room lit by a hundred-and-fifty monitors like his and a giant screen on the north wall. He had just broken Strategic Missile Squadron protocol—he'd entered an unapproved code, one not in the official, classified ICBM security operating manual. By doing so, Edgerton had committed an act of treason punishable by twenty years in a military prison and a dishonorable discharge from the Air Force.

But that was not why Edgerton's smile faded. It was not why he broke another rule by taking his eyes off his monitor and looking around the master control room. The reason Airman Edgerton's smile melted away and terror took over his face was because he realized his unauthorized *close-instruction* code could not do anything to Viking A-9 silo doors unless the *open-instruction* code also had originated in the master control room.

They had a mole.

CHAPTER **21**

"We cannot change the cards we are dealt, just how we play the hand."
Randy Pausch

Bismarck, North Dakota, 0700

"It is an industrial, all-purpose probe. I'm measuring core body temperature," Cage said from the long, purple shadows of the autopsy room.

Elliott stared at a nondescript mound of melting human flesh. A single wire ran from it into a box on wheels with a tail of printer tape to the floor. "This is different," he said. Three similar mounds were thawing behind him. The gruesome masses of flesh were at different stages of transformation. Autopsies could not begin until core temperatures were ambient, or what little physical evidence they had would be lost like an intricate snowflake on a warm fingertip.

"Roan Busey will be ready soon," Dr. Cage said. "We need to protect the integrity of cells the greatest distance from the external trauma. They could tell a story." He walked around the Roan Busey corpse. "Good to see you, Elliott. It's been a while."

"Yes, it has." The two men lapsed into silence as they stared at the greatest mystery they had encountered as forensic pathologists. "If I am right," Elliott said, "it was New York City eleven years ago, in December. December 17. You had just published your ground-breaking research, *Climatic Conditions and Decomposition*."

"Yes. You remembered! Then again, I would expect nothing

less. Your photographic memory is legendary, Elliott. It's the only excuse we have to explain your unparalleled success and our paltry accomplishments."

Elliott smiled. "I always wondered if people were talking about me behind my back."

"I doubt that," Cage teased. He slipped-on surgical gloves and grasped the temperature probe at the top of the mound. With a smooth motion he pulled it from Roan Busey. "I heard there were unexpected complications over Iowa."

"I'm surprised that information got out," Elliott said.

"Why?"

"I saw a plane shot out of the sky. Not something for the broadcast news."

Cage's eyes widened as he fiddled with the probe. "My God," he said.

"They said it was on a suicide mission. One of our F-4 Phantoms came out of nowhere. Took it out before it could collide with Albert's Falcon. Our evasive action is something I do not want to experience again."

"I didn't know about a plane shot out of the sky. The story we got was sudden loss of cabin pressure. Your plane had to drop to 5,000 feet. That was given as the reason for your delay."

Elliott smiled. "Seems our government keeps a lot of secrets."

"I can attest to that. This has been one strange week, to say the least."

Elliott leaned closer to Busey's thawing mass. He shined a penlight at the dead eyes that seemed to look back at him. "I was told these bodies were *heads-not-included.*"

"Well, that would be true for all except Mr. Busey. They cut it off and dropped it into their despicable compactor with everything but arms and legs. It's an odd departure from the others. May mean something more."

"I agree," Elliott breathed as he peered at the mound of decomposing flesh and bones.

"I assume—other than the head information—you know more about our crisis than I do. I've been kept down here like the *Hunchback of Notre Dame*. Our building has been crawling with suits and skinny ties for too long. I think the *local feds* aren't quite ready for prime time. They are hypersensitive, unwilling to share. They don't seem to grasp we are on the same team and sharing is a good thing."

"So you've not spoken to President Landon, I take it?"

"No. I have not. Have you? You have. Now my feelings are hurt," Cage teased.

"Who have you talked to in Washington?"

"Maureen Nye. Once. She didn't know much at the time. Said they were gathering in the Oval Office, getting the POTUS out of bed. They were at the front end of a national crisis. She used words like terminal breach, nuclear, and Minot. Our conversation was brief, cryptic. She did not trust our connection. Looking back, I would imagine just about everything was suspect."

"I'm not surprised. When someone hijacks a nuclear missile, you tend to question everything."

"Exactly." Cage inspected the tip of the extracted probe. He cleaned it with a sterile swab and put it under an ultraviolet lamp. "We'll let that sit there a few minutes. Where was I?"

"Dr. Nye. Did she provide any details on the terminal breach?"

"No. Not sure she needed to. I've been in North Dakota long enough to appreciate our rather unique notoriety. Minot is a big part of our nation's nuclear triad."

"Right," Elliott said as he continued to scrutinize Roan Busey.

"When Maureen and I spoke, I had an unidentified and

unexplained human ice cube thawing in the Decomp Room. She tried to explain why three more were delivered to my autopsy room without warning. She wanted me to get started as soon as feasible. Thank God she is a forensic pathologist by trade. She knew the transformation from a rock-hard block of ice required a slow thaw process. Any acceleration would destroy whatever we hoped to find. It would compromise—"

"—the forensics completely," Elliott said.

"Yes. She did say they were looking for *you*. Last night, I learned two more *connected* bodies were on their way from abroad. So now there's an international component. Your participation made perfect sense, given your experience with global forensic puzzles."

"We need to be on the same page," Elliott said. "I will tell you what I know. I did talk to President Landon. I see now why he is the president. The man stirred my patriotic sinews. I had no choice but to help. Do you know Albert Bell?"

"Yes. Mr. Bell subsidized my research in the early days."

"I did not know that."

"And I recently learned he is your biological father," Cage said. "It was in all the papers."

"Yes, he is. Another story for another time." Elliott walked to a different frozen human block and shined his penlight on the crystalline surface. He moved his small beam as if he had found something moving in the ice.

"Albert is a friend of Bill Landon's," Elliott said. "They go back a long way. Albert got the call from the POTUS. Yes. They were looking for me. Albert agreed to help find me. I think he is in this to make sure I survive. There are things I'm dealing with—"

"I know. Most of your forensic brethren know. You can move on."

"James Herbolt—director of the CIA—delivered a binder of

classified documents dealing with the nature and extent of this terminal breach. Albert met us in Miami with his plane and the binder—the GRAY WOLF file. We flew to Bismarck digesting the chilling document."

"GRAY WOLF. Interesting. Esoteric. I'm sure some vociferous general came up with that one. They love carnivores and Indian folk lore around here." He chuckled. "There were others on your plane to Bismarck?"

"Yes. Tony Wilcox, a private investigator, retired Memphis homicide detective and close friend. Tony and I worked several cases together. He was the one who found me in Key West. James Herbolt had convinced him this thing was more important than my health."

"Who else came up here with you?"

"Harold Turpin. Retired, Scotland Yard. The most gifted profiler I have ever known."

"That speaks volumes."

"Harold flew in from London and joined us in Miami. He was the first to connect the dots—Turkey to London to North Dakota. He recognized his homicide had to be a part of a larger puzzle, one with a torrid international agenda—I use *torrid* in the British sense."

"Full of difficulty and tribulation," Cage said. "I look forward to meeting both."

"That might take a while. They are on their way back to Key West."

"I don't follow. They just got to Bismarck."

"We didn't have Roan Busey's name until we were over Kansas."

"The name triggered the impromptu trip back?"

"Roan's father Milton was serving a life sentence at the Pingree Correctional Center."

"Pingree is just down the road from us," Cage said.

"And just up the road from Minot, and the stick in the hornet's nest," Elliott said.

"Please, tell me more," Cage said.

"Milton Busey got a couple of phone calls at Pingree four days ago. The calls came from our dead man in London, who got a phone call from our dead man in Turkey."

"Interesting," Cage said as he reinserted the probe into Roan Busey.

"The same day as the calls, Milton killed a prison doctor and left Pingree."

"I did the autopsy on Dr. Frank Rice. They didn't give me the name of the attacker. They were conducting an internal investigation. Pingree has had its problems."

"I am not surprised."

"The phone calls. Someone told Milton Busey about his dead son," Cage said. "That means this office has a leak. We've not released information of Roan Busey."

"We need to talk to Milton Busey. He's in Key West. I saw him," Elliott said.

"And you know Milton Busey how?"

"He killed five," Elliott said.

"A serial killer. I should have put that together on my own," Cage murmured.

"I saw Milton in Key West two days after he talked to London."

"Pingree to Key West in two days. He's a man on a mission."

"Minutes after Milton walked past the front window of a boat supply store—"

"—where you just happened to be," Cage added.

"Yes. Pure happenstance. I recognized Milton—last guy I'd expect to see in Key West. I was waiting on a part for my boat. I watched him stop on a curb in front of the business next door. Believe me; I had no desire to get involved. I had gone to Key

West to get as far away as I could from ... the monsters that haunt me."

Cage busied himself with surgical tools and drapes. "I understand."

"Busey went into a law firm. An explosion rattled the store window, and I ran out to see."

"Milton Busey shot someone?" Cage asked.

"Milton cut the throats of two lawyers and took one with him —disappeared. The explosion was sniper fire into the law firm. Hit a secretary."

"A sniper waiting for Milton Busey," Cage said.

"Yes. He out-maneuvered them."

Cage pushed Roan's gurney under the lights for the medical photographer. He was ready for autopsy. "Did you get a look at the crime scene, Elliott?"

"Not on purpose. I went there as a doctor to help. I guess it was a kind of knee-jerk thing. I saw someone injured, wanted to do something ..."

"The Good Samaritan always gets us in trouble," Cage sighed.

"I attended to the wounded secretary until the police and paramedics arrived."

"Then what?"

"I got out of there. I could not be involved. I would risk losing it."

"I understand. Your personal issue that is not so secret anymore."

"I'm learning that," Elliott said. "My effort to stay uninvolved didn't matter—I got sucked in. Whoever wanted Milton dead saw me at the crime scene. They decided I was a problem too. They came after me that night. Tony Wilcox showed up at the right time. I was lucky to escape."

"Unbelievable."

"That's what I thought."

"They had to know you weren't involved, Elliott. They just didn't want a world-class forensic sleuth talking to Milton Busey. But how do you think it connects to all of this?"

"Right now your guess is as good as mine," Elliott said looking back at Roan Busey.

"Maybe not. You have a theory?"

"I think Milton entered into a clandestine arrangement with an international entity. He probably did not know the big picture. He had something to sell, something they wanted."

"What?"

"Before his life of crime, Milton was a contractor with the government, a demolition expert. He helped with the construction of missile silos around Minot in the 1960s. Milton was invited back in the 1990s to participate in the demolition of some of those silos."

"You think he sold classified information to GRAY WOLF?"

"Yes. And I suspect Roan was his outside man."

"And the deal went south," Cage said.

"Milton was double-crossed. I know Milton, evil but an old-fashioned guy. He delivered on his promise. GRAY WOLF decided to eliminate Roan instead of paying. Probably felt safe with Milton locked up at Pingree. What could that old man possibly do?"

"Others dealing with GRAY WOLF learned of Roan's termination and started to worry about their own scalps. They told Milton GRAY WOLF had killed his son."

"I think GRAY WOLF miscalculated. They don't know Milton like I do. The man is a smart and tenacious, cold-blooded killer. Milton got out of Pingree and made a beeline to Key West to punish the people who killed his son and to get the money they owed him. I suspect it was a hefty fee."

"I wonder what he sold," Cage said under his breath looking at a frozen corpse.

"The man only cares about three things—respect, money, and family, in that order."

"Let's hope your friends can find him."

"He's down there waiting on his money. His message has been sent and received."

"We could use some help solving this puzzle," Cage said.

"You and I both know we don't have a lot here to work with here," Elliott said. "The President needs to know who commandeered his missile silos. If we can't identity GRAY WOLF soon, we'll all be gone and this place will be uninhabitable for decades—"

Squeaks from the swinging metal doors into the autopsy room got their attention. They turned and watched a line of surgical scrubs and lab coats enter. Behind them, the approved spectators started to take their seats on the observation ledge. In the eerie silence, all eyes were locked on the same things: the horrific blocks of frozen carnage.

CHAPTER 22

"The impossible is often the untried."
Jim Goodwin

Bismarck, North Dakota, 0700 CST

The news media could only speculate—because no one was talking. The daily White House Press Briefings were cancelled indefinitely. A plane had gone down over Iowa and the military was mobilizing.

Black SUVs with tinted windows, unmarked white vans, satellite dishes, and military helicopters surrounded the North Dakota State Medical Examiner's Office building as if staging another siege on Ruby Ridge. Anyone who came within two-hundred yards of the facility was escorted into one of a dozen army tents or a nearby abandoned building commandeered by the feds. All private and commercial flights were rerouted. No planes could enter the airspace of three Midwestern states. Flights were cancelled—they said it was the weather.

As the winter sun exploded over the snow-covered Great Plains of North Dakota, fifteen-hundred miles away the President of the United States and his National Security Council reassembled in the Situation Room beneath the West Wing. This time, there would be no leaks. This time, everything leading up to and including the highest-level gatherings in the free world would stay inside the confines of the 5,525 square-foot intelligence management conference center in D.C. and an autopsy room in Bismarck, North Dakota. Everyone on the inside now understood even an innocuous leak could trigger a nuclear event and alter the course of history.

Beneath Bismarck's snow and ice, the disintegrating basement of the old building on East Main looked more like a medieval dungeon than the official state morgue of North Dakota. The cracked tiled floors, whitewashed cinderblock walls, exposed pipes, crumbling asbestos infrastructure, water-stained ceilings, and broken fixtures did more than reveal the pitiful financial condition of state government. The failure to keep in repair and renovate one of their most vital facilities—the State Medical Examiner's Office—had put in jeopardy the most important autopsies of the century. Six bodies held vital secrets that could save millions of lives. The deteriorating facilities added variables to the already-impossible task.

Unknown to the outside world, four human blocks of oozing flesh thawed on gurneys in the basement autopsy room, and two cadavers lay supine on gurneys in the walk-in refrigerator. Specialists assembled at the epicenter of the international crisis. Medical photographers, dieners, histologists and toxicologists, and morgue clerks were in position to assist the three forensic pathologists. Sitting in metal chairs on a cement ledge five feet above the room were authorized observers—three U.S. Agents, Ward County Sheriff Deputy Raymond Gibbs, Albert Bell, and three armed military men in flak jackets and sunglasses.

Behind the observers—on the next ledge, three-feet up—were the state's histology-slide file cabinets, pathology references, medical-legal video archives, and twenty years of boxed autopsy records. Hanging from the ceiling were banks of broken and forgotten lights covered in dust and cobwebs. Dangling below them were the new halogen fixtures that lighted the autopsy table, work benches, and row of carts stocked with surgical instruments, specimen containers, and soft goods. The only other illumination in the room of shadows came from the broken laminar hood, long x-ray light box, and the small windows on the metal doors into the hall.

Roan Busey would be first. Steam rose from the gelatinous mass beneath the hot halogens. Dr. Cage stood on one side with hands clasped and eyes measuring the vital tasks ahead. Across from Cage, Elliott Sumner studied the carnage. The gifted forensic sleuth processed more information than most could ever comprehend.

Standing next to Sumner was Dr. Emma Osgard—the Manitoba ME. The three doctors were gowned in green surgical scrubs, paper masks and caps, and surgical gloves. Each wore a headset with adjustable mic. They had agreed to procedural rules in advance. Cage would take lead. The observations and surgical actions of each pathologist could be spontaneous and would be included in the official record. They followed standard protocol, verbalizing all actions and findings for the audio record. The three had conducted thousands of autopsies. They were ready for the GRAY WOLF carnage.

"The time is 0720 central, North Dakota Case File number 24991," Cage said in the quiet autopsy room. "The deceased, Roan Busey, is a forty-year-old white male pronounced dead on date and time of record. Health history of the deceased is unknown. Attending physician of the deceased is unknown." Cage adjusted his mic. "The pathology team conducting this postmortem includes Dr. Emma Osgard, Manitoba, Canada and Dr. Elliott Sumner, international forensic pathologist."

Elliott rested his palm on the bulbous mass like he was blessing the dead. With his other gloved hand, he felt several quadrants of the undefined form. "We find the body of Roan Busey brutally transformed from a recognizable human state to a gelatinous mound without structure or definition. This precipitous transformation is the result of exposure to substantial applied forces and pronounced temperature variances. The deceased was exposed to intense and confined compressive forces followed by an accelerated drop in body temperature to subzero levels, and then a graduated thaw process back to ambient temperatures.

"The external surface tension of this gelatinous mass is defined by a uniform mixture of ruptured cells, pulverized ostia, and liquefied tissue. A comparable texture equivalency would be the apical portion of the posterior horn spinal cord gray matter, a unique composition of very small cells and minimal myelination. This known biologic construct closely compares to the deceased's current gelatinous state—a membranous sack of biological gruel."

Cage walked to the long x-ray lightbox and turned on his mic. The observers in the autopsy room gasped as he slapped-up the radiographic image of the crushed man. "The x-rays of the deceased reveal the presence of certain skeletal parts and absence of others. All ostia found are shattered, crushed, or pulverized. This eliminated the possibility of following standard recognition protocol. "Based on preliminary radiographic assessments, we can confirm the presence of all bones including and superior to the pelvis. Absent are all bones inferior to the pelvis and lateral to both clavicles. For the record, missing are four appendages—arms and legs. The skull, severed at C-4 and C-5, was repositioned at the midsection of the torso and crushed. Adequate landmarks remain to confirm the head—while intact—had been repositioned."

"I concur with Dr. Cage's assessment," Osgard said. "Initial anatomical evidence confirms the amputation of four appendages and the decapitation took place prior to the application of compressive force. This physical evidence confirms the deceased's head and torso were introduced to the compacting device simultaneously."

"The four appendages are unaccounted for at this time,"

Cage added as the Histologist wheeled a stainless-steel cart to his side. On it were nine, 450 cc syringes connected to ten-inch plastic tubes with six-inch, 19 gauge needles. Cage inspected each setup positioned on the sterile drape. "Due to the liquefaction phenomena of the deceased, identification and inspection of internal organs and tissue will primarily be accomplished through microscopic examination."

"The deceased has been divided into nine quadrants," Sumner said. "A needle will be inserted into each quadrant. With Dr. Osgard's assistance, a 50 cc sample will be collected at six levels in each quadrant. This procedure will capture an adequate profile of all cells populating the biologic soup."

"Thank you Dr. Sumner." Cage picked up the first syringe and held the plunger. Osgard inserted the needle into the first quadrant. When the needle seated, Cage pulled the plunger. They watched the red/brown liquid climb into the barrel. At the 50 cc mark Cage paused and Osgard backed the needle out one inch for a second 50 cc sample collection ...

The sinewy U.S. Agent sitting next to Albert Bell held a handkerchief to his mouth. He leaned to the billionaire patriarch and whispered, "Excuse me, sir. Bill Aster, CIA. I understand you are the father of Dr. Sumner. You were responsible for getting him here—we thank you for your assistance."

Albert nodded.

"It appears we're going to be sitting up here a while. This is a new experience for me. Do you know what they are doing?"

Albert kept his eyes on the procedure below, his mind on two things: *Can Elliott find something to identify GRAY WOLF in time? Or will Bismarck be where they die?*

"I'm sorry to bother you. Clearly you are engaged," Aster whispered. "I wonder if you could take just a moment to tell me what they are doing down there?"

Albert kept staring at the monotonous process of collecting

fluid for microscopic study. Without thinking he said, "Necropsy. *Autopsia cadaverum.*"

"Excuse me?" Aster said. "Necro—what?"

"Mr. Aster, you are witnessing a surgical procedure on the dead. It is normally intended to determine cause and manner of death. However, under these unique circumstances, they are not necessarily seeking to understand either. There are other objectives."

"I don't follow."

"We now have six dead bodies. In life, they were somehow connected. Therefore, we have six opportunities to obtain something that perhaps assists in the identification of GRAY WOLF. You certainly would not be sitting in this room if you did not know of what I speak."

"Yes sir. I know about GRAY WOLF," Aster said. What I don't know is how we intend to learn anything from these—appropriately described—sacks of biologic soup. It appears to me GRAY WOLF did a good job covering their tracks."

Albert turned to Aster with a renewed interest in educating the CIA. Possibly the man could be of help to him later. "Dr. Sumner explained to me their navigation through these woefully transformed cadavers would be quite different from other autopsies. He explained the same principals of dissection applied."

"Dissection?" Aster asked.

"The process of disassembling and observing, sir. The aspiration of body fluids containing portions of cells is a *liquid dissection*. It is the way they will be able to observe and assess—microscopically. If there are clues to be found, they will find them."

"Doesn't look like disassembling to me. Looks more like emptying a kids' pool."

Albert smiled. "When you empty a pool, you might have an

opportunity to identify who was in the pool by examining the water left behind. Maybe GRAY WOLF left something behind."

"I sure hope so, Mr. Bell."

The last syringe joined the others on the tray. The histologist wheeled them out of the autopsy room for preparation and later microscopic review by Cage, Osgard, and Sumner.

"We can take care of toxicology with samples from the nine syringes," Cage said. "I suspect the use of a lipid disrupting agent during the compressing process. Viscosity suggests uniform dissolution of cellular membranes."

"Radioimmune precipitation assay," Elliott said.

"Is that what RIPA stands for?" Cage teased. "I'm sure we are dealing with one of the more aggressive lysing agents. The molecules might lead us to a manufacturer."

"GRAY WOLF could third-party source RIPA anywhere in the world," Elliott said. "More important is the *DNA testing* you pursued when each corpse arrived—"

"You mean the *lack of suitable DNA* for testing," Cage said. "I think the intensity of the radiation exposure was great. The residual dosage was relatively small."

"Almost undetectable," Osgard said.

"The ionizing radiation was a part of the compression process," Elliott said. "The perfect killing machine. If that is the case, the device is unique. If not for the device, the collective ordering of the specialized components would be trackable."

Cage backed from the autopsy table and looked to the observation ledge above the hanging halogens. "Mr. Aster. I suggest you take that piece of information and get someone in Washington on it."

Aster leaned over the railing. "Duly noted, Dr. Cage," he said with his small notepad and pen in hand. "I will do just that." Aster (gladly) eased out of the room.

With scalpel in hand, Elliott leaned over the bulbous mass on the autopsy table and turned on his mic. "I am now going to open Roan Busey with an incision sagittal to what we have defined as the midline."

Cage adjusted the halogens for Elliott.

"I recommend at minimal a fifty-centimeter incision," Dr. Osgard said. "We will need undisturbed internal access to each dismemberment site to optimize our opportunity to assess trauma. A substantial midline incision will relax the torso and improve exposure."

Elliott nodded and inserted the razor-sharp scalpel. As if he were cutting into a water-balloon, the cellular slush slid out and filled the tub of the autopsy bed. The taut skin behaved like an over-stretched elastic sheath. The release of internal pressure allowed the skin to contract and sag. As the flow of fluids slowed, chunks of damaged organs unfolded onto the table.

With the release came the putrid stench of decomposition. In seconds, the unpleasant smell—tantamount to a pile of rotting fish—had filled the room. A morgue clerk turned on the four laminar evacuation fans that protruded from the east wall. The familiar, rancid smell would linger for days.

Cage and Osgard focused on the torso. Sumner went to work on one amputated arm stump. With magnifying surgical loupes, he studied the remnant severed edges of tissue.

"A small proximal portion of the left tricep, the deltoid, and the teres minor muscles are present. Associated shoulder and arm ostia and connective tissues are absent—bone pulverized and tissue liquefied. Remnant severed structures reveal mechanical edges. Slicing by a sharp instrument noted, possibly a knife."

Elliott probed in silence for several minutes. "I think I've got something." He leaned closer with his tweezers and probe. "I need more light, please."

Cage backed out of the abdominal quadrant and aimed the halogens on Elliott's work area. With long-neck tweezers and lavage, Elliott cleared the lateral aspect of the ragged tissue. With his face inches away he announced, "We've got a tattoo."

"Tattoo," Cage said. "How much?"

"A portion. It appears to be part of a shield. On the shield is the top portion of a diamond-like design. Colors ... light brown, blue, red, and black ... the tops of black letters or numbers or symbols. Someone take a picture of this while I hold it."

The medical photographer leaned in with his camera and took a dozen shots with graduated focus and exposure. "Got it, doctor."

"A tattoo may give us valuable information," Cage said. "At minimum, we may be able to identify inks and artistic technique. If we're lucky, recreate the image."

Elliott removed the tissue with the tattoo. "We should focus on the other three dismemberment sites."

Dr. Osgard turned from the abdominal cavity. With hands dripping brown blood into the open wound she said, "These dismemberments make no sense."

Elliott dropped the delicate tissue section into 10 percent neutral buffered formalin and sealed the container. "Roan Busey is the smallest victim. Based on the consistent frozen cubic dimensions, all four were in the same or an identical device. There was not a *fit* issue."

"Exactly my thoughts. The largest reconstructed victim is a 245-pound male," Osgard said. "A reconstructed Roan Busey is 178 pounds, a sixty-seven-pound variance. Removal of his arms and legs would not be necessary to fit him into their device."

"I still have a problem with the great lengths taken," Cage said. "The arduous and grisly process makes little sense after death. These people were not tortured. They were processed."

"GRAY WOLF is mission-driven. They are on a timeline

and they're efficient. Why would they torture a once-contributing member of their team who was no longer needed? Disposal was their objective."

"It would have been more efficient to dig a hole and bury them somewhere in the vast wilderness. Or incinerate and spread the ashes," Cage said. "The traditional methods would still be needles in the forensic haystack."

"We may never know why they chose this approach," Elliott said. "All we can do is look for pieces to their bizarre puzzle and hope it tells us a story in time."

"Busey's head was included," Osgard said. "More proof these dismemberments and decapitations were not driven by the device. They were trying to hide something. I'm not sure we know exactly what yet."

"Yes. They had another reason," Cage said. "The most logical objectives are to eliminate identifiers: fingerprints, dental, facial recognition, and the like. Radiation appears to have taken the DNA off the table."

"I don't think DNA would have made a big difference," Osgard said. "Our victims were probably productive, uninformed members of the GRAY WOLF team. They were chosen based on their political leanings, skillsets, and universal anonymity."

"Disposables. Without criminal records," Cage said.

"I am interested in these dismemberments. They had a less than obvious purpose," Elliott said. "I think they were removing the common markers that lead back to GRAY WOLF. The tattoos have a story to tell."

"They could have cut out the tattoos," Cage said. Why take arms, legs, and heads?"

"Let's assume GRAY WOLF did not want to miss any of the tell-tale tattoos. Some members had tattoos on arms, some legs, and some necks. Their elaborate disposal method not only destroyed physical evidence quite thoroughly, it also reduced risk of error and served to misdirect people like us."

"That makes sense. We were not thinking tattoos until just now," Osgard said.

"I agree," Cage said.

CHAPTER 23

"If you do not expect the unexpected, you will not find it."
Heraclitus

Return flight to Key West, 1000 EDT

"Yeah, well I don't give a rat's ass about your procedures. We're on a tight clock. D.C. needs to light a fire. The names are Tony Wilcox and Harry Turpin," he barked into his mic.

"Harold ... old boy," Turpin insisted over the rim of his coffee mug.

Wilcox cold-eyed the retired Scotland Yard profiler, another one of those feckless, pontificating Brits he did not need slowing him down. "Like I said, *Harry* Turpin," he puffed into his mic. "Now go find someone important. Have them call me in ten damn minutes or I swear I will find you and hurt you. I got your name Fentworth, Fortinet, Fudewyler—the hell." He yanked off his headset, threw it on the seat, and seethed at the Brit. "What're you lookin' at?"

Turpin turned to the small window of the Dassault Falcon. He had met Wilcox a few hours earlier, on the ride from Miami to Bismarck. Now they were on their way to Key West to find Milton Busey—maybe the only man alive who could identify GRAY WOLF.

Over the years, Turpin had worked with a lot of American *big-city* homicide detectives, some good and some not so. As a gifted profiler, Turpin knew the difference in an instant. The good ones had a razor-sharp mind, missed nothing, had a short fuse, and were proficient in the art of colorful diatribe. One of them explained *the anger* to him once. He said each day, a little bit of hell rubbed off. Turpin learned to live with the downsides because the good ones never let pride or politics get in the way of hunting monsters.

"Appears the underlings in your capital are sitting in the dark," Turpin said.

"CIA newborns—the bastards," Wilcox fumed as he slid a cigarette in his mouth.

"You're not thinking of lighting," Turpin said.

Wilcox snickered. "Harry. We're moving 500 mph at 40,000 feet in a thin-skinned metal tube filled with compressed oxygen. Give me some credit. I will not ignite our sky torpedo."

"Good to know ... Anthony."

"Tony ... Harry," Wilcox huffed.

"Harold ... Tony," Turpin breathed into his mug.

"Well, shit." Wilcox stared at his iPhone. "Spyglass sent preliminaries on the law firm."

Turpin lowered his mug with eyes wide. "Carry on—"

"Bowman, Weller & Garcia on Caroline in Key West. They were on Wabash, downtown East Kansas City, their only home for twenty years. Office closed fourteen days ago."

"Six days before Roan Busey's death," Turpin said.

Tony scrolled with his nose inches from the screen. "There's a lot here."

"May I ask how you're able to transmit and receive in flight?" Turpin asked.

"Some expensive high-tech Wi-Fi setup, I guess," Tony mumbled. "You do know Albert Bell is a billionaire, right?"

"Yes. I do, in fact." Harold would not explain his longtime personal relationship with the Memphis billionaire patriarch, or his professional relationship with Elliott.

"Says here they promote themselves as *International Law Specialists*," Tony said. "Corporate, import/export, taxation, currency exchange, and accounting services. I would say these legal clowns are strategically positioned to screw a lot of people."

"Not the likely counsel one would expect a fellow like Mr. Busey to engage."

"I think it safe to assume that dirtball was sought by GRAY WOLF and these guys handled contractor payments for services rendered," Tony said. "My people are convinced they are a legit business in and out of suspect relationships over the last twenty years."

"It would be helpful to know what services Milton Busey provided," Turpin said.

"Maybe our CIA mollusks will get back to us on that before we land. I'd like to know how that old fart attracted the attention of the likes of a GRAY WOLF."

"Are we quite certain the BWG law firm is an unwitting participant?"

"The GRAY WOLF employee termination policy did not come into play with them," Tony said. "If they were insiders they would have been stuffed in a garbage compactor in Kansas. Instead, they got an all-expense paid relocation package to Key West."

"The timing precedes Roan Busey's death and Milton's Pingree exit."

"I don't think GRAY WOLF expected the old man to break out of prison. However, I do think they are people with backup plans. Key West was one."

"Disciplined," Turpin said softly. "Attention to details."

"GRAY WOLF knew Roan's value to their mission was limited. After he delivered they were going to get rid of him. If Milton found out and made trouble, I'm sure GRAY WOLF had a contingency plan or two to minimize the damage. The Busey boys had to go."

"Why relocate BWG to Key West?" Turpin asked.

"The first place Milton would go would be BWG in Kansas City."

"His only contact," Turpin said.

"Yes. GRAY WOLF moved BWG to buy time—make the old man drive a few thousand miles across country. They picked the farthest place from Pingree. They wanted to wear him out and give the cops a chance to catch him. Save them some work."

"Elliott said BWG leased commercial space in a tourist section of downtown Key West. The place had a big storefront window at the end of a long street."

"Perfect for a sniper," Turpin said. "They set the trap and waited."

"Sniper was three blocks away," Tony said. "Add all that to the fact Key West is not known for its homicides. Local law enforcement is inexperienced. They live in paradise on the edge of civilization. GRAY WOLF thought it out. If Milton did become a problem, they would take him out of the picture with a sniper and leave a baffling cold case behind."

"They did not count on Mr. Busey avoiding the sniper," Turpin said.

"Or killing two lawyers and taking one hostage," Tony said. "Now they have a pesky loose end. I bet Bowman is telling Busey everything he or she knows."

"And I'm quite certain GRAY WOLF did not anticipate there would be an international forensic investigator next door," Turpin said, chewing on his pipe.

"Well, that explains the relentless chase after I found Elliott down there," Tony said. "I thought my boy was holdin' back on me."

Turpin flipped pages in his tattered-leather notepad. "I want to see Caroline Street with my own eyes. Examine the likely sniper nests. You visit Miss Ramsey, the poor girl who took Milton's bullet."

"Penland Investigations," Tony said. "My people say it's legit. Out of Orlando."

"Their namesake was executed while talking to Elliott," Turpin said.

"We need to find out what they know about GRAY WOLF. Why was James Penland looking for Milton Busey? His partner agreed to meet us in Key West, if we run out of things to do."

"Time and place?" Turpin asked.

"Atlantic Suites, close to where his partner left this world. Man's name is John Smith."

"John Smith? Bloody wonderful," Turpin breathed.

"Hey. I'd use an alias if my partner ate a bullet on a quirky case," Tony said. "Maybe with our list, and the CIA getting back to us, we can actually track down this asshole."

"Elliott was quite certain Milton Busey would stay in the area a few days. I understand the Florida peninsula provides only a few exit options, all monitored."

"Yeah well, we need to keep that in mind while poking around," Tony said, his voice grim. "I'm sure GRAY WOLF operatives know we know they've got a loose end."

The speaker on the plane came to life. "Gentlemen, we are thirty minutes from touch down, Key West International. Mr. Bell has arranged for us to taxi into a secured hanger. Mr. Wilcox, the car you requested is waiting."

"Anthony, you asked Albert for a specific car?"

"It's Tony, and yes. The man's a billionaire, Harry. I have needs."

"I never—"

"Shit." The headset beeped and green light flashed. "Incoming. Bet it's the goddamn CIA. Guess I sufficiently motivated Fortnight, Fetner, or whatever." Tony slipped on the headset and adjusted the mic. "Yes. Go ahead." He rolled his eyes. "Hell yes, this is Wilcox. And it's *Tony*, not Anthony ... No ... Look, you're the ones who called me on this private line or frequency. My friggin headset lit up." He turned to Turpin with eyes wide. "Who are you connecting?"

Turpin reached over and flipped the toggle on the console where Tony had plugged his headset. Instantly, the conversation moved to the cabin speaker system.

"You can take off the headset," Turpin whispered.

After three pings, the next connection was made. "Hello, Mr. Wilcox. Hello, Mr. Turpin. This is James Herbolt, CIA."

Tony whispered, "It's the goddamn Director of the CIA."

"Hello James. Harold here," Turpin said.

"Harold, so good to hear your voice. We need you on the team. Your London/Turkey connection has already helped. I have been in discussions with Randolph and Bennett, putting those pieces together."

"What the hell's he talking about?" Tony breathed over his dangling, unlit cigarette as the Dassault Falcon descended into a bank of clouds over the Atlantic.

Turpin held up a finger. "James, we are a little more than twenty minutes from landing in Key West. Please tell us what you believe would be most beneficial for our mission."

"Yes, of course. You and Mr. Wilcox departed Bismarck to track down Milton Busey."

"Elliott Sumner is quite confident Mr. Busey is still in the Key West vicinity," Turpin said. "We have a few promising avenues to explore."

"Here's what we know about Mr. Busey. He was on the team

of 5,000 construction workers between 1963 and 1966, building 150 underground silos and fifteen launch control centers in and around Minot, North Dakota. Busey was a demolitions specialist."

"So he has intimate knowledge of the missile silos," Turpin said.

"To a degree. He may know some behind-the-scenes information. Mr. Busey is an expert on the geology of the area. I'm told knowing where the Missouri Plateau ends and the Coteaus Slope begins is important. And knowing geological secrets of the Souris Lake Basin and Glaciated Plains can be useful. Silos and LCCs throughout."

"I don't follow," Turpin said.

"Busey knows the underground terrain, Harold. He knows how to access the underbelly of our nuclear missile matrix. He knows the weak spots, the caves and caverns, and the shortest and easiest excavation routes to a launch control capsule and missile silo."

"So that's what GRAY WOLF wanted," Wilcox said.

"The subsurface geology is important to demolition people," Herbolt said. "They need to know the compositions—clay, rock and sand, volcanic ash, potash, salts and the like. It's not something I can fully appreciate. I do know it's easier to move sand than tunnel through rock.

"There's more. Milton returned in 1996 and participated in the relocation of a classified portion of our missile defenses from North Dakota to Montana. Again, he was on the demolition crew. He knows the silos and LCCs that were destroyed and those left intact. And he knows how they fit into the geological terrain.

"At this time, a third of the Minot missiles are in the Bakken oil fields. The experts tell us that would be Milton's preferred area. That *geological factoid* narrows our search for GRAY WOLF somewhat. The good news is, Milton was no part of the recent military program reinstalling 150 ICBMs in North Dakota. He would not know the details on most of the new silos, LCCs, and related networks."

"Is the dirtball from the Minot area?" Tony asked.

"He grew up in Cooperstown, North Dakota," Herbolt said. "It is relevant, to a degree. Oscar-Zero LCC north of Cooperstown was spared the wrecking ball."

"Could Oscar-Zero be Milton's port of entry for GRAY WOLF?"

"It is a possibility, but an unlikely one," Herbolt said.

"The state historical society stepped in and restored the Cooperstown LCC, a half-million dollars in state and federal grants. They restored everything but a nuclear-tipped Minuteman. I'm told they have a healthy tourist business, a surprisingly robust visiting population daily."

"What is your *working theory* on what Mr. Busey sold GRAY WOLF?" Turpin asked.

"Information about an underground passage to one or more of six Launch Control Capsules," Herbolt said. "It makes sense on a lot of levels and would explain how GRAY WOLF avoided surveillance."

"Six LCCs," Turpin sighed.

"It is a complex and convoluted path we take to the six, but we are confident. If they inhabit an LCC, it will be one of the six we've identified."

"Why not a surgical strike on those six and we all go home?" Tony asked.

"If we are wrong and GRAY WOLF is somewhere else; our action could potentially trigger a disasterous response. GRAY WOLF could send a Minuteman III nuclear missile anywhere in the world and start World War III. The POTUS will not risk it. We must know who we are dealing with and where they are."

"GRAY WOLF cannot allow us to talk to Milton Busey," Turpin said.

"Our intelligence confirms GRAY WOLF operatives are crawling all over the Keys looking for the man. Now they'll be watching for you two, for the reason you just said."

"Not a big surprise, Herbolt," Tony said, checking his gun.

"I understand. Here's some backstory that may give you more insight on who you're dealing with down there. We believe Roan Busey had one job: to deliver his father's expertise to GRAY WOLF, no questions asked. The man drove a tow truck. He visited his dad at Pingree once a week. No one thought to watch them. When GRAY WOLF had what they needed—"

"—Roan was tossed into a garbage compactor," Tony said.

"He was executed and Milton was scheduled to be executed at Pingree in a less obvious manner, probably by lethal injection not given by the state," Herbolt said. "But GRAY WOLF miscalculated—not something criminals at that level do often. They did not anticipate the power of their disgruntled employee network."

"Troubled people talk," Turpin said.

"Nobody pays enough attention to the worker bees," Tony said.

"Roan's *execution news* traveled fast. When London got it, the next calls were to Pingree. GRAY WOLF was just a few minutes behind each phone call. Turns out Dr. Frank Rice, the Pingree Psychiatrist, was ready to give Milton something to help his anxiety. The syringe found in Rice's dead, frozen hand was cyanide. It explains how Rice could afford a new Lexus. They found $400,000 in his house. We suspect he got offered a lot more to give Milton his shot."

"Milton turned the tables in Pingree. It only irritated GRAY WOLF," Tony said.

"We know now someone paid for the relocation of Bowman, Weller & Garcia from Kansas City to Key West. GRAY WOLF had launched a contingency plan before the Roan execution. They did have something in place should Milton somehow slip through the cracks. Turned out, their backup plan bought them more time. We hope that's all it bought them."

Turpin cleared his throat as they popped out of the clouds. He saw Key West International on the horizon. "Thank you for the backstory, James. I do believe we are set for the challenge ahead. We know GRAY WOLF is sufficiently motivated to keep us away from Milton Busey. And we know they are resourced."

"If GRAY WOLF makes a wrong move, you will know down there," Herbolt said. "I wish you both God's speed. This is a dark day in America. Goodbye."

The speaker popped off. Tony flipped the toggle and unplugged the headset. "You carryin', Harry?"

"Of course." Turpin lifted his coat revealing a black-leather shoulder holster and 357 Magnum revolver. "Among other things, my cane is equipped with a Cobra Arms Derringer. The handle releases here."

"Nice."

"Coat and vest are a tightly woven Kevlar—my newest experiment, I suppose. Certainly a man of your prowess knows the properties of para-aramid synthetic fibers—Nomex and Technora. I am told it will reduce impact and penetration when a projectile with my name on it finds me. They say it will stop a sniper's bullet, although I may be unconscious a while."

"Wonderful. A Kevlar suit. What next?" Tony looked down at his .45 caliber Glock. He slid it into his shoulder holster. "I only have this and four clips."

"Bloody lot of bullets to carry. Are you a bad shot, Anthony?" Turpin asked, amused.

The Dassault Falcon jolted and burned rubber as the wheels kissed the tarmac at Key West International. "Let's just say I like to shoot people, Harry."

Tony turned his first smile since Bismarck to the window, and Harold watched it fade in the glass. They understood their impossible mission. They would not be leaving Key West.

CHAPTER **24**

"You cannot find peace by avoiding life."
Virginia Woolf

Washington D.C., 1030 EDT

For most, an invitation to the Oval Office and audience with the President is a memorable experience. For the few, it is hell.

"I stand on the precipice of the most consequential decision a United States President could face, a decision that might decide the fate of our nation and the world."

Cabinet members had been summoned to the Oval Office, along with top military and national security advisors and selected experts in specific technologies. All were involved in the development, evolution, and management of the most destructive military force the world has ever seen—the Nuclear Triad.

On a cold winter morning, some of the few had stepped away from the Situation Room beneath the West Wing. They had walked through the "beehive"—the Tactical Command Center—to the next level of the nightmare that awaited them upstairs. A few others had sat alone in back seats of limousines as their drivers navigated the frozen streets and ignorant masses on their dreaded routes from the Pentagon, Joint Bases Anacostia-Bolling, Langley, and Fort Meade.

When they met in the Oval Office, they waited in quiet trepidation. The few knew the abominable secret now kept from the world. They knew their homeland, their family, and their friends now faced a greater threat than Pearl Harbor and

September 11. They knew if they failed this time, the death toll will be measured in millions.

President Landon sat behind the giant *Resolute Desk* with his trembling fist pressed hard against his thigh. The stress of the terminal breach had exacerbated his concealed medical condition. His advisors had said a POTUS must project strength in a dangerous world—but now he knew none of that mattered. He had refused his regimen of drugs a second day, and his condition was declining. The side effects of the medication were unacceptable at a time like this. Landon's early-stage Parkinson's would have to wait. As long as GRAY WOLF held the country hostage, Landon had to keep a clear head.

"Information I share may be new to some," the President said. "To others, maybe not. Regardless, I will be brief with my opening comments and swift to my purpose. I am confident you will find a way to keep up."

He panned the room with the chiseled face of a fearless leader. All eyes locked onto his, to bathe in courage. "Thirty-two hours ago, an unknown entity crossed the Canadian border and commandeered two—we believe—of our Launch Control Capsules in Minot, North Dakota. That alone is an extraordinary accomplishment," he said shaking his head. "These LCCs have authority over twenty silos. Each silo is the home of a Minuteman III Intercontinental Ballistic Missile, the most destructive weapon in the world."

He measured the room with his gaze a second time, to read in their expressions how many were strong and how many weak. "Based on your knowledge of the Nuclear Triad, I will dispense with the commentary on the order and magnitude of devastation to be realized should this occupation of our nuclear assets continue unabated.

"We have a terminal breach," Landon said. "This level of hostile penetration comes with its own set of rules of engagement and operational controls." With his good hand, he opened the leather binder in front of him and gripped the first page as if it were the only copy of the Dead Sea Scrolls. "Thirty-two hours later, we still do not know the identity of our invader—the one we call GRAY WOLF. Thirty-two hours into this situation, we still do not know their numbers, locations, capabilities, or intentions. But we are assuming their intentions are not good."

Only Landon's eyes left the page. He watched some heads drop and some of the officials squirm in their seats. The failure of any one of them might determine the fate of all. "Prior to the first contact by GRAY WOLF, we detected random manipulations of silo-door hydraulics. Prior to the second contact, we detected blast doors for two LCCs open and close. GRAY WOLF had our attention. Then they sent demands. They ordered us to evacuate all missile silos, all Launch Control Capsules, and all support facilities within one hour."

Landon leaned back in his chair and scowled. "They threatened to send one of our missiles into Canada, should we fail to comply—to demonstrate their capabilities. We did not believe they could do that. My experts told me our systems and procedures are too complex. Failsafe protections would prevent such a launch. Access codes change, procedures change. GRAY WOLF cannot launch one of our missiles.

"I made the decision to reject GRAY WOLF's demands. I was told the Minuteman III was designed to hit distant targets, those greater than 3,500 miles away. To hit a target a few hundred miles away, the changes in thrust, trajectory, stage jettisons, pitches and rolls, re-entry, warhead arming, and detonation were too complex to orchestrate. They would be impossible for GRAY WOLF to navigate. The Canada threat revealed their cards. GRAY WOLF was bluffing, I thought.

"Halfway into the allocated hour to comply-or-else, GRAY WOLF opened the silo doors of an intermediate-range ballistic missile. Opened them five damn inches. We have only two MRBMs. Both are off the grid. GRAY WOLF found one for Canada. I don't need to tell anyone in this room ... the depth of their knowledge is chilling. They found one in an 8,500 square mile area with 150 silos."

"We have a mole," the Secretary of Defense said under his breath.

CIA Director James Herbolt cleared his throat, addressing the room. "The President is right to be concerned about GRAY WOLF's familiarity with classified defense protocol and locations of specific assets," he said. "Prior to GRAY WOLF, six months of investigation put the mole at the Minot Air Force Base, 91st Wing Command. However, the trail ended there. We have been looking ever since."

"Mr. President, may I speak?" asked Major General Winston Gregory. Landon approved with his eyes. All heads turned. "In the last twenty-four hours, there have been developments. Hydraulic manipulations at the High Tech A-7 and Viking A-9 sites opened new avenues of investigation—and intensified our search for this mole. Due to the sensitive nature of the times, I have limited communications on this matter to Chief General Jamison and the 91st Wing Airmen who shined new light on this investigation. We believe the success GRAY WOLF enjoys is due to this mole manipulating our systems from inside the Command Center at Minot Air Force Base. We believe locating and then manipulating the mole may help us find GRAY WOLF."

The President sat up with renewed vigor. "General Gregory's work will not be discussed outside these doors," he said.

"Thank you," said the General. "This effort is only one of many underway to identify, contain, and remove GRAY WOLF, sir."

"The reason I asked all of you here is to address an aspect of the terminal breach, one that causes me great concern. I refer to the automated containment option."

"The computer take-over triggered by the degree of breach?" the Vice President asked.

"Yes. My gravest concern at this juncture is GRAY WOLF triggers a horrific action by mistake. I cannot leave it to a computer to distinguish between a hapless error and an intensified threat. I cannot let a computer launch an unapproved, devastating *containment option* response," Landon said. "Therefore, I am ordering the immediate deactivation of the terminal breach automated override."

"I'm not sure you want to do that, sir," said the Secretary of Defense.

"Convince me, Frank," the POTUS said.

"We are talking about taking our most powerful weapon off the table. Our network of the most sophisticated supercomputers in the world can process more variables faster than is humanly possible. Their computational capacity is so immense, it is measured in floating-point operations per second—FLOPS—instead of millions of instructions per second—MIPS. Our systems perform up to a hundred-quadrillion assessments and operations instantly. If we turn that off, we might miss an important piece of information and lose everything, sir. The use of supercomputers gives us a timing advantage. It can figure out better than we can what is coming, based on what is here."

"Frank, a lot of smart people are monitoring everything from Minot to the Pentagon," the President replied. "The Situation Room is assessing real-time information and military options, and deploying them accordingly even as we speak. Montana and Wyoming have missiles pointed at Minot. We have mobilized forces. We are ready to shoot a Minot-based missile out of the sky at launch—God forbid it comes to that."

"What's the international impact, Mr. President?" the Vice President asked.

"The State Department has opened lines with every nation in the world and they stand ready to evaluate changes in interests, and unusual activities. They have set the stage for negotiations, should they become necessary. Our Intelligence Services are at work here and abroad, identifying aberrations in behavior and foiling efforts suspected to be even remotely connected to this unidentified provocateur.

"The top forensic minds are closing in on the identity of GRAY WOLF. Even the news media has been successfully kept outside this crisis. All this is necessary, and it's been accomplished by a lot of people who love this country. As your President, I cannot allow a supercomputer to make the decision only a President of the United States should make. I will not allow a supercomputer to press the button!"

"Mr. President, GRAY WOLF has been silent for twenty-eight hours," said Major General Gentry. "This could mean they have been unsuccessful with their efforts to access any aspect of our missile control complex."

"Or it could mean they have found a way to penetrate our shields without us knowing it, Winston," the President added.

"Let me be perfectly clear. I am not abandoning the use of our supercomputers. I am only taking away their authorities to *initiate a nuclear strike*. That decision capability *must* be deleted now. All breach assessments by our supercomputers are to be brought to me and a team of military and technology advisors. At that time, I will determine the nature and extent of the threat, and only then will I decide the countermeasures to be taken. Is this understood by everyone?"

"Understood, Mr. President," said the room in unison.

"I want this in effect ASAP," said the POTUS. "Frank, handle it. No missteps."

"Yes, sir," Frank said. "I will implement immediately and advise, sir."

President Landon got to his feet and rounded his desk. "We will prevail, ladies and gentlemen. I want each of you to keep the faith. GRAY WOLF will be stopped. I thank each of you for your wisdom, your counsel, and your service to our country. Now let's all get back to work."

"Thank you, Mr. President." The words flowed in a steady stream as the experts filed out of the Oval Office just as they had entered: uncertain but determined to do their best.

As the Major General neared the President on his exit path, their eyes met. Landon's lips did not move. He whispered, "Stay back with me, Winston."

CHAPTER 25

"The road up and the road down are one and the same."
Heraclitus

Key West, 1130 EDT

The fresh plywood oozed amber sap. The board replaced the shattered storefront window beneath the swinging sign —Bowman, Weller & Garcia Law Offices. Two days had passed since the morning of mayhem in Margaritaville. Now, speculation and fear floated along the sidewalks and wafted into the eateries in the small resort town on the tip of Florida. Even the tourists stopped at the grisly crime scene for a family picture. No one knew why a sniper would shoot into law offices. And what kind of sick monster cuts throats and kidnaps lawyers?

The Sun Tribune had dedicated their front page to the carnage on Caroline. The bizarre blood bath soon became the most riveting story in Key West since Count Karl von Cosel slept with the murdered corpse of Elena Hoyos Mesa, which had happened in 1940. Newspapers flew off the stands and radio talk shows stirred the locals as the bloody grip of terror tightened. It was like the plot of a dreadful Hemmingway novel: Something horrible now lurked in the shadows of paradise. The glowing streets of *Shangri-La* were no longer safe. Who would be the next? How many had to die before Key Westers were told the truth? In spite of the denizen turmoil and demands for answers, the Monroe County Sheriff Mack Malone and Chief Medical Examiner Dan Hayes remained tight-lipped.

Their return to Key West could not remain unnoticed,

regardless of stealth efforts. Tony Wilcox and Harold Turpin had no other choice. Time was running out, and they had their marching orders: Find Milton Busey.

They knew the GRAY WOLF operatives in the Keys would be formidable, despite the setbacks they'd encountered off the coast of Cuba. Although it seemed there were no survivors, and the evidence had been obliterated and scattered across the expanse of the Atlantic Ocean, a last radio transmission from the target had been intercepted. Their dire circumstance had been communicated. Reinforcements were on their way. Then the Hellfire missiles struck.

GRAY WOLF might have made one miscalculation. They seemed to think the dying serial killer caged at Pingree posed zero threat to their mission. GRAY WOLF thought they could take the information they needed from Milton Busey and dispose of his outside man—his son, Roan Busey. GRAY WOLF was certain Pingree and a terminal medical condition would contain and dispose of Milton. And to be sure, they sent Frank Rice in with a special shot to calm his nerves forever. GRAY WOLF did not consider that their *insurance policy* would be Milton's ticket out of Pingree and into their world like an invisible swarm of army ants.

They did not consider that killing the son of a dying serial killer would give a man a reason to live. GRAY WOLF had killed and mutilated the body of Roan Busey, and they had failed to make their last (substantial) payment *for services rendered.* GRAY WOLF had broken two of Milton Busey's three rules. Even the devil has guidelines.

They had relocated the law firm as a precaution. They had sent a sniper to Key West for damage control. Now, at great expense, they had to contract a small army of independent thugs to locate, terminate, and dispose of their tactical error. If Milton Busey was still alive in the Keys, GRAY WOLF operatives had orders to stop Busey and everyone with an interest in the man. That included the Monroe County Sheriff's Office, the FBI, Wilcox and Turpin.

Wilcox parked their nondescript Tahoe five blocks from the Bowman, Weller & Garcia Law Firm and the two men eased into the flow of tourists on Caroline. Turpin would investigate the sniper nest and Wilcox the law office. They would rendezvous across from the Marine Supply Emporium to review surveillance video of the crime scene, compare notes, and move on.

Two blocks from the crime scene, Wilcox and Turpin left the crowd to go their separate ways. They would use the network of alleys, staying in the shadows of the tall fences, brick walls, and thick, tropical foliage. In the steamy shadows, they dodged puddles, garbage and rats.

Tony wove through the trackless maze to the dark side of the crime scene. When he saw the old, two-story building ahead, he backed up to a fence and hid in the foliage like a Navy Seal. He waited five minutes to see if he had been followed.

He saw the empty parking spaces next to the back door. *Had Bowman parked there? Is that how Milton Busey got away so fast?* Tony saw the green plastic garbage cans lying on their sides. They were empty. The sheriff would have bagged everything. They would have taken the trash for close inspection, often a treasure-trove of clues. Then Tony saw the aged algae that painted the rotten wood frame around the new, black metal door. *All of you guys knew he was coming. The only thing new here is the impenetrable metal door. You wanted him to come in the front. You guys knew about the sniper.*

Tony left the fence and approached the metal door. When he arrived, he froze on the rubber doormat, which was covered in slimy scum with a cloud of gnats. Tony stared at the fat yellow tape—the official line of demarcation between the authorized and unauthorized. Over the years, crime scene tape had served him well. It preserved evidence for a homicide detective. Unexpected clues were the keys to solving a mystery. Tony knew he had to go inside.

This time, he stood on the wrong side of the yellow tape, the wrong side of the symbol of his lifelong commitment to convention and the law. If he crossed the line, he would commit a crime. Tony had no legal right to enter an active crime scene, but he also did not have the time or patience to educate the Monroe County Sheriff's Office. They could not be told the reason for his mission. He had to find Milton Busey. Time was not on his side.

Tony lifted the yellow tape with the back of his hand and picked the lock. Seven seconds later, he opened the black metal door with an elbow and stepped into the god-awful familiar smell of a fresh kill. He followed the blood up the back stairs to the private offices where the two lawyers had been butchered. Tony walked in the dark through the stench. He would stay in the hallway. This time, he would honor the yellow tape on the office doorways. Only his light beam would violate the secured crime scene and explore the remnants of death.

He watched the same horror movie he had seen hundreds of times before—but this time, the bodies were gone. This time, the dead were not left in position, untouched and ready for the top Memphis homicide detective's inspection. This time, the victims had been removed, leaving behind only outlines on the floor. The dead were tucked in bed on a gurney in the Monroe County morgue. But Tony had not come to see the bodies. He wasn't there to solve a multiple homicide case. Tony had come to find that single, unexpected clue that would take him to Milton Busey.

Crusted splashes of brown and maroon hung on the walls like a twisted kind of modern art. The warped, wooden floors held coagulated pools of blood, as well as overturned furniture and scattered papers and shattered debris. Desperate battles for life had been lost here. Milton Busey had surgically released most of the blood both men possessed. It had sprayed like a firehose from their butchered bodies. Busey's knife had found all the major bleeders—the aortic, femoral, jugular vein, and carotids. They were each slashed open in seconds. The two lawyers had no time to be stunned. They dropped like rotten trees in a stiff wind. Paralysis came in seconds, death in minutes.

The carnage on the second floor of BW&G told Tony more about the man he hunted than the victims he had killed. Milton Busey cared about respect, money, and family. The rage in evidence on the second floor had transformed legal offices into a slaughter house. Tony learned he hunted an angry man, one who (this time) had put *family* at the top of his list.

The decision to split up with Turpin had two purposes. Two investigators moving in independent directions could cover more ground—and for Tony, spending less time with a doddering old Brit would speed things up. The retired Scotland Yard profiler shared a similar bias. Turpin had little use for yet another arrogant American homicide detective. He would find the sniper nest, assess its value to the mission, and meet the self-absorbed twit at the souvenir shop across from the Marine Supply Emporium as agreed. They would tolerate each other while they reviewed surveillance video.

Tony descended the narrow staircase to the first floor. He walked into the open room where the shooting had occurred. He stood at the back of the room and took it in with a slow flashlight beam. He saw the stacked boxes along the back, the law books nobody had had time to put on the shelves, and the two desks, each with a keyboard and computer monitor. Chairs lined the north wall, on either side of an empty fish tank.

Tony spotted a small hole in the plywood that had replaced the shattered storefront window. He went to it and peeked through. He could see straight up Telegraph Lane, the road that dead-ended into the law office on Caroline. He found two ideal locations for a sniper—the rooftop over the Key West Aloe Company on Telegraph and rooftop above Kino Plaza on Greene, three blocks away.

As Tony mulled over the possibilities, Harold Turpin popped out from an alley and strode into the center of Telegraph Lane. Tony watched the bumbling Brit in his three-piece suit. Turpin spun around and aimed his cane at BW&G.

My God, you fool, are you pretending that is a rifle? Streaming tourists parted to avoid the daft Englishman, like water parting around a rock in a stream. *That's it. I just made my decision. No way you're going to the hospital with me. I'll interview Ramsey alone. I do not need you doing something stupid like this, something that shuts the girl up tight as a clam. She's the last person to see Busey alive, and she could give some insight into the less-obvious practices of BW&G—*

Tony turned back to the room to escape the idiocy he had just witnessed in the streets. He grunted as his flashlight beam found the desk and computer monitor likely used by Helen Ramsey—the only desk with a letter holder and a flower in a vase. *That's where you met the monster,* he thought. Tony pulled a chair over to the left side of the desk—the scuffed section of the wood floor, the place where Busey likely sat in the beginning. All new clients must answer questions before they are assigned to a lawyer.

You sat there, Tony thought. *And Miss Ramsey sat behind the desk. She was at the keyboard looking at her monitor. She was asking you basic questions legal secretaries ask—who are you, where do you live, and why are you here?*

Tony sat in Busey's chair, his back to the storefront window. Tony rested his right arm on Ramsey's desk. *You sat in this chair in the beginning. You are outside a sniper's line of fire here. Did you know they were gunning for you, Milton? Or was it just habit?*

"You could not see her monitor, could you Milton?" he

whispered as he dropped the beam from the desk to his feet. *You played the information game. I bet you struggled to answer her questions because you don't have a life, Milton, and because you sure as hell did not want to reveal your true history—you sick bastard.*

But even more important, you didn't want to stir things up with a gatekeeper. You did not want Ramsey to sense trouble, to press a buzzer or call the police or alert the people you came to kill. You drove all the way to Key-damn-West from North-damn-Dakota to kill the people who killed your son, and to get the money they owed you. We can't forget about the money, can we? That's why your sick-ass is still down here. You gotta get the money, even if it gets you killed. I love the rationale of worms like you. Milton Busey can kill and screw with people, but they sure as hell are not permitted to kill or screw with you and yours.

Tony rolled his eyes and got back to the narrative. *You sat here all polite as you please. You didn't want to spook the horses in the corral. You don't know where those lawyers are yet. They could be off at a meeting somewhere and due back any minute. Or they could be upstairs, working behind locked doors with all sorts of alarm systems and cameras. Nope. Miss Ramsey's gotta help you bait the trap. She's gotta tell you where they are or bring them to you, because you're a new-damn-client. That's what you were thinkin' Milton.*

Tony moved his beam up the side of Helen Ramsey's chair. *Was she a pretty lady, Milton? Bet any woman would be pretty to you. You've been in prison for a long time. I bet you got side-tracked checking her out, you old dog. Is that why she had time to load all your data and have the system do its search?*

Damn! It found you, Milton. When she saw you had killed a man and that you broke out of prison a few days ago, I bet her eyes got big as saucers. Shit! A monster's sittin' right next to her, one wanted by the FBI. Poor Helen Ramsey, Tony thought. *She couldn't help reacting to the alert on her screen.*

What'd she do, Milton? Did she just get up and pretend she had enough information to go get you one of those lawyers you wanted to kill? Your guard was down, Milton. When she got to her feet, it broke your X-rated trance. You jumped up and grabbed her, didn't you?

Tony got up and reached for an imaginary Ramsey. He moved behind her desk to get a look at the screen, the way Milton would have. Then he aimed his flashlight toward the window. It hit the center of the plywood, the little hole. *Now you're exposed, you bastard. You're in the sniper's scope. Did you feel it, Milton? Or was there a flash of light on one of those rooftops that tipped you off? You had walked into a trap. The lawyers you came to kill knew you were comin'.*

Your instincts kicked in—survival, for God's sake. You knew you had a fraction of a second to react or die. You pulled Ramsey in front of you. She would be your human shield. You reacted like a damn terrorist. Boom! The poor lady takes your bullet you sorry son of a—

"Who are you?" The three words cut through the dark like a knife. Wilcox came back to his senses and the present moment.

"Answer, dead man." The next words were from someone else.

The overhead light popped on—the light Tony had left off on purpose. When he slow-turned his head, he saw the two gun barrels pointed at him, twenty feet away.

"Don't shoot," Tony said. "I'm a private investigator working a case. I know I shouldn't be in here, but the back door was open. I can show you credentials."

"You may not show us shit," said the wiry, sandy-haired man in the black t-shirt. His arms were wrapped in tattoos from his wrists into his shirt sleeves and out his collar up his neck. He approached with his gun in both hands and barrel pointed at Tony's head. "If you move one hair, I will shoot you." The other man, who wore a beige Panama suit, stayed in the back with his gun aimed at Tony. Dark hair, clean-shaven, and more polished, he watched his partner—Tattoo Boy—remove a Glock and four clips from Tony's body.

"Damn, you gotta be plannin' on shootin' a lot of people," Tattoo Boy said.

"No," Tony said. "It's standard. I can explain."

Tattoo Boy touched the tip of his gun to Tony's nose and smiled. "Back your ass to the plywood and pray I don't slip on any of this shit. I'd hate to get your brains on me."

Tony backed up with his hands still at his sides. "Why is the Tony Wilcox of Spyglass Investigations interested in Milton Busey?" asked the Panama suit as he lowered his gun.

"So you know me," Tony said. "I've been hired by Pingree Correctional Center. Milton Busey killed a prison doctor and escaped. They heard about these killings and asked me to take a closer look."

"Really," said the suit as Tattoo Boy snarled a few feet away with the gun. "So you are looking for Milton Busey. Tell me. You were a homicide detective for twenty-plus years in Memphis. You've seen a lot of crime scenes. You know how to put things together. What does this tell you about where Milton Busey might be?"

"Who *are* you guys?" Tony asked. "Put down the guns and we can talk."

"We're askin' the questions," Tattoo Boy bellowed.

"Shut up, Randy," the suit cried.

"I don't think we should be usin' real names, Billy," Randy said.

"Right." He rolled his eyes. "Where was I? You asked who we are. We are independent contractors like you. Then you suggested we put down our guns. Well, that's not gonna happen. You and I have met before."

"What are you talkin' about?" Tony asked.

"You don't remember?"

"No. I've never seen you in my life."

"You used karate or jujitsu on me. Driveway. Little house on Juanita a few nights ago."

"You got me mixed up with someone else," Tony said. *You're the guys tracking Elliott. Your people killed Penland. You gotta be workin' for GRAY WOLF, if you even know who it is.*

"We don't mix shit up, Wilcox," said Tattoo Boy, waving his gun like a finger.

"You were with Elliott Sumner," the Panama suit said.

"We lost him because of you, asshole."

"Randy, I told you to put a lid on it."

"Look, I don't know what you're talkin' about," Tony said. "I just got here. I'm working a case for Pingree—simple as that." He rubbed his face and watched the suit lean in. "Okay, you asked what I see here. I see a setup, everything staged. This blood looks like cow blood—way too much. I think these attorneys faked the whole thing. I don't believe Busey was here. Nothing adds up. This is a scam. It's fraud. These lawyers are running from someone. I suspect they have money and information someone wants back, maybe the people you work for. I suggest you look for the lawyers and not be fooled by this set-up. Could be a big payday for you."

"We watched them take two bodies out of here, Detective Wilcox," said the suit. "This was not staged. Milton Busey gutted two and took one with him."

"Did you see the bodies? I don't think so. You saw two body bags with something in them—probably garbage. Note the empty cans around here. You think one sick old man could overpower two young lawyers and make this mess? I'm telling you, this crime scene is fake. Who told you Busey was here, anyway? Who are you working for?"

"Our client is not up for discussion."

"Okay. I can respect that," Tony said. "If I am messing up your case, I'm sorry. I will leave and stay out of your way. No harm done. None of us should get caught in here, because it's still an active crime scene and it would be a felony being here. Or, this could be a trap set by the Monroe County Sheriff's Office. They left the back door open."

"Nice try. This is no trap. The back door lock was picked. You must think we're idiots. Sorry Wilcox, harm has been done. You are here, and that's not good."

"Yeah. You're here to find Busey too, you lyin' piece of—"

"Randy. Shut up, please! There's plenty of time for that when I'm done." The Panama suit set his gun on the edge of Ramsey's desk and ran a finger over the top of the monitor. "You know where Milton Busey is hiding. You studied this crime scene and got something."

"I got that Milton Busey was not here," Tony said.

"You are a lyin' son-of-a-bitch," Randy puffed. "Let me shoot him, Billy. This loser cop is a total waste. We need to go find and shake down that old guy, the one pokin' around Telegraph with the cane. He's the brains of this operation."

"You know you saw stuff here, detective," the suit prodded. "Just talk to me."

"Okay. I saw some stuff," Tony said with his eyes locked on Tattoo Boy.

"If you tell me what you got, I can let you go—no harm done."

Tony snickered at Tattoo Boy. *It will take two seconds, even with a bullet in me. I can spin your fat head, break your neck, and watch you hit the floor before I die.*

He turned back to the suit. In the periphery, he found the gun on the edge of Ramsey's desk two seconds away. *You're tempting me. You want me to go for it. A cold-blooded execution is not how you want to do me.* "You want me to tell you what happened here, Billy?"

"Yeah. I want you to tell me the truth."

"Are you sure you can handle the truth?"

"I want to know what you learned from this crime scene, homicide detective."

"I learned you and Tattoo Boy over there do not want to find Milton Busey," Tony said. Randy jumped toward him, enraged, with his gun cocked.

"Goddamn it! Back up, Randy. Tell me more, Wilcox."

"Milton is a professional. He has killed a lot of people. He's a serial killer—loves the art of the kill. You know what I learned upstairs? I learned Milton is not only efficient with a knife; he is one pissed-off guy. He has the knowledge, skills, and anger to kill anyone who gets near him. You might think you could outsmart this old man by putting a bullet between his eyes. You might think you can just walk up and kick his dead carcass and collect your money. This man kills people like you and Tattoo Boy in his sleep."

"Are you tryin' to scare me, Wilcox?"

"He found every vital artery in two men's bodies before they could make a move. He sliced open the aorta, jugular, femoral, and carotid arteries in both men with six moves in less than four seconds."

"That's four arteries in two men, dumb ass," Tattoo Boy scoffed. "That's gotta take at least eight moves, stupid."

"Right, Tattoo Boy. You got great math skills."

"You think that's gonna stop us, Wilcox?" The Panama suit said as a single drop of sweat left his hairline and hit his eyebrow.

"No," Tony said. "I don't think anything I say will stop you two imbeciles. I'm just a homicide detective from a major city who has hunted these monsters all my life. What do I know? You know what I really think? I think the people you work for are going to stop you, Billy. They're going to kill you and Randy whether you get Milton Busey or not. Either way, you boys are dancin' with the devil."

"You don't know what you're talkin' about," Billy shot back.

"We know the people you work for, Billy. We know them better than you do. I'm working for the federal government. Your employer's got the attention of the President of the United States, dumbass. Your employer is more dangerous than you could begin to imagine. Right now, we've collected a pile of bodies from a blood trail that began in Turkey. It goes through London into Canada, North Dakota, and now Key West, Florida. They don't just kill the people they don't like, Billy. They kill their private contractors when they're done with 'em."

"You're making this shit up."

"And they mutilate them—cut off their heads and arms and legs, and they're still not done. They throw all your parts into an industrial garbage compactor. They turn independent contractors into big bloody cubes of crushed human flesh. Then they put that block of death in the woods to feed the goddamn animals, Billy. Brilliant. No forensic evidence. Poof. Believe me when I say, I couldn't make this kind of shit up."

"Nice bedtime story, Wilcox. I guess you'll say anything to save your skin. You don't know who we're workin' for, and it doesn't matter if the President of the universe is involved. We have our job to do. Thanks for the info. Your life ends here."

"Are you sure I don't know what I'm talkin' about, Billy?" Tony asked. "Are you sure you don't want to be put into protective custody until we stop the assholes you work for?"

"Can I kill him now?" Randy asked, raising his gun. "Let's end this line of bullshit and go find the English dude. He'll take us to Busey. This dumb cop's got nothin'."

"You know, if I were you, I'd probably try not to think about the information I just gave you for free. Yeah, I would assume I don't know the assholes who hired you. I know the money is outrageous. But do you really think they'd pay you that money for killing some old man? You have had your doubts from the beginning, Billy. You're not stupid like Tattoo Boy. You also know a boatload of badass partners disappeared somewhere between Key West and Cuba."

"They went to Miami," Billy shot back. "That was the plan."

"Right. Keep telling yourself that. Don't you think it odd you've never heard back from them? They're gone, Billy. I watched their boat get blown out of the water by a U.S. Coast Guard Helicopter's missile. Do you really think they blow things up for the hell of it? Your boss is on a major shit list, the kind where our military shoots first and asks questions *never*. You'd best hide after you kill a retired homicide detective working for the president, dude."

"It's time for you to go," Billy said. Randy moved toward Tony with a smile and gun.

"If you two morons want to live, I suggest you put down your guns and put your hands on the top of your thick skulls. This is a one-time offer."

"You're nuts. Why would we do that?" Billy chuckled.

"If you do not comply, Mr. Turpin will kill you where you stand."

The Panama suit and Tattoo Boy turned. Harold Turpin stood in the doorway, his cane gripped over his shoulder like a spear ready to fly.

Pull out your gun, Tony sighed. *What in the hell are you thinkin' ...?*

Tattoo Boy turned his gun on Wilcox and Billy reached for his gun on the edge of the desk.

CHAPTER 26

"If the enemy is in range, so are you."
Unknown

Turpin's ebony cane flew across the room like a torpedo. Before Tattoo Boy could react, it pierced his shoulder and pinned him to the plywood nailed in the window frame. Tony slapped the gun from his hand and pressed it against Randy's head. When Tony turned back to Turpin, the Panama suit was spread-eagle on the floor and the Brit was dropping an extra gun into his coat pocket.

"Glad you could make it, Harry," Tony said.

"Harold. Please. I suggest you focus on the unpinning of the gentleman with the ink," Turpin said as he assisted Billy to Helen Ramsey's chair. "And you, sir. Should you twitch in the slightest, I shall be forced to hurt you terribly—possibly ending your wretched life. I am otherwise not a violent man."

Billy nodded with his hands clasped behind his neck.

The cane pinned Tattoo Boy's shoulder, the razor-sharp tip wedged into the plywood. Blood ran down his chest. "I think this one's gonna die," Tony said over the moans. "You're like a big insect in a shitty bug collection. You've gotta be the ugliest one I've ever seen."

Turpin punched a number into his phone and held it to his ear. "Yes. Turpin. Yes. We have two scoundrels. I suggest a discrete van of some sort to the rear of the building. You know the address. There is a small alley, trees, and that obnoxious tropical shrubbery everywhere."

With a wrenching motion that made both men gasp, Tony unpinned Tattoo Boy, removed the cane from the wound, and deposited Tattoo Boy onto a chair next to Billy. Turpin tossed a dusty rag. "Hold this on your little puncture wound or you can die a slow death," Tony said. "Really, either way works for me."

Turpin pocketed his cell. "They are sending a small moving van. We have ten minutes. Shall we torture these two now? Do they have anything for us, Anthony? You are the one who has spent time with them. I've only known them long enough to regain control of the situation you clearly lost."

Tony rolled his eyes and turned to their captives. "The CIA has ways to make terrorists talk. America does nasty things ... things the Brits cannot stomach." He turned back to Turpin. "You don't even let your cops carry guns, for God's sake."

"We ain't tellin' you shit," Tattoo Boy spewed.

Tony smacked the side of his head. "Shut up, Randy." *That felt good.* He turned to the Panama suit. "We're off the grid here, Billy. The people comin' to pick you up are off the grid too, and they're a lot meaner than us. There is some gargantuan shit going down right now. I'm talking national security nuclear shit that affects millions of lives. That makes you two less important than a couple of dung beetles carrying around a turd."

"They will step on you, and then hose you off their boots, sir," Turpin said.

"You now have nine minutes to convince Harry and me to put in a good word for you guys. If you choose to be the arrogant assholes I think you are, we will just say our goodbyes now and leave you for the CIA. No one will know you ever existed. The CIA makes sure people like you don't fuck up this country."

"Look, I don't know much," Billy said. "Don't leave us here."

"We'll be the judge of that," Tony said.

"I took on this job a few weeks ago. A friend of a friend said we could make fifty thousand bucks for sixty days of standby."

"Standby for what? And do not waste your eight minutes."

"Standby for this law firm. We were part of their back-up protection."

"Keep talkin'," Tony pushed.

"I didn't know much about the sniper. They brought him in from Detroit."

"Fine. Who hired you guys?" Tony asked.

"I was hired by Emily Bowman, one of the lawyers. I brought in Randy. I needed someone to watch my back. Randy doesn't know anything about the deal."

"Bringing this fruitcake along was your second mistake," Tony quipped.

"Fuck you," Randy shot back.

"Fuck you, Randy," Tony said as he poked the bloody rag with a finger.

"Can you please *shut up* Randy?" Billy said as he wiped his forehead. "Bowman gave me ten grand up front. She said they needed protection and we would get more instructions and the rest of the money at the end of the sixty days."

"When did you hear about the sniper?" Tony asked.

"It was a few days before the shooting, and the lawyers never told me. I have friends in the business. They passed on the contract. Said Detroit picked it up."

"Why'd your friends pass it up?" Tony asked.

"They said something about the whole setup stunk. There were outsiders involved."

"Outsiders?"

"Foreigners."

Tony turned to Turpin. "The timing of the sniper contract lines up with Pingree."

"It does," Turpin breathed.

"How did you rationalize a sniper in all this?" Tony asked. "Didn't that take your little financial arrangement to another place? It obviously was no longer about protection. It was about waiting and executing someone."

"Bowman said they had some really pissed-off clients in Kansas City—mob types. They made some heavy-duty threats. She said it got so bad they had to close their office up there. They came down here thinking they would be safe. I believed her. She said if these people followed them down here and got into their offices, a trained shooter would be their only defense. They leased the location on Caroline so they could be out in the open. Bowman said most international law firms keep protection like this. She said it's a dangerous world."

Turpin leaned closer to Billy's face. "You still did not find the arrangement and the story a tad bit peculiar?"

"Look. I get it. But the money was good. If I kept quiet and stayed low another forty-five days, I'd take home another forty grand. Easy money. I don't need to know all their problems."

"When did you first hear the name Milton Busey?" Tony asked.

"I heard it a day after the shooting on Caroline," Billy said.

"How?"

"I got a phone call from Bowman."

She's alive, Tony thought.

"Carry on," Turpin pushed.

"She was real upset," Billy said. "She felt terrible about what happened, their worst fears realized. Two of her partners dead. The hens came to roost. The shit hit the fan. The—"

"We get it," Tony barked.

"Bowman told me the bad people from Kansas City had followed them to Key West. She just happened to be coming in the back door when she heard two shots. She said she got back into her car and left. When she heard on the radio about her partners, she decided to stay in hiding."

"I'm sure she did," Tony said as he inserted clips into his belt, all the while staring at Tattoo Boy. *Make a move so I can hit you.* "Keep going."

"She seemed nervous on the phone," Billy said. "The killings pretty much ended my contract, I thought. She said she intended to pay the remainder of my retainer and even more if I would help her. She asked me to take on a new assignment, an additional twenty grand."

"And you believed she would actually pay you?" Tony asked.

"I was pretty sure I was screwed no matter what she said on the phone. I didn't have a clue how to find her, and I didn't think she had that kind of money hangin' around."

"So what happened to get you here?"

"She said I would get a phone call with instructions to pick up two suitcases at Key West International. One suitcase would not have a tag. Inside would be sixty grand for me. The other suitcase would have Milton Busey's name on a tag. Inside the *locked suitcase* were important papers and monies due Mr. Busey for services rendered."

"That's the first time you heard Busey's name?"

"Yeah. She said their law firm handled commission payments to contractors for an unnamed client. Milton Busey's commission had been sent to Cooperstown, North Dakota by mistake. She had to fix that as soon as possible."

"I bet she did." *With Milton holding a bloody knife to her neck,* Tony thought.

"She said the people who killed her partners would walk away when Busey's error was corrected. She had twenty-four hours."

"You were supposed to deliver the money to Milton Busey

down here?" Tony asked. "Did Bowman say when you'd get your instructions, the phone call?"

"Yeah. Today. She said I needed to pick up the suitcases and take Busey to Sunset Pier tonight after sundown."

Turpin lifted the bloody rag and checked Tattoo Boy's wound. "This does not appear too severe," he whispered. "However, there could be internal arterial complications—I'm not a physician. I suggest you continue pressure on the anterior wound. The posterior wound—the exit—appears to have slowed to a trickle."

"Why'd you come back here, Billy?" Tony demanded. "Don't lie to me."

"I was gonna look for money. I don't trust Bowman."

Tony turned to Turpin with his gun on Randy. "Harry, I just told the man not to lie to me. I gave him too much credit. I'm done."

"Yes. I do believe your assessment is an accurate one, sir," Turpin said.

"I'm tellin' the truth," Billy whined. "I've got no reason to be loyal to these people. They've done nothin' for me. They owe me money."

"You're lying!" Tony growled. "We're turning both of you over to the feds. You're a danger to society. I get no value here."

Turpin wiped the blood from his ebony cane. "And your friend made a terrible mess of my walking stick." Turpin slid a finger down the shaft and tapped a hidden button. The razor-sharp tip retracted with a snap. "I do believe I've grown to cherish discrete weaponry."

"And I don't like the foul-mouth of this punk terrorist," Tony said. You need to spend the rest of your sick life in a cell in Gitmo."

"No way," Tattoo Boy begged. "I'm not a terrorist." He looked at the floor. "I have anger issues. Ask Billy. I got one of those aggressive personalities. I say bad things. That's all. I don't do bad things. Look. I'll tell you the truth. I'll tell you why we were here."

Tony, who had turned his back on Randy, paused but did not turn back around. "Okay. Truth. One chance, Randy. Go."

"We came here for—"

"Shut up, Randy!" Billy shouted.

Tony spun around and addressed the tattooed man. "Ignore him," he said. "Talk. We'll let you go. He goes with CIA. I heard Gitmo is too good for the sickest shitheads. They're putting guys like you in intermodal freight containers now. You know, those truck-size containers stacked up on cargo ships. Yeah. They keep you in those. I heard they give you food and water, and you just get hauled around the ocean until you shrivel up and die. They hose out the container somewhere and wash your bones into the sea."

Randy swallowed hard. "Okay. Truth. We came to get the lady's address, the lady that got shot, the one in the hospital."

"Helen Ramsey?" Tony asked.

Randy looked around the room like the walls were closing in. "Yeah. Ramsey. We were gonna get her address and wait for her."

"Shut up, Randy!" Billy yelled.

"No, *you* shut up," Tony snarled. He yanked the cord off the computer monitor and tied Billy's hands, and then stuffed a bloody sleeve from Randy's torn shirt into his mouth.

"You were waiting for Ramsey—why?" Tony asked as Billy squirmed.

"We were supposed to get rid of her. When she got home from the hospital, we would be there. We would tie her up and drop her in the ocean a few miles out. The people didn't want her around. That's why we came here."

"Really?" Tony asked.

"Yeah," Tattoo Boy said.

"Just take her a few miles out in the ocean and dump her?"

"Yeah. Pretty slick way to get rid of someone."

Billy stopped squirming. With sizzling eyes he just stared at Randy.

"Dinner for one of those great whites, like in the movies," Tony said. "Very smart."

"Yeah." Randy smiled. "I thought it was smart, too. So I told you the truth, and now you know I can be trusted."

"Yes you can, Randy." Tony handed him his gun. Turpin smiled. Billy's eyes widened.

"We trust you Randy," Tony said. "Thank you for your honesty. You're with us now."

Tony turned back to Billy. "So you are going away for a while—"

Randy cocked the gun. Wilcox and Turpin slow turned to Tattoo Boy. Billy closed his eyes and shook his head. "You gotta be the stupidest cop in whole damn world," Randy crowed. He pressed his gun to Tony's nose. "You bought my whole lame-ass story. I lied. We were getting that Ramsey lady's address because that's—"

Billy kicked Randy. Randy pulled the gag out of his mouth. "Shut up, Randy!"

"You're right. Why tell two dead people where—"

Billy shook his head. "You stupid ass, the guns not—"

Randy pulled the trigger. The gun clicked on Tony's nose. Randy froze. Tony removed the empty gun from Randy's hand and punched him in the face. Tattoo Boy flopped back into the chair, unconscious.

"I really didn't think he was that stupid," Tony said. "I had to try."

Three CIA men came in the back door and froze with guns out. "Harold Turpin?"

"Yes, gentlemen. That would be me," Turpin said as he

passed credentials. "This is Anthony Wilcox—he is with me. And these are our prisoners, Billy and Randy. They will be departing with you.

"I might suggest you take the unconscious one first. Tie him tightly, sir. Relocate the scoundrel to a place far away from civilized society. I'm afraid he is a dangerous, hapless soul determined to hurt people. Unfortunately, the man is of scant intelligence value."

"What about the other one?" the CIA agent asked as his colleagues cuffed, gagged, and bagged Tattoo Boy, then carried him out like a rolled up rug.

"This is Billy," Tony said as he squeezed his shoulder and watched him wince. "We were on the fence with this one."

"Come on, man—"

Turpin lit his pipe in a cloud. "You are a heathen, sir."

Tony yanked him to his feet. He removed Billy's cell phone and tossed it to Turpin. "You guys can take him."

"Wait! Come on, don't. Wait a second!" Billy begged. The CIA agents flipped him onto his stomach and tied him. Tony and Turpin watched in silence as they poked the bloody rag back into the man's mouth and bagged him.

"Both are unprosecuted, self-confessed, cold-blooded killers," Tony said. "This one may have more info for you. After that, they won't be missed. Do what you do."

Minutes later, standing outside the metal door at the back of the law firm, they watched the unmarked white van pull away. It crawled down the narrow alley and disappeared into the lush tropical foliage. Turpin blew a smoke ring while keeping an eye on his pocket watch. "And what are your thoughts regarding the acquisition of Miss Ramsey's address?"

Tony watched Turpin pocket the watch and dip the bloody tip of his cane into a convenient mud puddle. "Interesting GRAY WOLF's southern contingency did not—"

"—have that address," Turpin said, nodding. "Someone dropped the proverbial ball."

"Maybe they didn't think that address was important," Tony said, feeling for his smokes.

"GRAY WOLF would not risk the deployment of untested independent contractors into an active crime scene," Turpin said. "Surely that would be unprofessional."

"I think these boys were working their own plan. I think they wanted Milton's money," Tony said. "They wanted both suitcases. I do believe—"

"—we just found Milton Busey," Turpin said.

"Busey knew Ramsey's place would be empty. It would be the ideal place—"

"—to hide," Turpin said.

"Milton has Bowman—leverage to get his money. Billy figured it out. He was gonna wait for the phone call. Get the suitcases at the airport. And he would go to Ramsey's house to kill Busey and Bowman—take care of all the loose ends so he could keep all the money."

"And Sunset Pier?" Turpin asked

"That's where Billy and Randy were supposed to transfer the money to Busey and get Bowman—an open place. I'm pretty certain GRAY WOLF will have people in place to eliminate all four of 'em. Doubt they care about Bowman or the money. It's about loose ends."

Tony passed a scribbled note with Ramsey's address. "She's still at Lower Keys Medical Center. Call your CIA contact and get them over there. They may try to eliminate her, too."

"They can watch our backs at the airport," Turpin said. "I'm too old for—"

"—this shit. I'm getting there too. Not a bad idea. I'm sure GRAY WOLF will have a shitload of twisted contractors like Billy and Randy runnin' around out there."

Tony lit a cigarette and dropped the match in the puddle of slime. "Nice work with the cane, Harry. I sure as hell did not factor in a spear-chucking skillset."

"Yes. Well. When you get to my age, you need something to keep the bloody edge. I'm slow, but have throwing strength. Must have practiced tossing it a hundred times before I could hit something."

The two chuckled in the empty alley. The steamy heat of the equatorial paradise would cut Tony's cigarette short. "I suggest we forget the surveillance video and go to the hospital. The phone call can come on Billy's phone at any time. I need air-damn-conditioning."

"We need to see Milton Busey," Turpin said. "We need more than a bloody photograph. You know, as an investigator, one must lift every stone."

"Well shit." The Scotland Yard sleuth was right.

They crossed Caroline and walked into *Treasures by the Sea*. The skinny, gray-headed hippy wearing shorts, a flower shirt, and sandals stood behind the counter. Eldon Frish had been sole proprietor of the cheap souvenir store for two decades.

"The Monroe County Sheriff's been here already," Frish said with an untrusting smile.

"I understand," Tony said. "I am a private investigator representing the Bowman, Weller & Garcia law firm." Tony spoke with a most proper and professional vocabulary, the one he rarely accessed. "We are conducting our own internal investigation."

"Internal investigation?" Frish queried.

"Yes. We are working in full cooperation with city and county law enforcement," Tony said. "As I am sure you can appreciate, the surviving members of the firm are still in shock. We were unable to mount an exploratory effort until now. We must understand this terrible tragedy. We need closure, Mr. Frish."

Turpin turned his smile and attention to a bobble away from Tony's pitch. "I understand. Of course," Frish said. "This must have been a terrible experience for all of you." He waved them to follow him to the back storeroom. They weaved between the bulging bookcases and boxes of cheap souvenirs made in China. "I never thought a surveillance camera would have value here. We live in a tourist town. Rarely do we have incidents. Maybe an occasional theft. Never worth the effort to apprehend.

"The camera feed out front was something my grandson decided to do. He's one of those IT geeks. I let him, to keep him involved in the business. I hope to leave it to him one day."

They approached an old computer monitor sitting in the middle of a cluttered desk in the darkest corner of the stuffy storeroom. "I think it's still set on the part that shows a man walking into the law offices. That part was real important to Sergeant Malone. He made a copy. Well, I guess he said only the important section. It starts here and goes for ten minutes or so."

Frish jiggled the mouse and the screen came alive. "Yep. My grandson put it back to the important time—a little after 9:00 AM a few days ago." Frish backed away. "I'll leave it to you gentlemen. Gotta be out front. Stay as long as you need." Frish disappeared.

Tony clicked play. "There he is, Harry. That's the infamous Milton Busey."

"A strange-looking chap," Turpin announced. "A wanker."

"Sure doesn't look dangerous." Tony leaned closer to the dusty screen. "How did that old man kill those two big-boy lawyers and drag Bowman out of there? He doesn't look strong enough. I've seen healthier people on the medical examiner's table."

"Those skinny legs. The poor man appears woefully

malnourished," Turpin said. "And with his raincoat and the silly hat with the feather—clearly he did not come dressed appropriately. For a serial killer, I am surprised. He appears quite unfamiliar with the art of blending."

"Maybe he's smarter than all of us. Instead of blending, stand out like a freak—

"There. He went inside. I'll fast forward."

"Stop there," Turpin snapped.

"Shit. Eight minute mark. The sniper takes the first shot," Tony said.

"Look!" Turpin lurched toward the monitor. "A bloody chair thrown out the window." They watched it settle on the sidewalk. "The old boy blocked the second projectile."

"Ramsey got hit and went down," Tony said. "The glass was out of the way for a clear shot. Busey knew it. He threw the chair to block the next one. Probably faster than getting out of the way of it."

"Mr. Busey is smarter and more agile than he looks," Turpin said. They watched another thirty seconds tick off. "There. Elliott going in to help. Just as he said."

"Yeah," Tony scoffed. "The man can't avoid this kind of stuff. He's his own worst enemy. You do know he had a breakdown, right? We were in Dallas when it happened. He almost died. Doctors said he has some kind of autonomic nervous system thing. Something he has zero control over. It shut down his heart —a cardiac arrest triggered by emotional overload. He's at capacity. Elliott has lived with monsters all his adult life because he's the best at tracking them down and feels responsible to use his gifts. But he can't carry any more of the emotional baggage, the terror, or the pain of the victims. He relives that shit all the time. It would tear any man's heart out and spike their blood pressure. The doctors said one more really bad experience could kill him."

"I know," Turpin whispered. "And I'm quite sure most of his friends do."

"Then you know why Elliott came down here in the first place—to Key West," Tony went on, staring at the monitor. "It's why I left him alone for more than a year," he added under his breath.

"Well then," Turpin said.

"Well then what? What the hell are you saying," Tony asked with hard eyes.

"You knew all that but came to Key West to engage him anyway, didn't you?"

"You bastard."

Turpin turned back to the monitor. "You're not alone, old boy. I came, too. Albert Bell, his bloody *father*, came. The President of the United States, he knew. He came, too. We all came for Elliott Sumner, didn't we? We share the guilt." He rested his hand on Tony's shoulder. "We all put Elliott in jeopardy. We did not have a choice—this wonky mess in the world. Evil has a foothold, Anthony. We all reached for the one man who might very likely be the difference. Elliott Sumner is far more than just a forensic pathologist, isn't he?"

Tony shook his head and pinched his eyes closed. "It's not right to do this to him. It's not our decision, Harry."

"He made this decision, Anthony. He knows it could be his last. "

Tony turned off the monitor. They stared at the black screen. "You seen enough?"

Turpin nodded.

"And it is *Tony,* goddamn it—"

Billy's cell phone rang in Turpin's coat pocket. "Crikey," he said as he pulled it out.

With eyes wide, they stared at it cradled in Turpin's hand. They had been absorbed in the surveillance video. For a split moment, they'd forgotten about Billy's phone and the instructions to pick up the suitcases. Loose ends swirled. Did the caller know Billy? Would they expect his voice? What about a code word? Is the phone traceable? Could GRAY WOLF operatives be on their way? Maybe Billy was supposed to call them from the crime scene? Maybe he did. Maybe he'd told them about Wilcox and Turpin already.

"God," Tony huffed as he searched pockets for his pack of cigarettes. "I don't have a damn code word. Shit! I didn't give that little prick a chance to tell me."

With the phone resting on the palm of his hand, Turpin said, "Off your bum, old boy. They're certainly not expecting a chin wag from a Brit."

"I'm not ready, Harry. I need to think. If this goes the wrong way, the place will be crawlin' with GRAY WOLF operatives. They'll know we're on Busey's trail. This could screw everything up. Maybe we let it ring and buy time."

The phone rang a third time. "Answer it, Anthony. We are out of time."

"I need a cigarette." Tony said. He grabbed the phone and swallowed hard.

Turpin pulled Tony's pack of smokes from his shirt pocket and held it up. "I'll light ya a fag. Answer now."

The phone rang a fourth time. Tony stared at the pack, tapped *accept*, and put the cell to his ear. "It's about damn time—"

CHAPTER **27**

"Because it is so unbelievable, truth often escapes being known."
Heraclitus

Bismarck, North Dakota, 1300 CST

Elliott removed another segment of ragged tissue from the stage of his 10X microscope. He pinned it in place on a white Styrofoam board with a dozen other fragments, and studied it like a rare find in a cherished stamp collection. He aligned the almost-invisible ink lines and the vague images of the mottled tissue, and then returned to the hideous mound of decomposing flesh to search for the next piece to the puzzle. He had to be certain.

"Welcome to the dead zone," Dr. Cage said, tongue-in-cheek. His words echoed from inside his laminar airflow hood and ebbed across the dismal basement laboratory. "If we're unable to identify GRAY WOLF soon, I'm afraid this old tin box will be my coffin."

Cage and Osgard worked on the histological morass—microscopic examination of gradient aspirates from the biologic mush of the four cubed cadavers. Sumner worked on tattoo reconstruction. The team had dissected suspect remnants of torn tissue from each appendage stub and neck of the six victims. All portions of the epidermis, from the *stratum corneum* to the *stratum basale,* with imperfections or discolorations were taken. Elliott would inspect each and attempt to reconstruct a morbid tattoo puzzle to shed light on the origin of GRAY WOLF.

After three brutal hours in the autopsy room with the horrific carnage, the three forensic pathologists had come to the same conclusion: The methods of GRAY WOLF had worked. Physical evidence was destroyed. Dismemberment, irradiation, lysing agents, crushing, and freezing, all contributed to the destruction of evidence. The gross anatomical examinations yielded nothing to assist their effort to identify the entity that occupied missile silos. Now the painstaking detail work in the forensic laboratory had to deliver something, or their worst nightmare would become a reality.

Elliott saw GRAY WOLF in a different way than the others —just one more twisted monster in a long line of barbarous adversaries in a world fraught with danger. In the depths of the dungeon-like basement of the state morgue, Elliott did not need to participate in the banter and forced humor to divert fear. He had lived in the darkest parts of the world most of his life as an international hunter of the most dangerous serial killers alive. Elliott knew evil all too well. He knew the places and things that cripple the strongest of men. Instead of engaging in hapless banter with blind hope, he placed another piece of inked tissue onto another glass slide and managed his demons the best he could. He put the glass slide on the stage of his microscope and adjusted his ocular lens knowing he was close. Elliott knew fear and pain were the distractors of the weak and the strengths of evil. He also knew his focus on the science of death weakened the associated experience of the trauma of death. It was another way to win his internal battle.

"Don't worry, Morgan. We will find a way," Dr. Osgard said as she sectioned tissue.

"If I had known you two were coming, I would have cleaned up the place," Cage joked. Only he could see his hand tremble as he zoomed in on the next sample of human aspirate. The fuzzy cells sharpened. He differentiated them with ease, even though most were lysed. "Kidney and liver cells—cadaver number four—

present and accounted for," he whispered as he checked two more boxes on the histological profile.

Elliott would not be distracted by thoughts of the catastrophic nuclear destruction of his country. Before he had accepted President Landon's invitation to the *Armageddon Dance*, he understood he would be needed in Bismarck, one of the first cities to evaporate should GRAY WOLF accomplish its mission. Elliott did the calculations on the Commander 44. One Minuteman III ICBM with the payload of one W62 nuclear warhead—a yield of 170 kilotons—would devastate a six-hundred-mile radius around Minot. Multiple Minuteman missiles would destroy most of the Midwestern United States and central Canada. Bismarck would be swallowed in seconds by the rolling molten nuclear conflagration. All living things in the firestorm's path would evaporate. In days, the residual nuclear contamination would quadruple the zone of death.

Unlike normal people, Elliott had taught himself to compartmentalize thought at an *absolute level*, in order to survive. In Key West over the last year, he developed (what he hoped would be) a failsafe capability to block traumatic emotions. If even one gained access to his conscious or subconscious thought process, he would risk an ANS event. That might trigger a cardiac arrest. Although he had not yet tested it, Elliott believed like meditation and self-hypnosis, compartmentalization of thought at an *absolute level* would be his best physio-psychological defense mechanism. Over the last year, he had honed the new skillset—but then the homicides on Caroline interrupted his plans. He wanted another year, to be certain. GRAY WOLF would be his test.

Osgard got up to exchange her rack of tubes of aspirates. As she walked by Dr. Cage, she paused to pat his shoulder and give him reinforcement. It had already been a long day of bleak possibilities. "We have twelve more racks to go, Morgan. Don't worry. We will get there. I think Elliott is onto something." She slid her rack of tubes under another laminar hood and glanced over at the bin by the door—a new report had been dropped off. Osgard picked it up and read in silence, flipping pages.

Cage backed out of his hood. "Is that the DNA update? I got a call it was coming."

Osgard approached Cage with the report in her hand and eyes darting across each line. On the other side of the workstation, Elliott got to his feet. In silence, he walked away. Elliott stopped at the opposite end of the empty lab and stared at the ceiling rubbing his neck.

Osgard looked up from the report. "We submitted the DNA on the two from overseas—"

"Right," Cage said as he watched Elliott. "What's he doing?" he whispered.

Osgard flipped a page. "According to this, we have successfully recovered DNA from cadavers Number Three and Four." She slid a pen into her coat pocket with a mesmerized stare. "These two were found in Canada. Number two was found in North Dakota, on the border southwest of the International Peace Garden. And as you know, Number One is Roan Busey. Now they are expediting DNA profiles on four. We should get information within the hour."

"That is incredible news," Cage said, still watching Elliott. "In spite of the use of lysing agents, radiation, compression, and exposure to extreme temperatures, we managed to excavate DNA from two of the four cubed cadavers."

"Yes," Osgard said. "And they are still working with the recovered cells we sent on Roan Busey and Number Two. When it is all done, we may have DNA on all victims."

"We won't learn much new from Roan Busey's DNA," Cage said.

"They'll run it last," Osgard said. "The five unknown IDs are priority."

"We can safely assume *no matches* on the international DNA data base," Cage said. "But we will get a look at ancestral profiles. That will help with ethnic background and may point to parts of the world. It will be helpful to know if we are dealing with people of North African, Russian, or Asian dissent."

"It won't be necessary," Elliott said.

Cage and Osgard turned to him. "What are you saying, Elliott?"

"This entity is cloaked in the deepest secrecy and externally directed. They specialize in deep penetration and sabotage. They are an espionage cell designed to assassinate top leadership around the world and destroy strategic infrastructure when the outbreak of war is unavoidable."

Cage looked over at the white Styrofoam board Elliott had been working on. The fragments of tissue had been merged. Most of the two-inch by one-inch tattoo had been reconstructed. It was an emblem. Against the backdrop of a bronze shield, a sword ran through the center of a diamond-like structure of blue and gold, a red pennant imprinted with letters, and three scrolls with more letters.

"What is the meaning of the diamond?" Cage asked.

"It's not a diamond," Elliott said. "It is a deployed parachute. They have one thousand operators and several special ops in all parts of the world. Physical training includes parachutes and hand-to-hand combat, diving and underwater combat, and climbing—Alpine rope techniques. I'm quite certain they are also trained for extreme climatic conditions and spelunking."

"Who are they?" Cage asked.

"Vympel."

"What the hell?" Cage breathed.

"And even more relevant, they are secretly deployed in cities with important nuclear facilities. In the past, they observed. Today, they took it further."

"Vympel is a Russian word," Osgard said.

"Yes it is," Elliott replied.

"How do you get all this from that tattoo?" Cage muttered. "Never mind. I forgot. Your perfect photographic memory. You remember everything."

Elliott placed the Styrofoam board on the table and the three stared at it. "I was in Russia five years ago, hunting an international serial killer. I suspected a member of the FSB, the Federal Security Service of the Russian Federation. Someone working on counterintelligence had access to the countries and places where brutalized bodies were found. The notes they left behind to taunt investigators were in Russian. I thought it would be a good idea to do my homework."

"You took a crash course in the history of the Russian Empire," Cage said.

"In a word, yes," Elliott answered as he pulled the white Styrofoam board closer.

"Your crash course took you to Vympel, their pennant, this tattoo?" Dr. Osgard said.

"Yes. The FSB was the main successor to the KGB after the collapse of the Soviet Union in 1991. The *Spetsgruppa* 'V' is Russian for *pennant*. This is an identifier for the Vega Group, the *spetsnaz* unit under the command of the FSB for the purposes I mentioned."

"We need to talk to the President, Elliott," Cage said. "This is what we've been looking for. You have identified GRAY WOLF. Since it is Russia, maybe there is a possibility for a negotiated end to all this."

"I agree, Elliott," Osgard said. "If you're certain, we can't wait."

Elliott studied the board of pinned tissue specimens, and

then pushed it away. He leaned back in his chair and ran a hand through his hair as if he was a million miles away.

"What is it, Elliott?" Osgard asked.

"Talk to us," Cage pushed.

Elliott blinked back into the room. "Right." He took a deep breath. "Okay. I am certain the reconstructed tattoo is the Vega Group pennant. What does not make sense to me is that we found pieces of the tattoo on Roan Busey."

"You don't think he was a stealth member of the Vega Group?" Osgard queried.

"Hell no," Cage huffed. "We have the life history on the man. He's a high school-educated, odd job kind of guy his whole life. We all read the man's dossier. Elliott's right. Why would Roan Busey have the Vega tattoo?"

"Russia defeated Napoleon and Hitler," Elliott said. "Their only huge mistake was getting into a forty-year Cold War with us. I know their economy is in desperate straits but—"

"But why come over here and commandeer our Minuteman missiles?" Cage said. "Why take the chance of being wiped out by the United States? They are smart enough to know that, in spite of their efforts to cover their tracks, we would find out and come for them."

"I've not studied changing geopolitical strategy," Elliott said.

"None of us have, Elliott," Osgard said. "That's a whole different world, and that's why we must turn it over right now. Our job is to follow the forensic trail to GRAY WOLF. I think that is how we treat this information. The tattoo is another piece to a puzzle—albeit a major one. It is something your President can do something with."

If I was going to take control of nuclear assets belonging to the United States, I would leave just enough of a trail to misdirect my enemy, Elliott thought. *My priority would be to buy as much time as possible to deal with the complexities that lay ahead. Maybe the bodies left behind were plants, intended to be found. Maybe the elaborate treatment of the remains was intended to shock and mislead. And maybe the tattoos were supposed to be reconstructed so we would think Russia was involved ...*

"Elliott. Did you hear me?" Emma Osgard pushed.

"Yes, Emma?" Elliott stood and took a deep breath. "Here's what we do. I want a spectroscopic analysis of the reconstructed tattoo. We need to know the chemical properties of the pigments in the inks. That could tell us when and where they were done. We need to know."

"That could take days, Elliott," Cage said.

"I have catalogued each tissue segment as to the victim from which it was taken."

"I get it," Cage said. "We can do that. It will need to go to DC. Still, we must get the President in on this. We have enough for them to work with. Time's running out, Elliott."

"Get the tissue to DC, Morgan," Elliott said as he paced a tight circle rubbing his chin. "Emma, get Frank Barth, the U.S. Agent in charge. And Bill Aster, CIA. They can set up the call with the President and whoever needs to be there. I will prepare—

"What do I say, Elliott?" Emma Osgard asked.

"Tell them we have GRAY WOLF identified." *For now,* he thought.

I need to get out of here. I need to go to Minot. Buck will help me—it's been five years, but he will work with me ...

Tony and Harold need to find Milton. Locating GRAY WOLF has always been most important. I never bought into the identity route. We've wasted too much time on it already.

CHAPTER **28**

"Only the insane take themselves seriously.
Max Beerbohm

Key West, 1300 EST

"Milton is not expecting his money until tonight," Tony said. With a well-practiced flick, he sent his cigarette butt soaring out the window and watched it land on the dirt road. They sat in the shade of a cluster of strangler figs, one block from Helen Ramsey's beach cottage. "The guy's smart, Harry. We can't just poke around Ramsey's place. If he's there, he's gonna be watching. We need to think through this daylight plan."

Turpin chuckled. "When did you become one to worry? Billy's cell phone, picking up the bloody suitcases at the airport, and now this? I thought you were one of those fly by the seat of your pants fellows. Contrary to your worst held fears, Anthony, everything has moved along quite smoothly."

"I'm not worried," Tony barked as he pressed a match to a fresh smoke. "I'm troubled."

"No one appears to have noticed the departure of Billy and that angry tattooed fellow. We have the money in our possession." He reached into the backseat and patted the suitcases. "We have our instructions from GRAY WOLF ops on delivery tonight. No, sir. I am pleased with our plan to pluck Mr. Busey before someone adds us to their bloody equation."

"I don't know," Tony said, shaking his head. "Somethin's not right."

"Our plan is quite simple. We are taking immediate

advantage of information extracted from two buffoons on Caroline Street."

"But what do we really know to be true?"

"The suitcases contain large quantities of money. One holds precisely the sum our Billy described for his payday. The other is an enormous sum for Mr. Busey's payday, the one we surmised GRAY WOLF had attempted to avoid. I see a $400,000 fishing lure. GRAY WOLF hopes to filet Milton Busey tonight on Sunset Pier."

"Assumptions, not facts," Tony said as he checked his phone for messages.

"Well yes, but they are reasonable assumptions, old boy, because they're corroborated by physical evidence," Turpin insisted. "And it is reasonable to assume Mr. Busey has chosen Miss Ramsey's abode because it would be available and a most unlikely hole for him to crawl into."

"Right," Tony said, looking down the narrow road. The ocean lay in relative silence beyond their side of the street and a wide berm of weathered scrub. Across the road, hard sand driveways cut through the same scrub and disappeared into dense groves. "That does make sense. He knew she wouldn't be coming home for a while. And, he did not know the area."

"Rather than wait until sundown, a high-risk Sunset Pier money transfer encounter with Mr. Busey and GRAY WOLF operatives in the shadows, it makes perfect sense to take the man now," Turpin proclaimed. "We can ship the heathen to the feds so they can do what they do, extract information. Remember, time is not our friend at the moment, Anthony. Providing your bloody government with an opportunity to identify and locate GRAY WOLF as soon as possible is quite important. Taking Mr. Busey now is our best chance to assist in the effort to avoid a nuclear holocaust."

"I get all that," Tony said with smoke falling from his mouth.

"I would say *that* is quite enough for one day, sir. A retired American homicide detective and a British profiler are small cogs in the massive war machine," Turpin said. "We do not want to bring the bloody thing to a standstill."

"But ... why was this part of the operation so smooth, Harry?" Tony asked.

"To what are you referring, sir?" Turpin asked.

"The call on Billy's phone. Getting the suitcases of money at the airport."

"They were not expecting us," Turpin said.

"GRAY WOLF mounted a major effort to draw Milton Busey into a trap down here. I get it. The man knows too much. They can't let him talk. They moved a damn law firm across the goddamn country and set up a goddamn sniper. After Busey kills in Key West and escapes, GRAY WOLF is relentless in their pursuit of Elliott. They followed him almost to Cuba. These people are on a mission. They're very organized. They have money, resources, and the numbers, Harry. They threw a net over the whole goddamn Florida peninsula."

Turpin nodded. "Every bit true," he said.

"Why would they use people like Billy and Randy to handle their most important job?"

"To transfer a half-million dollars to Milton Busey?" Turpin asked.

"Why wouldn't they know Billy's voice on the phone? Why didn't anyone stop us at the airport? They had to be watching. Somethin's not right."

"Put that way, it does sound peculiar," Turpin said. "On the other hand, GRAY WOLF may have numerous independent contractors looking for Mr. Busey. You said they lost their initial team when a boat sank in the Atlantic. They could be scratching the bottom of the barrel for clandestine personnel. And they might now be poorly coordinated."

"I don't know. Busey's too important. Maybe they want us to lead them to him. Maybe Busey is more involved than we thought. I think we're walking into a—"

The first bullet pierced the windshield between Tony and Turpin, leaving a half-inch-hole and an intact, two-inch shatter pattern. The second pierced the windshield and hit Turpin in the chest. He yelped and slid off the seat—his legs and arms limp, his eyes closed.

Tony slid low as two more bullets pelted the windshield and buried in the seat above his head. He reached for Turpin's wrist, but another bullet creased his arm. He yanked it back and reached for his gun. Turpin lay still. Tony saw blood dripping from his nose and mouth.

"Harry! You okay? Wake up, goddamn it. Harry!" Tony's awkward, bent position under the steering wheel made it almost impossible to reach his gun. As he struggled, a shadow fell over him. Then a tap on the window followed. Tony turned his head with a hand deep in his coat and fingers on his leather holster. He looked up and saw the end of a rifle and Milton Busey ...

"You killed my associate, you bastard!" Tony shouted.

"Stand up, right now."

Milton jabbed the rifle into Tony's back and pushed him up the driveway to Ramsey's cottage. "Quiet!" Milton seethed, scanning the area.

Any quick moves would mean immediate death. Tony had to be patient, choose his time. Busey had killed half a dozen men he knew about. The man had never been caught or charged for killing anybody. *People like him do not make mistakes when it comes to killing.*

"Why are you keeping me alive, you old coot?" Tony jabbed. Busey ignored him as he tied him into a chair. In a few minutes, Tony's hands were secured behind his back and his legs and body were wrapped in fifty feet of nylon rope. The bindings were tight enough to hurt and loose enough to allow blood circulation—the serial killer was a pro.

The room was dark. All windows were covered with heavy drapes. The kitchen bar was covered in food garbage, the remnants of foraging for two days. Busey slumped down in the only padded chair across the room. He lit a cigarette, and flipped through Tony's wallet.

"Those are my damn cigarettes, Busey. You got no class."

"They're looking for you, too, mister Memphis homicide detective."

"What are you talking about, you sick bastard?"

"You shouldn't have come back here. They're really mad at you and Sumner."

"Animals don't have emotions, prick. They just hunt to eat," Tony snarled.

"These animals are more like the wolf. They hunt in packs. They always got a plan," Busey said with a slur. "You should never underestimate the wolf."

"You just killed a good man, Busey. You didn't need to do that. I advise you to kill me now, because when I get out of these ropes, you're gonna wish you had sat in one of those electric chairs long ago."

"You still don't know what's goin' on here, do you?" Busey asked.

"Why don't you educate me, Mr. Asshole?"

Busey took a long drag and stared at the irate Memphis homicide detective-turned-PI. "You don't recognize my voice, do you?" He grabbed a half-empty bottle of beer from a group of six empties. His swollen, bloodshot eyes squinted with each painful swallow.

You were on the other end of Billy's phone, Tony thought. *You set all this up. Billy and Randy worked for you. You got Bowman to get the money to Key West. You were going to send Billy to get your money. It was never GRAY WOLF. They're still hunting you.*

"You workin' it out in your head, boy?" Busey poked.

Somehow, Billy figured out you were hiding at Ramsey's place. They were on Caroline to get her address. They wanted your $400K. But Billy knew you were one relentless son of a bitch. He knew you'd hunt them down. He had to kill you.

"Where's Bowman?" Tony asked.

"She's here. In the bedroom," Busey said.

"Got her tied up like a Christmas turkey too, old man?"

Busey blew a cloud of smoke that drifted in a lazy sphere. "Not necessary."

"You killed her."

"Took a while, but she told me where the money was—two suitcases and the counts. That's how I worked my deal for pickup and delivery."

"You killed Miss Bowman, didn't you?"

"She made me take off four of her fingers before she'd cooperate. Uppity lawyer criminal types ain't no better than me. They think they are, but they ain't. They're just smooth when they take your money but you know, they kill people, too. It's just business to them. I bet that stinkin' law firm's got more than a billion dollars off-shore. They clean dirty money all over the world, and they take care of eliminating risk—killin'—for lots of nasty people, includin' governments and politicians that don't like givin' up power."

"You're mean and you're crazy, Busey. Don't try to make yourself sound like a poor, misunderstood criminal. Now you sold out your damn country and got your son killed. You only have months to live and you're chasin' money you'll never spend."

"This country never did anything for me!" Busey bellowed.

"Aw gee. Blame the country for your sick-ass life. Give me a break," Tony snarled.

Busey lit another cigarette and reflected. "I never woulda done it, but I figured I could do somethin' good for Roan. I hadn't been around much of his life. I saw a way to get a lot of money to him before I died. It was simple as that. Then they killed my son for nothin'. He was a good boy—nothin' like me. He was just doin' what I told him."

"What did you do, Milton? We're all gonna die because of you."

Busey opened a new beer and returned to his cushioned chair. After a few swallows, he looked at the ceiling and said, "I can't get out of this place 'til tonight. They're watchin' every road out of here. Daytime would be impossible.

"I knew they'd never think to look for me here. Shit, I didn't think of it 'til I shoved my shank in Bowman's side in the car. She really wanted to live. She drove me right here."

"Good for you, old man," Tony mumbled as he picked at his knot.

"Only way out this damn resort town is saltwater. I found me a small sailboat out there in that scrub. I'm leavin' tonight. I figure I can sail out about a mile and go west for a day or so. There's nothin' to track—it's a little damn sailboat. There ain't much to pick up on anything.

"I'm gonna find me some empty shoreline. I'll wait to come in at night."

"You'll never make it, Busey. People have planes and fast boats. They'll be running up and down the coastline until they find you."

"I got more clothes and food all packed. Thanks to you boys, now I got my money—I'll need to bring your car up here and hide it. Can't forget to do that," he muttered. "When I land tomorrow or the next day on some empty beach, I'll steal me a car and go somewhere where I can dump it off and enjoy the last days of my life."

"Enough, Busey. Snap out of your stupid dream. It is not gonna happen. You told somebody—the Chinese, Russians, radical Islamic terrorists, or some rogue nation—how to get into missile silos in Minot. You think you're gonna have a nice moonlight sail. Hell no! The place you once called home is gonna be lit up like a Roman-friggin-candle, thanks to you."

Busey smiled. "That ain't gonna happen. Hell, that shit's so complex, ain't nobody gonna break them codes and mess with those missiles, no matter what I told them."

"Not true, Einstein. Thanks to you, some sick bastards are in our silos now fucking with them. They've opened silo doors. They've messed with launch control centers. They've got their hands on one medium range ballistic missile and they're threatening to send it into Canada to demonstrate their abilities."

Busey set down his beer. The smoldering cigarette dangled from his lips, and a snake of smoke curled up, covering one eye. Busey didn't seem to notice.

"Who the fuck did you put in our missile silos, Milton? And where are they?"

"They can't be—"

"They are, Milton."

"No. There's no way for them to—"

"You think we're all lookin' for you because you're so important? Hell, you're just a dying, two-bit, punk serial killer. Who gives a shit about you? Why do you think these people are so hell-bent on getting you, Milton? Why do you think the United States Government has Elliott Sumner in Bismarck, North Dakota doing autopsies to figure out who the hell is in those missile silos? Why am I down here? Why is Scotland Yard involved? You are one flaming dumbass."

"Shut up or I gag you," Busey said, scratching his head.

"You really screwed up this time."

"I was on demolition in the '60s," Busey said. "There were

hundreds of construction workers. I cleared the way for twenty of the hundred-and-fifty silos. I know the ground up there. When the military was done with their silos, there was nothin' for me. They said thanks, get lost. I did. I started drinkin' and drugs. Then the stealin' and rapin' and killin'. I fell apart. Then in the '90s, they call me. They need my help again. They want me to blow-up the same missile silos I made room for thirty years earlier. They said I knew the best way to take down the twenty I helped put there."

Tony worked the ropes behind his back as Busey relived his miserable life. *I'm gonna get loose and kill you—you bastard. Keep talking. Give me something to take back if I survive this. One of us is gonna die here.*

"They didn't call me when they decided to put some missiles *back* in Minot. Government spends millions doin' the same things over and over. Guess they didn't call 'cause by then I had a criminal record. I was too old to be of any use to them."

"You were never important, Milton," Tony announced. "Let that sink in."

"I still knew a lot. They made me sign them government papers sayin' I wouldn't tell nobody nothin'. Then I get the phone call in prison. Someone needed me."

"What phone call?" Tony pushed, but Busey didn't hear him. He was deep in his own memories. He'd been drinking all day. The alcohol was starting to numb his senses.

"It was a year ago. They tried to act like they were doin' some kind of geological survey in the Minot area. They said my knowledge of the missile fields would save them a lot of time and money—millions. They said if I helped, they'd put $400,000 in my bank account. I could leave it for my family. Do somethin' good for a change. They couldn't guarantee, but they said they'd try to get me out of Pingree for helpin' with the important surveys."

"You're not that stupid, Busey. You knew it was a covert operation. You knew it was a bunch of foreigners after our missiles. Surveys are bullshit. They had all that information before they put in the first silo. And surveyors don't have that kind of money to throw around."

"Yup. You're right. I knew it was somethin' bad. But the money was good and I wanted Roan to have it."

"Enough with the backstory," Tony puffed. "Who'd you deal with, and where are they?"

Busey struggled to his feet, clutching another empty beer bottle. "Not sure who they are. But I know where they are, and it ain't in a missile silo. Time for you to go, Mr. Wilcox. I got things to do."

Tony had worked the knots loose behind his back as Busey walked over to the rifle. "That makes no sense," Tony said. "They're lighting up the boards at the missile control center at the Minot airbase. Remember what I said. These people are opening silo doors and threatening to send a missile into Canada. They gotta be in a launch control capsule somewhere out there."

Busey picked up the rifle. "Got this from the sniper. They never think about targets back trackin' a line of fire. They think they're God almighty."

"You killed your sniper?" Tony asked.

"Well, I took him with me and Bowman—he was in pretty bad shape. The boy was comin' off the roof of some plaza area, the back of a building, in the alley. I ran him down with Bowman's car. The poor bastard didn't even see me comin'. He had his back to me. He was walkin' with a suitcase and his broke-down rifle. Now who the hell's carryin' a metal suitcase in an alley in the mornin'? I ran over him. Put him in the trunk. He's back there with Bowman."

The knot slipped off Tony's wrist. His hands were free but his legs and chest were still tightly bound to the chair. "Before you shoot me, I gotta know. Tell me where the bastards are hiding in North Dakota. After all this, I'm curious."

Busey blew into the empty chamber and slid-in three bullets. "They're outside Belden. Damnedest thing. There's an intact launch control capsule out there. It was supposed to be demolished. I placed the dynamite and detonated the area according to the book. It all caved in like expected. Every box got checked after full inspection by the United States 91st Wing Command."

"What happened, Milton?"

"Never told 'em 'bout the cavern. Wasn't on any of them geological surveys. You woulda thought all them smart people coulda found it one way or another, all that fancy equipment. I found the place when I was a boy, runnin' 'round. Use to stay at my aunt's house. Not much of a farm, north of Belden. I helped some. Grew wheat, navy beans, flax seed, and lentils. When I wasn't workin' in the fields, I'd go in that cavern with my cousin and a couple of friends—the Frenicolas. They're all dead. I'm only one knows how to get in it now. And I'm damn sure the only one knows how to get to that capsule.

"It runs a half-mile, 'bout a hundred feet underground. Turns out, one of them LCCs butted right up to the wall. Nobody knew. When I detonated the place, that big ole capsule musta spit into the cavern like a watermelon seed—intact and all. Looked like a big pill."

"It can't possibly be functional."

"It wasn't. Took 'bout a year to reconnect all them wires and conduits and stuff hanging down like a pile of spaghetti. That's why they needed Roan and me. Roan was an amateur electrician and my trusted surrogate. After we showed them how to get in there, they'd take close-up pictures each week and get them to me in Pingree. I'd give Doc Rice instructions. I remembered all that stuff. Doc would pass them instructions to Roan. Roan'd do the work and tests and things for me, when he didn't have a towin' job.

"You sayin' Roan did all that wiring stuff alone?" Tony asked. "I'm gonna be dead in few minutes. Why lie. He had help. Who helped Roan?"

Milton blinked over his rifle and then smiled at a memory. "The only man who cared 'bout me any my whole life. He helped. He's a smart man. I'll just leave it at that." Milton's smile melted as fire retook his eyes. "Doc Rice got greedy. Before I killed him, he told me he cut a new deal with Bowman. Said he got scared. Needed more money to get out of Pingree. Rice was alcoholic, ya know. A desperate man. His new deal took me and Roan out. I don't think we'd have had a problem if Doc hadn't messed with things like that."

"So Bowman, Weller & Garcia were in it from the start?"

"Yup. The sons-of-bitches screwed me out of my money and set up Roan. They didn't know this old man had friends. Us criminals got connections, too. One of mine in London told me he got some bad news from his man in Istanbul. We were gonna pool our money. The guy said they killed Roan in Minot. Said they cut off his head and arms and legs." Milton threw an empty beer bottle across the room. "They didn't have to do *that* to my boy—

"I knew right then that damn capsule was workin' somehow. But I think they did some things I didn't even know about," Milton said scratching his jaw. "They didn't need me and Roan no more. They had real smart computer people to finish things up for 'em." He stared at the ceiling. "I decided right then. I was gonna kill every one of 'em and get me my money."

"You didn't have to sell out your country, Busey."

Busey blinked back into the room. He raised his rifle. "You ain't never showed me no respect since I dragged your wounded ass out of that car. I coulda killed you with your friend. Instead I bring ya up here to find out what's goin' on, thinkin' I just might leave you here all tied up. I am gettin' tired of killin' people.

"But you done nothin' but bad mouth me. You're one of them people that goes 'round thinkin' you're better than everyone else. You're a killin' machine too, Mister Homicide Detective Wilcox. You like it, just like me, but you get to hide behind a badge."

"Fuck you, Busey. You're sick. And you didn't have to kill Harry Turpin—"

On his last word, Tony pushed off the floor with his feet. His chair started to fall backward as Milton pulled the trigger.

CHAPTER 29

"Never deprive someone of hope; it may be all they have."
H. Jackson Jr. Brader

Minot, North Dakota, 1400 CST

"It left the silo." Buck squinted at the ice-blue horizon and watched the burning tail and billowing plume climb the winter sky. With his heart beating in his throat, he confirmed the obvious on the secured line to the White House. "We're scrambling them now, Mr. President."

One hour before, the midday sun over Washington DC had seemed to hang higher than usual, and to be smaller than usual. Day Three after an unknown, hostile force had commandeered U.S. nuclear assets in Minot, North Dakota, the POTUS sat alone in the Oval Office. As the unthinkable haunted him, he read the new, official document—a confirmation memorandum that would one day be on display in the Smithsonian. Signed by all members of the Joint Chiefs of Staff, the Secretary of Defense, State, and Homeland, it established and preserved President Landon's most significant executive order issued in two terms. It was one no other president had to consider. Landon would not allow a computer to make decisions on the life and death of the American citizens. His executive order stated clearly that only the President of the United States is authorized to consider, select, and implement a *terminal breach* containment option.

The awaited forensic briefing from Bismarck finally came. Landon stepped out long enough to wash his face and manage his desperation. When he returned to the Oval Office, it was full and he had restored the confidence he needed to stir waning embers of hope. Even at the highest level, people need someone to tell them it will be all right.

As he entered, members of his cabinet and top military advisors stopped talking. President Landon stood tall and forthright, like a man born to lead a nation. He measured the mood and made eye contact with each person in the room—his Secretaries of State, Defense, and Homeland, the Director of the CIA, the Vice President, and two five-star generals. When he sat, the room sat.

"Dr. Sumner, I understand you have identified GRAY WOLF," said the POTUS.

All eyes turned to the speakerphone. "Yes, Mr. President. I won't waste time. Only the essentials. Questions as you deem necessary."

"Good. Please continue," Landon said, with one hand still trembling in his pocket.

"Based on our analysis, we believe the GRAY WOLF contingency is Russian in origin and purpose."

"The blasted Russians!" the Secretary of Defense huffed. "I knew it." More whispers rolled as cell phones emerged from pockets and leaders triggered new actions in their respective areas. Up until now, each had been developing multiple tracks pending action plans based on most likely scenarios with the Chinese, Russians, Iranians, North Koreans, and Islamic Terrorists.

"Please. Elliott," the POTUS nudged.

"The standard and customary forensic evidence was successfully altered or destroyed."

"Appalling," Vice President Pierce said.

"Therefore, our investigations were driven to the microscopic level at most turns. Our conclusion is primarily drawn from a tattoo," Elliott said.

"A tattoo?" The President said as confusion filled the Oval Office.

"Yes. We reconstructed a tattoo from tissue remnants recovered from each of the six victims linked to GRAY WOLF."

"A tattoo," the President whispered a second time.

"If I may explain," Elliott said to a room frozen in confusion, curiosity, and fear.

Landon panned the Oval Office with controlling eyes. He restored calm. "Yes. Please. That would be helpful, Elliott."

"I assume everyone present knows of the condition of the six victims, the grim postmortem processes employed by GRAY WOLF to destroy physical evidence and to mislead an anticipated forensic investigation."

"Your assumption is accurate. All present know," Landon said, watching the people around him.

"The heads, arms, and legs were removed from all six victims after death. Four of the six corpses were then infused with a cellular lysing agent. This infusion process was carried out much like the embalming process at a funeral home. However, a lysing agent is a combination of chemicals for the disruption of cells. It is not intended to preserve tissue. It is intended to destroy tissue at the cellular level. The objective of the lysing process is to make differentiation of one cell from another impossible. Solid tissue is liquefied. Lysing also helps in the dispersal of fractured mitochondrial and nuclear DNA in a biological soup."

"That's just evil," the Vice President scoffed.

"The four victims exposed to the lysing agent were also exposed to a lethal dose of radiation. They then were crushed inside a compressing device. The objective of irradiating the victims was to accomplish the wholesale destruction of DNA evidence. The compression step crushed bone and remaining solid tissue into a compact cube for unrecognizable disposal."

"DNA was not a factor in reaching your conclusion?" the Secretary of State asked.

"It was not," Elliott said. "However, in spite of the aggressive effort to eliminate it, we were able to find trace DNA evidence in all cases. We identified Roan Busey by matching his DNA on the national data base. We were not surprised there were no other matches. We did attempt to examine DNA profiles for ancestral lineage to help identify GRAY WOLF origins. Needed markers were too damaged to reach any meaningful conclusions."

"You said postmortem treatment of the victims had two objectives," the President said. "The destruction of physical evidence and to mislead ensuing investigations. I believe we now understand the destruction aspect. Educate us on the misleading aspect. And how were you able to find a path to truth?"

"The decapitations and dismemberments were not mechanically necessary to fit victims into their irradiating/crushing device. In the beginning, we reasoned decapitations were intended to eliminate access to dental evidence, and to nullify use of advanced facial recognition technology. In the beginning, we reasoned removal of arms—and therefore hands—was intended to eliminate finger/palm prints. The removal of legs made no sense. That action led us to reconsider our initial assumptions. We examined dismemberment sites and found remnants with tattoo ink.

"Tattoos and markings on a body assist in the identification process. At first, we approached the tattoos with the same thought process—individual identification. We discovered we were recovering remnants of an *identical* tattoo on all six victims.

"Was it possible a tattoo once worn proudly by members of a clandestine team had become a problem for this mission? Because anonymity is an obvious priority, GRAY WOLF had to find a way to eliminate the tattoo without drawing undue attention to it, and they had to do so without damaging morale. Failure either way might jeopardize their mission."

Elliott flipped a page in his notes and ran a finger down several lines. "The tattoo we reconstructed from thirty-two mutilated pieces of tissue superior to dismemberments is the recreation of a pennant worn by an elite force of warriors, a specialized Russian spetsnaz unit once under the command of the FSB and also known as a KGB Directorate, the Vega Group. The Spetsgruppa 'V' is referred to as Vympel."

"The Vympel was known for deployment in cities with especially important nuclear facilities. The Russians. It makes sense," Secretary of State Dabney said. "We know after the fall of the Soviet Union, they've been on the road to bankruptcy. This desperate move would confirm they see their future clearly. They have made a strategic decision to do something about it."

"They made a terrible decision when they tried to stand toe-to-toe with the United States. The Cold War gave them four expensive and wasted decades. Instead of working on their internal problems, they messed with the richest nation in the world."

"Russia has substantial geographic challenges and climatic problems," Dabney said. "Both limit them greatly. Basic transportation problems persist throughout their country to this day. Their rivers do not even provide an integrated network between population centers."

"And they don't have an adequate railway system either," Graham said. "By diverting time, money, and resources to a Cold War, they fell behind. Today there is no network to move agricultural products to market. They cannot build a sustainable revenue stream to support rural populations."

"Many parts of Russia have integrated with each other rather than with the Russian Empire," Dabney said. "That fractured reality further weakens—"

"—the empire," the POTUS broke in. "And it's because their military and security forces focused on holding the empire together, not on supporting the people and the economy. Today Russia depends on oil exports to fuel their troubled economy. Now we are an energy exporter, again their nemesis. Russia is hamstrung."

President Landon walked around his desk. State and Defense got the message—stop talking. The education process for the people in the room was over. It was time to focus on GRAY WOLF. "If I allow my cabinet and military advisors to relive Russian history and reconstruct geopolitical strategy, I'm afraid we'd be here into the night," Landers teased with a humble nod to the room. "Elliott, thank you and Dr. Cage and Dr. Osgard for excellent work in identifying GRAY WOLF. This will help define our next moves.

"Of course, and I understand," Elliott said.

"Elliott, this is Maureen Nye."

"Yes, Maureen."

"I was just notified we have located one of GRAY WOLF's human disposal machines in Canada—a semi-trailer in an abandoned barn twenty miles from Bone Lake. The device does include a radioactive-transmission component. There is a lysing infusion component as well. You are correct in your assumptions. The destruction of tissue at the cellular level and fragmentation of DNA across all cell types was carefully orchestrated."

"Tracking components of this human disposal machine may shed—"

"—new light, and is underway," Nye said. "You will be kept informed."

"Is there anything more," Landon asked of Elliott.

"In science, we navigate the unknown with knowns based on reproducible facts. In forensics, our mission is to bring objectivity to subjective matters. I caution all to receive our findings with measured caution. I have presented information we believe to be true. However, our findings express a level of *high certainty*, not an *absolute*.

"We know the Vympel tattoo is a revealing piece to this obscure puzzle. We are certain in our reconstruction and identification of it. However, we also are certain we are dealing with an entity—GRAY WOLF—that has demonstrated a consistent and predictable practice. GRAY WOLF is committed to manipulation and misleading."

"What are you saying, Elliott?" Landon asked.

"Although the Vympel tattoo points to the Russians, there is a chance GRAY WOLF is using it to mislead us. We should act on what we know, but must continue to seek more definitive information. May I make a recommendation—one outside my area of expertise, sir?"

"I doubt there are too many areas outside your expertise, Elliott. Please, recommend."

"As we move forward with the Russians, keep in mind there is a chance they are patsies. I must go to Minot to further hone the forensic tract, to be certain one way or another. We need to hear back from Tony Wilcox and Harold Turpin—the Key West hunt for Milton Busey, father of Roan Busey. We know Milton Busey engaged with GRAY WOLF. He is in Key West. He may be the only person alive who can identity GRAY WOLF for certain. And he may be able to tell us where GRAY WOLF is in the Minot area."

"What do you need from me, Elliott?" the President asked.

"I have worked with General Jamison in the past. I can help him on the ground in Minot. I need to be closer to GRAY WOLF. I cannot explain my methods—"

"You do understand that, at any moment, GRAY WOLF could cross a line. It might become necessary to contain them, to intervene in the Minot area," Landon warned.

"I do understand, Mr. President. That's not a factor for me. I need to go now."

"Very well. You have my approval. I will tell General Jamison you're on your way. I'm sure he would value your assistance.

"We will be in touch. Thank you, and God's speed."

"Thank you, Mr. President. Goodbye ..."

Several minutes after the speakerphone disconnected, a door opened into the Oval Office. Richard Parker, the President's Chief of Staff, rushed in and whispered into the President's ear. Landon's eyes sharpened as he took a deep breath. "Put him on the box now, Richard."

The President turned to the whirring room, which was engaged in modifying military and diplomatic plans and actions. "Excuse me." Heads turned. "Do not go. Sit. A missile has—"

"Mr. President, are you there?" Jamison scratched over the speakerphone.

Landon held a hand up. The room went silent. "We are in the Oval Office, Buck. You're on the box. Speak freely. Everyone here has top clearance."

"Mr. President, a medium range ballistic missile has left the silo, sir." The room gasped. "I am watching it climb now—"

"We've prepared for this," the POTUS said. "Were efforts to disarm successful?"

"We do not know, Mr. President. The Viking A-9 launch sequence was initiated when we were in the middle of the disarming protocol. We immediately redirected resources from other disarming assignments, but we didn't have a lot of time. The preset launch sequence jumped forward several minutes, for reasons unclear to us at this time. We don't know if GRAY WOLF circumvented standard operating procedure or if there was a programming problem as a result of our intervention."

"What the hell does all that mean, Buck?" the President barked.

"It means we lost precious time. She left her nest before we could confirm success."

"When will we know if it was a success?" President Landon asked.

"When she enters the downward trajectory phase toward the target," Jamison said. "That is when a missile is programed to arm itself. And that is when we know if our action to block that procedure has been successful. But, we do not want to wait until then."

President Landon stood in a cold silence with fourteen others in the Oval Office. He turned to the window and snow-covered Rose Garden. "Someone needs to talk to Canada."

The Secretary of State left the room.

Chief General Jamison stood with the top commanders of the 94th Wing. They looked out the tinted windows of the control center and across the Minot Air Force Base. On the ground, dozens of fighter planes moved onto the runways like angry bees leaving the hive. Jamison squinted at the ice-blue horizon and watched the burning tail and billowing plume and fire climb the darkening winter sky.

"We are in the boost phase, Mr. President. It will last three minutes. We have two thresholds available to take her down before weaponization. The first is the midcourse phase. About an hour ago we scrambled fighters armed with the appropriate antiballistic missiles. Several are waiting over central Canada."

"Is our technology there, Buck?" the POTUS asked.

"There is a massive speed handicap. Launching antiballistic missiles close to the calculated intercept point is crucial. It is to our advantage to know where GRAY WOLF is sending this one. We learned that information during the disarming process. Our guidance systems are more precise than ever before. We have the most advanced navigation on the planet. Top secret active-radar homing technology is in play. I believe we have a chance to hit her."

"And if we miss in the *midcourse* phase?" the President asked.

"She has a target 600 miles away. If we miss her in the midcourse, we will take her in the early stage of the downward trajectory, the free-fall, the final phase. The MRBM has a two-minute window of unguided vulnerability. We will get her there, sir."

"And if we don't?"

"We will pray we disarmed her in the nest," Jamison said, anticipating the next question from the President of the United States.

"And if our medium range ballistic missile is not disarmed?"

Jamison paused, and so did the heartbeats of everyone in the room. "Death and destruction like we've never seen, Mr. President."

Jamison and his commanders watched the tail flame fade into the northern horizon. *Lord, have mercy on us all ...*

PART FOUR

KILL**ALL**THE**MONSTERS**
DESCENDENTS AND GODS

CHAPTER **30**

"If you stop to ask, you'll be talking to yourself."
Anonymous

After the explosion, Tony slammed to the floor and the wooden, ladder-back chair cracked under his weight. *Where'd he get me?* He scanned his body as he struggled to get free. From experience, he knew a bullet wound always feels wet before the pain.

The smell of burnt gunpowder filled the room as he kept working the ropes around his chest and legs. *I don't need to die from a butt wound.* "What're you doin' Busey?" *You're awful damn quiet.* "You savorin' the moment, old man? I know you got two more rounds, you sick bastard. What're you waitin' for?"

Ramsey had a small cottage. The living room opened into the kitchen and a hall that led to the back—the bedrooms. Although he hadn't had the pleasure of a guided tour—as he was being pushed around by the muzzle of Busey's rifle—Wilcox had gotten enough of a look, even with the blinds down and curtains pulled. At the time, he was thinking that—if he got the chance—he would dive into the hallway and escape out a back window. Now, tied to a chair, lying on his back with his feet in the air, escape was the last thing on his mind. He leaned to see around the edge of the chair. *What're you doin' Busey? What the hell ...!*

Busey was in the shadows in the kitchen, his back against the refrigerator and the butt of the rifle on his hip. "Listen to me, Milton. We don't have to do this. There's a way out." Tony saw

Busey's eyes fixed on the hall to the bedrooms where he'd put the bodies of the sniper and Bowman. "There's things you know about the people in Minot, the people you worked with. That information's valuable, Milton. The feds want it bad. They'd forget all this mess and probably let you out of Pingree if you helped 'em."

Tony squinted. The old man's shirt was soaked in blood. He'd been hit in the stomach. *Someone else is in this cottage.* He watched Busey start to raise his rifle. The man's sick grin grew on his hideous face. Milton had found a target.

"You're supposed to be dead," Busey bellowed.

"I'm a ghost. I've returned for you ... sir."

Who the hell ...? Tony watched Busey take aim, his cheek pressed against the stock. Another explosion and more burnt gunpowder filled the room. Then the old man dropped his rifle and slid down the refrigerator to the kitchen floor.

A hand grabbed Tony's shoulder. "Sorry, old boy. I would have been here sooner but the bloody windows in the back have screens." Harold Turpin leaned his fat face over Wilcox. "You are bullet-free I assume," he said with eyes moving to the kitchen.

"I thought you were, ah—"

"—dead, I believe is the word you are searching for." Turpin groaned as he flipped Tony into a sitting position on the crippled chair. "It appears you've made considerable progress with your knots. I will leave you to it and check the status of Mr. Busey. He did not leave options."

"I hope you didn't kill the bastard," Tony groused, fighting his knots.

"Well then the man should have set his rifle down after the abdominal shot," Turpin said as he rounded the breakfast bar with caution. "Mr. Busey. Do not move, sir."

When Turpin leaned into the kitchen, he holstered his weapon. Tony kicked free of his ropes and jumped to his feet.

"Thought I lost you out there, Harry," he said as he padded himself down checking for injuries. "You were hit in the chest. I saw the blood comin' out of your mouth and nose. I tried to check for a pulse, but the son-a-bitch shot my arm—grazed me. Ruined a perfectly good sport coat."

Turpin pressed two fingers to Busey's carotid artery. "I did not want to shoot him. I paused. We would have benefitted significantly by turning him over to your CIA alive. I'm quite certain they would have convinced the old boy to spill all of his intestines, so to speak."

"Guts, Harry. Guts, for God's sake." Tony joined Turpin over Busey's bloody corpse. "The old guy wasn't about to leave here with anyone." Tony found the hole in Turpin's lapel. "I knew you were hit. What are you, some kind of English super freak?"

"Americans rarely listen," Turpin said. "They talk constantly. American homicide detectives never listen unless it is about one of their bloody cases. If you had been paying attention, instead of fondling your beloved 45 caliber Glock, projectile clips, and Japanese Nambu leather holster, you might have learned something new."

Tony pulled his gun from Busey's waist and grabbed a rag from the sink to clean off the blood. "Sorry, but I don't remember—"

"Well of course you do not remember, Anthony. You are a bloody American homicide detective busy with your toys."

"Point made," Tony mumbled.

"My Kevlar suit saved the day, sir, para-aramid synthetic fibers by Nomex and Technora. A new material designed to assist in the reduction of impact and avoid penetration." Turpin got to his feet and looked to the dark hall. "I did expect to be rendered unconscious for a time." He wiped blood from his nose with a monogrammed cloth handkerchief. "However, I do not recall a word being said in the accompanying printed materials about

Kevlar's propensity to cause a bloody nose and leave a horrid bruise."

"Oh for God's sake, you're alive. Try not to complain." Tony moved toward the dark hall and whispered, "We need to secure the place. I don't know what the hell's back there."

The two looked in the first bedroom, where Turpin had entered the cottage. It was empty. They opened the second door and found two bodies. Bowman and the sniper were dead on the bed. The last bedroom was empty. The bathroom was empty. They were alone.

"I gotta get some information to somebody fast," Tony said. "I think I can tell them where to find GRAY WOLF."

Turpin stopped in his tracks, and pulled out his cell phone. "Yes. This is Harold Turpin. We need you to come—now. I'm afraid I do not have the address. Ping my phone. Thank you."

"I have the address, Harry."

"I'm quite certain my way is faster. Your CIA has been tracking us since we landed. They should be here in—" The doorbell rang.

"Son of a bitch!"

"You may have won the war, old boy," Turpin chided.

The CIA agent set up the government modified AIRTERM KY-1000 on the coffee table. "This is a secured terminal for voice and data communications to the Pentagon. CIA Director James Herbolt insisted on direct contact the moment you and Mr. Turpin had something. He is standing by with his team."

"Good to know," Wilcox said as he found his pack of cigarettes next to the padded chair where Milton Busey had been drinking beer and reveled in his twisted life memories.

From the sofa by the terminal, Turpin watched the CIA team work the scene—taking pictures, bagging bodies, processing weapons, and gathering physical evidence. Wilcox joined him, lighting a cigarette. "Let's get this thing going. I have some vital information for Herbolt."

The agent flipped the last toggle and typed a half-dozen codes for satellite access. "We are on line with the Pentagon," the agent said. "We now wait for acceptance of transmission."

"2 4 7 2 2 clearance, over—"

"Agent Raven 42K7, Key West, Wilcox/Turpin priority, Minot, GRAY WOLF, over—"

"Hello, gentlemen. James Herbolt here. If this blasted gadget's working, I'm talking to Tony Wilcox and Harold Turpin."

"We are both here," Tony said through a cloud of cigarette smoke.

"Excellent. I understand you found Milton Busey ... and he is dead."

"Yes to both," Tony said. "We tracked him down and things got a bit dicey."

"Unfortunate, but not unexpected," Herbolt said. "The man does have a dismal record. What did we learn, if anything?"

"Milton Busey worked through the Bowman, Weller & Garcia Law firm for about a year. They represented the unknown entity. Busey claims he knows nothing about—"

"GRAY WOLF," Herbolt said.

"He told me he was offered a lot of money to provide information he gained from his work as a demolition expert in the ground-based ICBM program in Minot. Milton was employed by the government in the 1960s and 1990s. He participated in the construction of twenty missile silos and two LCCs in the '60s. We invited him back three decades later to demolish the same sites he helped construct."

"We can confirm all of that," Herbolt said. "Mr. Busey was on the government payroll. His role was as you've described. Do we know what information GRAY WOLF purchased?"

"Milton knew the location of an abandoned Launch Control Capsule."

"An *abandoned* LCC?" Herbolt asked.

"One of the two he was to destroy in the '90s survived the demolition process."

"I can't imagine that would be possible, but please continue."

"He talked about a cavern—a hundred or so feet underground and a mile long. He said this cavern is north of Belden, the place where he spent time as a kid on his aunt's farm. He said he and a few friends found the cavern. To his knowledge, there's only one point of entry. Until now, Milton was the only one alive who knew how to get in the cavern."

"I'm not following," Herbolt said. "You say there's an intact LCC, and then you're talking about a cavern. What am I missing?"

Tony dropped his cigarette into an empty beer bottle and lit another. "The Launch Control Capsule is near Belden, North Dakota. It was adjacent to this unknown cavern. When Busey blew the thing up, the whole damn LCC slid into the cavern intact, and then the ground settled like it had been obliterated. Government inspectors didn't know about the cavern. They signed off on the project."

"My goodness," Herbolt said.

That's an odd reaction, Tony thought. He shook it off and continued. "With the help of his son—Roan—Milton got GRAY WOLF into the cavern and to the abandoned LCC."

Tony watched Turpin slide back on the sofa, rubbing his chest. He watched the CIA people bagging everything that had to do with Milton. Some had already started to scrub the place. *You guys are erasing Busey from the planet before you know anything. What's going on here?* The unfolding process, and Tony's conversation with Herbolt, seemed off.

Maybe I'm not thinking straight, Tony thought.

"What else, Mr. Wilcox?" Herbolt asked.

"Right," Tony blinked back into the conversation. "GRAY WOLF took pictures of wires and conduits hanging in the cavern. Roan took those pictures to Dr. Rice who gave them to Milton. I think Milton gave some direction on reconnection. Roan may have implemented."

"You think, and may have?" Herbolt pushed. "Why are you struggling?"

"Milton said someone else was involved, someone who meant something to him growing up. He wouldn't say anything more. I doubt his truck-driving son had the expertise to work with the wiring. And I'm not sure what their objective with the wiring was. Just my impressions."

"I see," Herbolt said. "Tell me this. Is it your educated guess that GRAY WOLF possesses an abandoned LCC and are accessing our ICBM system, their location off the grid?"

"Yes. He said they had their own experts. I suspect Milton helped with the basics and others took over," Tony said.

"Anything else?" Herbolt asked.

Turpin cut in. "Harold Turpin here, Mr. Herbolt. "We do have in our possession $460,000 American dollars in two suitcases. Mr. Busey had orchestrated a transfer of funds tonight on Sunset Pier after sundown. We intervened. I believe representatives of GRAY WOLF will still be in the vicinity of the pier tonight looking for an opportunity to eliminate Mr. Busey."

"What are you recommending?"

"Anthony and I would be pleased to pass the project to your people, should you have an interest in a potential opportunity for more information."

"That is a substantial sum of money," Herbolt said. "We will take over tonight's assignment. We will sample the bills now so we can follow the money trail, too."

"Is there anything new we need to know?" Tony asked.

Herbolt cleared his throat. "Two things. First, Dr. Sumner identified GRAY WOLF. We are dealing with the Russians. Second, at the moment, we have a medium range ballistic missile in flight over Canada."

"Jesus!" Tony gasped. "Tell me we can stop it."

"We are attempting to do just that, as we speak."

"And tell me GRAY WOLF cannot launch another one."

"Although their selections are dwindling—we are disarming the Minot missile arsenal—I cannot say we are safe yet. I suggest you not talk to your friend, Elliott. He is extremely busy in Minot with General Jamison."

"Why in the hell would you send a forensic pathologist to Minot?" Tony barked.

"My feelings exactly," Herbolt said. "The President supports Dr. Sumner's decision to help. On occasions like these our military experts can miss the obvious. President Landon believes Elliott brings something to the equation, something that could make a difference."

"Thank you for your help. The return trip to Key West was worth it. Good bye."

The AIRTERM KY-1000 whistled and went silent. The agent flipped toggles and slid the dead terminal into the silver suitcase. "Thank you, gentlemen," he said on his way out.

When the cloaked communication line closed, Herbolt turned to his associates. "We say nothing about this. The Belden story dies here. Understood?" The room nodded.

"Get our people in place at the Sunset Pier. Nobody leaves there alive. I want our top snipers. This, too, is a project we will not share outside this room."

"Human history becomes more and more a race between
education and catastrophe."
H.G. Wells

Day Six, 1420 CST

"She's in free-fall, Mr. President." Jamison gripped his head
mic and stared at the monitor; the unthinkable unfolded
over Winnipeg. They watched, each second an eternity. "There
she is. We have a visual." The rogue MRBM from Minot
appeared on schedule.

"Where is my X-51?" The General asked. Then he touched
his lips like a father whispering to a child—*God help us all ...*

Somewhere between Bismarck and Minot, 1400 CST

"Why Belden?" Cage asked. "And why are we not answering our
phones?"

The white Range Rover sped across the treeless plains of
North Dakota on an empty Highway 83. Elliott squinted behind
his Ray Bans at the deep snow with the icecap that could hold a
herd of elk. The pounding sun and subzero temperatures
transformed or killed everything.

"I got a text from Tony. They found Milton Busey."

"And you're telling me this now?" Cage said.

"Didn't plan on you being with me," Elliott said. "Busey is
dead."

"Why am I not surprised ... the Busey part?"

"He claimed he didn't know GRAY WOLF. Worked with the Bowman, Weller, & Garcia law firm." Elliott adjusted the visor and glanced at the fuel gage. Running out of gas was not an option—they would be dead in twenty minutes.

"So he did sell missile-site demolition information," Cage said.

"Yes, and more. That's why we're going to Belden and not answering our phones. You've been up here twenty years," Elliott said. "What do you know about Belden?"

Cage sat up in his seat and smiled; at last he had something to do besides staring at snow. "I actually know something about the place. There's not much to do in North Dakota when I'm not working or doing my research.

"Belden was founded in the early 1900s. A small farming community that never really made it. No more than twenty-five people. It's a ghost town today. I visited the place a few years ago. Had an interest in regional Indian lore—great history up here. Belden was named after a man they called an *Indian agent at-large* back in the day. W. L. Belden was stationed at the Fort Berthold Indian Reservation—the home of the Mandan, Hidatsa, and Arikara Nations."

"Did you say nobody lives in Belden today?"

"There's one guy. Lives in an old gas station," Cage said. "A Lakota Indian. Gotta be close to a hundred now. Why're we going there? The place is on the edge of the earth."

"Milton Busey is credited for demolishing twenty missile silos and two launch control capsules. He worked in the Belden area. GRAY WOLF may be in one of the LCCs."

"If they were demolished, how's that possible?" Cage asked.

Elliott's phone vibrated—another call from DC. "I know they can track us. I don't want to talk to anyone, not now. They'll turn us around." He threw the phone in the backseat.

"Milton talked about a cavern," Elliott said. "He described it to Tony, a hundred feet underground and about a mile long. Said Milton blew up an LCC and it fell into the cavern—like spitting out a watermelon seed. The LCC is supposed to be intact in that cavern."

"And the military didn't know?" Cage asked.

"The ground settled like expected. Didn't know about a cavern. They ran standard seismic tests and concluded the LCC had disintegrated in the massive explosions."

"I can see how they—"

"Milton said he was the last man alive who knew how to get in that cavern. It does not appear on any geological surveys, although I haven't done any research on it myself. Milton and Roan worked about a year with GRAY WOLF. They handled reconnection of network wires and cables to the LCC or something else. They may have gained access off the grid."

"Well, that would explain why the 94th Wing can't find them," Cage said.

"Tony said there could be a third guy involved. Milton, Roan, and a guy who was once close to Milton. That's all he had."

"Someone with brains. I don't think Milton or Roan could pull all this off."

"That's a logical assumption. Another one is Milton could be lying about everything. I guess this is all we've got to go on. It's enough for me to take a closer look, regardless of what Washington or Minot have to say about it. I'm not dying in Bismarck, my friend. No offense."

"None taken," Cage said, chuckling.

"So, assuming Milton is telling the truth, you think we can locate that secret entrance. When we get inside, you think we can go a mile underground and sneak up on the LCC. When we get there, we can pull out our scalpels and convince GRAY WOLF—

the mean Russians who killed and mutilated their comrades—to cease and desist."

"Some version of that," Elliott said as he turned onto Highway 8.

"This is not what we do, Elliott. Why don't we give this information to General Jamison at the Base? He can wipe Belden off the map. Bye-bye GRAY WOLF."

"We don't know anything for certain, Morgan. We don't know who or what is out there. We don't have a lot of time. And we do not need to give Jamison another loose end to manage right now. This angle would be just one more distraction, maybe from the real problems—the disarming 135 Minuteman III ICBMs, managing nuclear surprises, and keeping GRAY WOLF talking. Anyway, I'm sure Wilcox and Turpin told them everything they told me."

"I guess when you say it that way." Cage looked out the window at the sun reflecting off the snow and ice. "I'm thinking like a forensic pathologist—everything is a tidy process. You're taking me out of my comfort zone, Elliott."

Cage rubbed his neck like a prize fighter struggling to climb back up from the canvas. "I don't know when I stopped taking chances in life. I used to look for adventure. Now I hide from it. I guess it takes the threat of a *nuclear holocaust* to open a man's eyes."

"Maybe the old man living in the gas station knows something about this cavern," Elliott said, moving on. "If he's as old as you say, a Lakota Indian should know the area better than anyone. What's his name?"

"Chankoowashtay," Cage said. "Did I tell you he was blind?"

"Chankoowashtay is Sioux for *good road*," Elliott said. "I would imagine lack of eyesight has presented little problems for him. Did you talk for a while?" Elliott asked turning on the deicer. The shadows were getting longer. The temperature was dropping.

"We did. At first, he didn't want to say much. Then he warmed up to me. I found him to be an interesting man. He had a lot to say about the Sioux Nation. I got the sense he was not one of the angry Indians. He was full, if you know what I mean. He also knew a lot about Lakota legend. I remember one about the gray wolf—the infrequent visitor to North Dakota today."

"How apropos," Elliott sighed. "Tell me about it."

"The Lakota gray wolf is nothin' like the GRAY WOLF contingency force we're trying to stop from starting World War III."

"General Jamison is a North Dakotan," Elliott said. "He had a reason for the code name—GRAY WOLF. I'm curious about why. Please, tell me the legend of the gray wolf."

Cage ran a hand through his hair and gripped his chin as if he had a beard. "Long ago, on the frozen banks of the Yellowstone River, *the one* was born and given the name *Jumping Badger*. He revealed courage and vision and patience. And he revealed an understanding of life unlike any before him. They believed one day *the one* would lead the resistance of the peaceful nomadic hunters against the erring ways of the flying eagle, and he would be known to all the Standing Rock Sioux Nation as *Tatanka Iyotake*—"

"—the buffalo bull who sits," Elliott whispered. "Lakota tongue."

"Very good. Yes. Sitting Bull," Cage said.

"And the elders spoke of another worthy nomadic hunter of the Great Plains," Elliott said. "This one stood vigil on that first day on the frozen banks of the Yellowstone, and again on the prairie the night Tatanka took his last breath and his spirit soared."

"*Canis lupus*—follower of an ever-changing course, hearer of the clouds passing overhead, and seer of two looks away—knows all the world's beginnings and all the world's futures," Cage said. "On the seventh day of every seventh winter after Tatanka took his last breath, the gray wolf speaks to the moon and touches his spirit and roams the Great Plains to evict evil and protect descendants of peaceful men." Cage turned from the window to Elliott. "It is said the sacred mission of the gray wolf can be heard in the whispering winds and only in the tongue of the Lakota—"

"—ktė iyúha hé Iya," Elliott whispered.

"I'm impressed," Cage said. "Your photographic memory is a true gift."

Elliott smiled. "*Kill all the monsters* sounds much nicer in the Lakota tongue."

"Then you have heard the legend of the gray wolf?" Cage said

"I have. A long time ago, when I was very young. I read everything I could get my hands on. I didn't fully understand why until much later.

"*Lakota Belief and Ritual* by James R. Walker was a book I valued. To this day, we do not understand or appreciate the American Indian's depth of knowledge of our world." Elliott lifted his visor and adjusted his sunglasses. "I have not thought about that for a very long time."

"The Lakota legend presents the gray wolf as a wonderful, protective force roaming the Great Plains," Cage said. "I don't know why Jamison gave the name to our hostile invaders."

I don't either ... yet. "On the seventh day of the seventh winter, the flying eagle drops his head and the gray wolf howls," Elliott said. Then he braked and pulled off the road. He threw the car into park. Staring down the glistening black asphalt that divided the white world, he removed his Ray-bans and said, "Sitting Bull died on December 15, 1890."

"I would not have committed that one to memory," Cage quipped. "Why'd you stop?"

"Today is December 22, 2016, one-hundred-twenty-six years after Sitting Bull's death. Today is the eighteenth event, Morgan. Today is the seventh day of the next seventh winter!"

"My God," Cage mumbled. "What're you thinkin' that means?"

* * *

At 1400 central time, the 94th Wing Command discovered GRAY WOLF had found a way to launch one of two offline, medium-range ballistic missiles—a feat they had once believed impossible.

The MRBM housed in Viking A-9 silo came alive. It lit up the boards at the Pentagon and the Central Command Center in the bunkers beneath Minot Air Force Base. The 94th Wing buzzed as their efforts accelerated to block the missile's automated arming system before launch. The medium range missiles had both been taken out of service one month earlier—scheduled for dismantling in the spring. That action made remote-intervention less-than-optimal. The 94th Wing Command had minutes to try to reprogram.

At 1420 central time, the hijacked MRBM left its silo, destination Winnipeg. Reprograming had been completed but not confirmed. The 94th Wing would know success or failure only when the rogue missile entered the last phase—free fall over its target. Only then could the warhead's arming protocol be initiated—and blocked.

"Hoping for success is not enough," Jamison bellowed. "We have 720,000 reasons why. Our efforts to destroy this commandeered missile in the mid-course phase failed. Now our only opportunity to stop her is in free-fall over the target. We must disable her before the arming protocol is initiated at a three-mile altitude.

"Where is my X-51?" the General demanded.

"X-51 EAGLE is on course, Mach 7." The robotic voice echoed in the otherwise dead-silent command center. The eerie absence of human emotion added to the fear and discomfort that hung in the dark room of monitors and giant screens in light of the unfolding catastrophe. Forty-two airmen, six commanders, and one five-star General watched the MRBM plummet toward Winnipeg as a new blinking light entered eastern Canada.

"Union ETA seventy-six seconds," said the robotic monitor.

Jamison covered his mic with his big hand and turned to Commander Troy, who was sitting a few feet away pounding a keyboard. "Did you send the message to the President?"

"Regarding GRAY WOLF demands, sir?" he asked, his fingers poised above his keyboard like a pianist pausing during the execution of a concerto.

"Regarding GRAY WOLF's *latest* demands, son," Jamison clarified.

Commander Troy lowered his hands and swallowed hard. "I did, sir. The President agrees with you. As ordered, all assets are pulling back. A hundred-mile radius around Minot will be void of military apparatus and personnel, within the hour demanded by GRAY WOLF. The Pentagon has confirmed deactivation or deterrence of satellite and air surveillance assets. That would include unmanned drones operating in the state. Private and commercial flights have been canceled or rerouted to eliminate any chance of misunderstanding. Nothing will fly into or out of the GRAY WOLF-designated zone."

"Good. We do not know the extent of their monitoring capabilities," Jamison said.

"No, sir. We do not."

"No military presence," Jamison said. "Zero risk taken. Only civilians permitted on the ground in the hundred-mile zone, Minot the center point."

"Yes, sir."

"The bastards have us by the balls," Jamison growled.

He looked at the floating time bars on the edge of the large screen, focusing again on the new flashing marker that inched on a line toward Winnipeg. The satellite on the eastern edge of the North American continent had a view of two-thirds of Canada. U.S. Chief General Buck Jamison had approved the use of the asset.

He let go of his mic and spoke as a leader. "We are fifty-seven seconds from union, Mr. President." Jamison shook his head, disgusted that he could do nothing more but wait.

The POTUS, his cabinet, and his military advisors sat in a bunker beneath the White House with all eyes glued to monitors and all ears straining to hear the speakerphone. Alternate strategies and tentative tactics were in place. All who needed to know were in the know—the rest of the world remained in the dark. All resources were in place. All military assets were deployed around the world on standby. Even a global nuclear war *started by mistake* required the most aggressive defensive actions.

"Thank you, Buck," the President said as he watched the blinking light enter the screen. It marked the movement of X-51 EAGLE. The MRBM light blinked over Winnipeg. Discussions with the Russians had stalled. The evidence had been shared—GRAY WOLF identified. The Kremlin had been informed that their secret force was inside a U.S. missile LCC —an untenable situation. The VEGA Group—a known spetsnaz unit under the command of the FSB—would be dealt with soon.

As anticipated, the Kremlin had denied culpability. President Landon had made it clear: Russia would be destroyed first if GRAY WOLF launched a second U.S. ballistic missile, or if the one on its way to Winnipeg could not be stopped. The death of a million people would be on Russia's hands.

Losing one million innocent people to a nuclear blast squeezed the life out of Landon's heart and pushed his Parkinson's to the limits. But his mission in life had never felt more clear. If the world survived this *terminal breach*, he would lead the charge to dismantle the world's nuclear arsenals.

"By definition, Sumner and Cage are civilians," the POTUS said with nervous eyes. Jamison and Landon had a long history, and Buck read between the lines. They both knew the two men on their way to Belden—pursuing a long shot—might die with millions of unsuspecting souls. If GRAY WOLF could launch one missile, they could launch more. Only the President's cabinet and a few top military advisors knew the *terminal breach containment options* once controlled by a computer were now solely in the hands of Landon, and he had decided that, if another silo door opened, he would send an armada of Minuteman III missiles to Minot to obliterate all nuclear assets and GRAY WOLF. Such an action would be a swift, effective end to the present danger. But the collateral damage would be horrific.

American *hypersonic technology* had been the best kept secret of the decade. The stealth Pentagon program produced game-changing aircraft and missiles capable of more than seven times the speed of sound. And they could avoid detection. Russian and Chinese moles penetrated at the highest levels, but they only obtained intelligence on the first iterations. They did not know the Pentagon had kept the name X-51 to hide their most advanced accomplishments.

The U.S. hypersonic program had advanced a second decade ahead of the rest of the world. The *newest* X-51 EAGLE aircraft traveled at speeds well above 7,000 miles per hour. Today, it would engage one of the American medium-range ballistic missiles over Winnipeg, a thought difficult to comprehend. The

EAGLE would release a missile of its own, something never done before, never contemplated, and another long shot for the General.

"We're at twenty-eight seconds and counting," Jamison said.

The robotic monitor took over. "The EAGLE enters Manitoba airspace. The EAGLE passes over Whitemouth. Vector adjustments, on course to Viking A-9. Twenty seconds."

Heads bowed. Eyes closed. Prayers flowed.

"Ten seconds."

The X-51 EAGLE closed on Winnipeg at an intercept altitude of 4.8 miles. Like an uninvited meteor streaking across the heavens, it left a plume of boiling mist in the subzero sky and a chain of sonic booms like infinite thunder from hell.

Jamison touched his earpiece. "I'm taking her in, sir," said the EAGLE.

The alarms went off in the Central Command Center. The sirens ramped at the Minot Air Force Base. The spinning red lights came alive in each corner of bunkers in Minot and DC. General Jamison closed his eyes. Only he and the pilot knew what had to be done.

The robotic monitor said, "Five ... four ..."

CHAPTER 32

"You've never had a problem until you've had a problem at
Mach 7."
Anonymous

Minot, North Dakota, 1443 CST

"She's arming! Viking A-9 has begun the arming protocol in
free-fall over target."

The giant screen in the 94th Wing Command Center showed
the EAGLE closing in at a phenomenal speed. The intersecting
lines had been plotted, the systems programed. It allowed for zero
variance. Inches or milliseconds would produce another miss.
Only General Jamison knew what would happen next,
something he could not stop.

Commander Richard Troy pounded his keyboard as the rest
in the room could only watch the lines and blinking orbs
converge over Winnipeg. From the corner of his eye Jamison saw
the four MPs enter the room. He held up a hand. They stopped
and waited.

The robotic voice continued its cold countdown. "Three ...
two ... one—"

The giant screen went white. The intensity of the blast
blinded the satellite and delayed the feeds. The room gasped and
then fell silent. Commander Troy stopped typing when there
was no more he could do. Minot and DC and the Pentagon
waited for the next words from Jamison.

He held his earpiece with two fingers and stared at the empty screen. Then he moved his head-mic into position and said, "We stopped Viking A-9."

The 94th Wing Command Center erupted into celebration as the base sirens silenced and the spinning red lights died and the alarms faded. Elation rolled through the bunker beneath the White House as cabinet elders and military leaders cheered and shook hands.

President Landon smiled and signaled calm. The room settled. "Talk to us, Buck," said the POTUS. "What's happening over Winnipeg?"

Jamison waved to the MPs. The four approached and stood behind him and Commander Troy as the giant screen came alive and more reports flowed into the general's earpiece.

"Mr. President, at 1443 central the EAGLE successfully intercepted a rogue medium range ballistic missile at an altitude of 4.7 miles above Winnipeg, Canada."

The room cheered again. The General smiled and held up a hand. "I am pleased to report four F-16 Falcons witnessed the intercept eliminating the threat. They are tracking debris projected to move fifty-four miles northwest. It will drop into Lake Manitoba—

"Mr. President, I am saddened to report one casualty. Captain Abbey Nevel, pilot of the EAGLE, gave her life to stop the rogue missile, sir." The room fell silent as the giant screen flickered and the aerial view of central Canada and the Midwestern United States returned, and a picture of Captain Nevel appeared in the corner of the screen.

"In the end, there were no good choices, sir. Too many inflight adjustments would have been required to keep the EAGLE moving within striking range of the target. Captain Nevel determined the planned release of our Q-40 Meteor Missile had zero chance for success. The changing variables were too great. Captain Nevel refused to abort the mission. She stayed with the EAGLE and took her to the target. Her decision accomplished the impossible, Mr. President."

General Jamison cleared his throat after a long silence and spoke with solemn candor. "Assessments and salvage operations have begun. We are working in concert with our Canadian allies. They have been with us every step of the way, Mr. President."

Commander Troy started to get up from his chair. The General placed a firm hand on his shoulder and whispered, "Stay with me."

"Congratulations to your team," President Landon said. "Every airman, missileer, and commander at the 94th Wing will remember this historic day the rest of their lives, a day few others will ever know about. And every one of us will honor Captain Abbey Nevel, an American who made the ultimate sacrifice for her country and saved perhaps a million lives today. The steady coordination of the EAGLE, stopping of a disastrous nuclear missile strike, and every effort by each who can hear my voice has achieved this success and given us another opportunity to stop those who wish to bring harm to the world."

"Thank you for those words, Mr. President. They will carry us forward as we continue our work to stop GRAY WOLF." Jamison said. "I have a few matters to attend to, sir. I will reconnect with you within the hour."

"More developments, Buck?" asked the President.

"Yes, sir." He looked at Commander Troy as Senior Airman First Class Frank Edgerton stepped up behind the MPs. The General disconnected and pulled out his ear piece.

"Is there a new problem, sir?" Commander Troy asked, looking at the MPs.

"You tell me," Jamison said.

"I don't understand," Troy said as the four MPs parted and Airman Edgerton stepped forward. "What is *he* doing here? Get back to your work station, Airman."

The General nodded. MPs pulled Commander Troy from his chair. "Airman Edgerton, do what you do, young man," Jamison said, pointing to the empty chair that sat before the keyboard and monitor.

Edgerton sat and snapped his knuckles, and then his fingers danced on the keyboard. He moved with speed and accuracy. Lines of numbers climbed Commander Troy's monitor. When the typing stopped, the numbers froze, and the big screen came alive for all to see.

"What are we looking at, Airman?" General Jamison asked as the room quieted and all eyes studied the giant screen. Every missileer in the 94th Wing understood the significance of the command sequence history displayed. Every airman sitting at a workstation with administrative responsibility for a launch control capsule and missile silo knew the significance of each stroke. They bypassed standard protocol. Some commands altered missile flight path. Other commands commandeered missile warhead arming protocol. The missileers had done it all in countless war game simulations. Most damning on the big screen were time log postings that tracked each issued command.

"Sir, Commander Troy talked to Viking A-9 prior to launch, in the cruise phase, and in free-fall," said Airman Edgerton. "Commands issued appear in the left column, each instruction sent to Viking A-9. The time log is the right column. This captures the initiation and completion time parameters for each command." Edgerton highlighted a block of commands. "This shows Commander Troy guided Viking A-9 MRBM from launch to—"

"I did nothing of the sort, Airman," Troy barked as he turned to Jamison. "This is manufactured data. It is some kind of set-up! I'm outraged. Are you accusing me of—"

The General held up his hand. "Continue, Airman Edgerton," he ordered.

"Yes, sir." Edgerton returned to the keyboard and a flurry of strokes. The page of commands and times on the big screen refreshed. A new column appeared labeled "Access Codes."

"These codes are required," Edgerton said. "They permit a missile to accept inflight guidance from here, the Central Command Center. Although a missile is released with preprogramed instructions, we reserve a capability of modifying flight path and warhead arming parameters. This shows the Viking A-9 missile accepted inflight guidance from *this workstation*. The unique access codes belong to Commander Troy."

"And this is why our efforts to block arming protocol in flight failed?" Jamison asked, knowing the answer.

"Yes, sir," Airman Edgerton said.

"Someone is doing this to me!" Troy barked. "There's a mole in this room."

"That's the first time you've told the truth, Mr. Troy," the General said. "I'm looking at the mole. You've managed to orchestrate much of GRAY WOLF's activities from the beginning. Your personal access code is right there. We looked back, sir. You have been involved in opening silo doors and now launching an armed MRBM. My God!"

Troy struggled to move, but the MPs held him firm. He was going nowhere. "Someone got my access code!" he insisted. "I've been set up. I did not do—"

"I changed your personal access code at 1400, Mr. Troy. Only you and I had it. I had to be sure. I could not believe a mole could have risen through the ranks at the 94th Wing."

Airman Edgerton scrolled through the commands sent to Viking A-9.

"As you can see, at 1401, your new access code appears," Jamison said. "You used it fourteen times. I watched you. You desperately attempted to manage an evasive flight path in the free fall. You had some success." The General stepped into Troy's face. "You forced Captain Nevel to abort our original plan. Captain Nevel could not get a lock on the free-fall phase because you managed to tilt the missile enough to move it inches off course.

"When Captain Nevel and the EAGLE closed in on the rogue MRBM, you were the only one in the room pounding a keyboard," Jamison said.

"We were on to you, but you still managed to disrupt the free fall. We ran out of time. We had no more options. The missile was arming. Abbey Nevel and I knew the damage was already done."

The General turned away from Troy and stared at the picture on the big screen. "I didn't want her to—but she said we had no other choice. You!" he said, unable to contain his rage as he poked Troy's chest. "You killed Captain Abbey Nevel, and she saved a million people this day."

Each missileer stood and turned toward the General. They stared at Commander Troy, the man who had demanded they not look up from their monitors and never talk to others. Now, in defiance, they stared at the mole with sizzling contempt in their eyes.

"You will be charged with treason," Jamison announced as he signaled the MPs. "Are we still hanging men for that?"

"This is not over!" Troy scoffed. "You don't know anything. You think it was just me. You're fools! GRAY WOLF is still in control."

"Get this traitor out of here," Jamison ordered. In unison, the missileers turned their backs.

When the MPs had hustled the squirming Troy out of the command center, missileers returned to their workstations, astonished by what they'd just witnessed. General Jamison left the 94th Wing central command center for his office. He needed a moment of reflection before calling the President—because he knew much more had to be done.

His walk through the hectic halls seemed longer than usual. Troy's wild claims had to be taken seriously. When the General's office door closed behind him, he stood alone at the window. He took in the supreme authority of the blazing orb above the glistening white horizon, a view that had not changed since the beginning of time.

Most knew General Brandon (Buck) Jamison's history. They knew he had been born in Grand River, South Dakota and had grown up on a ranch nestled in the Great Plains. Some knew about his Lakota Indian roots and about his great, great, half uncle, Spotted Elk. Everyone admired the General's passion for Native American culture and his knowledge of Lakota legend and lore. Only President Landon knew the General's greatest secret of all, a secret he had kept with a very few all his life.

As a member of the Joint Chiefs of Staff serving the most powerful nation in the world, he felt it even more important he keep to himself. The POTUS disagreed. He felt it was time the nation fully embraced its heritage. But Landon trusted the General to choose the right moment to reveal his ties to another great American leader born in Grand River, South Dakota—his great-great-grandfather, Sitting Bull.

As the sun warmed his face and hand touched the cold glass, the General pondered Commander Troy's choice of departing words: "GRAY WOLF is still in control."

The man never misused a word or made an idle threat. The stiff-necked disciplinarian and precision communicator had traits impossible to repress. He knew Viking A-9 had been disarmed before launch. He knew all the missiles in North Dakota would soon be disarmed. Why arm the MRBM over Winnipeg? Why alter flight path to avoid a missile from the EAGLE? Why did he think it worth the risk of detection? Troy must have known his unique access codes and commands would be screened. The high-level mole would be found. Why was this event so important to GRAY WOLF?

They are still out there, the General thought. *The terminal breach did not end over Winnipeg. GRAY WOLF did not come to simply send a U.S. missile into Canada. There had to be more.*

Why would you give us so many days—enough time to disarm all Minuteman III missiles in North Dakota? Jamison looked over the vast landscape and struggled with the logic of a monster. *Instead of sending a missile to Canada, why not make greater demands and send it to an American city? Why waste so much time and then sacrifice your highly-placed mole for a small target and no-fly zone over Minot? What is your real mission?*

Troy's parting words confirmed the General's suspicions—the horrific blood trail and terminal breach had objectives they still did not understand. GRAY WOLF had secured a position in a field of U.S. nuclear assets because they needed time. But for what?

Maybe you never intended to commandeer one of our intercontinental ballistic missiles, Jamison considered. *Maybe you brought something here!*

The General pulled a worn object from his pocket and held it like a rare diamond. He rubbed his thumb on the tooth of an alpha gray wolf, the tooth Tatanka had worn on a strip of buffalo hide around his neck. Buck Jamison squinted at the pointed fang, held it up to the sun, and whispered, "Today is the seventh day of the seventh winter. The flying EAGLE has dropped her head over Winnipeg—we lost a hero. Now the gray wolf howls.

"I've always known this day would come," he breathed onto the cold glass. Jamison closed his eyes and a tear left. *How do I explain this to the President ...?*

CHAPTER 33

"There are two ways to live: you can live as if nothing is a miracle; you can live as if everything is a miracle."
Albert Einstein

Belden, North Dakota, 1730 CST

The sun touched the horizon and shot orange fingers in all directions. Endless currents of ice crystals flowed over black asphalt. Sumner and Cage pulled up to the weather-beaten shack and stared at the worn, painted letters: Belden Union Oil Company.

They parked in a long shadow and sat in the warm car, surveilling their surroundings. In amongst the snowdrifts stood two large barns. In a patch of barren trees, a cluster of outbuildings crouched, crooked and bowed, crushed by brutal winters and time.

"Tell me more about Chankoowashtay," Elliott said. "Why would he be here?"

"Did I mention he's a nuclear physicist?" Cage asked.

"No. You did not. It might have been a nice detail to share a hundred miles back. I can only assume it did not impress you."

"Correct. I didn't think much about it. The old man's life in Belden was so different."

"Different?"

"He said he left Michigan State in his last year. There was an accident—he did not explain. Said it blinded him. He didn't want to talk about it."

"Did he come to Belden to escape?" Elliott asked.

"No. He *returned* to Belden. He grew up here, in that cabin. I got the impression he never abandoned his Lakota roots. I did ask, why nuclear physics? He told me the government paid his way. He took a proficiency test and was selected over all the other applicants in North Dakota. He is clearly a smart guy."

"Michigan State was established in 1855," Elliott said as he scrutinized the dark windows in the shack fifty yards away. "They've had one of the top-rated nuclear physics programs in the country for a very long time."

"I got a little curious after I left. Researched the man some," Cage said. "I have a friend, a Michigan State grad. We found Chankoowashtay. He told the truth. Because he was a Lakota Indian, he qualified for the government assistance program. He matriculated in 1957. He would have been in his thirties. Puts him in his early nineties today, if he's still kicking."

"And it would put a *nuclear physicist* in the middle of the U.S. nuclear missile program at its start in the early '60s," Elliott said. "I find that more than coincidental."

"A blind nuclear physicist who dropped out his third year. That's a reach."

They turned back to the shack. The glow of day had begun to fade. Snow shadows started to reveal the imperfections in the perfect blanket of white. "We might be walking into a nest of GRAY WOLF operatives," Elliott said with a touch of trepidation.

"If you're right, we'll be processed like the four poor souls in crash bags in Bismarck," Morgan said. "I bet the truck with their nasty compactor's in one of those barns."

"Could be," Elliott whispered. "Or we could walk in and find Chankoowashtay."

"If GRAY WOLF came to Belden—like Busey said—we might find Chankoowashtay dead. I doubt very seriously they'd leave even a blind old man around to tell tales."

"Let's hope we don't run into GRAY WOLF or Chankoowashtay's body. Maybe we can find something that points us to the cavern. We need to see the LCC for ourselves."

"I'm good with just finding an empty shack with a fireplace, a stack of wood, and a coffee pot," Cage teased. "In another ten minutes, the sun drops off the earth up here. The seventh night of the seventh winter drops to twenty below. We need to decide now. Should we go inside or drive away?"

After hiding the car in the nearest barn, they found the shack unlocked. They stood in complete silence for the first few minutes, taking in the room that looked abandoned. Agile as a cat, Elliott stepped over and around broken crates, stacks of firewood, and remnants of furniture. When he got to the back of the room, he saw signs of occupation. Someone had been in the room recently. Elliott eased up to the back door and paused. Cage stood behind him with a log held high.

When Elliott reached for the door, it flew open. On the other side was a gun. The tall, skinny man—wearing a fur coat with a rope tied around the waist and jeans stuffed in his mud-crusted cowhide boots—cocked the gun. His sunken, leather cheeks hung on sharp facial bones, and his white, marbled eyes quivered beneath shaggy brows.

"Best you not move," the old man said with his Colt pointed at Elliott's chest.

"I'm sorry. I was not expecting anyone to be here. The door was unlocked."

"Door's always unlocked 'round here," the old man said. "What do you want?"

"Chankoowashtay," Cage said. The old man paused and then lowered his gun. Cage continued. "We met two years ago. I'm Morgan Cage from Bismarck. I'm with Elliott Sumner. We just want to talk. We have a matter of some urgency."

The old man released the hammer and slid the Colt into his

rope belt. "I remember you. The doctor-with-too-many-questions," he said with a flat face. "Where's your car?"

"In one of your barns. Covered with an old tarp we found out there," Cage said.

"You see the truck?"

"What truck?"

"Never mind. Follow me. We can't stay here. They'll be back."

"Who?" Cage asked.

Chankoowashtay went to the end of the next room and felt along the edge of the wall. It popped and opened up to a narrow landing with a staircase dropping into darkness. As they descended, Cage whispered, "What about our tracks in the snow?"

"They'll be gone in minutes," the old man said. "Winds get real busy 'round here at sundown." He waited on a stone slab fifteen feet underground. They were deeper than a basement. Elliott and Morgan watched as the old man tugged on a rope looped over pulleys that ran up the wall. The metal wheels whined and squeaked as the top of the stairs went dark. The old man pulled a lever and turned back to them. "Two metal poles lock the wall. Nobody's coming in that way unless they drive a car through the wall."

They followed Chankoowashtay with a candle as he went deeper into the undefined chamber that smelled like old dirt. They approached a table with four chairs. Chankoowashtay lit a lantern and pointed. "Sit. We talk here."

There was a stove with a small fire and a coffee pot. *Where's the smoke going?* Elliott wondered. The light only reached ten feet from the table. *This is more than a basement.*

Time was running out. Elliott pushed forward. "Do you know why we are here?"

"I know some things to be true. I suspect other things to be true." Chankoowashtay poured three cups of coffee. "I am blind, but I see. I am deaf, but I hear. I am old, but I chose to live ... for now.

"You call me *Tay*." He took a sip. "My name is too long. Indians do that." He chuckled. "I know why you are here. You are late. Eleven months. They may return one more time."

"Are you saying people stayed here, in your house?" Cage asked.

"Yes. I am saying that."

"They can't be the people we are looking for. If they were, you'd be dead," Cage said.

"Not an accurate assessment," Tay said. "You're a forensic pathologist. You know better. I may be old and blind, but I am smart. You must factor in all evidence."

"I'm sorry," Cage said. "You are right. I did not mean to discount—"

"In the beginning, there were many in the rooms above. I knew they would kill me if they found me. They never found *this* place. I lived down here. I slept on the landing behind the wall, warmed by the fires they made with my wood. I have water. I stored all my food down here. I can come and go at night without detection."

"Why didn't you go and not come back?" Cage asked.

"I am a blind man. I have no transportation. No communications. I'm alone. I would wait for them to leave. Then it was eleven months."

"Tell us about the people," Elliott said as he studied the man with the marbled eyes.

"State-sponsored radical Islamic terrorists," he said. "They're part of a group that came here to launch a Syrian caliphate. In the beginning I counted twelve. Now I count seven. They have no problem killing their people when they are no longer needed. The caliphate is everything."

"How do you know this?" Cage asked.

"They talk. I listen through the wall," Tay said.

"Were they speaking in Arabic?" Cage asked as both scrutinized the old man.

"Sometimes Arabic. Sometimes English," Tay said. "I do not know the Arabic language."

Elliott leaned back in his chair as he shuffled more pieces of the puzzle. "We conducted autopsies on four people we believe were connected to GRAY WOLF—the code name given by the government. These bodies were severely mutilated. The limited physical evidence recovered pointed in a different direction."

"You believe them to be Russian," Tay said.

"Yes. That was our initial conclusion based solely on—"

"—tattoos," Tay finished the thought.

Elliott was stunned. "Yes. We reconstructed one shared tattoo from six linked bodies recovered."

"The Syrians spoke of this misdirection each time another *leave-behind* had been found by the Royal Canadian Mounted Police, CIA, or Homeland Security."

"That does not make sense," Cage disputed.

"The Syrian leader of this infiltration required members of the caliphate to have the tattoo. If they were captured or killed, the tattoo would implicate the Russians. This caliphate has been many years in the making," Tay said.

"In their first year, they came from Syria to Istanbul. In the second year, they lived in London. And then they rendezvoused at the Turtle Mountain Provincial Park in Canada just south of Boissevain. You found a leave-behind near Bone Lake. They crossed into the U.S. near Solper Lane and hid in a cabin on Devil Lake. Seven days ago, the remaining four came here to join the others, who were here for eleven months."

"The three members of the caliphate who were already here —who had been using up my fire wood for eleven months—had scoped the area. They thought this was an abandoned cabin. I kept a low profile."

"Tell us more about the leave-behinds," Elliott asked.

"I heard them talk about three tattooed bodies—Canada and North Dakota—and two tattooed bodies abroad. I believe London and Turkey."

Tay set his Colt on the table and loosened the rope around his waist. "Made Roan Busey get a tattoo. Killed him. Put him in the disposal device they have on the truck in one of my barns."

Cage and Elliott exchanged a look—*Tay was telling the truth.*

"The Syrian caliphate wants to get us in a war with the Russians!" Cage exclaimed.

"No they don't," Elliott said.

"What else could they possibly want to accomplish?"

"To confuse us, and to buy time," Elliott said into his tin coffee cup.

Tay got up and poured more coffee. "Today two were here. They talked about a missile going to Winnipeg."

"Jesus, they sent one of our missiles to Winnipeg?" Cage boomed.

"They did not," Tay said. "Someone sent it for them. Someone inside."

"They've got a mole at the Air Force Global Strike Command," Elliott said. "We need to get this information to General Jamison."

"You said they left your cabin and weren't coming back," Cage said.

"That is what I believed." Tay pulled something out of his pocket and passed it to Elliott. "I stepped on this up there this morning. A ring. I think they came back looking for it. They said it was a valuable Islamic ring. It belonged to their leader."

Elliott studied the ring. "It's made of a cheap silver alloy and colored glass. It's very old. There's an inscription, Kufic writing ...

'il-la-lah'. It means *for Allah*." Elliott passed it to Morgan. "They would not leave anything behind that could expose them. They will be back."

"This sure as hell is not a Russian ring," Cage said.

"They talked to others on a transmitter," Tay said. "That's how I learned about the missile sent to Winnipeg."

"Awful," Cage groaned. "A nuclear missile sent to a city of almost a million people."

"They spoke Arabic and broken English often," Tay said. "I made out a few things. They said X-51 and that the U.S. lost an EAGLE. I do not know what that means."

"We probably sent a hypersonic aircraft to take out the missile," Elliott said. "The only thing we have to intercept an ICBM. Sounds like we couldn't shoot it down. We sacrificed the aircraft—the X-51, the EAGLE." Elliott watched the blind man—something was not right.

"This discourse produced a most unlikely response from the Syrians," Tay said. "They laughed. Now I believe stopping the missile did not matter to them. Maybe it was not their goal."

Elliott got up and leaned on the back of his chair. The loose ends swirled in his head. The odd behavior of the Syrians said more to him than Tay could know, or did he know more? The blurred picture in Elliott's deductive mind had started to come into focus. "The missile launch was not important to their end game," he whispered and watched Tay.

"Yes. They have an end game," Tay said. "They spoke of—"

Elliott leaned closer and studied Tay. The old man was getting lost in his story.

With marbled eyes twitching, Tay rubbed his leather jaw. "They want the United States to *disarm* every ICBM in North Dakota."

"They want us exposed," Cage said. "Why?"

Our briefing before Belden, Elliott thought. *General Jamison*

told the President he was disarming every missile in North Dakota
...

Elliott jerked upright, as if someone had just plunged a dagger into his back. Cage turned. Elliott saw Tay jerk ever so slightly. "It's never been about commandeering a missile," Elliott said. "They didn't come here to send a missile into Winnipeg or anywhere else."

"What are you saying?" Cage said. Elliott watched Tay look to the floor. Not thinking, he brushed something from his leg.

"They had implemented a complex three-year plan just to get here. Every stage had been thoroughly mapped out, perfectly resourced, and implemented," Elliott said. "GRAY WOLF knew their chances of navigating top-secret U.S. systems to launch a nuclear missile were impossible. That's not what they would attempt. But they would use it to mislead us."

"All their demands were about limiting surveillance and buying time," Cage said. "They didn't want us watching them, and they needed time to do something. But why the *terminal breach* and why Winnipeg? Why are they here, Elliott?"

"They brought something," Elliott said. "Something they want to position in the middle of our nuclear arsenal. There is enough weaponry here to destroy a large portion of the North American Continent."

"What did they bring here?" Morgan asked.

"I don't know," Elliott said still watching Tay's every movement. "But I can tell you this: It is in the Belden cavern and it is intended to show the world their intense hatred of the west and the superiority of Islam."

Chankoowashtay held up a hand. Elliott and Morgan stopped talking.

He pointed up. Someone walked across the floor. They began to pound on the wall by the landing and staircase. "That is new,"

Tay whispered. "They found your car. They know you are here. We must leave, now."

Chankoowashtay lifted the lantern and led them into the dark abyss. The old blind Indian seemed to know every crack on the stone floor and every crevice on the rock walls.

Elliott and Morgan followed. A cold breeze lifted Elliott's hair as they left the table and stone walls behind. Then the lantern light spilled off the chiseled walkway and fell into an endless darkness.

The three descended into a cavern.

CHAPTER 34

"Anger dwells only in the bosom of fools."
Albert Einstein

Minot Air Force Base, 1900 CST

"We cannot risk sending anyone in for Elliott Sumner and Morgan Cage, Mr. President. We still do not know GRAY WOLF's surveillance capabilities. Any departure from our agreement could trigger another incident, one we now cannot stop. We lost our only X-51 over Winnipeg."

"I understand, Buck, but I do not like sending our forensic doctors into harm's way," Landon replied. "They're not soldiers. They have given me their time and talents without pause." The POTUS dropped his head. "How in the world does one get lost on the road from Bismarck to Minot?"

"We lost their signal at Belden, poor reception. Clearly, they got off track—at some point they went west instead of north. Isolated snowstorms on the Great Plains this time of year are not unusual. It's easy to lose your bearings when everything looks the same. I'm sure they'll find their way back on their own."

The General and President said everything they needed to say for the benefit of the Director of the CIA. He sat in the back of the Oval Office filled with cabinet members and military advisors. Jamison had spoken with Tony Wilcox minutes after the undisclosed satellite call with Herbolt. Vital information had not been shared by the CIA Director. GRAY WOLF had already sacrificed one highly-placed mole. Were they protecting one at a higher level now?

In private, the General had instructed Wilcox and Turpin to leave Key West. They were to go to the Naval Air Station on Trumbo Point. Captain E.C. Cardan would meet them at the gates and take them by helicopter to a boat at an undisclosed location. The two sleuths needed to get out of the Keys, and they needed protection. Albert Bell's Dassault Falcon had been compromised. The Secret Service had found a bomb. Someone did not want Wilcox and Turpin to tell their story about Milton Busey.

Belden, North Dakota, 1900 CST

The treacherous descent took an hour. Then the rugged incline leveled to a surface of flat, frozen sand and gravel. The three moved north. Elliott watched Chankoowashtay touch rocks and count steps as he probably had done many times before. The old Lakota Indian had grown up in the *Caverns of Han*. They were named after the ancient spirit of darkness banished to be under *Maka*, the earth spirit.

"This is the cavern Milton Busey spoke about," Elliott said as they kept a steady pace forward. "Is the entrance from your cabin the one he knew?"

"There are two ways into the Cavern of Han," Tay said. "There is only one Milton Busey would know. It is the one farthest north. It opens at the base of a plateau. In the spring, it is under water. In the winter, it is not. To enter, one must go down many feet and then go up many more. The overhanging rock guards the sanctity of the cavern. It is named *Anpao*."

"Do you know where the Launch Control Capsule is down here?" Cage asked.

"I know," Tay said, "but I have not seen with my eyes."

As the three moved through the cavern, it became clear

anyone following would be left behind. Chankoowashtay selected a single cave from a honeycomb of caves, and he often reversed directions to make progress through the underground maze. They stepped over skeletal and mummified remains of those lost before. The forensic experts could tell at a glance they had been preserved hundreds of years in the underground tomb.

When they reached the largest part of the cavern, Tay put out the lantern flame. The moonlight had found a way inside. Streams of soft white light passed through hundreds of small crevices and cracks in the mountains above. The blanket of light gave the massive cavern a mystical aura—as if they had entered a shrine. Elimination of the lantern also allowed them to move the rest of the way without risking detection by GRAY WOLF.

"There," Elliott whispered. They knelt on a rock shelf twenty feet above a basin. The enormous cement capsule seemed to glow, a perfect oval shape surrounded by sharp edges. It nestled in a sand bed like a sea turtle egg on a beach, half hanging over another cliff edge. An impression in the rock above was identical size and shape. The LCC once hung a hundred-feet above. The demolition had pushed it into the cavern. Mangled and crumbled debris from the collapsed elevator shaft and support structures cluttered the floor of the cavern. Most probably fell into the dark abyss on the western side of the capsule.

"It's like finding a dinosaur egg," Morgan mumbled.

"It seems we're alone," Elliott said. They panned the area for movement and saw nothing. "I need to go down," he whispered. "If this is where GRAY WOLF spent the last year, I need to find out why."

Leaning against a rock with his back to the LCC, Tay struggled to breath. The old man did not have much left. "There are seven. They could be near," he whispered.

Elliott heard more than Tay meant to reveal. "You two stay here. I'm going down."

He moved along the jagged rocks and avoided the staggered streams of moonlight. When he neared the capsule, he saw the massive crack along its base—damage from the fall, when the heavy capsule broke free of the rock mantle and crashed to the edge of the cavern floor, a hundred feet below. *Twenty feet to the west and you would have tumbled into the abyss. There would have been nothing here of interest to anyone, just a forgotten cavern ...*

Elliott moved around the LCC like a sand snake. He looked for members of GRAY WOLF and studied the forgotten, multi-million-dollar creation. It was just as Milton had described to Tony: intact. *Milton had to have seen this with his own eyes, or the eyes of someone he knew very well,* Elliott thought.

He crawled to the north end of the LCC and slipped behind a pile of debris at the edge of the foreboding abyss. He took several deep breaths and calmed his heart—so far he was still in control of his demons. When he opened his eyes he refocused on the opened blast door portal. The multi-ton concrete-and-steel slab lay on its side next to a scaffold that reached to the ceiling of the cavern. It stopped at the edge of the hole where the LCC had once nested. Massive bundles of wires and fat cables and colored tubing hung from the hole. His eyes followed the draped agglomeration down the scaffold to the floor and behind more debris.

Where does it go? He wondered. *I can't see from here.*

Time was not on their side. Elliott could not wait. He had to look. He had to find out what GRAY WOLF had done with the launch control capsule during the last eleven months. *Did you rewire this thing? Is it functional? What did you bring here?*

He eased up to the side of the opened portal into the LCC, his back against the cracked shell. Elliott looked over the piles of rubble and saw three bodies. They were next to each other by the blast door. *Tay said seven. Does this mean there are now four?* He inched closer to the portal, and then saw a light inside. Then he saw the shadow. The gun came out first.

The explosion seemed to echo endlessly through the cavern. Elliott fell back. Stunned and sitting on the frozen sand, he watched the man with the empty face fall out of the capsule. He watched him crash onto the frozen floor with the gun still in his hand.

Cage walked up with Tay's smoking Colt. "I ... I have never shot a gun in my life," he mumbled. "I ... I never—"

Elliott felt the carotid. "He's dead."

Cage stared. "I didn't aim for—"

Elliott took the gun and flipped the corpse over. Blood streamed from the man's left eye. "He is Middle-Eastern." Elliott got up and put his hand on Morgan's shoulder. "For someone who never handled a gun before, you're a pretty good shot."

"He was going to shoot you, Elliott. I had no choice."

"Morgan. This man was committed to killing millions of innocent people. Let it go."

They hid and watched. Ten minutes felt like hours. "It appears we're alone," Elliott said. "That shot filled this cavern. If GRAY WOLF was coming, they'd be here by now."

He pointed to the scaffold. "These guys spent a lot of time working with the wires and cabling. I need to find out why." Elliott went to the far side of the scaffolding and disappeared into a ravine. Morgan returned to the capsule.

When he emerged, he said, "There's nothing in there but beds." He discovered the other three bodies outside. "Makes four of the seven," he muttered as he grabbed Tay's arm and went down to Elliott. "Nothin' in that LCC but a battery-powered light. They didn't have electricity or water. It looks like they only slept in there. All the equipment had been gutted by the military before demolition. That launch control capsule is just a useless shell—no wonder the military had no concerns. Don't know what GRAY WOLF wanted with it."

"I think I can answer that question," Elliott said from behind the scaffold where he knelt next to a metal capsule the size of a Volkswagen Beetle. The wires from the ceiling of the cavern were connected to a circuit board on one end of the device. At the other end there were two computer monitors and a keyboard. A pulsating hum radiated from deep within the metal shell.

"For the love of God," Morgan said when he leaned over the edge of the ravine.

"We just found the lynch pin of the Syrian caliphate," Elliott said as he got to his feet and approached Tay. "Now is the time to talk to us. You can start by telling us you can see."

Morgan turned to Tay. "You can see?"

"Yes. He can," Elliott said. "And he has been more involved with this caliphate than he has shared—

"Tay, what you once thought was a good idea ... now you must know you were wrong. Don't let this play out. Don't punish the world because the Lakota nation lost their lands, and because the government put missiles on sacred grounds. You don't want this."

Tay removed his milky contacts and blinked. "When did you know?"

"When I looked into your eyes," Elliott said. "And the ring. It is payment. The Islamic ring you pretended to find, it is worth a lot of money. I remember everything—it's my bane. But sometimes it's helpful.

"The finger ring you showed me is a one-of-a-kind artifact. It was found in Birka, nineteen miles from Stockholm on the Bjorko Island. Birka was a premier trading center in the age of the Vikings. That ring ties the Islamic World to the Vikings. It helps define them. It helps justify their plan for the world." Elliott smiled as he took Tay's hand in his. "You've worn this ring on your little finger for the year. Like a cheating husband, your naked hand tells a story, my friend."

"I have seen many awful things in my life," Tay said. "My people lost everything. What was once magnificent and true is now gone forever."

"And you were given a chance to right these wrongs," Cage said.

"Milton Busey is your grandson, isn't he?" Elliott asked.

"Yes."

"He met people who wanted what you wanted," Elliott said. "They wanted to start a war. They wanted America to pay a price. You wanted America to pay a price, but you also knew we would find a way to stop the misery. You bet the new pain and the carnage would be enough. The U.S. government would finally end this nuclear nightmare in Lakota territory—

"Like in the '90s, when your grandson demolished some of the missile silos he had helped build thirty years earlier, you thought we would do it again. But this time we would never rebuild the silos. This time we would return the land to the Sioux Nation."

"Yes. What you say is true," Tay said.

"But something happened. There is a reason you left with us when they came."

"They did not keep their word," Tay said. "They killed Roan. They sent people to kill Milton. I warned Milton. I got word to his friend in Turkey. Milton got out of Pingree before they could kill him. They lied to me. They used my anger against me."

"They were going to kill you too when they were done with you, Tay" Elliott said.

"I would not let them have the ring back. It was mine. It belongs to the Lakota nation. It would help fix many wrongs."

"They said they did not want our missiles, didn't they?" Elliott said.

"They said they would disarm all missiles in North Dakota. And then they would disarm missiles in Montana and Wyoming."

"And they were willing to die doing their great work," Morgan said.

"They said they will die for their God." Tay's eyes met Elliott's. "What kind of God asks a man to kill for him, to die for him? This cannot be a religion. This cannot be a God. This is a twisted ideology of a few. Their God is a warrior leading them into battle."

"*Disarm* sounds nice," Morgan said. "Saints battling the evil empire."

Tay walked to the device with the wires and monitors and keyboard. He touched it with an open hand to feel the vibration. It beat like a heart. "This is a nuclear bomb, one-hundred kilotons of TNT." He reached up and cradled in his palm the fat bundle of wires that hung from the ceiling and connected to the bomb. "These wires have only one function. They do not tell. They listen. They wait for a very specific message. The moment the United States rearms one ICBM, this bomb is detonated by a miniscule electronic flutter."

"Oh my God!" Morgan cried.

"The explosion is ten times more destructive than the atomic bomb dropped in World War II," Elliott said. "It will set in motion a cascade of nuclear blasts that will—"

"—destroy much of the North American continent," Tay said softly. "I know. I am a nuclear physicist. I understand the power unleashed. I wish I had not—"

"Can you disarm this bomb?" Elliott asked.

"I don't know," Tay said. "I am not blind, but I have poor eyesight. My nerves are not good. My hands tremble."

Elliott's heart started to race. His head started to ache. His monsters started to stir.

"Where are they, Tay? Where is GRAY WOLF now?" Cage boomed. "You know. Tell us. We must stop them and we must fix this."

Holding his head, Elliott struggled to keep his balance. "You know you made a mistake, Tay. You need to help us or lose everything you have lived for."

"They will not be a problem ... here. They are leaving Belden on foot, the north end of the cavern," Tay said. "They never knew my way."

"On foot?" Cage asked. "You are lying. Nobody would attempt—"

"They will not risk vehicles in their escape. They do not draw attention. This is truth. They will cross the Canadian border north of Ambrose by morning."

"Ambrose, North Dakota," Elliott said. "That's a hundred miles. It's twenty below out there, Tay. I can't imagine ..." He winced. The pain grew in his head. He did not have the energy to fight. "Okay. How are they going to pull it off, and how many are there really?"

Tay let go of the bundle of wires and approached Elliott. "I lied about how many. I am sorry. There are now nine. You have seen four not going on their next mission."

"Nine armed radical Islamic terrorists," Elliott said. "Why do they think they can cross a hundred miles of snow in twenty-below weather in one night?" Elliott asked again.

"They are trained," Tay said. "They believe they can do this. It does not matter. They do not know their navigation equipment will cease to function within twenty minutes on the surface. They've not experienced this winter on the Great Plains. It is the worst I have seen in decades."

"My bet is they're smarter than you think," Cage grumbled.

"How could you do this, Tay?" Elliott asked pointing at the bomb.

"They said arming this would ensure cooperation—the disarming of all nuclear missiles on Lakota land," Tay said. "I'm an old man. Sometimes very stupid. I became lost in my sadness and my loneliness. Then, when I learned Roan had been killed and they were hunting Milton, I knew I had to come here and disarm it myself. I knew then they intended to use it. If I could not stop them, they would destroy everything I have lived for."

"We need to disarm this thing now," Elliott said with eyes squinted.

"And General Jamison needs to find GRAY WOLF before they cross the Canadian border and disappear into the Canadian mountains."

"I'll try to disable the bomb or disconnect it from the missile network." Tay shook his head. "The only way to call Minot is on top of the plateau above this cavern."

"I'll go," Cage said. "I'll do that. You two work on this thing. Elliott, you're the eyes and hands and jack of all trades. Tay's the nuclear physicist. I'm the youngest and best-looking."

Elliott chuckled. "You are the youngest," he agreed. Elliott passed his cell to Morgan. "Are you sure, my friend?" Morgan nodded. "Okay. Tell Jamison we don't want this thing going off on us. He can't rearm any missiles." Morgan pulled on gloves with fire in his eyes.

"The shortest route is the north exit," Tay said as he scribbled a simple map and passed it to Morgan. "When you think you are lost, look to the sand beneath your feet. Follow the path left by my ancestors. They will show you the way."

"I will do that," Cage said with wary eyes on Elliott.

"When you leave the cavern, you must climb to the top of the plateau on the north side. There is your best chance for reception."

Elliott and Morgan had no choice but to trust Tay. If they

were right, they had a chance. If they were wrong, it did not matter. There were no more options. Time was running out.

Morgan nodded to both men and disappeared over the next wall of rocks. Could he get to Chief General Jamison in time? Could Elliott and Tay neutralize the Syrian nuclear bomb, or would they launch the Armageddon? Would GRAY WOLF escape so they could carry out their twisted trifecta?

Tay and Elliott stared in silence at the humming nuclear bomb. Elliott's demons stirred more than ever as the terrifying realities of global catastrophe loomed. At any moment without warning Elliott could lose control. His autonomic nervous system might take over. And if it did, he would die instantly.

"If it means anything, I'm sorry for what was done to your people, Tay," Elliott said as his head world whirled and the nausea overwhelmed his senses. "In life, many mistakes are made, Tay. I choose to believe most people are good. I know we learn from our history, and we evolve together. No one is right all the time, Tay. We all struggle in life. We all carry burdens. I will not blame the world for the past errors of the few."

"I made a mistake," Tay whispered. He cleared his throat and turned to Elliott. "I was once a proud man. Then I allowed my pain to become hatred. It killed me inside."

"We all have demons, Tay, some worse than others. I almost died a year ago. The doctors said if I did not find a way to control my inner demons, the next time, I would die. I thought when I came to North Dakota I would die for sure. I was not ready for this test. My demons are very close." He looked to the ceiling of the cavern.

"You are ready, Elliott Sumner." Tay smiled for the first time. "And I am ready. I believe we were brought here at this time for a reason. We are stepping into a new river of life. We are not the same as we were."

"Elliott touched the side of the nuclear bomb. "Let's hope for some divine guidance."

"I trust the Gods have our world in the palms of their hands," Tay said.

"We will see." Elliott examined the complex circuitry like a surgeon looking for the cause of a new disease. "It is the seventh day of the seventh winter," he said under his breath.

"Yes it is," Tay whispered. Elliott looked up at the Lakota Indian as the old man looked into a moonbeam. "The gray wolf speaks to the moon, touches the spirit of Tatanka, and roams the Great Plains to evict evil and to protect the descendants of peaceful men."

Let's hope we are the descendants of peaceful men, Elliott prayed as his demons touched the door of his sanity and death.

CHAPTER 35

"What unknown power governs men? On what feeble causes do
their destinies hinge?"
Voltaire

J amison paced the war room on the third floor of the
Strategic Air Command Center at Minot Air Force Base.
"Explain yourself," he barked.

"We have identified an unauthorized connection, sir,"
Commander Peterson said. "We cannot be one-hundred percent
certain, but we believe we have located GRAY WOLF."

"You say an 'unauthorized connection'. I need more," the
General demanded.

His instincts told him the end game was near. GRAY WOLF
had played hide-and-seek long enough. Their demands were not
worthy of a six-day *terminal breach* in the Minot missile fields—
something big was about to happen. Commander Troy had been
removed from command. The despicable mole's parting words
had made it clear—GRAY WOLF was still in control ... of
something.

"One foundational construct of our secured network is *linear
resistance*—meaning constant resistance values over all applied
currents within our dedicated network," Peterson said. "Without
getting too technical, I can tell you we have found an
unauthorized connection, a drain. It is like lifting a phone in
another room to listen in on a conversation. It is a monitoring link.

"We did not pay much attention to this before because we thought it was a statistical aberration. After conducting a full systems sweep, it became clear. We are now certain we have found an unauthorized, managed portal into our secured network."

"Can you pinpoint the location of this portal?" asked the General.

"Yes, sir."

"Where is it?"

"Belden, sir."

Sumner and Cage are in Belden for a reason, Jamison thought. *They found—*

"We believe GRAY WOLF is in the Belden area, sir. We have reconstructed the monitor link but have not found a command-portal, one used to access and control missiles. We still have ten missiles not yet disarmed. We believe they could be commandeered like Viking A-9."

"I see," the General breathed.

"We recommend immediate neutralization, sir. Our network sweep is complete."

"What is the population, a five mile radius around Belden, Peterson?"

"Fourteen residents, sir."

"Arm the MRBM in High Tech A-7. I want to know when it's ready to go. We will send her to Belden. We have no choice. The President wants containment initiated from here."

"Are we evacuating, sir?"

"Evacuate by phone only. Explanation is *dysfunctional military assets in the area.* Tell them to leave immediately. No more information. We cannot send our people in. GRAY WOLF surveillance capabilities will be strong in the Belden area. I won't risk another Winnipeg. We don't have the ability to stop another missile. The only thing going to Belden is an MRBM on a short leash."

"We will arm High Tech A-7, sir." The commander left the control center.

Jamison's cell phone vibrated. It was Sumner. "Elliott, where the hell are you?"

"This is Morgan Cage. Elliott and I are in Belden. There is not much time. Do not arm any missiles, General. If you do, it will trigger a nuclear bomb brought here by GRAY WOLF. It is connected to your missile network. It is in a cavern in Belden. You cannot arm one missile."

"Hold a second, son," Jamison said as he turned to staff. "Do *not* arm High Tech A-7. That's an order. Stop all arming activity immediately. Stop Commander Peterson. He just left."

The command center jumped into high gear. The General's order rolled through the operation like a break in a dam. "Dr. Cage, your recommendation has been instituted. Let's hope we're not too late. What else can you tell me, son?"

Commander Gentzel dropped his head mic and turned to the General. "Done, sir. High Tech A-7 arming procedure aborted."

"Good. From here on out, no missiles armed until I say," the General directed. "What else, son? What can you tell me?"

To get reception, Cage had been forced to climb the plateau above the cavern's north entry. In the sub-zero conditions and gusting winds, he pressed the cell to his ear and struggled to speak between the violent shivers that rolled through his body every few seconds. He understood the medical impact. He would not survive his environment much longer.

"Elliott is in the cavern. Track this phone. I have a map to him in my pocket," Cage said. "Find me. I'm losing consciousness. I don't have long." He started to fade. "Elliott needs help. GRAY WOLF is not Russian. They're Syrian jihadist. There are nine. They're on foot from Belden to the Canadian border. They ... they—"

"Dr. Cage," Jamison yelled into the phone. "Morgan Cage. Can you hear me, son? Are you there?" The General spun around. "Find this phone. Move heaven and earth to do it now. The hell with surveillance. We're all going to Belden. Get my best team. Choppers. NOW!"

* * *

"Mr. President, we're dealing with a Syrian jihadist group," said the General on a private line. "We have located them in Belden, North Dakota. That information was gleaned from the Wilcox/Turpin interrogation of Milton Busey in Key West. It was information we should have been given by Herbolt."

"We have confirmed more disturbing transgressions involving James," Landon said. "They are bringing him to me. He should be here soon."

"We both knew Elliott Sumner and Morgan Cage went to Belden for a reason," Jamison said. "Elliott must have communicated with Tony Wilcox. He didn't need the CIA Director to tell him anything—typical forensic sleuth. Wilcox and Sumner have worked together for years. Wilcox got the Belden information and knew it was a key to finding GRAY WOLF. Elliott went there to confirm or deny. He knew we had enough balls in the air in Minot."

"He's not one to seek permission," Landon said as Albert Bell entered the Oval Office. "Let me put you on speaker, Buck. I have Albert with me. He needs to hear this."

"I just got off the phone with Morgan Cage," said the General. "A short call. I'm worried about him. He was standing outside a cavern for reception so he could call me. He said Elliott is in the cavern dealing with a nuclear bomb brought here by Syrian jihadists."

"Intelligence a while back, a Syrian caliphate in our country. The drums were beating three years ago but we did not hear much more about it," Landon said.

"Their nuclear device is triggered when Minot arms a missile. Naturally, we've ceased all such activity. Hell, our focus has been on *disarming* these missiles."

"Very creative," Landon said. "Put the trigger in our hands and skedaddle."

"Morgan Cage said there are nine Syrians heading for the Canadian border on foot. I've deployed a team to the Belden cavern. We are also sweeping the Great Plains north of Belden up to the border. I suspect they have prepared for this. They will have ample weapons and winter camouflage. Maybe the heavy snow and drop in temperature will slow them down."

"Albert here."

"Hello, Albert. Don't worry. I'll get your son out of there."

"I know you will, Buck," Albert said. "Elliott is a talented and resourceful man. He often surprises me. However, I can assure you gentlemen he is not well-versed in nuclear weaponry. Doubt he's had any occasion to study the matter, other than nuclear medicine and such. I bring this to your attention because it is my recommendation you deploy your top nuclear people with your fire power, Buck. I'm sure he will be grateful for some experienced help with whatever GRAY WOLF left behind."

"Done, Albert," Jamison said. "They're getting on the choppers now."

"Excellent, General."

"Buck, keep us posted. God's speed," Landon said. The phone disconnected and a door opened into the Oval Office.

"You have no idea what you're up against, Landon," spewed James Herbolt.

The President got to his feet as Secret Service walked Herbolt into the room. They had both his arms in their grip and one had an iron hand locked on the back of the Director's neck. Any effort to move would be met with a crippling squeeze. They didn't need handcuffs.

"What could make you *do* this, James? You're an American for God's sake."

"That's why. I'm an American who wants change. We're not so special."

"No one said we were," President Landon said. "But we are not monsters. You are the monster, James." The POTUS turned his back. "Remove him from the people's White House."

CHAPTER 36

"Reality is merely an illusion, albeit a very persistent one."
Albert Einstein

Belden, North Dakota, 2130 CST

Chankoowashtay seemed to age before Elliott's eyes as they studied the nuclear bomb in a fat beam of moonlight in the depths of the hidden cavern. The Lakota elder had spent most of his life alone in a forgotten time on an endless prairie with his legends and his loathing. Now he struggled for purpose and each breath as he stared at the beast in the belly of his world.

With his demons stirring, Elliott left Tay. He went inside the capsule and returned with a bag of tools, one overcoat, a working flashlight, and a tattered manual. After helping Tay into the coat, he went through the bag with numb fingers and blurred vision. Struggling to keep control, he itemized his meager discoveries between shallow breaths. Maybe something he said aloud would make a difference as they prepared to disable the bomb. Maybe something would help Tay find his way. "We've got a hacksaw ... two screwdrivers ... a hammer, wire cutters ... one adjustable wrench, and a manual." Elliott fanned through it. "It is electronics, circuitry, and computer programming."

Tay stopped shaking as his body temperature approached normal. "I don't know if I can do this physically," he murmured over the keyboard.

"You can and you must," Elliott slurred.

Tay turned to the forensic sleuth. "We will die down here. Even if Dr. Cage is able to halt the rearming of U.S. missiles, these people will not leave the launch of their caliphate in our hands. When they are out of range, if North Dakota still exists, they will trigger this bomb."

"It's not about us, Tay. We may not leave this place, but we must try to stop the wholesale death and destruction of millions of lives. We can do anything we believe we can do."

"Said the man who battles inner demons," Tay whispered.

"This is within our reach, Tay. My demons are not," Elliott bellowed.

"No," said the Lakota elder. "Your demons have always been within your reach. You invented them. They are an illusion, not a reality. The monsters you hunted no longer exist. Their memories haunt you because *you allow them* to haunt you.

"Simply tell them to go away. And do not wait for a response. Move on with what is real in the world. Leave behind your inventions, your illusion."

Elliott stared at the old man. Their eyes locked. Elliott saw truth borne from the pain and wisdom carried by the old Indian. For the first time since entering the cavern Elliott felt warm blood flow from his taut chest into his cold extremities. Cramps left his limbs. Fresh air filled his lungs. His vision cleared. *What is happening to me?* Was it possible? Did Elliott need to touch the edge of cataclysmic death in the presence of a sage to hear his truth, one he could understand and believe?

His demons were never real. They were the illusions of a lifetime, Elliott's way to cope with the magnificent gifts he always felt unworthy to possess. Did he always have control? Could his nightmare be over minutes before his life was taken from him?

Tay turned on the monitors and started punching the keyboard. "I need a password."

Elliott snapped out of it. With confusion and doubt and renewed energy, he blinked back into the cold cavern and the impossible task. His logical computer-like brain raced through all the possibilities and weighted all the relevant data. "Try il-la-lah or Allah or caliphate." He pulled a screwdriver and adjustable wrench from the bag, and slid the flashlight into his back pocket. *I need to get inside this bomb.*

"According to the old manual, I'm sure we will need to get to the master circuit board in this thing sooner or later," Elliott yelled back as he disappeared from view.

"Go in through the largest panel on the other side," Tay said as he typed Allah and hit enter. "Well. That was easy." The small screen populated, and the hum deep within the metal shell got louder.

His eyes avoided the dark abyss behind him. Elliott skirted the crumbling ledge. He gingerly unscrewed the access panel. The thick metal door dropped into the empty darkness behind him without a sound. Elliott leaned in. "It appears our jihadists did not get their hands on modern weaponry. There's a date and lot number on the inside housing—June 1959."

Elliott eased his hand into the web of wiring coming in from the top of the metal shell, the wires hanging from the ceiling of the cavern. Only a dozen were connected to the master circuit board. He leaned in deeper with his flashlight. With a measured breath, he blew off the dust and read the next metal tag hanging. "Made in the USA," echoed inside the metal shell. "Our Syrian terrorists didn't bring this with them, Tay. It's *been* here a while."

Elliott climbed out, leaned over the top. He found Tay's troubled eyes staring at the monitors. "Tay. You can't do this. You must decide ... or maybe you have. We do not have much time. Unless you want to blow us up, tell me what you're not telling me?"

He looked up. "This is my bomb. I built it."

"What about Milton and Roan? What about the eleven months?"

"Milton and Roan only handled the capsule wiring hanging

from the ceiling," Tay said. "There are more than a hundred wires. There are only twelve that listen."

Elliott stared at the old man who happened to be a Lakota sage, a hermit, and a nuclear physicist. "What do you want to do, Tay? If you want to follow through with your obvious dream to punish America, there is nothing we need to do. Go ahead. Obliterate North Dakota. Slaughter millions of people. You will really show the world they were bad. You will teach them a lesson they will never forget. Boy, your ancestors will be so proud … that you killed so many and you destroyed their sacred grounds."

Chankoowashtay looked at the monitors he knew well. "This is one of the tactical nuclear weapons from the Nevada Proving Ground. I was part of Operation Tumbler-Snapper. The code name was *Fox*. Not many people know one of the first bombs did not go off. I had to climb a three-hundred foot tower on the Yucca Flat to figure out what went wrong."

Elliott stared in silence in the darkness outside the moonbeam that lit up the Lakota Indian like a God. Tay shook his head and took a deep breath. "This is a fifteen-kiloton device." He rubbed the metal shell as if it were an old horse. "I had to disarm it. I was disposable. There were five-hundred military observers and a thousand troops—the 701st Armored Infantry Battalion. Out of all those people, they chose the Indian to climb the tower with a hacksaw and a screwdriver."

"You were all expendable in the early days," Elliott said. "I read about the 701st soldiers. They were called the 'guinea pigs'. Back then, we did not know what would happen when that atomic bomb went off. We didn't know about flash or burn or the effects of a shock-wave."

Tay shook his head, his motions weary. "I got up that tower and heard the sizzle—it was ready to go. We were testing a new polonium-beryllium neutron initiator." His eyes looked a million miles away. "I reached in there and pulled random wires. I deactivated the pit systems and initiator. Did it with my bare hands. I neutralized the plutonium core. Turns out, the only problem was with the connection to outside sensors ... a lot like the bundle of wires that were once connected to that LCC."

"None of you were disposable, Tay. You weren't sent up that three-hundred-foot tower because you were a disposable Lakota Indian. You were sent up there because you were the only man who could save the day."

"And who would believe the seventh day of the seventh winter mattered?" Tay said under his breath. "And who believes the gray wolf howls and evicts evil men?"

"Maybe you are here to stop evil men again, Tay. Maybe the bombs are not evil. Maybe the bombs have a place. Remember, men like you ended World War II."

Chankoowashtay looked at his hand a long time, and then closed it with tranquil eyes.

Elliott straightened up in the shadow of the bomb. "Do I need to climb into this thing and cut some wires and pull out a plutonium core?" he asked.

"I am sorry for what I have done. Now I am grateful to right my wrong." Tay turned to Elliott with a humble smile. "You need do nothing. It is done, Elliott Sum—"

The shot rolled through the cavern. The old Indian fell, the back of his head covered with blood. Elliott rounded the bomb and ran to Tay, but there was nothing he could do. The old man who had just killed the iron monster in the sacred cavern was dead.

Dazed, with Tay's head in his lap, Elliott leaned back against the cold shell of the neutered bomb. He would be next. GRAY WOLF had come back.

Elliott lifted his eyes. He saw the face of the young Syrian rebel thirty feet away. He saw the winter fatigues and the barrel of the smoking revolver. He saw the crooked smile and the dancing eyes.

"I come back," the man said. "We know old man attempt to stop us. He weak. We strong. I finish this now. I detonate bomb—death to infidels." He looked up with hollow eyes. "I celebrate victory in my heaven."

Now Elliott was alone more than ever before. His demons did not stir—they were gone. He heard the metallic click. He would be the jihadist's next joyful kill. Elliott started to get to his feet. *I will stop you. I can take your bullets and live long enough to—*

The giant gray wolf flew from the darkness into the moonlit haze like a ghost from hell. His teeth caught the light as his jaws locked around the neck of the Syrian terrorist. They crashed onto the hard sand and rolled. Elliott fell back and watched the surreal struggle until both were still. Then, in the darkest recesses of the cavern, something came alive. A hundred eyes stared and blinked as brawny shadows mingled and passed by. They slinked and undulated in complete silence.

The giant gray wolf left his kill and padded over to the feet of Chankoowashtay's body. Elliott saw the wolf tooth on the palm of Tay's open hand, and the peace in his glazed eyes. And then came a whisper of wind. Elliott was alone.

EPILOGUE

THREE MONTHS LATER

Guantánamo Bay, Cuba

Walking on the sand-dusted cement in the blazing afternoon sun felt good after his five-hundred mile boat ride. The captain had stopped briefly at Cárdenas and Gibara on the coast of Cuba, but only for gas and supplies. Elliott would not rest until he reached Guantanamo. He had to see with his own eyes the one GRAY WOLF jihadist who had survived. Chief General Jamison would be there at 1400 hours.

"Is Herbolt down here, too?" Wilcox asked, an unlit cigarette wagging in his mouth. He dropped his sunglasses from his forehead to his nose.

"The Director of the CIA and the 94th Wing Commander are both here, but they're not talking to anybody."

"Who gives a shit? I hope the bastards rot in hell," Wilcox sneered.

"President Landon is satisfied James Herbolt was the primary infiltrate. Herbolt brought Troy inside via an elaborate process. Now they're looking at everyone he touched."

"I'm sure they'll find more moles," Wilcox said. "Nature of the world now."

"They found the terrorist cell in Syria by backtracking encrypted communications from GRAY WOLF. I've been told the nest and feeders have been neutralized. Drone strikes."

"That's what happens when you mess with our nuclear-damn-missiles."

They stopped at the chain-linked fence and took in the razor-sharp coils of barbed wire and strapping armed guards. Elliott passed papers and IDs to a guard. The military eyes studied the forensic sleuth and retired homicide detective in their khaki shorts, Adidas, and Prada shades.

"You are expected, Dr. Sumner. Chief General Jamison left orders. You are free to walk the base without escorts or encumbrances. GRAY WOLF is in isolation courtyard 241X. You can observe from elevated walkway TITO. The General just arrived." He passed a small map.

"Thank you," Elliott said, looking for the section with courtyards.

"We know what you did in Belden," the guard said. "Thank you for your service."

Elliott managed a nod and awkward smile.

"Excuse me. What about me?" Wilcox huffed with arms extended and open hands.

"Yes sir, Mr. Tony Wilcox. I was getting to you, sir. We welcome you to Gitmo too, sir. Chief General instructed you have freedom to walk the base without military escort or encumbrance ... as long as you are with Dr. Sumner, sir."

"Well I'll be god—"

Elliott grabbed Tony's arm and pulled him through the open gate as the guards saluted. "Let it go, Tee. It's not important. We don't want to walk around anyway. I'm only interested in one thing—241X. Then we get back to my Commander 44, compliments of the U.S. Navy."

"Yeah. Well, I talked to Chief-friggin-General Jamison on the damn phone after they discovered Herbolt was screwin' them. I told him we never trusted the fat, little bastard."

"Is that when you and Harold told him about Belden?" Elliott asked.

"Belden and Sunset Pier," Wilcox said. "Jamison put a team

of Navy Seals on the pier in twenty minutes. Carried their weapons under their flowered shirts, although none of them needed a weapon. Their whole body's a weapon." He chuckled. "I gotta admit. I like that old Brit, Turpin. He got a kick out of the American way. I was proud of us. We covered Sunset Pier like a burkha in the wintertime. I think everyone was military except the bad guys, me, and Turpin.

"They caught all six of the idiots. Five were local contractors paid to take out Milton. I can't believe they thought the guy who killed three lawyers and hid from GRAY WOLF in itsy-bitsy Key West would just saunter onto some pier to get a suitcase of money."

"One was not a contractor?" Elliott asked.

"Right. Worked for Bowman, Weller & Garcia. They couldn't shut him up. He told the feds everything. That law firm was a money launderer for Syrian rebels."

The two walked and watched as prisoners in orange suits (three fence lines away) watched them. "By the way, what's Morgan Cage's status?" Wilcox asked.

"Good. We almost lost him. He should be 100 percent in a few weeks." Elliott said.

"I heard another five minutes could have killed him," Wilcox said as they rounded the corner and approached wooden steps to a catwalk. "Ops track TITO," he read. "This is where we go up. Should be interesting."

They climbed the stairs to the catwalk above fencing and barbed wire. From there, they could see the extent of the detention center as the afternoon sun beat down on the small tract of land on the Island of Cuba. For the orange jumpsuits, Gitmo would be their last residence on earth. The people were too dangerous to ever leave alive.

"I know we talked some about it on the way down, but I find it hard to believe a ninety-year-old man had the wherewithal to build a nuclear bomb. I don't care how much money the Syrian rebels gave him and his tribe. It seems an impossible task."

Elliott kept the pace. Fifty yards ahead, General Jamison stood with his back to them. He leaned on a railing in the shade. His military entourage of five armed officers stood on either side, two looking the same way as the General and three honed in on Elliott and Tony. Any threatening move and the shouldered rifles would drop into position.

"Chankoowashtay did not build that bomb from nothing. He commandeered parts from the Nevada test site he knew well. The rest he pulled together from clandestine sources by way of GRAY WOLF. Tay was unhappy with the United States. We have a terrible history, our treatment of Native Americans. We disrupted their lands and ignored their sacred sites. The Belden launch control capsule and missile silos violated the sanctity of the *Cavern of Han*. That eventually pushed him over the edge. Syrian Rebels approach Milton Busey. Milton connects with his grandfather, who had been playing around with his bomb in that cavern for decades. Now he could do it. He could get restitution. If Tay had not seen the errors of his ways, we would not be here, Tony."

"Amen to that, brother," Wilcox said.

"Worse than that. After the military got to me in the cavern, they realized they were disassembling something that would have triggered a chain reaction of nuclear explosions that would have decimated the upper third of the country. A lot of people would have died."

They approached General Jamison. "Hello, Elliott. Tony. Good to see you boys." He waved to his men. "We're good. Privacy."

Elliott looked past the General into the courtyard below, where there was little to see but sand and sparse scrub and one man in an orange jumpsuit. He cowered in a corner, his arms covering his head. He trembled.

The General followed Elliott's eyes to the lone survivor of GRAY WOLF. "I know. He is scared to death."

Elliott stepped up to the railing and removed his sunglasses. He watched the man jump to his feet and run to the next corner of the small courtyard. Again he turned away and buried his head in his chest and arms. *What did you see out there,* Elliott wondered?

"He's been like that ever since we found him," the General said. "He was alone, running in the snow, twenty miles from the Canadian border. And twenty miles from—"

"—the others," Elliott added.

"They were all dead," Wilcox said.

"Yes," said the General. "Nine left the cavern for the border. One returned; the one who shot Chankoowashtay. The one who—"

"—had his neck broken by a—"

The General turned to Elliott. "Are you sure about what you saw?"

"We've been over this." Elliott watched the man run to another corner and again bury his head. "I am a forensic person, General. We are trained observers. It is time you accept my observation and focus on figuring out how it could be possible."

Wilcox inserted himself into the conversation. "I've known Elliott twenty years. We've investigated and solved hundreds of homicides together. Elliott has stopped fifty serial killers all over the damn world based on dealing with reality at a level few can comprehend." Wilcox looked at his smoldering cigarette. "If Elliott said he saw a giant gray wolf chomp down on the neck of a radical Islamic terrorist, it happened. So here's what I think you should do. Send some of your people to North Dakota to find this gray wolf, the one who saved my friend's life. When you do, give him a moose or an elk. Something nice."

The General smiled. "Well said, young man." He turned to Elliott. "Let me try another way. I did not ask you here because I doubt your experience or observations. I asked you here because I need your professional help as a world-renowned forensic pathologist. Help me understand how a giant gray wolf kills a man by breaking his neck without leaving bite marks."

"I cannot explain it, General," Elliott said.

"We found the other eight Syrian jihadists forty miles from the Canadian border. Their weapons had not been used. Their necks were broken the same way—snapped. It had to take a great external force. Again, there were no teeth marks. No signs of external trauma."

"There's gotta be some explanation," Wilcox said, puffing his cigarette.

"General, I cannot explain the size, speed, or strength of the gray wolf I saw," Elliott said. "It appeared and killed the man who shot Chankoowashtay. I cannot explain the legions of eyes and shadows around me. They were there and then they were gone. And I cannot explain how the eight Syrian rebels died.

"We think we know a lot, when we actually understand very little in this world. And I suspect you are less surprised than me about all of this. I think you expected an unexplainable outcome. After all, you named the terminal breach GRAY WOLF. Maybe you already have the answers you seek from me."

The General watched the Syrian run to another corner and bury his head in his arms. "I know Lakota legend. It is my heritage." He took a deep breath. "This terminal breach truly threatened our existence. I ask myself why it came on the seventh day of the seventh winter.

"A member of the Joint Chiefs of Staff for the United States wields enormous power. With it comes an even greater responsibility to serve all Americans. I could not allow Lakota legend to enter into my decision process, although of course it was always on my mind."

Elliott turned to the setting sun with fond memories of an old Indian, the Lakota elder that showed him the way to evict his demons forever. "After the horrors of the *terminal breach* and the mysteries of the Great Plains, I am reminded of an old American Indian proverb. Men have responsibility, not power ..."

General Jamison and Tony turned to the sunset. All three smiled.

ABOUT THE AUTHOR

STEVE BRADSHAW is a forensic field agent and biotech entrepreneur writing his unique brand of mystery/thrillers. Steve's training and experience investigating thousands of unexplained deaths for the medical examiner's office, and as the founder-President/CEO of an innovative biomedical device company enables him to put his readers on the front row in the fascinating worlds of fringe science, modern forensics, and the chilling pursuit of real monsters.

Steve enjoys sharing his experiences and perspectives as a forensic investigator, President/CEO, and mystery/thriller author. Visit his website and join MEMBER GUEST so you can interact with the author, get insider information and updates, arrange for an author visit, and to be the first in line for new releases.

For more information:
www.stevebradshawbooks.com
steve@stevebradshawbooks.com

www.ingramcontent.com/pod-product-compliance
Lightning Source LLC
Chambersburg PA
CBHW020818180626
46814CB00001B/10